Escape to the Northern Lights

ALSO BY CARRIE WALKER

Escape to the Swiss Chalet
Escape to the Tuscan Vineyard

Escape to the Northern Lights

CARRIE WALKER

HEAD OF ZEUS

An Aria Book

First published in the UK in 2025 by Head of Zeus,
part of Bloomsbury Publishing Plc

9 7 5 3 1 2 4 6 8

A catalogue record for this book is available from the British Library.

ISBN (PB): 9781035918669;
ISBN (ePDF): 9781035918645; ISBN (eBook): 9781035918652

Cover design: Gemma Gorton
Typeset by Siliconchips Services Ltd UK

Printed and bound in Great Britain by Clays Ltd, Elcograf S.p.A.

MIX
Paper | Supporting
responsible forestry
FSC
www.fsc.org   FSC® C018072

Bloomsbury Publishing Plc
50 Bedford Square, London, WC1B 3DP, UK
Bloomsbury Publishing Ireland Limited,
29 Earlsfort Terrace, Dublin 2, DO2 AY28, Ireland

HEAD OF ZEUS LTD
5–8 Hardwick Street
London, EC1R 4RG

To find out more about our authors and books
visit www.headofzeus.com
For product safety related questions contact productsafety@bloomsbury.com

For you, Dad.

Creative, poetic, romantic and full of imagination.
Always dreaming the big dreams.

The best dad in the world
and the apple of Carrie Walker's eye.

'You and me against the world, kid.'

Always and forever xxx

One

Friday 28th August

'Sara? Can you hear me?'

Unfortunately, I could, but I was mid-way through answering an email and determined to clear my inbox before the working day *officially* started.

'Ignore me till nine,' I said. 'I'm a figment of your imagination.'

Bobby huffed loudly as he scribbled on a Post-it and slapped it on my screen:

Partner meeting moved to 2 p.m.

'Has it? Why?' I shouted after him as my mobile buzzed.

'Ask me after nine,' he drawled, flipping me the bird. Dickhead.

HIIT me up Group Chat

Abi: Just landed. Can't wait to see you girls. Still on for dinner later?

Kat: YES. Always yes.

My desk phone started ringing and I could see it was reception.
For the love of God.
I cradled the handset to my ear as I typed. 'Hey, Pete.'
'Morning! The cab's here to take you to court.'
'Already? He's early – can you ask him to wait?'
'Will do.'
My stomach growled and I searched my drawers for snacks. Red Bull and coffee would only get me so far. I needed a proper, protein-rich breakfast, but had to settle for a packet of Frazzles and a loose Polo.

HIIT me up Group Chat

Me: Count me in. It's Mark's week for the dogs so I can stay out late. Promotion meeting later, so I might have good news.

I could barely acknowledge the possibility that it was within reach. That today could mean the triple F: financial freedom forever. The partners at CSH made more money in a year than most people earnt in a lifetime and this promotion would be like a lottery win if I got it. After all the sacrifices I'd made, the weird jobs I'd worked through university, all the beans on toast and Super Noodles I'd eaten, the decision was now made, and it was either me or Bobby. Heads or tails. If they chose me, I'd be the youngest appointed partner in the history of CSH and the second woman, after our HR partner, Cheryl.

I'd been on the promotion fast-track for two years now and had thrown everything I had at it. First in each day, last out, working crazy hours and weekends; even more so since splitting up with Mark. Work had been the obvious way to fill the void. Criminal law was all-consuming, and I'd lose myself for hours, researching, preparing and scenario planning. Spending time in other people's messy lives, so I didn't have to think about my own. Then as soon as one case finished, I'd take another, sometimes two. Filling my boots with as much work as I could handle.

Promotion to partner had been the only thing I'd ever dreamt of. It was my living, breathing dream. And today it might finally happen. I was ready for it. I craved the recognition and I'd more than earned it. My career could at least have the decency to skyrocket if the rest of my life was going to fall apart.

'Come in, both of you. Come in,' Antony said, opening the boardroom door. The partners were sat around the chic, concrete table, with Antony at the helm and Cheryl by his side. Twelve pale faces with half-smiles and disinterested stares. But they wouldn't put me off. This was *actually happening* and I was going to enjoy every single second of it. I flashed them a winning smile while Bobby cleared his throat.

'Thank you for joining us at such short notice,' Antony said, folding his hands in front of him. 'We are mindful of you waiting to hear the partner promotion news and wanted to talk to you together.' I leant forward, ready for the gold confetti to fall from the ceiling.

Cheryl nodded gently, as if Antony was reading off a script. Surely we weren't both being promoted. Were we? I glanced at Bobby with excited eyes.

'Due to a number of factors, we've unanimously voted *not* to add another partner to the board at this time.'

My stomach lurched. *No.*

'I know this will be a huge disappointment to you both, but it isn't a forever decision. It's just for the time being.' He smiled benevolently, as if he'd revealed a fabulous surprise, as opposed to handing the pair of us a double-ended shitty stick.

I'd officially been dumped by work *and* my husband in the same calendar year.

'When will the next review be?' I asked, deflated.

'There's no definitive timeline,' Antony said. 'It could be as soon as next quarter. We'd like to see you both land a high-profile win and then we can look at it again.'

It didn't make sense. The boardroom was hot, and I zoned out as he carried on talking. I'd heard all I needed to hear. One more minute of Antony's patronising pity-faces and I'd be in tears.

My watch flashed to flag my blood pressure, then vibrated as another email came in.

'Thank you, Sara, Bobby,' Antony said, dismissing us. 'We've got a couple more points on the agenda to discuss, so if you wouldn't mind leaving us to it.'

I followed Bobby out, completely thrown. I had a banging headache and my eyes were fuzzy. I needed a cheese sandwich. We walked down the corridor in silence until it was safe to speak.

'What the hell was that?' I hissed, ready to scream.

Bobby was fuming. 'This place is fucked. That promotion had my name all over it.'

'Or mine, more likely.'

'As if you're ready to be a partner,' Bobby sneered.

'What would you know? You've been trying for five years and still no joy.'

He quickened his pace. 'The timing's always been off,' he blustered. 'It's complicated being promoted to partner, you know.' He pulled his trousers up over his gut and tucked in his tie.

'Yeah, well, I don't like to be on the losing side.' I flopped into my chair and turned to face my computer, frown already in place. *Just get through the day. Then get through next week.* And then I was off on annual leave. I hadn't wanted to take it, but now I knew this was the situation, I was grateful it was booked.

My gilet fluttered in the wind as I made a beeline for Hicce to meet Abi and Kat. Coal Drops Yard was buzzing with people, the fountains lit up in a rainbow of colours, and fairy lights strewn across the square. King's Cross had transformed in the two years I'd lived with Mark in Chelsea, but I still managed to orientate myself in the right direction, like a hungry homing pigeon.

The maître d' beamed as I walked in. 'Good evening, Ms Pearson!' he said, with an exaggerated bow.

Ouch. That was going to take some getting used to. I glanced at my wedding rings and faked a smile. I hadn't taken them off yet, but this was the problem with being a regular – people got to know you, and it was difficult to pretend.

'Hi Franz!' I said, handing over my gilet. 'Looking handsome, as always. I'm meeting some friends.'

'Of course,' he said, peeking through the blue feathers. 'The ladies in the corner are waiting for one more.' He pointed to the back of the restaurant, where Kat's blonde locks glowed gold against Abi's mahogany blowout. The LA lifestyle suited her.

'That's them,' I said, waltzing over and giving Kat a kiss. 'Evening, girls!'

'Here she issss! How did it go?' Abi asked, reaching for a hug and searching my face for good news.

I shook my head. 'Not today. '

Kat groaned. 'Bastard. I'm so sorry, babes. Did he say why?'

'Apparently I need another significant case under my belt.'

'What?!' Abi said with a frown. 'There's no more room under your belt.'

'White wine?' Kat asked, pouring me a glass. 'It's chardonnay I'm afraid. Sorry.'

'It's all I deserve.' I laughed, then covered my glass. 'Not too much. I'm taking it easy on the booze.'

'Are you? Why?' Abi's frown deepened.

'My blood pressure is off the charts,' I said. 'My nutritionist has put me on a strict regime of green powder and pomegranate seeds.'

'Well, *my nutritionist*, AKA my mother, says one glass won't hurt,' Kat said, topping me up.

'How long are you back, Abs?' I pivoted. It was so lovely to see her smiley face.

'Two whole months!' she squealed. 'Tony's filming in Brazil and the neighbours are dog-sitting. I'm taking Mum to see *Hamilton* tomorrow, then I'm available for brunch, lunch and dunch for the foreseeable.'

'LA ain't all it's cracked up to be, eh?' Kat shimmied her shoulders. 'Tottenham girl, back for a hit of the London Badlands.'

Abi giggled. 'There's just *too much sun* in California, you know?'

'Uh-huh.' Kat nodded. 'I've heard it's a hot mess.'

'And the showbiz parties are tiresome. Swimming in the infinity pool, swanning around in the Jeep – it's doing my head in. Give me the pissing-down rain any day.'

'Stop it! Like we weren't already jealous! *I* want to swan around,' I groaned. 'Even my watch is telling me to relax these days. Can we please do a life swap?'

'Your watch is an idiot,' Abi said. 'Relaxed has never been your thing.'

'Which is why you're such a good barrister,' Kat added. 'If you were all chilled out, you wouldn't be half as pernickety.'

I took a sip of vinegary wine and shuddered.

'*Particular*,' Abi covered quickly. 'A woman who knows her own mind.'

'If only I knew how to calm it down.'

'You haven't had a lot of time for calm recently,' Kat said. 'Defending half the criminal minds of London, a wedding in Greece, moving house – twice.'

'And now the divorce...' I whispered, forcing down more wine. 'I've nearly gone full life cycle.'

Kat winced. 'You have. No wonder you're stressed. Anyone would be.'

'The flat is a state as well,' I said, thinking about the empty space waiting for me at home. I'd only been back in it a month, but it looked how I felt. Unloved and used up.

'I can help with that,' Abi said, clapping her hands together. 'Me and my paintbrush! Let's mood-board some ideas and choose some new colours.'

'You're a sweetheart, Abs, but you can't waste your holidays painting my flat. I was going to ask your mate Jimbo to decorate it for me.'

'Oh, well, he'll do a great job. But I'm happy to help too. I love painting and I'd get to hang out with you. Win, win! I can even do you one of my murals.'

I thought about the beautiful cityscape Abi had painted in Tony's LA living room. The canals of Venice full of tourists: couples being serenaded on gondolas, St Mark's Square with an opera singer mid-aria and tables of people eating breakfast al fresco. It perfectly represented Abi and Tony. Venice was where they'd finally got together and the mural was totally *them*. Intricately painted details and metallic flecks that gleamed in the sunshine. It was magical. But what would my mural be? What was *me* enough to have it painted on my walls? A Deliveroo driver balancing a pizza box on his handlebars? The inside of a courtroom? Not exactly great inspiration.

'Honestly, Abs, it's cool. I've already decided to use the same colours I had at the house.'

'At Mark's house?' Kat asked, slowly raising her eyebrows.

'It was my house too when we decorated it.'

'Of course it was – sorry.'

'What about trying a new look?' Abi said, gently. 'Something that doesn't remind you of him. There are

8

so many cool wallpaper designs to choose from. Or you could paint the whole flat one colour? Sunshine yellow is very in?'

I didn't want to piss on her chips, but I wasn't about to panic-vomit colour all over my flat. 'I'd rather stick with what I know for now. I haven't got the brain space for anything new, and I don't want to hate it.'

'Fair enough.' Abi squeezed me tight. 'If you change your mind we can just paint over it and start again.' Her peppy cheerleader vibe was kind and comforting.

'Keep things easy for now,' Kat said, looking into my eyes. 'All these little steps will get you there eventually.' Wherever *there* was.

'Thanks, guys.' Tired of having all the attention on me, I changed the subject. 'How are things with you, anyway? PR on the up?'

'Same, same,' Kat said. 'Work is up the wall, and my sex life is woeful. I've been on three terrible dates with an actuary, and I've got a coffee in with a hot-bod builder tomorrow.'

'I thought you'd been through all the builders on Tinder?' Abi said.

'He's new. Separated,' she said with a wink. 'Oh, God, sorry, Sara – me and my big mouth.'

'What? Don't be sorry. It gives me hope there'll be men on the market when I get round to dating again,' I said. 'As long as Mark isn't on there.'

Kat and Abi exchanged a look.

'Er… and what was that?' I asked.

Kat took a breath, and my heart sank at her worried eyes. 'I wasn't sure you'd want to know.'

I rolled my eyes. 'Tell me everything *immediately.*'

'I haven't seen him on there, myself,' she said. 'But my sister has.'

I laughed in shock. 'What? She can't have done. When?'

'Yesterday.' Kat held up a photo of Mark inside a Tinder frame, handsome and grinning behind the wheel of his boat. I felt sick.

'Mark, 35, Real Estate,' Abi read aloud. 'Is he American these days?'

'He'd like to think so. Too many episodes of *Selling Sunset.*'

I zoomed in on his profile. 'Six-foot-one? Hmm. Maybe in heels.' I sighed. He looked so handsome, so full of life. Show me a girl who wouldn't swipe right for those dimples. 'Relationship status: separated. Has children: no. Wants children: no.' My heart raced as I swiped through the screenshots and Kat topped up my wine.

'At least he's being honest this time,' Abi said. 'Three years too late.'

'Do you think he was lying to me, at the start?' I asked, feeling miserable. 'That he never wanted kids?'

'Either that or he was going along with it because he loved you so much,' Kat said.

'I'm such an idiot.' I handed back her phone. 'He's already moved on and I'm avoiding unpacking in case he has a change of heart. What's wrong with me?'

'Absolutely nothing,' Kat said, twisting the end of her blonde ponytail. 'You are the cat's cahoonas, baby.'

'Obviously not.' I closed my eyes to hold back the tears, but they found a way out anyway.

'Babes! Don't cry!' Kat said, grabbing my hand. 'You're smart and fun and cool. And you'll meet someone a thousand times better than Mark *the estate agent*.'

'You will,' Abi agreed. 'A handsome hunk who'll give you everything you want.'

'I can't believe he's already out there, advertising himself to the world.'

'False advertising,' Kat quipped. 'That photo is at least five years old.'

I could feel the wine softening my resolve and reached for some bread. 'It just feels so fast. I'm still in the denial stage. Or is it grief? I'm certainly not in the over-it stage, yet. Is that bad?' I buttered a wedge of baguette and covered it in salami.

'Not at all! Take it at your own pace. You don't *need* to be at any stage, any time, ever.'

'Of course I do! If he's out on dates, then I should be too. On the hunt for a Magic-Mike type to throw in his face.'

Kat laughed. 'Let me know when you find one – I'm in the market for one of those, myself.'

'The classic rebound shag.' Abi nodded wisely.

'Yes!' I said, eyes shining. 'Ideally with a global megastar.'

'Or Mark's boss,' Abi suggested.

'That's more your *revenge shag* territory,' Kat said, sounding like a used car salesman. 'In which case you'd be better off with his brother – or his dad.'

I shook my head. The whole thing was too surreal.

'When was the last time you went on holiday?' Abi asked. 'Would it help to book a few days off work?'

'I've got a fortnight off the week after next, but I'm dreading it. The thought of going on holiday alone, like a sad old spinster, is too much. I haven't even booked anything yet.'

'What are you talking about?' Abi said. 'Solo travel is the best! You can do whatever you want, whenever you want. Sleep in, read books, eat ice-cream all day – indulge yourself entirely.'

'Hmm, that does sound nice, I guess. Mark did tend to be quite bossy on holiday. He wasn't one to deviate from his itinerary.' I thought back to our last holiday where we'd played tennis in the rain, because it was in the plan.

'This time you can make it all about you, but there's no rush to decide,' Abi said.

'Sorry girls, I don't know what I'm doing. I can barely decide what I'm having for breakfast these days, let alone organise a holiday. Dad has been looking after the dogs on my weeks while I sort myself out, but everything feels hard, you know? I need a spa day. Or spa week, or month, until I feel better. A full body massage and some healthy food. Actually – unhealthy food would be better. And bottomless margaritas.'

'Hang on – I'm getting *déjà vu*. I had this same conversation with someone recently.' Abi massaged her temples to summon the memory. 'Yes! It was Emma Stone.'

'The actress?' Kat piped up.

'The very one. She was in make-up telling me about the most unbelievable forest retreat she'd been to in Norway called... flying something. No, hang on, I'll think of it... fiery something.' She snapped her fingers. 'Firefly!'

'Interesting.' I picked up my phone and typed in 'firefly', 'retreat' and 'Norway' and up it came. Firefly Forest, a family-run retreat nestled among the fjords, close to the

Folgefonna glacier. Two hours from Bergen. *A hidden gem* was scrawling its way across the homepage, followed by a carousel of stunning Norwegian scenery. Drone shots winding through the fjords showcasing the lush greenery either side. Wooden lodges tucked in among the conifers, camouflaged by the forest. Reindeer chilling in the sunshine, huskies sledding through the snow and wild swimmers in enormous waterfalls decorated with rainbows. It looked calm, clean and fresh. Idyllic.

Abi was still talking. 'Yeah! She said it was like nothing she's ever experienced before. Amazing treatments, hot springs and Michelin-star food.'

'Really?' I said, swiping through the photos. It was beautiful, but I wouldn't have pegged it as an A-list hotspot. It was probably one of those places only the PRs knew about. I tapped through to the booking page to check out dates. Sold out, sold out, sold out. Of course it was.

'Ever heard of it?' I asked Kat, who was piling up a cracker with brie.

She shook her head. 'I can ask at work though and get you some other recommends?'

A spa trip wasn't a bad idea at all. I wouldn't feel strange being there on my own and I could hide behind my sunglasses. People might mistake me for a reclusive celeb. I could do that. Hmm, yes... I could absolutely do that.

Two

Thursday 3rd September

'In the red or the black?'

The shop assistant had a Jimmy Choo in each hand, and I was torn. Both pairs were beautiful. Should I go classic black for work, or sparkly red for client drinks? Which was also… work. I could always buy the black now and come back for the red. But would I? The clock was ticking, and I couldn't decide.

'I'll take them both,' I said, and her eyes widened. I was on a Zoom call in twenty-three minutes and didn't have time to mess around.

She placed the stilettos in their marbled grey boxes, wrapping each one in silver tissue, then skipped off to the cash desk to ring them up.

I ran out the back of Selfridges and across Portman Square, grabbing a sashimi plate from the food hall to eat at my desk. The bronze gargoyle on our office door grimaced as I typed in my passcode and pushed my way in.

'Back already?' Pete called from behind reception as I whizzed past.

'No lunch for the wicked,' I replied. 'Well, just some quick sushi.'

'Sushi Sara – isn't that a restaurant in Liverpool Street?' he said with a chuckle.

I checked my watch in the lift and ripped off the plastic lid. Five minutes to quickly scoff. It was a shame to ruin these tiny works of art. Each piece had been carefully sliced and shaped, using delicate flavours and different textures to justify the twenty-quid charge. I squirted a piece of tuna with soy sauce as I sped down the corridor.

'You're on this call, Sara!' Antony shouted from his office.

'I know. One minute,' I replied, mouth full of fish.

Antony Taylor was a stickler for the clock. We were charged out in fifteen-minute slots at eye-wateringly high rates, so every second was important. But I hadn't been late for a meeting in six years and today wouldn't be any different. I was back at my desk and logged in with one minute to go. Ready, waiting and on time.

I paused for a second to check my reflection. No kimchi in my teeth. Nate had done a lovely job on my weekly blow-dry, but my ginger roots were starting to twinkle. Invisible to the untrained eye, I could always spot them sneaking up on my darker bottle-auburn. The screen dissolved to show Antony next to the leathery face of Danny Jackson, who was sat by his pool in Mauritius looking as smug as ever.

'Are you there?' he barked, squinting hard.

'Yes, Mr Jackson. You've got Sara and Antony from CSH.'

'CSH – just missing an A.' He snorted with laughter and took a slurp of his cocktail. 'Can't beat a pina colada. Or as I like to call it – the taste of freedom.'

'How are you, Danny?' Antony asked.

'Can't complain – the food is a marked improvement on Wormwood Scrubs. Nah. Let's get serious for a second. You guys were expensive, but your work was very much appreciated. Thank you for saving my arse. Again.'

'There was a lot of circumstantial evidence when it came down to it,' I said. 'The prosecution didn't have enough of a case.'

'That's because you tore it apart piece by piece,' he said. 'Don't think I don't know how lucky I was to have you in my corner. If there's ever anything I can do to show my gratitude – on or off the record—' he winked. '—don't hesitate to ask.'

'That's very kind of you, Mr Jackson, thank you.' The mind boggled at the kind of favours he could pull.

'Danny, please. And success breeds success,' he continued. 'I've got another piece of business for you. Friend of mine – Micky Moo. He's had a run-in with the blues, and I've recommended you lot for the job. Kinda member-get-member ain't it? Do you do a referral scheme? Stamp my loyalty card?' He laughed again.

'Is Mr Moo under arrest?' I asked, googling on a side window.

'Sorry, sweetheart. First name Micky, last name Maloney. Another case of false accusation I'm afraid,' Danny said, shaking his head. 'There's a lot of it about.'

My screen filled with red-top headlines. *Magpie Maloney caught red-handed. Diamond geezer fails diamond heist.* His mugshot showed a chunky man with perfect teeth, in a sharp brown suit.

'He's in the clink at Scotland Yard, no less. Can you pay him a visit and put it on my account?'

'Consider it done. Any background you can share?' Antony asked.

'He's an old man with a diamond fetish and he ran into some trouble down Leather Lane by all accounts. Stood in the wrong place at the wrong time when a loot kicked off in the jewellery quarter and it didn't end pretty.'

'Got it,' I said, my AI Otter transcribing as he spoke.

'Innocent of course,' Danny added.

'Of course,' Antony said. 'Thanks for recommending us. We'll take it from here and be back in touch once we've got the measure of the situation.'

'Sure. Then we can talk real money. Mick's a mate, so I want your best people on it.'

'Understood.'

'And by that, I mean you two.'

Whether it was divine intervention or pure luck, this was too good to be true. I gleefully slammed my laptop shut and ran down to Antony's office.

'No!' he said, resolutely. 'Not a chance. Cheryl will have my bollocks for Christmas baubles if you take on any more cases.'

'But he specifically requested me! Well... *us*. And this is exactly the kind of case that will help me make partner. You can't say no to Danny, surely?'

'I can say whatever I like to whomever I like – I'm the boss around here, remember?' Antony said. 'You've already got far too much on your plate and you're on leave next week.'

'I'll cancel it. I'm not going anywhere anyway. *Please?* Let me take this one. Whoever this Micky guy is, I'll get him off. I promise.'

Antony leant all the way back in his leather chair and folded his arms. 'Absolutely not and that's my final answer.'

'Who's getting who off?' Our HR director appeared in the doorway in a skin-tight minidress, all lithe-limbs and knee-high leather boots. She needed to have a word with herself about dressing appropriately for work.

Antony jumped. 'Cheryl! Your ears must be burning. I was just reinforcing your, I mean, *our* party line when it comes to duty of care and making sure staff take time off.'

Staff was a bit rich.

'Mm-hmm…?' Cheryl eyed the pair of us, suspiciously.

'In fact, Sara was just saying how much she's looking forward to her holiday.'

What a lie.

'Then the rumours are true,' Cheryl said, tapping a hot pink nail on the door frame. 'Where are you off to?'

'Half-true. I'm not so sure I can go anymore – we've had a request in, haven't we, Antony?' I flashed him a pleading look. I was desperate to take this case.

'Of course you can go. We're a law firm, Sara, not A&E. A fortnight will fly by, and Bobby will watch over your cases while you're away.'

Urgh. That *snake*! Always lurking around, waiting to open his big mouth and eat the rest of us. He'd be wrapped around Antony's neck the second I was gone, then slithering all over my clients. I couldn't bear it. My breathing went shallow, and I plastered on a smile, afraid I might cry.

I didn't *want* to take time off; I wanted to work.

'Bobby's got enough on his plate. Honestly, it's better if I stay and do it – I don't mind rescheduling my leave.' The air started to flicker, and my throat felt hot as I clutched Antony's desk to steady myself, sinking into the chair across from him.

'Sara?' He jumped up. 'Are you OK? Cheryl – grab Pete, will you?' I scoffed. He couldn't do anything on his own.

'I get like this sometimes – it'll pass,' I said, dropping my head between my legs and regretting the raw fish. 'I skipped breakfast this morning, so it's probably that.'

Pete came rushing in with a glass of water and hovered by my knees.

'Get her a couple of biscuits as well, will you? She hasn't eaten.'

This was a disaster. I didn't want Antony thinking I couldn't handle any more work. I absolutely could. I was FINE. I sat up and smiled, but my heart was pounding and my head hurt.

'The lights are on but no one's home,' Antony whispered to Cheryl, over my head.

'I can hear you,' I said, looking up.

'Sara? It's me, Ch-er-yl,' Cheryl said, looking into my eyes. 'Are you about to faint, lovey, or do you think it might be a heart attack?' It was a reasonable enough question, but I couldn't answer while in the middle of one of the two.

I took several raggedy breaths and put my head back down. I was raging. I didn't want Bobby *anywhere near* my cases. I'd worked solidly for months, to get as much done as possible before this enforced leave and stop him tapping up my clients. I didn't give a shit about Micky Maloney and his dodgy diamond dealings, but it was exactly the big-ticket case the partners needed to see me win. There'd be plenty of publicity for the firm and Danny had specifically *asked for me*. There was no way anyone else was taking it – least of all Bobby.

Pete reappeared with a coffee and a packet of custard creams, luring me out of the brace position with caffeine and sugar. 'Get a couple of these down you,' he said.

Antony flicked through the first aid manual and studied me closely. 'You've lost all the colour in your face. Are you experiencing symptoms of heartburn?'

I shook my head and dunked a biscuit in my coffee, swallowing it whole. Followed by another, then another. Custard creams were so small these days.

'Her digestion seems fine,' Pete murmured.

'How do you feel inside?' Cheryl asked, side-eyeing Antony, in alarm.

'Woozy,' I said honestly. 'I can't get a full breath.' Panic crept up my spine.

'Could you be pregnant?' Antony tried.

The question caught me unawares and I felt a visceral pain in my gut. I shook my head, sadly.

'Chest pains?' Cheryl continued.

I shrugged. 'Maybe.' The thudding in my heart was getting louder and my heart *was* in my chest, wasn't it? Behind my boob and take a left. I'd always had a high tolerance for pain though, so I was useless in these situations. I'd end up accidentally dying in Antony's office, dismissing appendicitis as indigestion.

'Right, let's get you checked out,' Cheryl said, snapping into action. 'Pete, call us a cab please. We'll be downstairs in two minutes.'

I stuffed another custard cream in my mouth and downed my coffee. That'd pep me up. Or would it kill me if I was mid-heart attack? Too late now either way.

'Mind how you go, Sara,' Antony said. 'We'll expect you a fortnight on Monday if all goes well at the hospital.'

'What about Micky?'

'Leave Micky to me. I'll sort him out.'

'OK, well, update me later,' I said, with a weak smile, following Cheryl down the corridor.

'Your work ethic is admirable, but entirely misplaced. No.'

'Tomorrow then,' I called.

'Still no.'

I wobbled towards the lift and tried to keep it together. Head up, shoulders back, like Mum always said, but I couldn't get enough air in my lungs to take a proper breath. My legs were heavy, and my tongue was too big for my mouth. I stumbled then stopped to lean against the wall and get my balance, the hot feeling back in my throat. Then the twinkling took over my eyes and I slid all the way down to the floor.

Three

Thursday 3rd September

I woke to a cacophony of noises and the smell of vegetable soup.

A slow, steady beep, a high-pitched irregular bleep, a loud continuous pinging… I was in a hospital bed surrounded by corrugated curtains. Cocooned in duck egg. I took a deep breath, and it was a relief to feel the oxygen fill my lungs.

I was OK, I was alive, and I'd somehow made it into a hospital gown without my bra. There were wires stuck to my chest and a plastic tube poked out of my hand, surrounded by purple bruises. At least I still had my knickers on.

An eye appeared at the corner of the curtains, followed by a hand. 'Ah, good evening, Sara. You're awake.'

'Hi,' I mumbled, my mouth parched.

'My name is Dr Fielding. You fainted in the office, do you remember?'

I nodded.

'We've been monitoring you for the past few hours. We suspect it was a type of anxiety attack.'

I frowned. 'Nothing to do with my heart then?'

'No. Your ECG was clear, so no problems there. It looks to have been more of a vasovagal response.'

I leant forward to hear him better. Did he say *vaginal*?

'In layman's terms, your blood pressure and heart rate dropped at the same time, and you fainted. This kind of reaction is usually triggered by stress and exhaustion.'

'Right.'

'Your colleague Cheryl Garner admitted you and informed your husband. Mark, is it?'

My stomach flipped at his name, and I nodded. I didn't need to correct him. Mark *was* still technically my husband and by default my next of kin, but I could imagine the confusion on his face when Cheryl called. Like – why was she telling him? No doubt he put her straight on to Mum.

Dr Fielding tapped away on his iPad. 'I spoke with him earlier and he gave us full permission to go ahead with whatever treatment we deemed necessary.' *Course he did*. A timely reminder to update my will. Not that I had anyone to leave it to – not in the next generation, anyway. Abi and Kat would have to draw straws.

'Your bloods are all fine, but your cholesterol has been flagged as high.'

'Really?' I croaked, thinking of the wine and cheese fest I'd had with the girls.

The doctor ploughed on, despite my one-word answers. 'Do you exercise regularly?'

'Yes,' I said, affronted. 'Swimming, HIIT classes, running occasionally.' *Very occasionally*. And I hadn't been to HIIT for months, now I thought about it.

He frowned. 'Typically, we'd associate this kind of episode with a trauma reaction. Has anything happened recently we should take into consideration?'

You could say that.

'I'm a lawyer, so work is always full-on. Criminal defence.'

'Mm-hmm. We don't usually class work as *trauma*,' he said with a wry smile. 'Anything else?'

'Not really,' I whispered, scared to say the words out loud. I smiled into the silence, as Dr Fielding scratched his head, then I made myself tell him. 'Apart from the divorce.'

My heart ached as I said it and I really didn't want to go through it all again. Reliving the split and that awful, *awful*, conversation with Mark.

'*We got married too quickly,*' he'd said, and I froze. I could tell immediately this wasn't just one of those conversations. He was serious this time. '*I got carried away and that's on me. We barely knew each other.*' I'd heard the words, but I couldn't believe he was saying them. '*I love you in principle, of course I do, but this isn't going to work.*'

'*You love me in principle?*' I'd repeated, as he smashed my precious memories to smithereens. '*What the hell does that mean? It wasn't quick – it was a beautiful, romantic whirlwind.*'

'*It was,*' he'd said sadly. '*But the whirling has stopped now, and we still have a fundamental issue... you know it as well as I do.*'

Mark had said he was open to having kids when we'd first started dating and the same when we'd got engaged and tied the knot. *There's no rush though*, he'd said. *Let's wait and see what happens*, he'd said. But then nothing happened. And the more nothing happened, the more it became clear Mark didn't want anything to happen.

'*We barely have time for the dogs with our careers, and I don't want to commit to any more responsibility. The truth is, Sara, I'm just not interested in being a dad, and I know I never will be.*'

It was Mark's go-with-the-flow vibe that had attracted me to him in the first place. Sailing high on the open seas at Cowes, his ginger curls blowing in the wind while he shouted instructions at his race team. He was laid-back and easy-going, open to different scenarios. But his view on family life became more and more fixed once we were married, until eventually there was no turning back. And I'd been devastated. I would forever be devastated.

But the doctor didn't need to know all that.

'Divorce?' Dr Fielding repeated. 'A stressful time then, no?'

'Yeah, but it's nearly done now,' I said, with a shrug. 'Soon to be signed and sealed.'

Dr Fielding's typing picked up pace. 'It's likely a contributing factor,' he said gently, perching on the end of the bed to talk on my level. He looked genuinely concerned. 'These big milestones can take a while to land and it's important we consider all aspects of your life. Your general health, work stressors, family situation… these layers add up and have a cumulative effect on your nervous system. You may need to think about some lifestyle changes.'

I scratched the flaky skin behind my ear, and it felt deliciously satisfying. One dry patch had turned into two and then somehow spread to my elbows. Where had it all gone wrong? My throat constricted at the thought. I'd killed myself getting into law school, passed all my exams, dated carefully, married well and been an excellent wife – even if I did say so myself – and where had it got me? Itchy, overworked and nearly divorced. It was hard to make sense of the version I now knew of Mark, and the version I fell in love with. We were strikingly similar, au naturel, with our red curls and Roman noses. Noble noses, he always called them. We'd been drawn to each other at the regatta that year; I'd been with clients on the VIP terrace and Mark had skippered the winning crew. CSH sponsored the Captain's Cup each year, and I'd been the one to present it to him. His green eyes had a sparkle about them I'd wanted in on, gleaming bright against his freckles. He was vibrant and alive and so different to the potato-faced legal eagles I usually surrounded myself with.

'*Congratulations!*' I'd said, handing him a methuselah of Moët.

He'd kissed me on both cheeks, the mix of sea salt and spicy aftershave giving me a rush.

'*Fancy helping me drink it?*' he'd whispered in my ear. He was wild and sexy and rugged all at once, so it was a surprise to find out he was a city boy and only twenty minutes in a cab from the office. I'd locked myself in the loo to check out his LinkedIn profile and make sure he was legit. After a bad Tinder date with a creative director who turned out to be an unemployed hairdresser, I always did my due diligence. Real estate seemed so boring for such a firecracker, but he was more of a property scout when it came down to it, which he loved. Non-stop travel and lots of networking – it played to all his strengths.

I hated that I was still thinking about him so much. But if the doctor had called him, maybe he'd come and visit. It was certainly one way to get his attention. The thought of losing me forever might jolt him into action. Make him backtrack. The paper curtain flickered again and Dad's nose poked in.

'Hi, lovely,' he said, balancing a slice of cake and three coffees on a tray. Mum wasn't far behind, marching with conviction, despite all her bags.

'I'll leave you to it,' Dr Fielding said, disappearing discreetly.

'Sara! Sweetheart! What happened?' Mum rushed over and put the back of her hand to my forehead. 'You're boiling hot. Jeff! She's boiling hot!'

'She's alright, love,' he soothed, handing me a coffee and kissing me on the cheek. 'Decaf, I'm afraid. Doctor's orders,' he said, nodding silently at Mum.

I held it gratefully to my chest. 'Thanks, Dad.' It felt good to have a little piece of normality in my hands. 'How did you know I was here? Did Mark call?'

'No, he did not,' Mum snorted. 'The chicken-shit.'

'Technically he did inform us,' Dad said, quietly. He was a stickler for the truth.

'A voice note is the coward's way out, Jeffrey,' Mum snapped. 'And tells me all I need to know about that boy. My baby girl is on her last legs in hospital, and he's left her for dead.'

'Has he?' I sat up, panicked. 'Do you know something I don't?'

'No. But you could be for all he cares. Thank God you saw fit to leave that marriage. You're so much better off without him.'

Mum liked to rewrite the narrative to suit her version of the story.

'I told him we'd come and get you,' Dad whispered. 'He's just got back from Finland and was exhausted, otherwise he'd have been here.'

My heart slumped. Exhausted? Mark didn't know the meaning of the word. He was a human jumping bean. When we'd first started dating, he'd drop everything if he could see me for even half an hour at lunchtime. He couldn't get enough. Neither of us could. And now not even a call from A&E could lure him over. He hadn't even sent a text to see if I was OK.

'As if,' Mum snapped, whipping out a velvet pouch from her bag. 'You can't believe a word he says.' She loosened the dusky pink strings and emptied the contents onto the bed. Three tiny bottles of oil: lavender, sandalwood and jasmine, a wodge of sage wrapped in purple ribbon and a gold bell.

'Viv...' Dad warned, under his breath.

'Leave me. Someone needs to clean the aura around here. It's filthy.'

'Mum! For goodness' sake!' But it was too late – she was already tinkling her bell and clapping in the corners.

'Come on now, love, this isn't good for Sara's stress levels,' Dad said, while Mum pulled out a box of matches. 'Vivian do *not* light that sage. This is a hospital!'

Three matches in a row snapped under the strength of Mum's mania, before she gave up and wafted the sage bundle around as it was. 'It's precisely because this hasn't been done that she's in this mess.'

'Er... hello? I *am* here?'

'Yes, Sara, we can see that! And how do you think it makes me feel, knowing I'm to blame?'

'You're not to blame, Mum.'

'I am. I should have cleansed that dreadful office of yours months ago. It stinks of decay and bad decisions, and don't even get me started on your flat. God knows what those tenants were up to while you were at ours; it's filled to the brim with negative energy.' She bit her lip, and Dad put his arm around her.

'No point going through the should'ves now, is there, love? Let's keep the focus on Sara, shall we? On the here and now.'

'What do you think I'm doing?' she said, brandishing the sage at him like a shaman expelling a demon.

I closed my eyes to shut out her nonsense, but the bell was too loud. There'd be no peace until she'd finished.

'What have the doctors said, then?' Dad asked, while Mum carried on carrying on.

'They think it was a panic attack, which is ridiculous – what have I got to panic about?' The beeping from the heart monitor picked up pace and Dad gave me a look. 'What?!'

'Let's be real, love; it's only us here now,' he said, gently. 'You've been running yourself ragged and you know it.'

'You're worn out,' Mum agreed, her energy finally spent. 'Working sixty hours a week, with all this Mark stuff going through on top. It's been too much. Staying with us probably hasn't helped.'

'It has! I'd have had nowhere to go otherwise. I've really appreciated having you there, and it was only a temporary solution – I'm back in the flat now.'

'That you are. Which is a step in the right direction,' Dad said. 'As long as you don't spend the hour you've saved working. You need time to rest and play too.'

'It's been a lot for me and your father, so I can only imagine how you must feel.'

'You're a stress sponge, Sara,' Dad said. 'Absorbing it all in with no complaints, and now it's too heavy to carry. Time to put it all down.'

'Knock, knock,' Dr Fielding called, whipping back the curtain to reveal several other people on the ward. He immediately clocked the sage bundle in Mum's hand.

'Just giving the space a quick cleanse,' she said, with a reassuring smile.

I shrank under the sheets, as the monitor kicked in again, my heartbeat back to normal.

'Can we take Sara home?' Dad asked.

'I think so, yes. There won't be any medication dispensed, but please think about your lifestyle and try and make good choices when it comes to diet and exercise.'

I instinctively took a deep breath to oxygenate myself.

'Exactly,' he said with a smile. 'You might also consider taking some time off work. I'd be happy to write to your GP.'

'This is what we've been saying, Sara,' Dad chided.

'I am taking time off – I'm on annual leave for the next two weeks.'

'Right. Well then, that's a good start,' Dr Fielding said.

'It is,' Mum said, solemnly. 'Sara, you must do exactly as the doctor says. He's here to help.'

'Of course, I can only advise you.' The doctor finished tapping his notes into his iPad. 'Entirely up to you what you choose to do with it.'

I breathed a sigh of relief. Advisory was fine. A fortnight pottering around the flat and I'd be right as rain. I just needed a bath and a Snickers.

'Most people would be thrilled to have some time off work,' Mum said, fussing dramatically. 'You'll stress yourself into an early grave at this rate. No one "makes partner" in heaven, you know.'

Dad nodded his agreement. 'No pockets in shrouds.'

'I don't want any pockets – what are you two talking about?' The heart monitor started beeping. 'Why can't you understand how important this promotion is to me? I'm at a critical stage in the process and I just need your support.'

I wanted to scream, but I was conscious of three sets of eyes on me and the heart monitor giving me away. I swallowed down my panic and smiled sweetly. 'Thank you for the advice, Doctor. I'll get myself home, then see how I feel.'

No one could force me to stay off work. I'd have my two weeks at home and that would be that.

Four

Friday 4th September

I flipped the pillow onto the cold side and snuggled down into the duvet, glad to be back in my own bed. Another half an hour wouldn't hurt. Another hour wouldn't hurt, either. I could stay in here all day for all anyone cared – I had nothing to get up for. I shut my eyes and tried to force more sleep, but it wouldn't come, so I got up and made myself a coffee. The familiar grind was comforting as I checked through my emails, filing the FYIs and red-flagging anything I needed to follow up on.

Twenty minutes later and I was still scrolling. Right. Stop that. I'd take my vitamins, have a wee and *then* try and relax. The carpet was soft on my feet as I wandered into the bathroom and threw the windows open. Mum must have turned the heating up when she left, and the flat was sweltering. I tipped *Friday* out of my pill box and plinked a Berocca in a glass of water. Extra strength C, double D, magnesium and zinc, knocking them back one by one with the fluorescent fizz. My standard morning ritual.

And then I got back into bed. There was no point getting too pumped up when Antony had insisted there be no work contact until I got back. Unfortunately, it wasn't that easy. My body was pre-programmed to get going the second I opened my eyes and it was already nearly seven. I was *resting* as agreed with Dr Fielding, but that didn't mean I couldn't read.

My phone pinged.

Mark: Hey. How's the patient?

Finally. Ever the early riser. Another thing we had in common. My heart flip-flopped at his name on the screen. So, he *did* care. Well – he didn't *not* care, which was almost the same thing. He'd changed his profile picture to the one he was using on Tinder. The whole time we were married he'd used our wedding photo and now it seemed to be a different photo every week.

Me: Feeling much better – thanks for speaking to Cheryl and the hospital.

Mark: Least I could do. Sorry I couldn't swing by. Hope it wasn't too serious.

Me: Me too. Doc said it could be heart-related, so I've been signed off work.

A slight play on the truth, but a little guilt trip wouldn't hurt.

Mark: Shit, sorry to hear that. Want me to keep the dogs?

Me: No, no, I miss them! Dad will pick them up tomorrow
as normal.

We'd been doing a week on week off trial with Twiggy
and Dots, our two daxies, ever since we'd split, and Dad
was officially obsessed. Having never been a 'dog person' he
now much preferred them to Mum and me.

Mark: Great. Take care of yourself, OK?

Ugh. So polite and banal. All the best, Mark. Even a
suggested heart condition didn't get much of a response
these days. My phone lit up again with his name. Hopefully
something more caring and concerned.

Mark: Might also be worth updating your next of kin info
when you get chance.

Charming. I puffed up the pillows and lay back with my
coffee, looking around the bedroom. It was not a pretty
sight. The paint had been sparkling white when the tenants
had moved in and was now a grubby, chewing-gum grey,
with scuff marks where their furniture had been. With
marks on the carpet and a couple of cracked tiles, the
flat was dog-eared and tired and needed a good tinkling.
I messaged Jimbo to get him over asap and immersed
myself in the Farrow and Ball colour chart, trying to
remember if it was Mole's Breath or Pigeon we'd had in
the kitchen. No time like the present to kick off the refurb.

I could even pop down to B&Q this afternoon and order the paint.

I'd moved back in with two suitcases and just enough home comforts to get me to work and back each day. Most of my stuff – and a lot of *our stuff* – was in boxes at Mum and Dad's, so it was good timing for some redecoration. Maybe it would shake me out of my going-through-a-divorce limbo. Waiting for Mark to swing by with one of his bashful smiles and say he'd changed his mind wasn't getting me anywhere. But I missed our beautiful home in Chelsea. We'd spent ages doing it up when I moved in. Debating different colour combinations and choosing all the fabrics to get the look exactly right. And I wanted it all back, even if it was just a mini version for now. Icy blues and greys on the walls with indigo velvet cushions.

I watched half an hour of HIIT with Millionaire Hoy before my shower. He was one of the only constants left in my life and his YouTube videos kept me company all over the world. I wasn't doing the HIIT so much anymore, but I couldn't start the day without him. I turned the shower up as hot as I could bear it for ten seconds, then blasted myself with cold. Abi said it was the best way to get the circulation going in the morning and she knew all the Hollywood tricks. It always left me breathless, and I hated doing it – but I forced myself to. Mark used to say *there's no change without challenge*. And I wanted my life to change. Back to the way it was before, that is.

I threw on a tracksuit, Deliveroo-ed a bacon and egg baguette, then started a rigorous vacuuming session. The decorating planning would continue after the cleaning. And there was a lot of cleaning to do. I'd been desperate to give the flat a thorough going-over, ever since I'd moved back in, I just hadn't had the time. The cleaners had done an OK job with the end-of-tenancy clean, but there was nothing like doing it yourself. Remnants of limescale under the taps, yellowing grout in the shower, spatters of fat on the extractor fan. Nothing like a bit of surprise cardio to get the heart racing. I cleaned the windows, then mopped the bathroom and kitchen floors and had moved on to scrubbing bleach between the tiles with a toothbrush when I started to feel light-headed.

I stopped for a second and took a deep breath, waiting for it to settle. But it didn't. And the air started to flicker like it had in Antony's office. *Shit*. Maybe I'd taken it an espresso too far. What if I collapsed on the floor right now? How long would it take for someone to find me? Would anyone even miss me? I clicked onto FaceTime as a precaution and could just about make Mum's face out as it connected.

'Hello?' she mumbled, pushing back her *DON'T YOU DARE* sleep mask and blinking into the light. She didn't get up much before ten these days. 'Sara? Love? Are you OK?'

'I'm not sure,' I said, taking another shaky breath. Which was the closest I'd got to asking for help in ten years.

'You're not sure? Jeffrey! Wake up, you lazy lump! Sara isn't sure!'

'I'm OK… I think…' I swallowed, as the sparkles came back. 'I think I'm OK…'

'Open a window, Sara, quick! Take a big breath of fresh air. Have a drink! Splash some water on your face!'

'I can't, Mum, I can't. I'm…'

And with that, my phone fell towards my face, and everything went blank.

Dr Fielding loomed over me and shone a torch into my eyes.

'Back already, Ms Pearson?'

'Mhmm,' I murmured, shifting under his gaze. Mum and Dad were ashen, sat either side of me, holding my hands. 'Am I going to be OK?'

The doctor frowned; his stethoscope suckered to my chest. 'It seems we need to shift my recommendation from advisory to *mandatory*,' he said, firmly. 'Your body is trying to tell you something and you really need to listen.' My heart sank. Either that or it was being dragged down by saturated fats. I itched for the bacon and egg butty that was probably being pulled apart and enjoyed by foxes on my doorstep. Was this the kind of thing he meant?

'You need to take some time to rest, or these episodes will keep happening. And I'll be writing to your GP to say the same.'

'Is this a diet and alcohol thing?' I asked, just to be one hundred per cent clear.

'Of course it is, Sara!' Mum butted in. 'You need to eat all your greens and drink lots of water. Live the life of a... of a goat!'

Dr. Fielding nearly smiled. 'As I said before, your cholesterol is flagging as high, so it won't hurt to look at clean eating, but it's more holistic than that.'

'You need to start looking after yourself, love,' Dad added, gently. 'This self-destruct mission has got to stop.'

'Rest is key,' Dr Fielding said. 'Meditation. Fresh air. Water. These attacks are an outward symptom of inner chaos, so you need to concentrate on your wellness for a while. The effects of stress are reversible, but it will take a concerted effort on your part.'

I gulped and nodded. Dad was right – I had kind of let myself go. Six months in my teenage bedroom filling up on home-cooked meals and takeaways hadn't helped. I'd been using all my energy to keep it together for work, and everything else had gone out the window. In the early days, I'd just about managed to put my make-up on and brush my hair. It had all felt so pointless.

'Half a goat is more than fine,' Dr Fielding said, signing my discharge form with a squiggle. 'Your GP will take it from here, but the taking care of yourself part is down to you.'

Five

Monday 7th September

So that was that, then.

Cheryl had been crystal clear on the video call, despite the look of despair on Antony's face. My annual leave had been extended to a month, plus another month signed off work. Ha! How's that for duty of care for your *staff*? Bobby juggling my workload for a fortnight was just about manageable – two months was another thing altogether. And I'd already been locked out of the email system, so I couldn't even keep a cursory eye on things. Corporate wellness dictated it. I had to rest and recuperate in whatever way worked for me and they wouldn't hear another word on the subject. Those red follow-up flags would have to stay waving in the digital ether until I got back.

I gave the company portal login a try, but that was blocked too, and when I closed the page, the Firefly Forest website was sitting open behind it. CANCELLATION was flashing in the corner of the reservations page with one green dot now available to book. I clicked into it out of curiosity. A double cabin on their four-week mind and body transformation programme, starting next week. Which was no time at all to get myself organised and over to Norway.

No. It was too soon. I couldn't be spontaneous in my current state of mind. I couldn't even *think straight* in my current state of mind. I needed some air and a walk to think things through, and I needed to eat. Yes. Food. My brain was all sixes and sevens, and I could tell my blood sugar was low again – not a great start to my wellness journey.

The lunchtime bustle was in full swing on the walkway below, the city workers like busy ants off to get their breadcrumbs and grains of sugar to take back to their nest. I didn't much fancy being out and about in King's Cross, but the fridge was empty, and my stomach was growling. I could be down to Greggs and back in ten minutes if I got a sweat on. Tuna mayo on white, salt and vinegar crisps, a four-pack of sausage rolls and a Sprite. The working woman's thinking food. I caught sight of myself in the mirror and did a double take. Pale and tired, my hair in the same bun it had been in all week. I added blow-dry to my mental to-do list. I'd dressed up for my video call with a wide hairband to hide my curly bird's nest. Business up top and casual on the bottom. My spotty blouse looked fresh, but my leggings were faded and baggy. Horrible to look at, but *so* comfortable, I sometimes wore them in bed. They'd be fine for a quick lunch run. No one in Greggs would care. I zipped my big coat up, ready to run the gauntlet.

'*Big Issue*, love?' Ron was waving his bundle of mags in the freezing cold as people rushed past him on all sides.

'I've already got one,' I said, dropping my hood at the first challenge. 'It's me.'

'Sara! Sorry, I didn't recognise you under there. I don't usually see you this time of day.'

'Well, you will do from now on – I'm off for a few weeks.'

He frowned, concerned. 'Everything OK?'

'Yeah, in the grand scheme of things. Just need a reboot.' My breath had turned to smoke in the cold air. How could he bear to stand outside all day in this weather? 'I'm getting some lunch, Ron. What would you like?'

'Oh no, I'm fine. I can't ask you to do that.'

'You're not asking, I'm offering. Sausage roll? Coffee? Sandwich? All of the above?'

His eyes softened. 'Thank you.'

I could have eaten my arm off I was so hungry; I grabbed two of everything and a bag of doughnuts for luck. With three bags full, I hurried past Harry's and the al fresco diners huddled under the heaters. Rather them than me.

I sensed Mark before I saw him. Something in my peripheral vision made me double-take as he leant back with his hands behind his head and pulled a funny face. The shiny blonde he was sat with laughed, and I couldn't help but stand and stare at the two of them, happily wrapped in woolly blankets and drinking red wine.

He looked up and our eyes locked, but my feet wouldn't move.

I was frozen to the floor, stood there in my saggy leggings and Crocs and socks, laden down with Greggs carrier bags. Then I lifted myself up, stuck my nose in the air and marched myself over.

'Mark? Is that you? What a lovely surprise!'

'Oh... er... hi,' he stammered, looking like he might throw up. 'What are you doing here?'

'What am I doing here? I live here. What are you doing here?' I was enjoying watching him squirm, even though he looked gorgeously handsome in the pale blue blazer I'd bought him for the Henley Regatta.

'You're back in your flat?'

'Yep. Three weeks now.' His date looked from him to me for clues as to what was going on. 'Dad is looking after Twiggy and Dots while I get myself sorted.' I smiled at Millie. 'Our babies,' I said, to clarify.

She snorted into her wine. 'You have *babies*?'

'No! Of course not!' Mark said, going bright red.

'They're grown up now, I suppose, but they'll always be babies to me.'

'Sara! What are you doing?' he hissed.

'Sorry, I don't think we've met? I'm Mark's wife.'

'*Ex*-wife,' Mark added vehemently. 'Sorry about this, Millie, she's talking about our dogs.'

'You have *dogs*?!' she said, alarmed.

We both stopped at that.

'Yes. The sausage dogs in my photos. Do you not like dogs?'

Millie wrinkled her tiny nose. 'I'm allergic. Like, *really bad*.'

'Oh. That *is* a shame.' I couldn't help but smile. 'Mark loves the girls, and their wiry hairs are all over the house. And in the bed, of course,' I said, with a wink. 'And, darling, I've been meaning to tell you – I'm going away for a few weeks, so you'll have to play single parent until I'm back.'

'Away where? When? I thought you were ill?'

'Norway. One of those Scandi spas – you know the type. Impossible to get into normally, but Abi managed to pull a few strings. Mum and Dad will have the dogs on my weeks so it shouldn't affect you too much, but I thought you should know in case there's an emergency. It's only for a month.'

'A *month*?' he blustered, eyes bulging. 'But I can't possibly do any more than…'

'Well, you might have to,' I interrupted, with a smile. 'Dogs are for life; we both know that. I'm sure your mum will help if you get stuck. Have you met Mark's mum?' I turned to Millie, who shook her head. 'Nightmare,' I whispered behind my hand. 'Anyway! Take care, or *ha det bra* as they say in Norway. Enjoy your lunch.'

I needed to book that last slot to Firefly Forest, and fast. I strode off, handing Ron his lunch as I went past and filling my face with mine while I waited for the lift. I ran in, propped my phone against a bottle of wine and proceeded to payment.

Focus, Sara, focus, I thought, trying to steady my mind. Nothing was more important in this moment than securing that place. My hands were shaking as I auto filled my credit card details, panicking that someone else might book on that green dot before me. Click, swipe, face scan and it was done. It was too easy to spend money these days. My phone even recognised my face when it was stuffed full of sausage roll. Yes! I was IN. My brain flooded with dopamine as I poured myself a glass of wine to celebrate. This would be an excellent way to busy myself for a month. If I stayed here, I'd only stalk Mark's Instagram day and night, obsessing over who he was with. Then I'd look up Millie, and her friends and family, and her ex-boyfriends and their ex-girlfriends… I was driving myself mad even thinking about it. No. I was going to Emma Stone's spa and that was the end of it.

HIIT me up Group Chat

Me: Ladies – I've only gone and booked it! I'm off to Norway!

Abi: Random. Why?

Me: To that retreat you recommended! The Emma Stone one.

Abi: No way.

Me: Yep. Firefly Forest. I'm being spontaneous. Thank her for me when you see her.

Kat: YESSS! You go, babes!

Six

Tuesday 8th September

Dear Mrs Pearson,

This is confirmation of your booking with us at the Firefly Forest retreat:

- 1 x Double Cabin (single occupancy)
- Check in: Monday 14th September
- Check out: Saturday 10th October

We acknowledge receipt of your payment for 55,000 NOK, with thanks.

You have been enrolled in our mind and body transformation programme for four weeks and I have attached a flipbook of information, so you know how we operate and what to expect. I hope this answers any questions you have, but please don't hesitate to email me if you need anything else.

As it is less than a week until arrival, your booking is non-refundable.

We look forward to welcoming you.
All the best,
Tore Nilsen

I read the email with one eye open, then turned the light on and read it again as a text came through from the bank:

A payment of £4,010.24 has been made to Firefly Forest Retreat, Norway.

Oh, fuck. It all came flooding back as my brain woke up. Shit, shit, *shit*.

What a ridiculous thing to do. Four grand? My post-wine head was thumping. When was I supposed to be going again? Monday?! For fuck's sake.

My phone started ringing and Mum's sunny smile appeared on screen, her ginger hair in rollers.

'Morning darling, how are you feeling?'

'Tired and hungover.'

'What? Dr. Fielding said no booze!'

'I know, I know, but I ran into Mark *on a date* – can you believe it, Mum? Right under my nose.' My voice cracked. 'He didn't know I was back in the flat, but still.'

'A date?' Mum's jaw dropped. 'The cheeky shit! You're not even divorced yet! That boy needs to stay single for a few years and think about what he's done before breaking anyone else's heart.'

'It won't last – she's allergic to dogs – but I went rage-shopping when I got home, and now I've got buyer's remorse.'

'Don't worry, darling, I do it all the time. Your father nearly lost it when the half-price Christmas hampers started arriving in January. He wouldn't know a bargain if one bopped him on the head.'

'I wish it was just a hamper.'

'Anything you buy online can be sent back within seven days for a full refund. Nothing to stress about. I'll help you with it if you're worried, darling. I know my rights.'

'It's not really something I can send back,' I sighed. 'I've booked onto a retreat in Norway for a month. Leaving on Monday.'

Mum stopped at that and frowned into her phone. 'Okaaay... that's a new one. Tell me more.'

'It's this cool celeb haunt that Abi recommended. Scandi heaven apparently. I'm sure it'll be amazing, but I haven't really thought it through properly. I'm going to need a new bikini and some furry boots and a yoga outfit. And I know it's cheeky, but I kind of assumed you guys would be OK to cover my weeks with the dogs while I'm away?'

'Doesn't sound like we have much choice,' she tutted. 'Not that I can prise your father away from them, anyway. That man's a sucker for a waggy tail. He's been throwing the ball for over an hour now.'

'Amazing, thanks Mum. I better get shopping then; I can't downward dog next to Jennifer Lawrence in my current get-up.'

'Will J-Law be there?' Mum asked, excited.

I laughed. 'I doubt it, but there should be some celebs – it's that kind of place.'

'Maybe I can book in too and leave your dad to it?'

'There was only one space left – sorry Mum. And it's quite pricey.'

'I dread to think. You've lost all touch with reality when it comes to money. Your teenage self wouldn't recognise you.'

I felt slightly ashamed. Fancy moaning because I was off to an expensive spa. I thought of Ron outside in the cold, selling *Big Issue*s and coping with actual life issues. 'I know. I think with all the promotion disappointment and then this health scare, I wanted to treat myself. I've used my bonus to pay for it.'

Mum shook her head in despair. 'Money's money, Sara. Just because it's a bonus, doesn't mean it doesn't count. I suppose you work hard enough, though. You deserve to enjoy it.'

'Thanks, Mum.'

'It's not really me, anyway, that type of thing. I can't relax when holidays are too expensive. I'd know exactly how much each minute had cost me and be messaging your dad non-stop to see if he thought it was worth it.' I laughed. 'No. There's a perfectly good jacuzzi at Enfield swimming baths that does me fine.'

'If you don't mind sharing it with five men.'

'Of course I don't!' Mum chuckled. 'Why do you think I go there? You've got to get your kicks where you can at my age.'

'Eww, Mum.'

'Don't you *eww* me, young lady, your time will come,' she said. 'You better get yourself in gear if you're flying on Monday. Get shopping and packing. Don't stress and don't drink. Love you.'

After Mum hung up, I dragged my Louis Vuitton suitcase off the top of the wardrobe and flung it open. Presumably I'd be in my swimming costume with a fluffy spa robe on most of the time, so I wouldn't need too many clothes. A couple of sparkly numbers for dinner and a few jumpers. If ever there was a time for the Jimmy Choos, it was now. I put them in the case, still in their shoeboxes, and there wasn't much room for anything else, so I grabbed Louis' little brother and made a matching pair. Uggs, oversized angora jumpers in pink, yellow and black, three pairs of jeans. Forty pairs of knickers and forty pairs of socks. Biblical. Three bikinis, one tankini, one wetsuit, my kimono, karate outfit and skiing thermals. A solid baseline pack.

Trainers? Hmm. Three dresses or four? Shorts? I pulled out hanger after hanger. An embarrassing number of garments still had their labels in. Maybe I didn't need to go shopping after all. Crisp white T-shirts, tulip jeans, a leather jacket. I performed a one-woman fashion show, trying on everything I owned and rediscovering treasures I'd long forgotten. It's the sort of thing Mark would have enjoyed when we first got together. Slowly dressing up for him then taking it all off. Lacy underwear in black and red, with a low-cut silky dress, a feather boa and a faux-fur coat – the more glamorous and outrageous, the more he liked it. I'd dance for him while he'd sit and watch, peeling off layer after layer until there was nothing left.

Packing to go away without him didn't feel right. We'd travelled as a team for such a long time. I always organised the sun creams and liquids, and he'd take care of the tech. Chargers, adapters, speakers. Anything with a plug. And now I had to think of everything myself again, having trained my brain away from it. I'd never been on holiday on my own before and I couldn't decide if it was terrifying or liberating. What if I got lost? Or went missing? Would anyone care? Would anyone realise? I pulled out a notepad and wrote down where I was staying, then took a photo and sent it to Mum and the HIIT Group Chat. My friends and family could consider themselves briefed, whether they liked it or not.

The doorbell rang, interrupting my thoughts.

'Alreet? Sara? It's Jimbo about the decorating job.' A deep Geordie voice boomed through the speaker, and I buzzed him up. I did a quick sweep around the flat to make sure there weren't any knickers on the radiators. My electric candles looked barely on as they glowed faintly in lines along the windowsills and dotted across the mantelpiece. They needed new batteries. Another thing Mark was always in charge of. He had all the tiny screwdrivers.

I swallowed down a sob and opened the door.

'Jimbo! How are you? Thanks for coming over on a school night.'

'No problem, pet. Every night's a school night for me, like.'

'OK, well, I won't keep you long. As you can see, it's all on one level. Entrance hall, two bedrooms, the bathroom and this open-plan living space.'

'Lovely. The walls and the woodwork, is it?'

'Yes, the whole lot please. Mole's Breath in the kitchen and bedrooms, White Swans in the bathroom and Green Goose everywhere else.' I handed him the colour chart with the numbers circled.

'Thinking of starting an ark?' he chuckled. 'Yep, nay problem. I can pick the paint up on Monday and be here for ten if you like?'

'Anytime is fine. I'm away next week, so you'll have the place to yourself. Let me grab you a key.'

I rummaged around in the kitchen drawer of doom, where the tenants had left the instruction manuals, the meter readings, three boxes of matches and all the keys. Mark's set were on his precious Chelsea keyring. It felt strange handing them over to another man, knowing Mark would never need them again. These daily reminders of our split were torture. Each one another tiny link in the divorce chain.

'Here you go. Help yourself to anything you need and call me if there's a problem.'

'Champion.' Jimbo pocketed the keys with a nod. 'I'll text you some photos once it's done.'

The flat was virtually empty apart from the clothes explosion in my bedroom, just those few half-dead candles and my plastic plants. A fresh lick of paint would make a world of difference; I'd get the carpets replaced and new furniture after Christmas, and start single life again in the new year.

Seven

Monday 14th September

I boarded the flight to Bergen with ten minutes to spare. Old habits die hard, and I wasn't one for hanging around in airports – get on the plane, get the job done and get home. Like a legal hitman. Well, hitwoman. I'd spent my student years travelling up and down the country on the Megabus for a quid, and I didn't fly anywhere until I was twenty-five. My entire focus as a teenager was on getting into law school and any spare money I managed to scrape together went in the pot marked 'fees'. I'd started saving when I was fourteen after watching a particularly fascinating episode of *Suits*. I decided there and then that I was going to be a barrister and that was all there was to it. Mum and Dad helped me out as much as they could, but a career in law was expensive and it was my bill to pay. It meant saying *no* more than *yes* to holidays, clothes and nights out at uni, but the delayed gratification had been worth it. Now I was qualified, I could afford to do things properly, and I made damn sure I did.

I looked like Dora the Explorer walking down the tunnel, in my pink puffer jacket and waterproof trousers, turning left and settling into my regular seat: 6A. Next to the window and far enough away from the bustle of the trolleys to be able to concentrate.

Ahhh. Business class. One of life's true pleasures. Or so people said. It had mostly been a necessity for me, so I could stay online, charge my phone and have enough space to work during the flight. The clock never stopped and Antony needed to allocate those fifteen-minute slots.

A stewardess dressed in navy with a big blonde bun came sauntering over with a tray of drinks, a huge smile plastered on her face. 'Welcome on board, Ms Pearson. Champagne?'

'Yes please!' I said, taking two. Dr Fielding could do one. I unwrapped my pillow and blanket and made a little hamster nest, then plugged my phone in, whipped out my laptop and connected to the Wi-Fi before remembering I didn't need to do any of that this time. I was pre-programmed to work when travelling on my own, and it felt alien to me that this time I couldn't. The flight was only two hours, but on Kat's advice I'd popped a couple of CBD gummies and was already feeling warm and snoozy. Medicating myself to force some chill. I planned to tick every treatment off the spa menu while I was there – I had a whole month to try them all, and they were bound to have all the latest therapies and techniques to keep the A-listers coming back for more. Massages, facials, reflexology. I couldn't wait to get in there and loll about. Oil me up boys, then rub – me – down. I took a photo of my set-up, making sure the business class logo was visible in case Mark was watching, and posted it:

Seatbelt sign ON. Out of office ON. Time to take OFF. #TimeOff #TakingOff

*

I was off the plane and breathing in the fresh Norwegian air within ten minutes of landing. The sky was clear and blue, with stunning greenery in every direction as I clomped down the steps and onto the tarmac.

I felt healthier already. I jumped in a cab to the harbour and bought a ticket for the fjords trip that would take me to Firefly Forest. There was only one boat a day that did the route I needed, so I had to be on it. The drive took over an hour and I much preferred the thought of arriving by boat. I had some time to kill, but it was a relief to be in the right place and well ahead of time.

Bergen was beautiful. Bright and cold, with a rainbow of wooden buildings along the waterfront and a cable car taking people up and down the mountain. The sun felt hot on my face as I took a seat in one of the outdoor bars and slid my coat off.

'*Hallo!*' A gangly teenager with flawless skin called over. 'Would you like to order something?'

'White americano, please.' It was nearly six, but I needed some caffeine. I was only halfway to heaven and there was so much more to see. I wanted to be awake for it.

'Coming up!' the waiter said with a shiny white smile. How were the Scandis all so bloody gorgeous?! They must have teeth brushing parties to pass the time instead of going to the pub. Lots of running and swimming while brushing their teeth, then trekking up mountains in oversized skis – presumably to avoid paying for the chair lift. Nothing else made sense.

I finished my coffee and wheeled my cases down to the waterfront which was still and shiny, mirroring the shoreline. An old-fashioned riverboat with a waterwheel chugged into the harbour, cutting gently through the sea.

'Is this the boat for Firefly Forest?' I asked the girl on the dock as it parked in front of her.

'*Hei-hei! Ja* we stop at Firefly. Are you booked in with Tore?'

'Yes, under Sara Pearson. He's expecting me.'

'Excellent. I'll let him know we have you,' she said, the sun bouncing off her white-blonde hair. Bergen was a small place. It made sense that everyone would know everyone else. 'Jump on and make yourself at home. You can leave your bags there. Lars! Two cases, please.' A salty sea dog with bright blue eyes grabbed my cases and hopped onto the boat, holding his hand out to help me.

'Thanks,' I said, pulling my sleeves over my hands to keep them warm. An icy breeze whipped along the water, and it was a relief to get out of the wind and under cover, where the heaters were on full blast. I sat by the window and stared out at Bergen from the boat, with its pretty harbour, old buildings and narrow alleyways – so vivid and full of colour, it looked like a photoshopped spread from a holiday brochure.

The wooden huts on the waterfront, or *Bryggen* as it was famously known, stood gable to gable, smart and sharp in muted tones of red, yellow, orange and white. Mother Nature provided a stunning view, with the mountains protecting the fjords on both sides like enormous steel gates, leaving half an inch in the middle for the boats to pass through. The rock was its own work of art, the sheer size of it awesome to look at: dark grey and blue-black stone with a broccoli of moss covering the lower levels in a salad of different greens. A sliver of turquoise then separated the two sides, the water sparkling in the sun. All the beauty of the ocean, without the worry of a hungry shark snaffling me up for lunch. Norway was an absolute vibe of nature and wholesomeness so far – and even better that I could admire it from the heated passenger deck, before I got to the hotel and ordered a cocktail.

The trip was billed as a sunset cruise to the South Rock Fjords, with a chance to spot puffins and whales, and there was a buzz of excitement as the seats filled up with silver-haired couples in waterproofs, carrying binoculars. Two guys in orange jumpsuits walked past with tripods and helped each other carry them up onto the top deck. There was a mass feeling of anticipation as people stared anxiously out the window, but I didn't have that pressure – I was just hitching a lift and in desperate need of a martini. I wondered if Emma Stone had got on this same boat when she came over. Surely not. There must be a helipad at the airport to chopper in the elite. Although I hadn't seen it as an option when I'd booked.

The boat sounded its horn, belching bright white clouds up into the sky as it reversed out of the harbour. Even the pollution looked clean over here. And with the chocolate-box promenade of Bergen soon in the rear-view mirror, I was relieved to be on the final leg of my journey, gliding through the glassy water towards Firefly Forest.

A loud clicking interrupted my thoughts, and a lady started speaking over the Tannoy.

'Ladies and gentlemen, welcome on board this Bergen Ferries Wildlife Cruise. We are happy to have you with us today and will be keeping you updated on any animal activity we spot from the captain's deck. Please use your eyes to update each other also. If you look starboard, to the right of the boat, we are passing a bearded seal. There are plenty of seals in this region and people come from all over the world to photograph them.'

There were lots of excited ooohs.

'If we are lucky, we will see the puffins and maybe a walrus, and of course I know you are all hoping to see the whales. There are five different pods living in this part of the fjords, so I hope they come out to play with us today.'

The water didn't look wide enough to hide one whale, let alone five different families. How was it possible *not* to see them? I imagined their massive bodies bobbing up to the surface against their will as they tried to hold their breath and hide.

'And of course the wildlife on land is just as exciting as that in the ocean,' her clipped voice continued. 'Keep your eyes up and you will see the famous white-tailed eagles flying above us, and perhaps there will be an Arctic fox or two on the mountains. The reindeer and elk also graze at the edges of the forest. A common sight in Norway, but not so much everywhere else.'

I was following the route on Google Maps and could see my blue dot getting closer to Firefly Forest as a shriek sounded throughout the boat, and everyone stood up to see what was happening.

'Whale!' a little boy shouted, pointing out to sea. 'Over there!'

There was an excited scupper and shouts of 'where?' and 'I can't see!' as the boy pointed emphatically.

The Tannoy clicked back on. 'Hello, everyone. We heard a call of whale and are looking to see if one of our animal friends is close by. We are using sonar radar, as well as our professional spotting telescope, which has a large, objective lens.'

The photographers were already clicking away, hoping to land that one shot that would make them a fortune should Moby Dick decide to leap out of the water.

'We now have confirmation of the animal,' she said, continuing the slow reveal. 'And if you look to the left, by the pink buoy, you will see some disturbance in the water.' The binoculars went up as everyone tried to see. 'Around ten o'clock from the buoy. If you look *very* closely you can see a w... walrus.' There was a collective groan. 'A fantastic example of a beautiful creature, I'm sure you'll all agree.'

It wasn't even a full walrus. It was a break in the surface where we had to imagine a walrus was chilling underwater. The photographers might have bagged themselves a photo of his nose and whiskers if they were lucky. There were lots of disgruntled mutterings and one of the team was handing out sick bags. The further we went, the bouncier the ride, and the roiling lurch of the boat was playing havoc with my stomach.

Lars appeared out of nowhere and flashed me a silver smile. 'Your stop is next.'

I followed him down to the lower deck, out into the bitter cold, relieved to be on the move. The wind rattled through the tarpaulin, ruffling up the blow-dry I'd managed to fit in before I left. I could just about see as I shuffled forward, using Lars as a human shield. Emma Stone couldn't possibly have suffered all this.

'Firefly ahoy!' the girl shouted, getting her rope ready. The boat edged towards a wooden jetty surrounded by conifer trees, and the soft scent of pine reminded me of Christmas. A man stood waiting by the steps, bundled up in a fur hat and ski jacket, with his hands in his back pockets. He watched as the rope unfurled in the air, then stepped forward to catch it.

Eight

'*Hei*, Tore!'

'*Hei*, Ana!' He wound the rope around a metal post and dragged the boat in slowly, looping the slack to pull us in. 'You must be Sara Pearson. Welcome to Firefly!'

'Thank you,' I said, taking his warm, calloused hand and hopping onto the jetty. He was similar in age to my dad and his hair had the same steely tinge.

'The snow is on the way,' Ana shouted, as Lars grappled with my bags and threw them off the boat. 'Do you have enough reserves?'

Tore nodded, with a furrowed brow. 'Yes, we are ready for it,' he said, scratching his beard. 'We've plenty of supplies, and we've talked through the evacuation procedure with the guests.'

I half-listened with an eye on my luggage, which was now on the ground getting soggy. The wind had been joined by some drizzle, and it was wet and miserable. My bags were squidgy, Italian leather and weren't designed for a difficult life. Surely Tore would notice them soon. There didn't seem to be a trolley or a bellboy to help.

'Call me if you need anything. Filip will come in the speedboat if you get stuck.'

'*Takk*, Ana. We are good. The boys have been preparing for it all week. Chopping logs and locking everything down.' Tore untied the rope and threw it back to Lars, then picked up a suitcase in each of his shovel-sized hands.

'Get stuck?' I repeated, paying proper attention now my bags were safe.

'*Lykke til*,' Ana called. 'Have a wonderful time, Sara.'

'*Farvel!*' Lars pulled his hat over his ears as the boat grunted into reverse, its engine grinding noisily under the water. Ana and Lars were in matching gold puffer jackets and red mittens, waving in time like a pair of Japanese lucky cats. *Maneki-neko*.

'There is a weather warning in the area but it's nothing to worry about,' Tore said. 'We are used to extreme weather here. The ice storm will come tonight and then the snow will fall.'

I shuddered. The cold was already seeping into my bones, so I sped up to get a move on. Tore was like a giraffe, his neck forward and long legs stalking along. It was hard to keep up.

'I'm not worried – the hotel must have been built with snow in mind, right?'

Tore smiled. 'The hotel?'

'Oh, sorry.' I shook my head. 'Do you call it something else out here?' I couldn't wait to get into the central heating and pop on a fluffy robe. Twenty minutes in the sauna would sort me right out.

'There isn't a hotel as such. All our guests have individual lodges.'

'Oh yes, of course, and they look beautiful, but I assumed the main experiences would be in the hotel? The restaurants and the bar? The spa?'

Tore didn't reply immediately, the crunch of his boots on the frosty leaves interspersed with my double-speed steps filling the silence. I looked over as I trotted along, my ankle boots working hard.

'When you say spa, do you mean the sauna?' he asked, his breath fogging in front of us.

'Yes! Exactly! And the steam room, jacuzzi, swimming pool…' I breathed a sigh of relief. It was obviously just a translation thing.

'It is all in nature,' he said. 'Each sauna is individual, built in the forest, next to the water.'

'Wow, that sounds amazing. And the restaurant?'

'We deliver a *frokost* basket for breakfast every morning so you can enjoy your food in your own time and wake with the daylight, into your own rhythm.'

'Oh! So, there isn't a cooked breakfast?'

'Absolutely. It can be cooked – in your kitchen.'

I hoped this was also a translation thing. He surely wasn't suggesting I cook my *own* breakfast on holiday. There must be a private chef who goes from lodge to lodge in the mornings.

'And lunch and dinner?'

'Are in the Orangery.'

'Ooo, that sounds lovely.'

'Lunch is eaten in silence, to respect our guests and their healing process.' *Huh?* This was getting very weird.

'Dinner is shared tables: three courses, cooked to order, and alcohol-free.'

That got my attention. 'Sorry, what?'

'This is all on our website,' Tore said, looking puzzled. 'And in the welcome information I sent with your confirmation.'

I'm pretty sure I'd have remembered the words *alcohol-free*. What the hell kind of hotel was this? Oh well, I'd just have to buy it from the supermarket and drink behind closed doors.

'Here we are. Hygge Three.' We walked down a winding path and Tore held a branch back and waited, so I didn't get slapped in the face. 'This will be your home while you stay with us.'

We were stood in front of a cute wooden cabin, with smoke piping out of the chimney and a bright light shining above the door. There was a pyramid of logs on either side of the entrance and a small metal table with two chairs out front. I couldn't see much else – the rain was now coming down in sheets – but I'd seen enough to know it wasn't quite the five-star celeb haunt I'd imagined. I'd have to double-check the details once I was in the bath. It was freezing cold, and I was too knackered for any more back and forth.

Tore opened the door and ushered me in out of the rain. It was the sort of place I imagined a human-sized squirrel would live. Everything seemed miniature. A tiny kitchen to the left, a tiny sofa in front of a wood burner straight ahead, and a tiny door that presumably led to the bedroom on the right. The hearth was pale grey stone, decorated with a vase of pine-cone-laden branches next to a pair of old wine bottles wedged with yellow candle nubs.

'Looks like someone forgot to replace the candles,' I said, handing one of them to Tore.

He chuckled. 'Not at all. These are beeswax and have plenty of life left in them. We don't throw candles away until they are finished.' he said, putting it back down. 'This is your living space. Fully equipped kitchen, lounge, dining area, and your bedroom is through here.'

The cabin was covered in pictures of the Northern Lights. Huge swathes of electric green on a canvas in the lounge, a Polaroid of swirly pinks pinned up in the kitchen, and a framed print of purple skies as I walked into the bedroom.

To the right was Mrs Tiggy-Winkle's bed – advertising it as a double was a stretch – with a thick duvet, garish, multicoloured blankets and a pile of square pillows. Bloody Scandinavians and their made-up sizes. IKEA had a lot to answer for. Our student house had been full of odd-shaped mattresses and lamps that only worked with Swedish lightbulbs. I'd have to sleep on my back, like a vampire, and stay still to avoid rolling onto the floor.

'And the bathroom is in the corner,' Tore said. I walked past a wooden chest, lifting the lid to find more crocheted blankets and a hot water bottle wearing a knitted Christmas jumper. The en suite was more of a wet room: a tiled box in shiny black, with a shower head in the centre and a toilet next to the sink.

'Is the, er... bath in another room?' I asked, already knowing the answer.

'We only have showers in the cabins, but there are plenty of lakes for you to bathe in.'

'Are the other guests bathing in this?' The rain was now torrential.

'They can if they choose to. Otherwise, it's the shower.'

Someone had obviously made a mistake somewhere, but there wasn't much I could do about it tonight. It was nearly nine, so I'd nip out and get some wine and crisps and have an early night. There was no TV, but I could watch Netflix on my laptop.

'Lovely. Well, this isn't quite what I'd imagined, but I'll see how I get on. Can I have the Wi-Fi code please? And how far is the shop? I'll pop out and get some supplies.'

Tore was looking increasingly awkward. 'Most of our guests want a tech-free environment for their wellness break, so we don't have Wi-Fi in the cabins. The signal isn't good I'm afraid – by design.' I was starting to get palpitations. 'But there is a small lounge with Wi-Fi next to the restaurant – for emergencies.'

'And I can use my laptop in there?'

'Yes.' Tore was running his coat zip up and down, a worried look on his face. 'If there is something urgent, of course.' There were plenty of urgent things I needed to do. Watch the final episode of *Severance* for a start. 'And I'm sorry, but there is no shop on site,' he said, bending to straighten the tiny cushions on the tiny sofa.

'What?' I was incensed. 'How can it be self-catering, with no option to buy food? Or drinks?' More importantly.

'Well, as I said, the kitchen is for cooking breakfast if you want to, and we deliver the food to your door each morning. To drink, there is coffee, juice, hot chocolate...' He opened the cupboards and fridge to show me. 'And it's no problem to request extras for your breakfast basket. We can add anything you need to our shopping order from the mainland each week.'

'Then can I request some Crunchy Nut Cornflakes and a box of wine?'

Tore nodded slowly. 'I'll see what we can do,' he said, clearly not wanting to say no a third time before I'd even been here an hour.

'In fact, I'll put a shopping list together and give it to you tomorrow.'

'Fine,' he said. 'For tonight, there is vegetable stew in the fridge and homemade sourdough in the tin.' I cheered up at that. 'And *brunost* marshmallows by the fire for something sweet. Big and chunky, with caramel layers. They are very nice.'

Now we were talking.

'Enjoy your *hyttekos*, Sara. Your "cabin cosiness" in Hygge Three. Goodnight.'

I doubted I'd be enjoying anything of the sort and didn't want to get into a verbal contract.

'Goodnight, Tore.' I closed the door and breathed in the smoky air as the fire crackled in the silence. The sound was kind of nice. I mean, it *was* cosy. If cosy meant small. I closed the blinds in the lounge and stood as close to the fire as I could without setting myself alight, enjoying the burn on my thighs. It was pitch-black outside and I couldn't see anything through the darkness. What if I was murdered in my crocheted bed? Invaded by wild reindeer or a blubbery walrus somehow smothered me in my sleep. I couldn't even tell Mum and Dad I'd arrived safely. Would they be worried? Should they be? I was thirty-two after all. It wasn't really their problem that I'd signed myself up to who knows what, who knows where. I eyed the marshmallows suspiciously. Could I trust them? They might be laced with a hallucinogenic or powdered with ayahuasca to alter my mind. I could be knocked unconscious... and then smothered by a blubbery walrus.

I sniffed one and gave it a tentative lick. No effect, but it did taste sugary and marshmallow-y. I cautiously bit into it, and it was... bloody amazing. A tiny cloud of gooey deliciousness. I stuffed another two in and pushed them into my cheeks.

'Chubby bunny,' I said to myself in the mirror and half-smiled, my eyes still and sad.

Then I shoved in a third.

'Chubby bunny,' I said again. It was more of a struggle this time but still would have been clear enough to pass. Mark and I had always played it on bonfire night – he could put away six marshmallows in his chipmunk cheeks, but four was my limit.

I was ready for my small, definitely-not-a-double bed. I jumped in the shower, which was surprisingly hot and powerful. I stayed under the jet far too long, feeling dizzy as I dried myself on the fluffy towels and put on my silk pyjamas, which were slightly impractical as I slithered under the blankets and turned off the lights. It had been A DAY. I'd worry about the Wi-Fi and the food and drink situation, and the weather and the retreat not being fit for purpose, tomorrow. For now, I was safe and warm, and in bed – at last.

A piggy in hygge (three).

Nine

Tuesday 15th September

I woke up in the middle of a tangled blanket doughnut, warm and snuggled, like a happy little kitten.

Slivers of light peeked into the room as I rolled up the blinds, and I was greeted by the most beautiful view: a large patio area with a wood-fired hot tub and a thick blanket of virgin snow leading all the way out to the forest. The trees were weighed down with lumps of icing and everything glittered like a Christmas cake. But however pretty it looked, my breath was making smoke rings in the air, and I couldn't feel my nose; it was bloody freezing. I lifted my duvet and blankets as one and hulked into the lounge to put the fire on. I was not a natural fire-starter. I was more of a thermostat turner-upper. I liked radiators and underfloor heating, any kind of heating in fact, where you flicked a switch and it immediately worked. The wood burner felt alien to me, but I was an intelligent, logical woman – how hard could it be to bung a few logs in and light a match? I piled in the fattest logs I could find, crumbled in a wedge of firelighter and threw in a match. Double of everything so I didn't have to do it twice. But rather than the blazing inferno I'd imagined, the match licked the firelighter's face for thirty seconds, then closed in on itself and fizzled out.

So I did it again. And again, and again, and then *again*. Like a crazed arsonist. What kind of firelighter was this? Why wouldn't it bastard-well light?

There was a knock at the door, and I caught my reflection in the window as I tiptoed across the cold tiles. I felt like a queen on coronation day, clutching my full-length cape to my chest, but in reality my hair was frizzy, and I had creases on my red cheeks from burrowing too tightly into the sheets. I wasn't made for emergency situations. Lighting fires and answering doors. *Whatever next?*

'Hello?' I called suspiciously, cracking the door open half an inch.

'*Hei*, Sara, welcome to Firefly Forest!' With one eye, I could just about make out a man on my doorstep. Tall and tanned, with a soft Viking beard, holding a wicker basket covered in red gingham cloth.

Mr Red Riding Hood. I had no plans to open the door any further.

'Thank you. Can you leave the basket there, please? I'm just… in the shower.' I couldn't go out in my blanket dress. What if J-Law saw me?

'Sure, take your time. I'm Henrik, Tore's son. My brother Jonas and I help run things around here, so if you need anything, just let me know.'

'Will do!' I said, starting to close the door.

'Have you got the fire working OK?' he asked. I was torn between telling him the truth and having him, or anyone, see me like this.

'Erm… sort of,' I replied, turning to look at it. There was no sign of fire. Fucking thing.

'Can I help you with it? There is a knack I can show you.'

'Well, I'm not really decent at the moment…'

'I can come back in ten minutes if that's better for you?'

'Yes, actually, ten minutes would be great.' I needed warmth and I couldn't even YouTube 'how to make a fire' and get tips from strangers. It was just me on my own trying to work it all out. Where was Bear Grylls when you needed him?

'See you then, then,' Henrik said, and I watched him through the spyhole until he disappeared into the forest. He took big strides in his stonewashed Levi's and battered boots, off to find his next Grandma.

I waited a full minute to be sure, then dragged the basket in like a hungry raccoon. It was filled to the brim with treats and the sugary smells made my mouth water. Fresh sourdough, croissants, raspberry jam, nutty granola and a bag of juicy clementines. It all looked so good, I didn't know where to start. I dipped a croissant in jam and ate it on the way to the shower, luxuriating in the hot water and the power massage on my back. My TikTok jeans and pink angora jumper were both more fashion than function, so I layered them up with my skiing thermals to stay warm. It was obvious only a few of my clothes were going to cut it, so I'd just have to wear all of them, *all the time*. And more fool me for presuming I'd be lounging around in a robe all day inside a brick building with radiators.

By the time Henrik returned, I was back to feeling fresh again and looking much more 'me'.

'Hi,' I said, opening the door fully this time. 'Sorry about that – I wasn't quite with it. I overslept and forgot where I was.'

Henrik laughed. 'This place will do that to you,' he said. 'You'll get plenty of deep sleep – that's for sure.' A taller, broader version of Tore, with the same chocolate button eyes, he was gorgeous, with his dark blonde man-bun and golden tan. A Norwegian He-Man. 'Let's get some heat going on in here, shall we?' he said, rubbing his hands together. *Yes, please.*

He opened up the wood burner, whistled at the charcoaled mess, then started taking the logs out one by one.

'Sorry, I'm not very outdoorsy,' I said, embarrassed. 'I'm a barrister.'

I winced as a chunk of wood fell out and scattered soot all over the floor.

'Enough said. More the indoorsy type, then.'

'Not really that either to be honest. Incourtsy. Is that a type?'

'Not a type that can build a fire, it seems,' Henrik said, smiling. 'But it's easy when you know how. You just need a couple of these small sticks piled up with some paper. I build a kind of Jenga tower to keep it all together, or make a cone and point everything up.'

'Mm-hmm,' I said, sliding another croissant out of the basket and into my mouth. 'I see...'

'Then it's a case of putting the firelighter in the right spot, and... hey, presto!'

He stood and watched as the bundle of sticks burst into flames, waiting until a mini fire got going before adding a small piece of wood, and then another, until he eventually got a full-sized log in there.

What a bloody faff this was going to be. Couldn't he just swing by and do it for me each morning? Surely it was basic customer service to make sure guests didn't freeze to death in their Firefly beds. And it wouldn't hurt to have some early-morning eye candy to start the day off strong.

'I've been doing it all wrong. Stuffing a tree in there and trying to light it. No wonder it wasn't doing anything.'

'Ah, no. It takes practice,' he said, holding the door ajar and blowing on it gently. 'I'm doing this all day every day; you'll get the hang of it. Are you happy with everything so far, otherwise? Let me know if you have any questions.'

Where to even begin? 'Oooh, yes, I do have a couple. Is there a laundry service?' I was here for a month after all; how could anyone manage on one suitcase of clothes? Or two, even?

'Not a service as such, but we have a washing machine and dryer that guests can use up near the main house.'

'Ahhh – so there *is* a main house. What a relief! I was beginning to think I'd be stuck in this tiny shoebox the entire month!'

'Well, yes, we have a farmhouse, but...'

'Sod the fire in that case, I'll mosey on up there for a macchiato and people-watch for a couple of hours.'

'...it's our family home,' he finished, quietly.

'Oh. I *see*,' I said, awkwardly changing tack. 'Can you show me where the Wi-Fi lounge is then instead? I can get a coffee in there.'

'Erm...'

'Your dad said I could?' I said, feeling desperate.

'Sure, I can take you there, but it's not what you might think of as a lounge. Is that what Tore called it?' Henrik smiled to himself, his teeth pearly white against his sun-kissed skin. 'The retreat is advertised as tech-free, you see, so the Wi-Fi is really just in place for emergencies.'

'And is Netflix classed as an emergency?' I asked, half-serious.

Henrik's eyes sparkled as he laughed. 'I wouldn't say so, no. Watching TV goes against the vibe of the place. People come here to switch off from all that,' he said, swerving me off topic. 'There are loads of activities instead though, to get you into nature – I have your programme here in fact,' he said, handing me a booklet. 'Today we have a laughter workshop at ten, in the Sun Hut.'

I cringed. That sounded like my idea of hell, but I didn't want to be a spoilsport. 'What does that involve, exactly?'

Henrik smiled. 'Lots of laughing, ideally. It's very fun and silly, and everyone always leaves in a happy mood. You know how it is when you get the uncontrollable giggles?' I nodded. 'It's a real high, right? Complete release.' The fire was now at full throttle, flames licking at the glass door, grappling to get out. Henrik gave it a sharp prod with the poker and threw on one last log before locking it up. 'There, that should keep you going.'

'Thank goodness for you! I was about to set fire to a pillow to get it started.'

He shrugged. 'Come on, I'll take you to the Wi-Fi *lounge*,' he said, the twinkle still there. 'Bring your map, and I'll give you a tour at the same time.'

Finally – access to civilisation.

We trudged through the snow and into the forest where I spotted a couple of other cabins camouflaged into the woodland. Each one was in its own space, far away from any neighbours. All of us together, in the middle of nowhere.

'You're from London, aren't you?' Henrik asked, his hands stuffed in his back pockets as he walked.

'Yes, the King's Road – I mean, King's Cross – do you know it?' Freudian slip. The King's Road was where I'd lived with Mark. Before.

'Like in Monopoly?' He had a flirtatious glint in his eye. 'Yeah, I've heard of it.'

I laughed. 'The very one. It's been done up over the last few years, so it's much nicer than it used to be.'

'What made you come out here if you're not an outdoorsy person?'

Bloody good question. 'It's a funny story actually. Did Emma Stone stay here a few months ago?'

Henrik frowned for a second then shook his head. 'I don't think so. I'm pretty good with names and I don't remember an Emma. Is she a friend of yours?'

'Emma Stone, the Hollywood actress?'

He looked at me blankly. 'Sorry – no idea. The signal is bad out here, as I said, and I'm not really one for watching films.'

Good God. 'Not even on your laptop?'

'My laptop is very old,' he reasoned. 'I've spent too much of my life staring at a screen; I mostly avoid them. When I'm not working, I like to take the boat out.'

The farmhouse came into view, and it was very clearly a family home. Beautiful red brick, with a cutesy porch and white shutters on every window. Picture-perfect from a distance, but as we got closer, I could see the paint was peeling on the shutters and the roof was missing a slate or two. Henrik walked me down a dirt track and my phone picked up the Wi-Fi network before we'd even reached the lounge.

'What's the password?' I asked, thirsty for distraction.

'Audhilda,' he said, taking my phone and typing it in. 'Do you want to sit inside while you do whatever it is you need to do?'

I nodded. 'Yes please. I'm quite attached to my fingers.'

Henrik laughed and punched a code into the keypad, granting me access to the lounge of tech shame. It clearly hadn't seen much action in a while. The shutters were closed, and the tables and chairs were covered in a thin layer of dust.

'Amazing, thanks.' The group chat was pinging off the charts and I couldn't wait to read all the gossip.

'And what was it you wanted again? A macchiato?'

I blushed, feeling like a prize chump. 'No, I'm fine. I didn't realise this was the set-up.'

'I'm teasing. I'll get you a coffee from the kitchen. Milk? Sugar?'

'Splash of milk, half a sugar, please.'

HIIT me up Group Chat

Abi: Don't hate me, but there's been a slight miscommunication on my part.

Kat: Go on?

Abi: Not for you – Sara.

Kat: Oh. Well, she's not online so tell me – I won't hate you 😊

Abi: So, it turns out the retreat Emma Stone went to was in Sweden, not Norway.

Kat: Oof, so close.

Abi: I know. Do you think she'll be cross?

Kat: Not at all, babes! It's an easy mistake to make after half a bottle of wine. You weren't expecting her to book it.

Abi: True. I feel bad though. Where the hell is she? Sara??? Where the hell are you?

I knew this didn't feel right. FUCKETY FUCKING FUCK. *Where the hell was I?* This was where spontaneity got me: in a mud hut in the middle of nowhere, setting fire to my Jimmy Choos to stay warm.

Me: Abi!!!!! WTF! I'm getting the next boat out of here. There's no spa. Or heating!

Kat: Hey, Sara! Hmm, that sounds bad. Abi isn't online, but I'm sure she'll get the message soon. She's really sorry 🙁

Me: I'm going to kill her. Abi!!! I'm going to kill you.

The door creaked open, and Henrik appeared with two mugs and a plate of biscuits. 'One very basic coffee with milk,' he said, putting it all down.

'As long as it's hot and caffeinated.'

'Oh yeah. It's all of that. Cookie?' he offered. I took two in case he didn't come back. 'Is it legal work you're doing?'

'Er… yes, a couple of urgent emails. Shouldn't take long.'

I tilted my phone away slightly as I quietly clicked out of Instagram. I'd already posted my photos of the fjords and the farmhouse and made it clear I was at an amazing top-secret spa #amazing #topsecretspa.

Henrik sat opposite with his coffee and I wondered if he had to supervise me while I was in here. To make sure I didn't overdose on TikTok.

'Henrik? This is a bit of a strange one so bear with me, but having checked a few things online, I seem to be… on the wrong retreat.'

He slowly raised his eyebrows. 'The wrong retreat?'

'Yes.' I laughed. 'It turns out, I'm supposed to be in Sweden. Can you believe it?' I took an awkward sip of my coffee, then stopped for a second to enjoy it. Perfect taste, perfect temperature, creamy and strong. 'Oooh – this is nice!'

'Isn't it? That's the coffee you've got in your cabin. Jonas grinds the beans by hand. He's obsessed with it. Wait till you try the biscuits. Freshly baked in the Nilsen kitchen this morning by the big man himself.'

I bit into one and it melted on my tongue. Crumbly and oaty with choc chips, it immediately leapfrogged Fortnum's double-choc chunkies as my favourite biscuits of all time. Henrik watched my face change with a shy smile.

77

'Good, aren't they? *Mor's* secret recipe. My mother. Sorry, you were saying… you were heading for Sweden and took a hard left?'

'It's a long story; I won't bore you with all the details. Obviously I'll still pay in full – I wouldn't want you to be out of pocket.'

Henrik looked completely bewildered. 'But you only arrived last night. How do you know you won't like it here?'

'Oh no – it's not that! I already love it here, but it's my friend's birthday. My Swedish friend.' I could smell freedom. A quick swipe of my credit card and I'd be out of here. We could sweep this misunderstanding under the carpet and forget it ever happened. 'If it's OK with you, I'll settle whatever I owe and get out of your hair today. Can I book a boat back to Bergen harbour?'

'Not likely, I'm afraid,' Tore said, from the doorway. 'Good morning, Sara. How did you sleep?'

'Morning!' I said, surprised to see him. 'I slept well, thank you. Really well.'

'I'm pleased to hear you got some rest,' he said. 'The Bergen boat only comes once a day, and ordinarily we could take you to the mainland in our dinghy, but not in this weather.' He looked out at the heavy clouds. The snow was falling thick and fast against the window, adding to the chunky layer already on the ground. I didn't want to get stuck here.

'How long will it last?' I asked, repeatedly tapping my weather app and getting nothing. I was being held hostage by a lack of technology.

'A couple of days. Maybe three.'

'Three days?! You mean we're trapped?' I already *was stuck here*. My heart raced as I tried to think logically. Three days was totally doable. Seventy-two hours. Two more sleeps. I wasn't trapped; I was safe, and warm and completely fine. But I couldn't catch my breath.

Henrik eyed me with concern. 'Are you OK?'

I nodded silently and he jumped up and ran round the table.

'Look at me,' he said gently, taking my hands. 'Into my eyes. It's fine. You're fine. Now, take a breath in...' I followed his voice and mirrored his breathing. 'And out...' He nodded as he spoke, keeping eye contact and calmly repeating the words until the feeling passed.

'Thank you,' I said, relieved and full of adrenaline, once I was out the other side. 'I've been having these breathless episodes. It's stress, I think. I'm OK now.'

'Are you sure?' Henrik's eyes were full of concern. 'Take your time.'

I kept the deep breathing going and pushed into the soles of my feet, feeling the floor solid beneath me.

'I'll just have to be patient, I guess. The weather is the weather. Can I book on the next boat whenever it makes it through? And I'll settle my bill now, so at least that part is done.'

'But you've already paid,' Tore said, confused. 'Upfront when you booked.'

'Have I?' Well, that explained why I'd thought it was a ten-star spa. Four grand wasn't the deposit – it was the full amount. I just hadn't quite realised that this was what I'd paid for. 'Great, well that's sorted then. No hard feelings and maybe someone else will book in and you can sell my room twice.'

Henrik shook his head in disbelief. 'You don't even want to try it out for a week when you've already paid? How bad can it be?'

Father and son both looked at me, one hurt and the other offended.

'It's not bad at all! It's beautiful and I'd love to stay, but as I said, I'm supposed to be in Sweden at a different Firefly altogether. Is it er… Firefly Lodge?'

Tore shook his head. 'I've no idea.'

'Never heard of it,' Henrik seconded.

'The Firefly Hotel and Spa?' They both shrugged. 'I'll double-check. I'm not great with names.'

'A barrister with a bad memory, eh?' Tore smiled. 'Not many of those around. If the weather is clear we can take you back to Bergen on Thursday, but give us a chance to change your mind, hey?'

'Starting with my laughter workshop,' Henrik said. 'If you're up for it?'

'Absolutely!' I said with a big smile. I absolutely *wasn't*, but if I was only here for a few days, it wouldn't hurt to throw myself into it. 'Lead the way.'

Ten

*H*ow? How had this happened? I was a good person and didn't deserve this on my holidays.

I'd walked with Henrik to the Sun Hut and was now crossed-legged on the floor in some kind of 'let's all have a breakdown together' circle. A pile of shoes had been left at the door, and there was a sour, sweaty smell about the place. It was the first time I'd encountered the other guests and there were twelve of us in the circle. Will and Celeste were to my right, a shiny Canadian couple on a gap year who were bursting at the seams with youth and positivity. All nut-brown hair and dewy skin. Lucky bastards. Ethel was on my left, a woman who was well into her seventies and walked with a gold cane. Her chunky, mustard cardigan looked handmade, and her silver necklaces jangled as she told me about her drive over from Oslo. Ethel had been to Firefly every year since she'd retired and was looking forward to her annual zen top-up.

I didn't get chance to meet the others, but we were all embarking on this 'transformational experience' together, so no doubt I would. Although it would just be the three days of transformation for me. Which would be plenty.

'Good morning!' Henrik called. 'I will be running the laughter workshop today.' He flipped his hair into a bun and slipped off his shoes.

'Good morrrrn-ing, Hen-rik!' the group parroted back like cheeky schoolchildren.

I started to worry that this might be an interactive session. Would I be expected to explain why I couldn't laugh anymore? To sit and think about where my giggle had gone?

Henrik stood in the centre of the circle, slowly turning to look each of us in the eye. 'The aim of today is to have fun and let ourselves go,' he said, lingering a second longer than necessary when he got to me. His gaze was so intense it made me flutter. 'There is no pressure here. Simply go with the flow and let's see what comes. The only thing I ask is that you try not to block your feelings. OK?'

There was a collective exhalation as we nervously smiled at each other.

'Right. Are we ready? Everyone up,' Henrik said, stretching out his hamstrings. We stayed in the circle, mirroring his moves as if he were an aerobics instructor. 'Now, I want you to breathe into your feet. Feel the ground holding you up. No one is judging you here.'

Celeste nodded emphatically, gripping the mat with her naked finger-like toes. I was *totally* judging her. I'd planned to have a pedicure when I got here, so my feet weren't really fit for public viewing, and from what I could see, neither were Ethel's. Foot Finder would have a field day. I stood strong in my socks as Henrik moved on to some vigorous all over body shaking to expel the bad energy. I didn't need bare feet to laugh.

'We'll start with some simple ha, ha, ha, hee, hee, hee,' Henrik said, completely straight faced. Wizbit himself. I willed myself to join in with enthusiasm and vim, but I just couldn't do it, so I silently mouthed along with the others and tried to get away with it.

'And now an evil laugh. Mwah, ha, ha, ha, haaa.' Tongues lolled about all over the place and there was a whiff of coffee breath in the air as everyone copied Henrik, panting like a pack of dehydrated dogs.

The Japanese couple opposite were already giggling away.

'And clap in time!' Henrik called. 'HO. HO. Ha-ha-ha. HO. HO. Ha-ha-ha.'

I couldn't pretend to clap, so I surrendered to the process and got involved with ho-ing and ha-ing. It was strangely liberating to go all in – and much easier than faking it. And once I relaxed and let myself go, I felt something inside me shift.

'Now walk in a circle.' Henrik's eyes were twinkling again. Was this a wind up?

I followed Will, who marched behind a skipping Celeste, and the repetition of sounds punctuated the air like a drumbeat as we moved. The chanting felt almost meditational to start with, but once Henrik added in the walking, it was like being in a zombie apocalypse.

I stifled a snigger, and Henrik caught my eye.

'Don't hold it back, Sara,' he shouted across the room. Ethel snorted in my ear, and I lost my composure. A guttural guffaw started rumbling in my chest as a happier version of myself tried to get out. It didn't really sound like me, but it had been a while since anything had properly cracked me up – maybe I didn't recognise it anymore. Whatever it was, I couldn't hold it back. The sight of this mad, gurning circle of strangers and the ludicrousness of even being in this situation was too much. My snigger turned into a chuckle and then I got the giggles, until I was double chin laughing with my whole body. My cheeks pushed into my eyes as I shrieked at the hilariousness of it all and *I couldn't breathe*.

We took it in turns to be the person losing control of our faculties. The hysteria was infectious, and by the end of the session, tears were rolling down my cheeks and I couldn't really remember what it was that had tickled me so much in the first place. The laughter stopped in the same way it had started, gradually going back down to silence. Bubbles of excitement filled my stomach, and I felt elated. Was this another gratis way the Norwegians got their kicks?

'Amazing work,' Henrik said, beaming around at us all. 'Enjoy all those endorphins coursing through your veins. People forget to laugh when they become adults. Children laugh all the time. Loud and without fear. It's incredibly good for you.'

'Kinda cool,' Will said with a smile.

'Better than sex!' Celeste added and everyone cheered. Except Will. 'Not really,' she said, giving him a hug.

Maybe I didn't need a box of wine, after all. Not for the next few hours anyway. Although realistically, how often were we going to stand in a circle, laughing for no reason? I'd be needing a drink in between times.

'Lunch is being served in the Orangery if you'd like to make your way over,' Henrik hollered over the chatter as everyone came down from their natural high.

The mention of food had my stomach grumbling. It had been quite a morning.

'I'm so hungry,' I said, falling into step with Ethel. 'I could eat a horse.'

'The food here is fabulous. Are you a practising vegan?' she asked, raising her eyebrow at my phrasing.

'Ugh, no,' I said, aghast. 'I don't know how they do it, do you? What is life without a bacon and egg buttie on a Sunday morning? And milk and cream – and butter! No, it's not for me. I'll be having the carnivore menu.'

Will stopped suddenly and turned. 'You'll be having the *what*?' he snapped. 'Celeste! You told me there was "no meat at the retreat"?'

'There isn't!' Celeste replied wide-eyed. 'It's one of their slogans.'

'Is it?' I said, equally surprised.

'What have you heard?' Will whispered, clearly desperate. 'How do I get it?'

'I don't know! Sorry, I assumed...'

'It's her first day, remember,' Ethel said with a chuckle as the restaurant came into view. It was a huge, wooden building, festooned with dotty bunting and fairy lights.

Tore stood in the doorway and welcomed us in one by one. He nodded, then I nodded, although I was slightly freaked out by his overenthusiastic smile. Weird. The dining area looked set for Valentine's Day, with candlelit tables for two dotted between the fir trees, each one made from a different type of rustic wood and decorated with jars of dahlias. The air felt fresh and green, yet cosy at the same time. It reminded me of Dad's old greenhouse, a labyrinth of leaves decorated with shiny, red tomatoes. He'd slice them up and sprinkle them with salt, and we'd eat them with crusty bread and butter.

A hush descended as I followed Ethel up to the buffet. 'Am I missing something?' I whispered.

She put her finger to her lips and pointed to a handwritten sign next to the cauliflower rice.

Please observe silence during lunchtime.

I looked around and realised everyone had gone quiet. Only the clinkety-clank of cutlery and the shuffling of chairs could be heard. It was stifling. It took me back to a failed twenty-four-hour sponsored silence in high school, which I'd accidentally cocked up by answering my phone. My brain wanted to run outside and shout into the sky, but my stomach was gurgling away and talking a lot of sense, so I decided to zip my mouth and grab a quick bite.

I moved along the line like the Little Mermaid, using my body to communicate. Big, excited eyes at the man spooning out jacket potatoes, and after several encouraging nods from my side, he eventually gave me a second. I wrinkled my nose at the aubergine lady and smiled at the bean chilli girl, then took a seat at an empty table and looked around. Would it be frowned upon to get my phone out? Nobody else had, so probably. Although I couldn't do much on it without any Wi-Fi. Flick through photos and reread old messages. What was the point of that? I'd just have to sit and eat quietly, with nothing to distract me. Like a sociopath. I smiled at Celeste and rolled my eyes – like *what the helll, gurlll?* – but she stared straight through me, then turned away.

Ethel was far too busy with her broccoli to notice me trying to make eye contact, so I gave up and ate my food instead. Celeste was right – no meat at the retreat – and my potato was devoid of dairy. I'd have liked it slathered in butter and cheese, but my churning mime hadn't resonated with the chefs. Instead, they'd given me an onion stuffed with jackfruit, and a pepper sauce. I was determined to hate it, but it was annoyingly delicious. Meaty, even. Maybe I was hallucinating because I was so hungry. Or maybe they knew what they were doing in that kitchen. The sound of my own chewing rang through my ears, and I felt overly conscious as I swallowed each mouthful. As if everyone could hear the gulps. Scoffing sushi in the work loos had become my norm, and being so far down the other side of the spectrum felt very weird. I'd never had so much time and space to consider my food.

Once we'd all finished our beetroot brownies, Tore wandered through the restaurant like an exam invigilator, silently putting a note on each table as some soft piano music started to play. We were being gently woken from our tranquillity, and it was a relief to have something to focus on again.

We hope you enjoyed your lunch, proudly vegan and cooked from organic ingredients grown in Firefly Forest. This afternoon we meet at the sauna pods at 4 p.m. Please wrap up warm and bring swimwear and towels.
   Tore, Henrik and Jonas

Yes. Time for some luxury. A sauna would warm me up, if nothing else. I trudged back to my cabin through the snowstorm, knowing it would be almost as cold inside as it was outside. I'd have to get the feeling back in my fingers before I could attempt another fire. I braced myself, but I was hit by a delicious heat as soon as I opened the door. Bizarrely, the fire was still going strong. But it was more than that – the cabin felt homely and welcoming, and I was warm enough to take off my coat and bobble hat. In fact, I was suddenly desperate to get them off. The wood burner was roaring wildly, like a mini bonfire in the middle of the room, and there was a note under a stone on the hearth:

Sara,
    Apologies – there was a problem with the heater in your cabin, which is why it was so cold.
    I've fixed it and built another fire, so it should be plenty hot from now.
    Henrik :)

Amazing. I had not been looking forward to shivering in my PJs and burying myself in blankets. The hot air thawed out my bones, starting with my toes and working its way up. I was a real-life Ready Brek kid glowing warm from the inside out.

I had a few hours to kill before my sauna session, so I made one of Henrik's delicious coffees and hunkered down in bed with my Kindle. I was exhausted from all the laughing and crying and eating. Reading was my only entertainment option, and I couldn't remember the last time I'd picked up a book for pleasure. My life was spent scanning bricks of paperwork for case-winning nuggets and staying hypervigilant in case there were inconsistencies or mistakes. Reading for fun just didn't happen anymore. I'd been a voracious reader as a child, reading with a torch under the covers after lights out. The morning was always too far away to find out what happened next. And I'd taken that level of compulsion into my work. I *had to know* what the story was and how we were going to win as quickly as possible.

There was always a way to win; it was just a case of working out how.

Eleven

The snow was still falling as I left for the sauna, piling up against the door and weighing down the trees. Stalactites on stalactites hung precariously from the roof and the wind howled as the blizzard swirled overhead.

I couldn't imagine the storm stopping anytime soon. Although staying longer didn't seem half so bad now the cabin was warm and cosy. In fact, I wasn't sure I wanted to go anywhere for a while. But I'd make an exception for the sauna.

My tankini with the missing jigsaw pieces seemed inappropriate under the circumstances, but it was the best of a bad bunch. Ordinarily I liked a cheeky flash of flesh on holiday, but it was out of place here and felt ridiculous. I'd layered my thermals on and had less than five seconds before I started sweating, so I pulled my hood up to protect my hair and got ready for a cold, dark walk. My phone torch wasn't much use, but at least it was a light in the mist as I kept my head down and walked into the wind. Into nothingness. And I suddenly felt vulnerable on my own in the middle of a strange forest.

Man, or bear? *Man, or bear???*

I was half considering turning back when a turquoise umbrella bobbed towards me, hiding whoever was behind it.

'Hello?' I called.

Henrik peeked around the side with a smile, looking like a Teletubby in his red snowsuit. '*Hei*, Sara. Are you joining us for Fire and Ice?'

'Yes,' I shouted into the wind. 'I was just on my way.'

'Great! I am accompanying guests down as the weather is so bad. We don't want anyone to fall.' He held out his umbrella and nodded me under, which I was grateful for on behalf of my blow-dry. What was left of it, anyway.

'Norwegian service,' he said, offering me his arm. I tucked in tight to make it easier for us to bundle along together. Henrik's snowsuit was soft and puffy, but I could still feel his arm through the feathers. It almost felt like he was flexing under my grip. Muscular and taut, he was holding me up as I skittered on the ice. My boots were designed more for style than practicality, but they looked cute, so no regrets. I'd just have to watch my step.

'The Swedes do it differently, eh?'

'Oh, yes. It's extremely poor over there.' He smiled. 'You won't get door-to-door service in Sweden.'

'I'll let you know when I get there.'

'These are for you, too,' Henrik said, holding out two sachets. 'Hand warmers.'

And they were already hot. 'Oh wow,' I said, popping them into my gloves and immediately feeling better.

'Nice, huh? They help distract from the rest of the cold.'

'Amazing,' I said, shuddering. 'How far is it to the sauna pods?'

'Five minutes' walk from here. They are next to the lake. Well, it's a lake in the summer. Right now, it's an ice-skating rink.'

Each step felt precarious as my boots tried to get some traction. I leant my head into Henrik's shoulder and trusted him to lead the way as the wind tried to push us back. He was strong, so I wasn't worried I'd fall, but I had to stay focused. A sauna seemed entirely frivolous given the circumstances, but I *was* supposed to be on holiday – I couldn't sit inside all day reading.

Henrik stopped and left me to balance on my own while he opened the door, then he took my hand and led me into the calm and warm.

'Another bird in the nest,' Celeste said as I pulled back my hood. 'That's three of us, then.'

Celeste and Will were sat in matching Dry Robes cradling hot chocolates, ready to go.

'Hey, you two,' I said, anxiously eyeing their outfits and feeling entirely underprepared. I only had my towel from the cabin to cover up with.

'I think three is going to be it for today,' Henrik said. 'I'm impressed by all of your commitment to wellness.'

I was immediately suspicious at that. *Commitment* and *wellness* as buzzwords didn't do it for me. Even though we were going for a sauna – and a sauna was a sauna, surely? – I could sense some kind of socially embarrassing test was coming.

'The saunas can be seen through the window, over there,' Henrik said, pointing in the direction of some fairy lights. 'I suggest that instead of swimming today, we run from here to the sauna for our first burst of ice. Then two minutes in the sauna and back outside for two minutes. Repeat, repeat, repeat.'

And there it was. I'd been tricked, again. Henrik saw my face and thought I was disappointed.

'Unless you want to do the swim?' he said.

As if. The wind looked about ready to pull the trees up by their roots and start hurling them around. 'No, no. I'm good, thanks.'

'Storm chasing! Yeah!' Will shouted, flexing his muscles to make Celeste giggle.

I had to say something.

'I didn't see the part about the swimming,' I started.

'*Ja.* It's the cold to the hot,' Henrik said.

'Which sounds fun, and I *love that* for you guys, but I'm not massively keen.' I was increasingly mindful of my teeny-weeny jigsaw tankini and wishing I'd worn my wetsuit, or even just some shorts.

'No pressure to do the ice part of fire and ice, but you might find it a relief after the sauna. It is extremely hot in there,' Henrik said. 'Deliberately so.'

'Of course. And missing out is totally on me. I thought the fire and ice would be in different huts.'

Will snorted. 'Why would they put the ice in a hut, when it's already on the ground?'

Smart-arse.

'The last time I did this kind of thing, we moved between two rooms in the spa. Cold, then hot, then swim.'

'Which is what this is, but without the swim so we don't get hypothermia,' Celeste said with a frown. 'But it's a better *experience*. We're in nature. This is the real deal. You don't get snow in a spa.'

'They sit you in an overpriced freezer, then pop you in the oven,' Will said.

'Both experiences will have their advantages,' Henrik laughed, coming to my rescue.

'It's just what I'm used to,' I said, feeling defensive. There was nothing wrong with the spa version.

Celeste slipped off her Dry Robe. 'Shall we get on with it, then?'

'Absolutely. Sara, do you have your costume to change into?' Henrik asked, taking in my waterproof trousers and thermal combo.

'Yes. No. I've got it on underneath and then this to wrap myself in.' I held up my green bath towel and Will and Celeste exchanged *who is this idiot?* glances. 'Sorry, I thought towels would be provided.'

Henrik paused. 'There's a robe in the changing room you can put on between saunas, if you don't want to run into the snow. You'll still be more than cold enough to feel the benefit.'

There were signs everywhere insisting guests wash themselves while naked – with soap –

before using the sauna. 'Naked' was in capital letters. It was like a boot camp. They wouldn't know though, would they? If I left my bikini on while I showered? The poster glared at me as if it could read my mind and I quickly stripped off – *please wash your face, bits and pits* – then I patched my bikini back on and slipped on the robe. I knew they'd have guest robes somewhere. Bright orange, with

Firefly stitched across the back in tiny green dots. It didn't look anything special on the peg, but it was velvety soft inside, and heavy. A dressing gown version of a weighted blanket. It somehow took the pressure off my shoulders and grounded me at the same time, connecting me with the moment. I popped my purple Crocs on and went back out, feeling like I was dressed the part.

'Ready?' Henrik was in his swimmers and wearing the same robe as me. We looked like competing couples on a TV challenge. Me and Henrik versus Will and Celeste. I didn't want to let Team Firefly down, but I also didn't want to freeze to death. So...

I plastered on a smile. 'Yup! Let's go.'

Henrik jumped up and down like a pogo stick, suddenly invigorated, then flung open the door and disappeared into a cloud of snowy smoke. 'Follow meeeeeee!' he called behind him, and Will and Celeste followed with a whoop. I went as fast as my little Crocs would carry me but I was already slower than everyone else and we were only on the first challenge. I toddled out into the snow and couldn't help but shriek as the cold smacked me in the face. Blinded by the wind and breathless from the shock – this was what commitment to wellness got you.

'Sara! Over here!' Henrik called as my body started to cryogenically freeze. I'd be found mid-stride once the storm was over, like the White Witch in Narnia. I ignored the fact I couldn't feel my legs and kept doing the motion of walking, like Theresa May dancing in the snow. Henrik grabbed my hand for the last few steps, a silhouette against the heat and glow of the sauna behind him. Like an alien grabbing an earthling and pulling them into the spaceship.

'Ahhuhuhuu.' I shuddered involuntarily as I made it inside. The dry heat was delicious, enveloping me all over and making me shiver. I rolled out my tiny towel on the bottom rack to lie down for a snoozy sauna and hung up my robe. The others were sat on the edge of their seats with bright red faces and an egg timer between them.

'It is *extremely* hot in here,' Henrik said, stating the obvious. My eyelids were already sweaty, and they were always the last to go. 'We recommend no more than two minutes at a time.'

The sands ran out and Team Canada leapt up.

'See you out there,' Celeste called, as they ran back into the snow.

'I'll wait with you,' Henrik said, looking at me with concern.

'I'm not sure I can do two minutes,' I croaked. 'I'm already too hot.' I felt heady and dizzy, and my throat was dry. Henrik handed me some water, and I pressed the glass to my face for a second, before pouring it all over my head. The water mingled with the sweat, slow broiling me. I needed to get outside and cool down.

'You're meant to drink it,' Henrik chided, though the corner of his mouth quirked up. 'Time is up. You can put the robe back on.'

I couldn't think of anything worse than putting a heavy, velvety robe *back on*. I wanted to remove everything, including my hair. 'No, I... I... can't. I'll have to come out like this.'

He shrugged, grabbed his own robe, and we dashed outside.

'Ye ha!' Henrik shouted, leaping off the steps to join Will and Celeste, who were lying on the ground doing snow angels. Adrenaline junkies. The cold was absolute bliss for half a second, then quickly plunged me into frostbite territory and I was freezing once again.

The shouting, running and rolling must all be part of distracting the brain. I stood outside the sauna panicking. Too cold to go forward, too hot to go back. It was a temperature rollercoaster and neither option was enjoyable for more than a few seconds. If only the snow could be warmer, and the sauna could be cooler, it would be perfect. Which was probably where the swim came into it.

'The pleasure is in the extremes,' Henrik whispered, as if reading my mind, draping his robe over my shaking shoulders. I wrapped myself up, snuggling into his hood. The warmth was orgasmic, running down my spine and making me tingle. He had a point. These little moments of heaven were almost worth the agony either side.

'Back to the fire!' Will shouted, and the four of us ran into the heat of the sauna and glared at the egg timer for two minutes, willing the sand to go faster, *faster, faster*, before going back out into the snow. Back and forth, back and forth, challenging ourselves to sit in the uncomfortable. I extended the number of seconds before putting my robe on each time and it was excruciating. Five seconds suddenly felt like forever. I couldn't decide if it was getting easier or harder as we dared each other to keep going, but after forty minutes Henrik called it.

'That's enough for today. Well done, all of you, an excellent session – most wouldn't have kept going for so long. You have more than earned your dinner. Go back, enjoy a shower and relax.'

I was exhausted from the adrenaline of being in survival mode and so, *so* happy to get into the heat of the changing room and put my woollies back on. Feeling warmer and happier with every layer, like a human pass the parcel. End to end it had been an hour of focus on something completely different; something other than Mark and the dogs, and work and what I was doing with my life. It was impossible to think about anything other than the seconds ticking by while running between the fire and the ice.

Twelve

Wednesday 16th September

Yes! I was finally close enough to the Wi-Fi lounge to pick it up and my phone was pinging rapid-fire in my pocket.

I didn't want Tore and Henrik to think I was some kind of tech desperado, so I hid behind a pine tree to check my messages. Over fifty likes for my photo of the fjords. Including Mark. Still watching what I was up to. And so many comments:

Beautiful! / I've always wanted to go to Norway. / Refreshing to see somewhere new. / Looks amazing! / Fab photos. / DM me to collab.

I'd become a travel influencer overnight but didn't have time to reply to my new fans. I zipped through and liked all the comments, then homed in on Mark's.

Are you in Bergen?

I didn't want to publicly answer, so I sent him a DM.

Hey. Yes, well spotted. Vegan spa. Very exclusive. I'll send you a pin and you can check it out.

A pair of birds were scrapping above me as I swiped through to TikTok, and a branch full of snow emptied onto my head. The icy sludge slid past my neck and I screamed as it shimmied down my back.

'Sara? Is that you?'

I peered around the trunk, my hair now full of snow, and Henrik was leaning out of a window up at the farmhouse.

'Yes, only me! Morning!' I waved my phone by way of explanation.

He chuckled. 'I recognised the scream. You can sit in the lounge, you know. You don't have to Wordle in the bushes.'

'I didn't want to disturb the tech-free vibe,' I replied. 'I was just looking at flights.' The snow had started up again, settling as tiny snowflakes on my fingerless gloves and melting on my cheeks.

'Really? Are you still keen to leave? I didn't think the flights were running. We don't like to take chances with these flash Arctic storms.'

I logged in to check my flights and the website was covered in red. Cancelled today and delayed tomorrow. Bloody hell! I'd be stuck here forever.

Henrik frowned. 'Are they not showing up as cancelled?'

'Hmm... yes, it does look that way,' I said, trying to play it cool while I worked out another route home. Maybe I could tap Danny Jackson up for that favour and ask him to send me a private jet. I needed airlifting out of here. Or some vodka and beefburgers airlifting in.

'We'll get you on the first flight we can – don't worry,' Henrik said. 'Jonas knows one of the guys at the airport, so we'll get a heads-up when things start moving. Until then, you'll have to try and enjoy yourself.'

'I am enjoying myself. It's just…'

'…not Sweden?' Henrik finished, his brown eyes sparkling. Was he laughing at me?

'It's not Sweden, no, and it's also not quite what I was expecting.'

'The snow won't stop the programme activities here – we are quite used to it. Are you joining us for the geothermal pools later? It's a wonderful, healing experience.'

'Anything *thermal* sounds good to me – I love being outdoors in the water. I did some wild water swimming out in Greece a few years ago and was obsessed.'

'These pools are small, but I can take you to the swimming lakes another day if you like?'

'That would be great!' I said, knowing full well I wouldn't be around long enough for it to happen.

'And the heating in your cabin is all sorted now? It is nice and warm?'

'Toasty,' I reluctantly admitted. 'The bed is so soft. It snuggles me down somehow, then lulls me into a deep sleep as soon as my head hits the pillow. I woke up this morning and felt like I'd been drugged.'

'That'll be Greta's blankets. My sister-in-law to be. She crochets them by hand and says they are full of moon magic, so once you're under one, it's impossible to have a bad night's sleep.'

'I can testify to that,' I said, smiling.

'Not all bad here, then?'

'Not even half bad. It's beautiful.'

He nodded slowly. 'It really is. Well, see you at the Sun Hut in half an hour.'

There was just enough time to dash back and pop my tankini on, which had been drying by the fire. It was the only one I had with full bum coverage – I wouldn't be able to relax in a G-string. The wood burner was glowing bright, despite the vegan firelighters, and I'd felt so proud this morning when the ashes still had a tiny spark. I'd somehow kept the fire going overnight, like a vigilant cavewoman, by doing nothing more than sleeping under a magic blanket.

I slipped inside the Sun Hut on the dot of 10 a.m. and quietly stomped the snow off my boots. Ten of the guests sat cross-legged at Tore's feet, staring up at him adoringly, waiting for him to speak.

'Good morning. Today you will get to experience the geothermal pools here that are etched into the mountain. There are eight in total, each one with a different level of heat and velocity. Some are hot, some are mineral-heavy and very buoyant, some have a lot of pressure running through them, but I'll leave you to discover which is which for yourselves. Please enjoy.'

Everyone stood up and started milling about.

'Oh, and to remind you all,' Tore shouted over the din. 'You must have a naked shower – with soap – before you get in the pool.' *Obsessed.* 'The PH balance of our pools is extremely delicate and very precious to us. Perfume, deodorant, body creams and oils, anything like this, can ruin it.'

I sidled over to Ethel, who was the only other person standing. 'Morning,' I whispered.

She briefly lowered her ear trumpet to acknowledge me, looking the height of silver-screen sophistication in her long-sleeved swimsuit and fabulous tartan cloak. Super Gran on tour.

Henrik walked in, followed by a muscly double who could only be his brother. They were wearing matching red swimming trunks that left little to the imagination and Firefly robes. I'd been too distracted by possible death in the sauna the other night, and then possible death in the snow, to properly appreciate Henrik's body. I needed to get back in the saddle and holiday was always the best place to let loose. No recriminations. I flashed him a smile to test the water, and he looked back at me confused.

'If the pool feels hot on your skin, get out immediately and take a seat in the relaxation area,' Tore said. 'We don't want to take any risks. No jumping, diving or splashing. And if you somehow get water in your mouth – spit, don't swallow.'

That got a few titters.

'Sounds like this will be a right laugh,' I muttered.

Ethel gave me a sharp look.

'It's a lot of rules for a hot tub, isn't it?'

'You're always complaining,' she said, with a frown. 'Try being a little more positive. You might surprise yourself.'

'Me?!' I turned round in case she was talking to someone else. 'I'm not complaining… I was just *saying*.'

'Far too much *saying* going on then, if you ask me. First the weather and the food, then the Wi-Fi, and now this. The rules are there to keep the pools clean, so we can all enjoy them. Don't go in if you're going to spoil it for the rest of us.'

The other guests were looking at us, and I could feel my cheeks burning as Ethel strode off towards the showers. It had been a while since I'd been told off like that and my heart was racing. How dare she! I was supposed to be on an uber-glam spa break, *never knowingly not* being massaged and half-cut on dirty martinis.

'Are you OK, Sara?' Tore asked, a concerned look on his face.

'Yes,' I said, forcing a smile. 'I was just telling Ethel how much I'm looking forward to this.'

'And you are having a naked wash?' he asked.

Like I had a choice. 'Absolutely. I'll just wait until some of the others come out.' I was starting to worry they had cameras set up and we were being livestreamed on the dark web.

I poured myself a glass of water for the stress and Henrik came over with his sausage-smuggling sibling.

'Sara, I'm not sure you've met my brother, Jonas?'

'I haven't. Hi – lovely to meet you.'

'Likewise,' Jonas said, shaking my hand. Another tree of a man with the same melt-in-the-mouth chocolate eyes as Henrik, but with bottle-bleached hair, as opposed to Henrik's dark blond, professional surfer vibe.

'Jonas is the head chef here and makes all the cakes and pastries for breakfast – and the sourdough, of course.'

'You bake the bread fresh every day?' I was impressed. 'Can't you just bulk-buy it from the Euro Spar and whack it in the freezer? No one would know!'

'I would know,' Jonas said.

'Well, yes, but it'd taste the same and you'd get more sleep.'

Jonas looked at Henrik as if I were mad. 'It wouldn't taste the same. My bread has a special ingredient in it.'

'This is why Jonas and Greta are such a good couple. Magic blankets and magic baguettes,' Henrik said, with a chuckle. 'You sprinkle the dough with love, don't you, Jo-bro?'

'Among other things,' Jonas said, tapping his nose. 'I can't give away my culinary secrets.'

I had to admit the sourdough was deliciously moreish. I hoped the special ingredient wasn't cocaine or magic mushrooms. It certainly wasn't a preservative of any kind as the bread was always rock-hard by bedtime.

'Is it OK to borrow one of the Firefly dressing gowns, again, for today?' I asked, realising I once again had nothing but a cabin towel to wrap around my middle. Henrik slipped his robe off and handed it to me. 'Oh no, sorry, I didn't mean yours!'

'We don't have any spares, I'm afraid – you were in Jonas's last night. It's fine, honestly. I'm used to the cold.'

I felt bad, but I *wasn't* used to the cold and *was* very worried about getting hypothermia. What kind of retreat didn't provide dressing gowns? This one. 'I'm happy to pay you to hire it?' I said, trying to appease my inner guilt.

Jonas laughed. 'He can't charge you for that old thing – it's never been washed.'

'Course it has,' Henrik said, getting him in a noogie. 'Ignore him – it looks better on you anyway.'

'Are you sure?' I asked, knowing as soon as it went on, he wasn't getting it back. The woody, musky smell was homely and comforting. If he hadn't ever washed it, he shouldn't. It was like Santa, Prince Charming and a handsome woodcutter had all got together and collaborated on a scent.

Jonas wriggled his way out of the headlock and ran into the changing rooms, and Henrik caught the door before it slammed. 'See you out there,' he said, his beard and hairy chest connecting to give him a natural fur coat.

I had a shower and made my way out to the thermal pools, which were bubbling away, blowing steam into the air. Each one glowed a different colour. The eggy smell of sulphur was unavoidable as I held my breath and headed for the turquoise pool – it was the furthest away and the only one still empty. I wasn't in the mood for small talk, and the thought of any leg touching or an accidental toenail scrape gave me the ick.

The water was divine, with pockets of hot and cold swirling around my body, the minerals stinging my skin as they did their thing. I lay back on a ledge in the rock, letting the bubbles come up to my chin, and could feel three other seats covered in natural sponge, oscillating in rhythm with the jets. The snow was still pelting down, and the clouds were so low, I was practically breathing them in. The steam mingled with the mist making it impossible to see, but it was strangely calm and relaxing. Submerged in the heat and thinking about nothing, I floated in a surreal, dreamlike state as I enjoyed my one-woman bath in the sky.

Until someone else showed up.

A red beanie poked through the smoke followed by Henrik's face. 'Oh! *Hei*, Sara. Sorry, I thought this one was free.' He started to back away.

'There's plenty of space! I can't hog a whole pool to myself.'

'Of course you can. You're on holiday. Please. Enjoy.'

'Honestly, it's fine. See it as a thank you for giving me your robe.'

I was loving the space and quiet, but why not add a Nordic hunk into the mix? I didn't want him to disappear back out into the fog.

'Fine. It's too cold to argue.' Henrik dipped a set of neat toes into the water, then jumped in. 'And to be clear, I've *loaned* you my robe for the day. It's not a forever thing.'

'Can I not buy one from somewhere? Or order one in? I thought I was going to an actual spa where there would be thousands of robes; not two between twenty, like some kind of biblical nightmare.'

'They're not meant to be shared, the two we have are mine and Jonas's. I *can* order you one, of course, but it won't arrive until the snow clears and you've already said you're leaving as soon as it does.'

'Order me one anyway, in case I decide to stay. Can I borrow Jonas's in the meantime – when he's not using it?' What had I become? A desperate woman, begging for men's clothes. This place was destroying my street cred.

Henrik bobbed down, leaving just his eyes and nose above the waterline, the pair of us blinking at each other like hippos. Gold flecks swirled around the brown as he looked at me from under his lashes. He had a beautiful face, but there was only so long we could stare into each other's eyes without speaking, and eventually I had to look away. The intensity was too much, and I could feel something beginning to stir in my stomach. 'Sure. Jonas won't mind.

Greta goes to the mainland all the time, too. I'm sure she'd bring you back some clothes if you asked.'

'Amazing! Yes please – whatever she can. Jumpers and jeans would be great. The clothes I've got won't last me a month.'

'Have you changed your mind about leaving then?'

'I'd rather be overprepared than eating dinner in my karate outfit.'

Henrik laughed. 'Karate, eh? Impressive. What level dan are we talking?'

I had no idea. I mean, I had the outfit, but I wasn't a dan. Whatever that was. 'Now let me see… it's been a while.' *Think, think… what colour belt did they give me.* 'I was er… orange dan last time I went.'

'Orange dan?' Henrik said, puzzled. 'Is that something these days? You can handle yourself, then, can you?'

'Absolutely.' I thought back to my karate lesson. Singular. I'm still not sure if it was me who had accidentally booked the kid's class, or the sensei had decided I was only at an eight-year-old level. I'd imagined a few cool Shoreditch peeps getting involved in some self-defence and chopping a couple of blocks in two, then going for margaritas. Instead, I did some very basic arm moves and repeatedly said 'Yes, Sensei,' for an hour with a load of schoolkids. And in hindsight… no, Sensei. No.

A whoosh of hot water started whirlpooling around me and I found myself pushed towards Henrik, unable to control my legs.

'Ooh, sorry, argh, I can't…' I put my hands out to stop a full-frontal hug but still ended up cuddled into his big, broad chest.

'So much for being able to handle yourself,' he chuckled. 'Or is it my magnetic charm?' Was he… flirting with me? He certainly wasn't trying to stop me, or moving away. Although it would have been weird if he'd started moving around as well, like two crabs playing kabaddi in a puddle. 'It's easier to go with the flow until the water changes direction.'

'This happens a lot, does it?' I asked, feeling safe in his arms. I leant against them slightly, just to check. Yep. All that wood-chopping wasn't for nothing. Rock-solid.

'Not really. But the water has its own plans, and I've learnt not to get in the way of nature. It always knows what it's doing.'

Henrik's skin was warm and smooth, but it felt strange to be so close to a naked chest that wasn't Mark's. Hard and muscly with a dusting of hairs, it was like bathing with an elf king and I imagined myself as one of his many lovers.

A flurry of snow shook me from my thoughts and I shuddered underwater, pressing into him further. My nose was numb and I could feel my eyelashes crisping up as the snowflakes fell, but one patch of cold wasn't enough to override the pleasure of the thermal pool on the rest of me. The aggressive jet of water had eased off, but I stayed in Henrik's arms a few seconds longer, enjoying the heat of his body next to mine. He didn't move either, lying back with his eyes closed. It had been a while since I'd been tangled up with a man like this, and I liked it.

'Anyone in here?' Jonas appeared through the mist, squinting to see, then backtracked when he saw us snuggled together. 'Sorry, sorry, carry on.'

I leapt up and moved to the other side of the pool. 'What? We're not…'

'No carrying on here,' Henrik said. 'Get in, Jo-bro.'

'Room for me, too?' A petite blonde with shiny plaits peeked out from under Jonas's arm.

'Hey, Greta,' Henrik said, with a wave. 'We were just talking about you. This is Sara; she's over from London for a few weeks. Sara, Greta – Jonas's fiancée and soon to be my sister-in-law.'

'And a person in my own right,' Greta said, smiling.

I laughed. 'Nice to meet you. I'm only staying until the snow clears but I'll be here for at least a few more days by the looks of it.'

'How come?' Greta asked, climbing onto Jonas's back as he slithered into the water.

'It's not quite what I was expecting.'

'Is that a bad thing?'

It was a good question. I shrugged. 'Not necessarily.' I hadn't really thought through my reasons in any detail. My fight-or-flight instinct had kicked in the second I'd felt uncomfortable, and my knee-jerk reaction was to go straight home. It wasn't the luxury break I thought I'd booked but I didn't want to sound like a spoilt brat. So far, it had been challenging and cold and relentless, and I was way out of my comfort zone.

'Give it some time,' Jonas said. 'Transformation doesn't happen overnight.'

'Especially for you Brits.' Greta giggled. 'No offence, but they usually have the most unwinding to do. The first week is for sleeping only.'

'Well, that's working, I've been like a little dormouse – the bed is too comfy.'

'That's my magic blankets at work. You're welcome lads,' Greta said, reaching over the side of the pool and putting a tiny teabag in her mouth. Probably LSD. She offered it round. 'Do you snus?'

'No. I don't think so. Is it... drugs?'

The three of them laughed. 'No, it's not *drugs*, Sara,' Jonas said, doing a scary, theatrical face. 'It's nicotine.'

'Arguably a drug,' Henrik batted back.

'Oh, well, yes, I do occasionally do nicotine.'

'You do, do you?' Greta said. I took one of the little pouches and copied Jonas, who popped it in his cheeks like a lop-faced gerbil, and carried on talking.

'The nicotine goes straight into your bloodstream, so you don't need to do anything,' Jonas said, but it was too late, I'd already started chewing.

'Cool,' I side-mouthed, tasting the grossness and looking for an appropriate spittoon.

Henrik was lowering himself into the water, which was now just below his chin. 'Got it,' he said, bouncing back up and holding a stone in the air. Blue and bronze-green with gold-tinged edges, it twinkled in the light as he held it out to me. 'Labradorite for the lady.'

'There's loads of it in this pool,' Jonas said, feeling down and pulling out another piece. 'It polishes up really nice.'

'I prefer it natural and raw,' Greta said, finding her own rock to admire. 'You should take them for your cabin, Sara. Labradorite is very calming – it gets rid of negativity.'

'Facts,' Jonas said, putting his piece on top of Greta's and giving them both to me. 'It'll take away *all* your stresses. Guaranteed.'

'Thanks,' I mumbled, trying to smile, my mouth now full of nicotine spit.

'All included in the mind and body transformation package,' Henrik said with a wink.

I considered coughing the snus into my hand and washing it in the pool. But I couldn't bring myself to contaminate the water. Not when Tore had beseeched us all so earnestly to follow the rules. There was obviously a tiny eco-warrior inside me, somewhere.

I rolled onto my front, letting the water massage my legs, then put the tiny chewed-up bag on the edge of the pool. Yuk! There were a lot of things to like about Norway, but snus was not one of them.

Thirteen

Thursday 17th September

The Firefly greenhouse was more of a green mansion, making it easy to spot from a distance. A glowing hotbox of humidity, at odds with its wintery surroundings. There was nobody about as I wandered in, and the sweet, zesty smells hit me from all sides. Lush and fresh, it reminded me of Columbia Road flower market as I unravelled my scarf and whipped off my layers. The floor was split between fruit and vegetables, with a small section at the front for salad-y things. A row of trees stood tall along the back wall, and I spotted baby apples, pears and plums nestled in among their leaves. The vegetables would have been less easy to identify had it not been for the hand-drawn pictures scattered among them: rhubarb, basil, lettuce, onions. It was much the same vibe as my colour-coded filing cabinet and I loved it. The greenhouse was full of good energy and the plants were flourishing in their patchwork of freshly watered plots, with plenty of space to grow.

Tore had been adamant we would carry on with the retreat programme despite the weather – even though most of the guests were hiding in their cabins, loath to leave the warm. Somehow I'd managed to do the opposite and in trying to enthusiastically prove I'd *given it a good go*, I was the only idiot who'd turned up for the gardening workshop.

Henrik emerged from behind a cherry tree wearing a long apron and carrying a spritzing bottle in each hand. 'Sara! Sorry, I didn't realise anyone was in here.' He walked towards me, spraying the lettuces as he went. 'Looks like it's just me and you for this session.'

'Is it safe to be in here?' I asked as the wind whistled through the glass. The vibrations reverberated across the ceiling and I wondered how long we had before the roof caved in.

'Completely safe. I won't let anything happen to you – don't worry.' He said it with complete sincerity, but I could feel my cheeks turning red. 'This building has survived worse storms than this, believe me. It's solid.' He handed me an apron and a pair of orange gloves. 'Put these on and let's start. We could do the growth and grounding workshop you missed on the Monday you arrived?'

I shrugged. 'No idea what it is, but yes. Let's do it.' I pulled the gloves on and they felt gross and rubbery inside.

'The others planted spinach, cucumber and carrots, so shall we do the radishes?'

'Yes, chef,' I said, wiggling my eyebrows cheekily.

Henrik rolled his eyes with a smile, his muscles rippling through his T-shirt as he grabbed a sack of topsoil and slapped it down next to a tower of cardboard pots. 'Each pot needs filling halfway and patting down. Then we bury the seeds and add a touch of water.'

'Is this the growth part of the workshop or the grounding?'

'Both.'

We worked in companiable silence, patting tiny handfuls of cold soil into each pot in a productive rhythm. Henrik put some classical music on, and I inhaled the oxygenated air, enjoying the calming effect as we lost ourselves in the repetition of the job.

'Our menu is all plant-based, as you know, and most of the food is grown here,' he said proudly. 'We are working towards self-sustainability, but it'll take time. I want us to get to carbon negative and give back more to the environment than we take.'

He looked so earnest and genuine. I felt ashamed of my plastic soy sauce marlins.

'Wow. That's a very worthy goal. Is it possible in a place like this when you can't control how much hot water and heating everyone is using?'

'We control what we can. Starting with this. Not just standard versions either, I've been cultivating new varieties of beetroot, lettuce, cucumber, cabbage, spinach… all sorts. Jonas wants our food to have a specific taste that nowhere else can replicate.'

I was genuinely impressed. 'That is such a cool idea.'

'We think so. Assuming the taste is good.' He laughed.

'True. You don't want Firefly to taste of smelly feet.'

'That is one of the beetroot varieties I'm testing,' he said with a cheeky smile. 'We've put a lot of effort into our growing programme, and Jonas is experimenting with all the flavours. I've even developed a secret sauce for the soil, to make sure everything gets the same set of nutrients. And so far, so good. The greenhouse is thriving.'

It certainly was. The fruit and vegetables were plump and plentiful in a glossy mix of colours. It was mind-blowing to me that Henrik was keeping so many plants alive at once – and they were bearing fruit. The yucca in my lounge didn't look half as shiny, and it was plastic.

'Do you meditate back home?' Henrik asked, once we had the first line of pots complete.

'Not really,' I said, being honest. Unless I could count swearing under my breath. 'I find it hard to empty my mind. I know you're supposed to acknowledge the thoughts and let them go, but I've got too many going on at once. I just spend the whole session imagining myself as air traffic control.'

'We've got a morning meditation on Sunday, if you want to try again?'

'I'll be back home by then, if this snow ever stops.' Although the thought of going home was slightly less appealing today. 'I'll do it if I'm here, for practice. But it'll only be a one off – I'd never fit it into my real life.'

Henrik nodded while he potted. 'The gurus say you should meditate for twenty minutes a day. Unless you're too busy. And then you should do it for an hour.'

I rolled my eyes. 'I'd need two hours then. My brain is honestly too full. I don't find it very helpful.'

'That's London for you. All that city noise takes a while to quieten down.'

'Have you been?'

He gave me a look. 'Yeah, plenty of times. I'm not some country bumpkin, you know.'

'I wasn't suggesting you were!'

'Did you think I'd lived my whole life in this forest?'

'It was an innocent question.'

'I was working in New York until a few years ago and travelled all over the place. Australia, Japan, London.' He waved like a magician as if it was some far-off land. 'I came home to help *Pa* and Jonas with the retreat – it was getting too much for them without my mother.'

I didn't ask where she'd gone; we hadn't known each other very long, and it felt wrong to pry. He'd tell me if he wanted to. 'What were you doing in New York?'

'Trading. Day and night, up to my neck in pressure.' His eyes glazed over at the thought. 'I was so ready to move back home when the time came. I was completely burnt out.'

'I can't imagine you doing all that 'buy! Sell! Sell!' up and down the trading floor. It doesn't seem very... you.'

'It wasn't. And I wish I could say it felt right at the time, but it didn't. I finished my PhD in Oslo and was offered a shit-tonne of cash to be a trainee trader in New York, and I took it.'

Well, this was a turn up for the books.

'It must have felt like a different planet compared to all this.' I gestured out at the silence.

'It did. It was brutal. I could never have prepared enough for that kind of lifestyle. The pace, the panic, the anger; it was everywhere, and it was relentless. I had no idea what I was getting myself into.'

He grabbed a bag of radish seeds from the wheelbarrow and tipped a small pile out onto the table.

'I get it. It's hard to resist when they dazzle you with cash.'

Henrik shrugged. 'I could have said no – I'm a big boy. We all knew the money was a stick dressed up as a carrot, but it worked. Every time I got a payout I'd think *three more months and then I'm gone*. But the bonuses got bigger, and each quarter was more tempting than the last. I should have quit while I was ahead, but I stayed in the game too long and ended up having a breakdown.'

'I'm so sorry to hear that.' Why was the corporate world such a shitshow? I wanted to put my hand on his and reassure him it wasn't his fault. 'These hellish jobs creep up on us all. The moneymakers have a way of keeping you close and chewing you up at the same time. Holding our noses to the grindstone until we can't take anymore.'

He gave a mirthless chuckle. 'In a funny way I'm glad I got ill. It was a relief to have a get-out. I'd still be there, otherwise. Crawling through tunnels like a lab rat trying to find the light. I'd lost all sense of myself and wasn't thinking straight.'

'A perfect case study for the Firefly mind and body transformation programme!' I said, baffled by this new information. 'A PhD, no less. He's fit, smart *and* loaded, ladies and gentlemen. The original triple threat. Come and get him while he's hot.'

'Hardly.' He gave me a bashful smile. 'I'm certainly not loaded anymore. I had the New York job and the New York girlfriend to go with it, and my money went on living the high life – if you can call it that. A penthouse apartment, weekends in the Hamptons, expensive dinners, a driver – the lot.'

Curiouser and curiouser. Who was this guy?

'It wasn't all bad, then.'

'Not all, no. The slices between work and sleep were amazing. But I was exhausted pretty much continuously.'

'Like the rest of us, then.'

'I made a lot of money for a lot of people and when you make it rain, they'll do anything to keep you working. You're a lawyer, I'm sure you know what I mean.'

His lovely bright eyes were now dark and flat.

'I really do,' I whispered. 'The American dream, eh?'

He nodded despondently. 'Jonas calls it the Norwegian nightmare. In the end I had no choice but to stop. I physically couldn't do it anymore. Migraines so bad I couldn't see, my back was totally fucked – you get the idea.'

'Did the bosses care?'

'Nope. Paid me off and replaced me with the next guy on their list. Another grad with fresh eyes and a full tank of nerve, while I got on a plane back here, completely broken.'

'Sounds like you got out just in time. Sometimes I wonder if my work is breaking me, but it's hard to see it when you're in it.'

He opened his mouth to say something, then shook his head.

'What?' I asked.

'It's none of my business, but the panic attacks are a big clue, right?'

I stopped at that. I had been trying to convince myself that they had nothing to do with work and everything to do with everything else. The divorce going through, forgetting to eat then eating and drinking too much, moving back home... the non-stop juggle of life. It was bound to stress me out every now and then. But if Henrik could clock it that easily...

'Work is fine. I've just had a lot of big changes recently.'

'Fair enough,' he said, but he didn't look convinced.

'It must have been a culture shock coming back to all this quiet,' I said, looking around. I wanted to keep talking about him, this unexpectedly fascinating man. 'From the city that never sleeps to a handful of people at a time.'

'I much prefer the peace,' he said, pouring another bag of soil across the pots. I followed behind to smooth the tops, tucking in our radish babies.

'Just call me your gardening sous chef,' I said, standing back to admire them.

'They look good, don't they?' Henrik spritzed them with his water bottles, managing two full sprays before it started to sputter. 'Can you turn the hose on, at the wall?'

I walked to the back of the greenhouse and turned on the tap. Henrik stood there with the hose, but nothing happened. I waited a few seconds then turned it up, just as the water shot out all over him. The hose leapt out of his hand and thrashed around on the floor like an angry snake, pissing water everywhere.

'Sorry!' I yelped, turning it off and running back to where Henrik and the radishes were now drenched. He'd wrestled the hose into a watering can but not before it had soaked him through. His T-shirt was translucent, and he had to wring out his beard.

'Luckily I needed a shower,' he said, smiling as he untied his apron and stripped off his wet shirt.

I smothered a giggle. 'I didn't think it was on.'

'Well, now you know it was.'

I couldn't help but stare at his big arms and smooth, muscly back as he disappeared into the bathroom to dry off. I wondered if he had a Norwegian girlfriend these days to go with the hip, Scandi lifestyle. Surely he couldn't be single?

'Do you want to borrow my scarf?' I called, not that it would be much use on its own. 'And gloves? Or I can run up to the house and get a jumper from Jonas?'

'Don't worry, I've got a spare. Just don't tell anyone you saw me in it.' He reappeared in a T-shirt that was far too small for him with a glittery Cinderella on the front. As he got closer I could see it was covered in shapes and scribbles.

'Big Disney fan, eh?' I said. 'Your secret's safe with me.'

He laughed. 'Greta's goddaughters came to visit in the summer and brought me a present. It was the biggest size they sold apparently – in kid's sizes – but I managed to squeeze it on.'

I couldn't help but smile. 'How cute. What did they write on it?'

'Uncle Hen,' he said, pointing out the letters. 'Then there's a carrot, an apple, some broccoli and a chocolate cake.'

I melted at the thought of this big handsome Viking letting two little girls draw all over him.

'Are they vegan as well?'

His eyes were back to twinkling. 'No chance. But they know I do the growing and Jonas does the cooking. They like to help me water the plants when they come, and on a good day they are angels. On a bad day... chaos, of course.'

'You can't beat the chaos of kids,' I said, wistfully.

'Too true. Do you have any?'

'No. But hopefully one day.'

Henrik nodded. 'Ella and Kaja are Greta's flower girls so we've been seeing them a lot recently, for dress fittings and to explain what will happen where. It's been fun having them around – I'll miss them after the wedding.'

Could this be? A man who actually liked spending time with children. A proper family man. So they did exist. Henrik's New York girlfriend must have been an idiot. Fancy having this tall drink of water by your side and letting him go.

Fourteen

Friday 18th September

The magic blankets were very much doing their thing, and I woke up refreshed and ready for the day as the sun warmed my face through the window. It seemed the long, four-day-winter was over, and the cyclone had passed. The snowstorm had been fun for a day or two, to decorate the trees and hide the reindeer droppings – Celeste and Will had even built a snowman. But it had gone on long enough and the cold winds and hunkering down had started to get tiresome.

Today was perfect though. Sunny and fresh, with a thick snow carpet twinkling in the light. There was a knock at my door, which could only be my breakfast delivery, and I felt like I was starting to get into the Firefly flow. It wasn't what I thought I'd booked, but it had its charms. The ebb and flow of breakfast, lunch and dinner, with activities in between, was keeping me busy and I didn't feel alone or out of place. We were one gang following the same routine and everything was pre-organised. I didn't have to worry about making plans or eating on my own, and I was so grateful for that. Having a framework to follow made me feel safe.

The law was just one big framework after all, and once you had rules to follow – or interpret – it made everything so much simpler. Was it this or that? Right or wrong?

I answered the door to another wicker basket full of goodies, with a note pinned on top.

Good morning Sara! It's a beautiful day.
   For breakfast we have:
   Fresh sourdough
   Orange and rosemary cake
   Homemade raspberry jam
   A pineapple, turmeric and ginger shot
   Fruit salad
   Enjoy!
   Jonas

Thank you very much, Jonas, I bloody well will.

I hacked into the bread and slathered the crust in raspberry jam while a proper slice toasted, and my coffee brewed. Still no Crunchy Nut Cornflakes or wine, but they actually sounded quite grim in comparison. Now that I'd gotten used to the *frokost* it was my new favourite thing. The wood burner was still crackling away, much to my delight, fifteen hours after it had been lit – just call me Brown Owl. Although, what did that mean for my carbon footprint? Was it better to douse it out and start a fresh one each day? Or should you always have it on low, like Dad did with the central heating?

I poked the morning spark and threw a brittle log on to get it going. My phone had zero bars and no connection, and I was sick of looking at it. It had been silent ever since I'd arrived, only springing to life when I hovered near the Wi-Fi lounge, like an attention-seeking loser. I wasn't expecting to hear from anyone. I just liked to know what was going on… *generally*. I hated to admit it, but I wanted to see what Mark and Millie were up to – if they were even still a thing.

I fleetingly wondered how Bobby was getting on with Magpie Micky. Did Danny really care who took his case on, or had business as usual carried on without me, like Antony said it would? They'd made it clear I wasn't partner material – not yet, anyway – but could it be that I was so easily replaceable?

I hadn't heard from Mum or Dad either and Abi had gone quiet since the mix-up. Was anyone missing me at all? It seemed I was out of sight, out of mind on all fronts. Insignificant to my significant others. I cracked a window to let some cool air in and spotted a plane trail overhead. The flights were back up and running again, which made sense; the storm had passed. Although I didn't feel as desperate to go home now, eating jam on toast in front of the fire, with the sunshine on my face. Especially as nobody was missing me anyway! But I didn't want to mess Tore and Henrik around after making a big deal about being in the wrong country. I kicked myself for making up such a stupid lie.

I crunched over to the farmhouse to ask about boat timings and flights. The path had already been cleared of snow, and it felt good to breathe in the mountain air and feel some rays on my skin. There'd be no sun when I got back to London – that was for sure.

There was a flicker in the trees, and I froze, my heart beating in my ears as a baby reindeer stepped out from the forest, followed by his mum and dad. The three of them nosing their way through the snow to get to the grass. I'd never seen a reindeer so close before and there was not a red nose between them. I wanted to call the others to come and see them too, to share the experience, but I didn't dare in case I scared them away. They were so calm and gentle, nibbling away together, the daddy reindeer lifting his snout at the slightest sound.

I slowly pulled out my phone to take a couple of snaps and popped them up on Instagram. I spotted Henrik and Jonas watching the reindeer show from the farmhouse, and I didn't want to spoil it for them by moving so I checked on the flight situation to distract myself from the cold.

Swipe, swipe, hmm. There was one heading back Monday evening, which would work. Not quite as soon as I'd like, but it wasn't a bad thing to have a couple more days while the sunshine was out. That way, I'd have done a full week and could in all good conscience say I'd given it a go. I switched myself onto it and paid the £200 change fee. The robbing bastards.

A flurry of likes came through on my reindeer post, including one from Mark. I couldn't decide if I felt flattered or watched. Why was he still inserting himself into my day? Like some weird hologram standing next to me, looking where I was looking at the exact same time.

An eagle spread its wings mid-air and started fluttering, getting ready to pounce, and Rudolph the brown-nosed reindeer ushered his family back under cover. I watched breathlessly as the eagle swooped down, snatched up its prey and flew off. What a way to witness nature.

I waved at the boys and pointed at the front door, waiting patiently for them to let me in.

'Morning,' Jonas said. 'You know this isn't really a guest zone?'

'Oh.' I had sort of forgotten. 'Er... yes, sorry. I was just checking flights and looking for Tore.'

'Back on the Wi-Fi again? Weren't you in the lounge yesterday? And the day before that?' I didn't appreciate his tone. I'd told them I was leaving, so they couldn't fault me for checking the flights home.

'Jonas, relax – Sara's our guest, remember,' Henrik said, slinging an arm around his little brother.

'This is supposed to be a tech-free retreat. She won't get the benefit if she's on her phone the whole time.'

'We are not here to judge.'

'True, but it spoils it for everyone else! Rules are rules.'

'Well, don't worry, lads, I won't be ruining the vibe for much longer – I've changed my flight home to Monday. Can I book the dinghy to take me to Bergen harbour at 1 p.m.?'

'Consider it booked,' Henrik said with a nod. 'But it's a shame we couldn't convince you to stay.'

'Couldn't handle it, huh?' Jonas said. 'Not everyone can. Transformation is painful.' This guy really had it out for me.

'But then so is staying the same,' Henrik said. 'You have to choose your pain.'

'It's not that at all – I'm just looking for something a little more *luxurious*. With a pool and beauty treatments. And... er... cocktails.'

'Numbing your feelings with alcohol isn't the answer,' Jonas replied piously.

'Don't be so superior,' Henrik said, rolling his eyes. 'You numb your feelings plenty. Sara, I'm not sure if it's classed as a beauty treatment, but Greta does reiki and Hopi ear candles.'

'And reflexology now, as well,' Jonas added. 'She passed her qualification a few weeks ago.'

'Really? Why hasn't anyone mentioned it? How do I book?'

'The system is quite archaic,' Henrik said, eyeing his brother.

'We're supposed to line up the appointments,' Jonas said ruefully. 'She's only here at the weekends and hasn't done the last two because of the weather. I couldn't risk the Spa Hut flying off into a cyclone with Greta inside – we're getting married in a couple of months.'

'OK, well, that all sounds good. Have you got a treatment list I can take with me?'

Jonas and Henrik looked at each other, then Henrik spoke. 'Not printed out, but I can write it down for you if you like. It's reiki, Hopi ear candles…'

'…and reflexology,' I finished. 'Right. OK, well book me in for all three. At least I can get my feet done.'

'Sure,' Jonas said, checking the schedule on his phone. 'Sunday afternoon?'

I nodded.

No wonder Greta was struggling for customers if this was the sales patter. I turned to go, and Henrik put his coat on and followed me down the path.

'Will you keep going with the activities until Monday, then?' he asked.

'One hundred per cent. It's not a question of it being too challenging for me here, believe me.'

'Great! In that case, we can walk to the morning session together.'

'Is there something on right now?'

'Yup. Are you coming?'

Ah. I was being coerced into more woo-woo and I wasn't sure what. I should have studied the timetable more carefully instead of staying up all night reading.

'Try and stop me! Are you running it?' I was hoping a couple of vague questions might get it out of him.

'As much as it needs running, yes. Normally we do it every day, but it's best in the sunshine.'

'Makes sense.' *What could it be? Yoga? Bike riding? Weightlifting?* What's better in the sunshine? Well, everything.

I followed him into a forest nook, where Will, Celeste, Ethel, and the rest of the guests were already waiting.

'Good morning!'

'Morning, Henrik,' they chorused.

'Now. I think everyone here already has their tree. Raise your hand if you don't know what I'm talking about.' They all looked at each other and smiled. 'As I thought. OK, no need to wait any longer then, off you go, and I will introduce Sara.'

The group scattered, running in different directions and launching themselves at the trees. One by one they crashed into them face first as I watched in horror.

'What are they doing?' I asked, bewildered, until I looked a little closer and realised they'd stopped and were clinging onto them. *Oh no*. 'Erm… it's not tree-hugging, is it?'

'It is.'

'Right,' I said, exasperated.

'Incredibly good for the cortisol levels, you know,' Henrik said. 'To physically connect with nature each day.'

'I'm sure it is, but I don't think this one's for me.'

I was a walking, talking cliché.

'This way.' Henrik ignored my protests and pointed at a couple of unhugged trees. He lowered his voice to a whisper. 'You must stay curious, Sara,' he said urgently. 'Take your time to walk around. Inhale the trees, try out their trunks for size. *Feel* the bark against your hands. Don't rush. Use all your senses to find the right tree for you. It'll be out there somewhere.'

I started to reply but he put his finger to his lips and pointed to the others, who were silently enjoying their cuddle-puddle. Still and quiet and calm. I felt like a right idiot, although I wasn't sure what I was afraid of. The tree didn't mind if I hugged it or not, and everyone else was clearly into it, so they weren't going to judge me. Henrik walked off into the forest and left me to it. To hug or not to hug. Let's face it, no one cared either way.

The nearest tree was stuffed full of branches from top to bottom and I couldn't see a way to get in there without doing myself some damage. *Sorry, tree, no hot lovin' for you today.* The forest was full of trees, as you'd expect, so there were plenty to choose from, but not many on brief. I didn't want to stray too far from the group and was just about to turn back when I spotted Henrik mid-hug, practising what he preached. It was a relief to see him. I hadn't gone too far into the forest, but I was way beyond my comfort zone. Some of the trees were damp and mossy, some were rough to touch, some were too wide to bother with, but I eventually stopped at a funny-looking one, tall and skinny and wearing its leaves on top, like hair. I wasn't really going to hug it though, was I?

Oh, bloody hell.

I looked both ways to check no one was watching, then stepped forward and patted it on the bark like a dog. Was this my tree? Did it have to choose me as well, like a wand? I expected it to feel cold and dirty, but the trunk was in a suntrap and had sucked up all the heat from the rays. It was warm and smooth, and I put my other hand on it, then took a step closer and awkwardly pressed my cheek against its body.

My eyes were open, and a million thoughts raced through my mind. *This is so embarrassing. What was I even doing here? Had I hugged it for long enough? Was I hugging it right? Could anyone see me?* I closed my eyes, as I'd seen the others do, and gave it thirty seconds, allowing the warmth of the tree to absorb into my body. For self-heating purposes. Then pulled away. Done. I stood back and looked up, making sure I'd remember which one was 'mine'. It was just the right size to hug in a satisfying way and all the branches were above my head, so no chance of a poke in the eye. I looked closer and could see some letters etched around the middle. W-I-L-L-O-W. It didn't look like a willow tree, unless they grew them differently in Norway. It was well established though, that was for sure. This tree had been rooted to this spot for a long, long time. Growing in the sunshine. No worries or stresses, just absorbing the elements and doing its thing.

I walked back through the forest and caught the tail end of Henrik chatting to the group.

'Enjoy your tree while you are here. Hug it, talk to it, sit next to it. You all know their names. Sara – yours is called Willow.'

'Cool, thanks,' I said. Willow was her name then, not her species. They'd christened the trees on top of everything else... and clearly someone *had* seen me hugging her. I thought it was meant to be a private moment.

'Connect as much or as little as you like, but I promise you will notice a difference with two heartfelt hugs a day.' He shrugged. 'Have a go and see what you think.'

Celeste nodded enthusiastically, but Will didn't seem entirely convinced. He had scratches all over his cheeks and a bloodshot eye.

'You mean we've got to do it again later?' he groaned.

'Not if you don't want to, but why not? Ten minutes a day is nothing when you consider the benefits,' Henrik replied.

'All this complaining from you young ones,' Ethel piped up. 'You don't have to do anything. But why are you here if not to try something new?'

Will shrugged sheepishly.

'I will be guiding the alpine touring session after lunch. We're meeting at three in the farmhouse car park, to give everyone time for digestion. It's a short drive in the minibus to get to the mountain.'

'Skiing?' I whispered to Celeste, excited.

She nodded. 'The Norwegian version.'

'Do we hire the kit?'

'From where?' She laughed. 'I'm not sure you've got the measure of this place yet, Sara. No, the kit's all included. They have a ski hut with everything in it at the bottom of the mountain.'

My insides did a little dance. Skiing was one of my favourite things to do and another reason Mark and I had got on so well at the start – we were both sailing-skiing shapeshifters, depending on the season. Nipping over to Chamonix or Val-d'Isère for a cheeky weekend whenever the snow report looked good. Blue skies and powder, with brand-new kit from the hire shop. I liked to have the latest skis, sharp and waxed and ready for action. The idea of a ski hut full of shared, used gear filled me with dread, but if that was all there was, I'd have to make do and mend. I followed the others down to lunch, giving my knees the occasional bounce to check my suspension levels. Today was full of gorgeous sunshine, with soft, deep snow after the storm. *Perfect* ski conditions. I'd always been more of a fair-weather skier than a throw-myself-down in a white-out and keep my fingers crossed type.

Henrik was already up at the buffet table when I got to lunch. I wanted to ask if we'd get anywhere close to the glacier. Now *that* would be amazing.

'Henrik!' I called, and the entire line turned and frowned. Ethel rolled her eyes and zipped her lips.

'Sorry!' I mouthed at everyone as they carried on clattering about, filling their plates with cheat balls and herb-roasted potatoes. I'd catch him on the way. I suddenly felt lighter and brighter. Skiing today, reflexology on Sunday – my last few days were shaping up nicely.

I helped myself to lunch, then took a table by the window. No tech, no noise, and the food was delicious. It was a relief not to have the pressure of talking. Permission to sit with my own thoughts in peace while still being part of the group.

Fifteen

'Everyone onto the minibus, please,' Henrik shouted. 'And put your seatbelts on. One, two, plus three of you, is five. Six, seven...'

I didn't like to interrupt while he was counting. Everyone was going skiing except Ethel – which was fair enough with her leg – and when he got to eleven, he jumped behind the wheel and gave us a thumbs up. Like a dad taking us all on a road trip.

'Morning!' I was sat next to the Japanese couple. 'Sara,' I said, pointing to myself.

'Good morning. My name is Kimi,' the lady replied. 'And this is my husband, Yuto.'

'Nice to meet you.' They had a machine that translated my words into Japanese, and Yuto grinned and waved. What witchcraft was this that they were operating tech on the move?

'Is that 5G?' I asked.

Kimi shook her head. 'No internet needed. It downloads the languages then translates sounds offline. It is very clever.'

'Wow!' I said as they watched it, and they both nodded. 'Do you ski in Japan?'

Yuto spoke slowly. 'Yes. Plenty skiing on Mount Fuji.'

They were on a round-the-world trip, celebrating their retirement. Although they didn't seem old enough – they were in such great shape. I'd overheard Jonas saying how excellent they'd been in the rock-climbing session. Bending themselves around the tricky bits to find the best grip.

'Henrik, will we be able to see the glacier from the mountain?' I called.

'Yep, you'll see everything. There's a three-sixty view from the top all the way out to *Folgefonna*. Hope you've all brought your cameras.'

Camera and phone in one. There was bound to be signal up there, as we'd be closer to the satellites. That was how it worked, right? I might even be able to make a call.

The minibus lumped along the road, weaving and sliding to avoid the ice. Henrik was like a go-slow racing driver, doing his best to keep it smooth as he drove towards the mountain. I pulled out my phone and by some miracle I had two bars! Actual signal connecting me to the real world. I scanned through my apps and could see Mark had sent me another message. He was such a contradiction. He either didn't want to talk to me at all, or he was on my case every other day. I toyed with leaving him unread for about thirty seconds, but I couldn't help myself.

He'd screen-grabbed the Firefly homepage where Tore, Jonas and Henrik stood side by side, arms-folded in front of the farmhouse.

Mark: Is this where you're staying?

Me: You know it is – I sent you a pin. Checking up on me?

Mark: Any good?

Me: Gorgeous. On my way to ski the glacier. Worth checking out for sure.

Mark: You always choose the best places to go on holiday.

Me: Yep, I'd highly recommend, but it's fully booked till Jan – I got lucky with a cancellation.

He didn't need to know the whole truth. An eco-resort was Mark's idea of hell. And that would be without the vegan, no-alcohol situation. Mark liked all round luxury when he went away – ideally with a butler on call.

After a bumpy half hour, Henrik pulled over and the minibus lurched to a stop.

'OK, guys, this is it. The ski hut is over there to the right. Those who have been before, get your gear on while I park. Those of you who haven't, ask those who have. I'll be back in ten.'

We staggered off the bus, slow and dozy, like a coach trip tipping pensioners out onto Blackpool promenade. Phil Collins had lulled us into semi-sleep, and it was a shock to be back out in the cold. The ski hut was hot and a musty smell lingered in the air. It was a wooden shed with a closed hatch at the front and just enough room for us all to cram in. The kit was a jumble of skiwear from the nineties with sweaty-smelling boots. I looked around, panicked, to see if everyone else was thinking the same as me, but it seemed they were not.

Kimi and Yuto had already stepped into matching onesies, red with white stripes. Which was kind of cute as an old married couple. Until I realised that all the ski outfits were the same.

No. Absolutely *not.* I would not be seen dead in one of those. There must be something else to wear. Celeste was next to me, wrestling hers on.

'Psst. Girl to girl. Are there any other options?' I didn't want to be difficult, but I couldn't wear a giant Babygro. It would ruin the experience. Thank God Ethel wasn't here to witness me flapping about.

Celeste shook her head. "Fraid not, sister. It's these or nothing. They're not sexy, but neither is frostbite.'

'No one will see you,' Will butted in. 'There was literally no one on the slope last time. The aim of the game is to keep warm.'

I was torn between sunny ski time on an empty mountain and wearing a ski suit that gave me the ick. Henrik wasn't back yet and everyone else was ready and raring to go.

'You are coming?' Kimi asked, sweetly.

'Henrik won't leave till we're all ready,' Will said a little too loudly, and ten pairs of eyes turned to stare at me, piling on the peer pressure.

'Yes, yes, of course. Sorry, I'll be quick.'

What else could I do, other than wait on my own while everyone else had a great time? I kicked off my Uggs, chose the least depressing pair of ski boots and took a onesie from the pile. *No one cares, Sara, just get on with it.*

Fine. I gave the ski suit a final once-over, then slid it on over my thermals and zipped it up. It was like wrapping insulation around every part of my body: thick, cosy, full of feathers, and deliciously warm. Then the ski boots snapped on nice and snug and felt sturdy and comfortable. I bounced around the hut like an astronaut, and it felt amazing. Like one-wear fancy-dress. I knew I looked as ridiculous as the others, but I couldn't see myself, so I didn't *really* know. I'd just have to focus on how I felt inside instead.

Henrik bounded in already suited and booted. '*Hei*, OK!' he said, looking around. 'You all found what you need? The skis are at the bottom of the piste to save us carrying them, so if everyone is ready, we can go!'

We shuffled outside, boinging from foot to foot on the wooden floor. Henrik waited at the back to lock the door, then led the way to the locker to dish out the skis and poles.

The mountain was covered in fresh powder and looked beautiful in the sunshine. Perfect ski conditions, but I couldn't see the lift. I was starting to worry it might be a button. The mountain was quite remote after all. The piste hadn't been bashed, but the red flags were visible, so it would be just the right level of challenge for me to fly down.

Henrik clapped his hands together. 'Please check your skis have fresh Velcro on the bottom and remember to strip it off before you ski down.'

'What for?' I asked, turning my skis over. There was a black sticker running straight down the middle. Weird.

'Too much friction otherwise. You won't get a speedy, smooth ski.'

'Right.' I wasn't sure what he meant, but everyone was clicking on their skis, so I followed suit. We must have to ski to the lift, which would be a nice practice run as I hadn't done any for a while.

'Everyone ready?' Henrik called, and we all clanked our poles together, like performing seals. 'Good. Now, remember, don't waste your energy talking. We can do this together, right? Let's go!'

We formed a natural queue behind Henrik and followed him step for step, the twelve of us moving as one. *Left, right, left, right...* I had my head down, towards the back of the line, so it took me a second to realise the gradient had changed and we'd started walking *up* the piste.

'Will?' I shouted. 'Can you hear me?'

'Yes,' he replied, marching on like a compliant Orc.

'Where's the ski lift?'

'There isn't one.'

'What?' I took another look at the unkempt piste. 'Sorry, what are we doing here?'

'Alpine touring,' Will said. 'The Norwegian way.'

'It's skiing though, right?' I gasped, trying to breathe.

'Yes! Once we get to the top,' Will replied as it finally dawned on me what was happening. We were walking up the bastard piste and I was already too high up to break away and ski down. The Velcro comment suddenly made sense. Norwegian skiing.

'Keep going!' Henrik shouted from the front, as I dug in with my trekking sticks. 'Heads down, focus on your breathing, stay mindful.'

My mind was full of something alright, and about to shut down entirely. I couldn't feel my legs, and the mountain looked like Everest as it stretched up above us. No wonder the piste had been empty when they'd come last time:

Alpine touring was only meant to be for those who were fit or determined enough to drag themselves up it in the first place.

I huffed and puffed my way along, using my outrage as fuel. Each little step was getting me closer to the top and there was nothing anyone could do to help the situation. It was my choice: either keep going or give up. And I was desperate for the skiing-down part. The cosy warmth of the onesie was a lot less attractive now, and there was a layer of sweat between my body and the material, making it even hotter, if that was even possible. I considered taking it off and climbing up in my thermals. If I threw it into the middle of the piste, I could pick it up on the way down.

'Let's hold it here!' Henrik called, and everyone stopped, collapsing on the ground to regroup and rehydrate. There was no point complaining now – we were all in it together.

'You know what?' Celeste panted, leaning back on her elbows. 'There's nowhere else on earth I'd rather be right now.'

'Agreed,' Will said, putting his arm around her.

'I could sit here all day,' I said, turning my face towards the sun. It was absolute bliss now we'd stopped. I was just missing a deckchair and a cold, Norwegian lager.

Henrik stood up. The team leader was ready to go. 'Good work, everyone! We're halfway there.'

'Alright, Bon Jovi,' Will shouted, and everyone laughed.

'The same effort again and then you get your reward at the top. Ready? Let's go!'

I was not ready, but he wasn't really asking. Left, right, left, right, I kept my head down and dug deep. Trying to find the inner strength to get my arse up the hill. Kimi and Yuto were inspiring me at the rear – if they could do it, I could do it: there was no excuse for me not to shift my bum.

Half an hour later and I was ready to raise the white flag. It felt like we'd been walking forever and I had nothing left to give. Nobody had spoken since the break, but the silence was masked by heavy breathing, the odd grunt, and the continuous clatter of skis. I was seconds away from giving up when we rounded a corner and the peak came into view. There were a set of metal steps we'd have to walk up, but it was close enough to believe it was possible.

'Not far now!' Henrik said, turning sideways to get up the steps. The final climb to the top. 'Keep your legs moving. Don't stop.'

We all got a second wind and pushed each other on, to get there together. I felt completely broken as I walked up the steps – all twenty-eight of them – and crawled over the summit. Clicking off my skis and lying on the ground, I was physically and mentally exhausted.

'You did it!' Henrik said, clapping his poles together. 'Congratulations. You have all earnt your dinner tonight.'

I peered over the edge and couldn't believe I'd done it. The drop down to the ground was huge. It had seemed impossible when we'd started, like any difficult thing, yet here we all were. My breathing returned to normal as I lay coddled in my ski suit, staring up at the sky. I'd been exercised like a prize cow and needed an hour or two to sunbathe and recover.

'Take your photos and drink some water, and we'll all ski down together,' Henrik shouted, as everyone ran to different spots to check out the view. I stayed put, sitting up to take it all in.

We were on top of the world. As close to heaven as it was possible to be. Snow-dipped mountains poked through wispy clouds and I could just about make out the fjords down below. Bergen looked spectacular in all her colourful finery, and I took a few snaps then stood up to check out the other side. And there she was. The *Folgefonna* glacier. Thousands of layers of snow packed tight on top of each other, forming this miracle over thousands of years. It was like seeing a different planet. Will and Celeste were taking selfies in my eyeline as I admired the view, and I found myself getting irritated that they couldn't just enjoy the moment for what it was. Their tech and noise were ruining my first glimpse of this awesome natural phenomenon. Look how far I'd come.

I carried my skis to the edge and peeled off the Velcro, excitement bubbling in my belly. It wasn't a piste at all. Not like the wide, bashed, regulated runs I was used to. It was more like a shovel of snow going downhill, and there was nobody else on it.

'Are you sure this is safe?' I asked as Henrik walked past.

'I am,' he said with a reassuring confidence. 'People helicopter in to ski this mountain every day. It's a well-kept local secret and very easy to ski. I promise.'

The snow was untouched and looked incredible. I was torn between relishing every second and skiing down as fast as I could. It was the one and only time I'd ever do it – there was no way in hell I'd be trekking up that mountain again.

The others had already click-clacked over and were waiting for the official nod.

'Everyone ready? Follow your nose as far as you can see, then the piste goes to the right and round, then down and to the left. We walked up the short part of the mountain, but we'll take the long route home. Off you go!' He watched as one by one we tipped over the edge, like penguins chasing each other into a swimming pool. I waited till the end so I could hoon it down without anyone crashing into me. I liked to know where everyone was.

'After you,' Henrik said with a smile. 'Unless you're afraid?' He was teasing, but there was an undercurrent of real concern. He was so sweet.

I found myself wanting to impress him, to show him that this was one activity I would be good at. 'Not at all – I can't wait! I just like to go either first or last, but I suppose you're playing teacher, so you get to go last. See you down there!' With a wink, I jumped into the powder. My muscle memory got straight to work as I swooshed left then right, the soft snow already up to my calves. I was gliding through it, gunning down the mountain with the wind in my hair. The climb up was totally worth it. I slowed slightly to veer right and realised Henrik was skiing next to me. He gave me a cheeky wave and the two of us skidded around the corner, regaining our balance at the same time before carrying on down the mountain. I couldn't shake him off, and I wasn't sure I wanted to, so we skied side by side instead.

I was used to being alone on the slopes. Mark liked the black runs and the board park, so I barely saw him on our weekends together. It felt strange to be skiing in a twosome like this. I already knew Henrik was strong and fit, but it hit different seeing him out on skis and I had to work hard not to get distracted. Using every inch of his body to get down the mountain, he clearly knew it inside out, zipping off to do little jumps on the side, while I went left to right in huge circles of eight.

We arrived at the bottom, where everyone was waiting, breathless and full of adrenaline. What. A. High. I could see why the Norwegians loved it. The release at the top was so worth the effort of getting up there in the first place. To have the whole piste to fly down and feel so completely free.

I wanted to do it again.

Sixteen

Sunday 20th September

'Imagine yourself standing in a garden.' Henrik's voice was already giving me the feels, and the meditation had only just started. 'Surrounded by plants. *All* your favourite plants, in bright colours, big leaves, beautiful flowers... and you spot a hammock hanging between two trees.'

I was on a heated yoga mat in the forest, covered in Greta's blankets, so the idea of a garden full of plants wasn't too far-fetched. But I wouldn't have really said I had a *favourite* plant.

'I want you to climb into that hammock,' Henrik said softly, giving us time to make the mental move. 'Nice and slowww. One foot, then the other, easing yourself in comfortably to rock in the warm breeze.' I hadn't once in my life eased comfortably into a hammock. It always ended in an aggressive swinging tangle.

A bamboo screen had been put up to protect us from the wind, with bio-ethanol fires to keep us warm. Chunky church candles in huge glass jars surrounded us in a circle for some extra zen. Unless we were being sacrificed? Mum would say we were all insane, lying on the floor in the cold, but I felt safe and coddled. And Henrik's voice was really doing it for me. I tried to sneak a peek of him in action, but his eyes found mine with a faux-disappointed shake of the head. Watching me watching him. I couldn't do anything but close my eyes and lie there feeling exposed.

'There is nothing to worry about. Empty your mind of any thoughts and if something tries to creep in, just acknowledge it and send it on its way. This is *your* time. Your hammock time.'

My brain automatically heard Hammertime and MC Hammer entered the hammock in his baggy pantaloons. I acknowledged him and sent him on his way.

'You are calm and relaxed. Safe.' His Norwegian accent lilted. 'Feel the ground beneath you. Breathe in... and out. Be in this moment, breathing in... and out.'

You can't touch this.

Now he came to mention it, I *could* feel the ground beneath me, and there was a stone digging into my back. 'You are at one with nature. You are from nature. In... and then... out.' Nature was not very comfortable to lie on. 'You are enough. Think of the words and say them in your mind. I am enough.'

There was a lot of deep breathing going on and Yuto was snoring next to me. Henrik's voice was sending everyone off to sleep, but it was having the opposite effect on me. I was far too conscious of him standing over us to relax. I couldn't risk sleep-talking or dribbling on Greta's blanket. I tried to focus on the mantra.

I am enough. Am I enough? How much exactly was enough these days? STOP thinking.

ESCAPE TO THE NORTHERN LIGHTS

'And now I want you to…'

Every time he said those words, I lost myself a little bit more. His voice was so smooth and sexy – I'd have done anything he asked. I was imagining his lips saying the words and his body next to mine. His strong arms, and how easily they could scoop me up and carry me off. We'd be back in my cabin in less than ten minutes…

'Now slowly start to acknowledge your breath and feel the ground beneath your back. Wiggle your fingers and your toes…'

Bugger. It was just starting to get good and now I was back to thinking about that stone.

'Hi again,' Greta tinkled, opening the door to the Spa Hut and welcoming me inside.

'*Hei*,' I said, trying out my Norwegian. 'I had no idea this place was here! Tore only mentioned the sauna when I asked about the Firefly spa.'

'Honestly! Those Nilsen men!' Greta laughed. 'They don't believe in the holistic side of things, or that it could be good for business. Tore especially. He thinks people only want the physical activities and forgets the part I do. And then no one knows so no one books.'

'What a shame. I'd have been in here every day if I'd known.'

'I only work weekends, so you haven't missed out – it's your first weekend here, isn't it?'

I nodded. *First and last*, I thought to myself.

The hut was warm and lavender-scented with a massage table covered in fluffy blankets and a trolley-full of oils.

Candles flickered from all the nooks and crannies and Greta led me to a snug seating area, poured me a herbal tea and handed me a clipboard.

'You're booked in for everything. Have you had reflexology before?'

'Yes,' I said, feeling very spoilt. 'A few times.' *A few hundred times.*

'Good. Well, have a read through and sign at the bottom and we'll get started.'

'Great!' I was so ready to relax.

She tinkered through her bottles, eventually selecting one and giving it a sniff. 'I like to do a combination of reflexology and aromatherapy massage on the feet and legs, and a Reiki session at the end. Does that sound alright?'

'It sounds amazing.' She was talking my language. I had a quick scan through the form, ticked panic attacks and blood pressure and squiggled down my signature.

'If you'd like to get under the blankets and stay face up,' Greta said, pulling a curtain out of nowhere across the middle of the hut. 'You can leave your clothes on the chair.'

'All of them?' I asked in a small voice. Did Scandinavians do everything in the nude?

Greta looked confused. 'Just your socks and trousers. Unless you'd rather roll up the legs.'

'No, no. Trousers off is fine.' I was so tense! Of course she meant trousers – it was reflexology, not gynaecology.

Some calming violin music started as I climbed into the bed.

'Ready?' Greta called.

'Yes.'

She slid back the curtain, and I kept my eyes closed as she adjusted the blankets and tucked me in. The music was just loud enough that there was no question of having to talk, giving me permission to completely relax. She uncorked the oil with a pop, and the air filled with jasmine as she started massaging my feet, working through the pulse points in each of my toes to get rid of the toxins. Re-energising my ankles and calves, then finishing with some reiki magic. She rang a bell to signal the end of the treatment and I immediately felt bereft.

'There's some water on the side for you,' she whispered as I lay in post-massage bliss. I was taking this woman back to London with me. 'Take your time getting dressed; there's no rush.'

The music clicked off five minutes later and I was still sat there in a daze. I shook myself up and got dressed. 'That was such a treat.' I said with a yawn, sliding back the curtain.

Greta smiled. 'I'm glad you enjoyed it. Put this on over your clothes to walk back.' She handed me a big, fleecy jumper and I did as I was told. 'It'll help keep your body heat in.'

She'd thought of everything. Five and a half stars.

I put my head down and walked fast to try and stay warm. My phone vibrated as I marched past the Wi-Fi lounge, but I didn't hang around. My only focus was getting back to the cabin to sit in front of the fire. This was my life now, going from one extreme type of relaxation to the next. I stumbled in, got my pyjamas on, then noticed the messages flashing.

Jimbo: Paint looks cracking :) I've given it three coats.

He'd sent some photos and the painting was all finished, the creams and browns now covered over with the Chelsea colour palette. I hadn't expected it to feel so weird, seeing my old life painted into my King's Cross pad. My marital home infiltrating my single girl flat.

Mark: I've booked to come and check it out like you suggested.

Mark: Arriving a week Wednesday.

I was jolted out of my reverie.
What?
He'd booked to come here? No. He must mean something else. I re-read his message. *Like I'd suggested?* When? I scrolled back through our messages. What the hell was he talking about? My post-spa zen had gone and I couldn't even call him to find out. What to do, *what to do*? If I told him I was heading back to London, he'd know I'd lied about how amazing it was. Although I had to admit it had turned a corner. If I carried on as planned, he'd turn up a week on Wednesday and I wouldn't be here, but if I stayed, he'd completely ruin any relaxation vibes. What did he want? There was only one way to find out. I'd have to change my bloody flight again and write off another two hundred quid.

Seventeen

Wednesday 23rd September

'Sara? Are you OK?' Henrik pulled me out of the snow *again*, lifting me up by the arms, like a rag doll.

It was the third time I'd fallen on the way to the husky station, and I was feeling bruised and exhausted. My boots were struggling to cut it on the ice and I was dreading the rest of the walk.

'Sorry about this,' I said as we came nose-to-nose.

'Do you want some help?' he asked, that flirtatious glint twinkling in his eye.

'I'm not sure there's anything more you can—'

In three quick moves he had me off the ground and in a fireman's lift, dangling over his shoulder.

'Argh! What the...? How did you do that?' I squealed into his bum. 'I'm not sure about this!' But I got used to it fairly quick. Turns out it was much more fun hanging onto Henrik while he did all the hard work than wading through the snow and falling on my face.

'Last one here, Kaspar!' Henrik shouted as he turned me upright and placed me on the floor.

'*Hei.*' An old man in a well-worn sheepskin smiled over as I got my bearings. We were stood next to a wooden sled covered in black furs, with eight, beautiful blue-eyed huskies ready and raring to go. 'Oh, wow! Hi, doggies!' I said, rushing over to stroke them.

'*Nei, nei,*' Kaspar said, intercepting me. 'They are working.'

'Oh! Of course, sorry. I'm a dog person,' I said, to explain it.

'Where are the others?' Henrik asked as a second sled disappeared over the horizon, its sleigh bells ringing loudly.

'Gone,' Kaspar said. 'They waited, then Tore said to go. He tried to call.'

Henrik checked his knackered old phone with a frown and nodded. 'Oh. *Ja.* He did. Must be on silent,' he muttered, shaking it.

'Were we that far behind everyone else?' I said, embarrassed he was having to make a second trip for me. 'I'm so sorry – it's my fault for being slow.'

'It's good exercise for the dogs,' Kaspar said, offering up the front seat and helping me in. 'I take the two of you, OK?' The sled was like a pram for twins, with one chair in front of the other. Henrik hopped in behind me, and we belted up as Kaspar jumped on the back.

'Let's go!' he shouted, cracking his whip, and the dogs set off, hurtling across the snow at a thousand miles per hour.

'Hold on, Sara!' Henrik shouted as we juddered over the snow.

'I am!' I yelled back, although I wasn't sure I needed to. The G-force had pinned me to my seat. Once the huskies made it up the hill, we slowed right down, and I loosened my grip on the sides. I'd imagined a leisurely jaunt through the snow, not Olympic-level bobsledding.

'You alright up there?' I felt Henrik's hand on my shoulder and squeezed it tight.

'I hadn't realised it was an extreme sport,' I shouted as the sled hit a rock and jumped through the air.

Kaspar laughed. 'Sit back and enjoy the ride,' he said. 'The dogs know the way – they'll get you there safely. Unless you'd rather walk?'

It was a good reminder to live in the moment. Instinctively, I wanted to close my eyes until it was all over, but I had to remember how lucky I was to get to do this. Eight powerful dogs were working hard to give us this unforgettable experience, and I most certainly did not fancy a ten-mile walk through the snow instead. I'd already proven I wasn't very good at that.

The view from the sled was breathtaking, and it was like flying through a Christmas card as we whizzed along, past frozen lakes lined with Nordic firs while reindeer watched from the sidelines. The snow reached up to the mountains and the fjords, and tiny white boats glimmered in between, sparkling in the sunlight.

'*Hike! Gahhh.*' Kaspar shouted commands over our heads and the huskies galloped in sync. I felt like a Disney princess on a mission. The other sled was no longer visible, so it was just the three of us and nothing else for miles. Racing along the edge of the world.

Henrik's hand reappeared with a mini bottle of schnapps. 'For the cold,' he called.

'Is this allowed?!' I replied, secretly delighted as I cracked it open.

'Don't worry – it's alcohol-free.'

I inwardly groaned and took a swig. Of course it was. Although... if he hadn't said anything, I'd never have known. It tasted spicy and delicious and I felt it go all the way down, warming up my insides.

'Cheers!' Henrik shouted.

'To an awesome day,' I said, holding it above my head for him to clink. Never had a soft drink tasted so good.

The huskies veered right suddenly, throwing us to one side, their panting getting louder as they pulled towards the home run. They were starting to get tired, but the end was in sight.

'*Videre!*' Kaspar shouted, cracking his whip. *Onward*.

We kadunked aggressively over the snow and half my 'schnapps' went up my nose. I was desperate to capture this moment and the magnificent view, but we were bouncing around all over the place and I didn't dare risk my phone being knocked to the floor.

The sled rounded the final corner towards Tore and the rest of the guests and not a second too soon. The temperature was dropping fast and an icy halo had formed around my hood – even my nose hairs were crispy.

'There you are!' Tore said with a big smile. 'Did you enjoy it?' I nodded, breathless. 'Good! That's everyone back and accounted for now then.'

'Where have you two been?' Ethel asked as Kaspar helped me out of the sled.

'We were only a few minutes behind you.' I couldn't understand why they'd left without me, not that I'd have fancied a twelve-man sled-conga, if that's how they'd travelled.

'We waited over twenty minutes. Henrik must have taken you the long way.'

'Henrik did nothing of the sort,' he said, appearing next to us and shooting Ethel a look.

'Time must have stood still,' she replied, with a knowing smile. 'I saw the pair of you frolicking in the snow while the rest of us waited in the cold.'

'Sorry Ethel. It was my fault. Inappropriate footwear as usual,' I said, showing her my boots.

She didn't look impressed. 'For someone so smart, you're not very well prepared.'

'I wasn't meant to be coming here,' I said, getting agitated. 'It was...'

'Firefly in Sweden,' Henrik sing-songed. 'We know, we know.'

'Ludicrous,' Ethel said, shaking her head. 'Booking the wrong retreat is one thing – I can almost see how that happened if they have the same name. But booking the wrong retreat in the wrong country? I'm not sure I'd want you representing *me* in court.'

'She's got a point,' Henrik said with a snort.

I laughed. 'Yeah, fair enough. I'd had a few wines – it was an honest mistake.'

I took a detour through the forest for a tree-hugging session, transfixed by a pair of dragonflies who led the way. The husky ride had put a spring in my step, and I was proud of myself for sticking it out here when I'd wanted to cut and run. Firefly Forest had jolted me out of myself in more ways than one, and if I'd rushed back home I'd have missed out on so much. I thought of Henrik pulling me out of the snow and felt warm inside; it was nice to have a man to pick me up when I fell down. Kaspar must have thought I was a new member of staff when the two of us arrived in matching Firefly jackets – but I was thankful Henrik had found me one or I'd have frozen my arse off. Not that it really mattered what I'd worn as there was no evidence either way. The only proof I had of travelling by husky was now forever locked away in my memory, where I could wear whatever I liked.

I was weighed down with an armful of battered old sticks when I finally spotted Willow across the clearing, but somebody else was already there, the two of them in a clinch. My own tree cheating on me in broad daylight! I lightened my footsteps to get a closer look.

It was Henrik. Of course it was. Melded into the tree with his eyes closed, completely content. I gave him a few minutes to come back to himself once he'd stepped away.

'Oi! That's my tree,' I whispered, smiling.

He looked up in surprise, then smiled back. 'She was mine first,' he teased. 'We'll have to share.'

I playfully shook my head. 'Only child, I'm afraid. That's not how I do things.'

'And how do you do things?' he asked, moving towards me. The intensity in his eyes made me shiver. We were finally alone and away from prying eyes.

'I decide what I want, then go after it hard.'

'I like that,' he said, raising his eyebrows. 'And you want Willow. Anything else? Maybe we can come to an arrangement.'

'Maybe,' I said coyly, looking up at him from under my lashes.

'I go hard after the things I want, too,' he said, his eyes full of longing. He stroked a stray curl away from my cheek, making me tingle. I could barely breathe as his lips found mine, kissing me slowly, the passion almost lifting me off the ground. I clutched my firewood to my chest as he pulled back.

'What kind of arrangement were you thinking?' I asked.

He laughed. 'I'm open to offers. Although Willow really is *my* tree. Tore planted her the day I was born.' He looked up wistfully while I got my bearings back. 'And that one over there – Elmo – was for Jonas. My mother decided ten was a good age to start tree-hugging, when Willow was the right size and shape for my little arms.'

'That is *so* cute.'

'I know. Although Jonas has his struggles with the wych elm.'

Elmo was thick with branches from top to bottom. I couldn't imagine it was easy to get in there and find the trunk for a hug. I giggled. Poor Jonas.

'Do your mum and dad have trees too?' I asked, looking around.

'Yep, over there.' He pointed to a pair of fir trees; one stood taller than the other. 'Tore and Audhilda. Their trees didn't get pet names.' He paused, seemingly lost in thought. 'We lost her a few years ago. Cancer.'

I reached out to squeeze his hand. 'I'm so sorry.'

'I can feel *Ma's* energy in Willow,' Henrik said, nudging a pile of stones with his foot. 'It's a comfort, you know? To connect with her in nature, have something tangible and rooted in the ground, growing stronger every day.'

My heart hurt for him. 'Makes sense,' I said, squeezing his hand once more before letting go. 'Sorry for interrupting; I'll leave you to it.'

'No, no – were you here to hug?'

I shrugged. 'Sort of.'

'Then please… go ahead. I insist. Proof the madness in my methods works. Occasionally.'

I hesitated. After that kiss my head was in a spin. 'I'll come back later. I don't want to interrupt you and your… er, mum.'

His eyes sparkled as he smiled. 'You're not. I promise. And this conversation is crazy. She would laugh her head off if she could hear us. I'm done anyway, so it's up to you.' He looked so desperate not to ruin it for me, I couldn't walk away. It felt disrespectful somehow.

'Sure, I'll stay for a few minutes then. Thank you for… sharing,' I said, quietly. 'Not just Willow. All of it.'

'You're easy to talk to,' he replied, before turning and disappearing into the trees.

I took a couple of deep breaths, then put my arms around Willow and gave her a squeeze. She felt even warmer today. Henrik must have transferred his body heat into her. Maybe that's what had happened the day I chose her as well. It was something he'd been doing ever since he was a little boy. I nuzzled into the tree and closed my eyes, imagining how it would feel to nuzzle into Henrik. That fireman's lift earlier had caught me by surprise, and being so close to him had been fun and exciting. I'd never had a man sling me over his shoulder like that. He was packing some serious muscles. I could barely pick up a twelve-pack of Diet Coke these days.

But then he couldn't just leave me behind, buried in the snow. It was basic customer service. I cuddled in further, pretending otherwise in my little Viking fantasy, breathing in the greenery of the forest and feeling my feet on the ground. Would it be inappropriate to invite him over for a drink? I didn't want to be accused of workplace harassment.

I wandered slowly back to the cabin, my body throbbing as I thought about the two of us together and what we might get up to, his soft lips on mine. And as I walked up the path to my cabin, I already knew the note stuck to the front door was from him.

Sara,
I'm still worried your fire isn't lighting fully.
Check it when you get in and let me know if you want me to have a look at it.
Henrik

Eighteen

There was a knock at the front door, and my stomach flipped.

It could only be him.

I was ready and waiting in my Firefly jacket, with just my underwear on underneath. Was that too slutty?

Oh God.

'Just a second!' I shouted as I lost my nerve and pulled on some jeans. It had been a while, and I had zero confidence in my old seductress routine. I'd shaved all over and slathered myself in oil, and I already felt naked without my body hair.

'Oh hi!' I said, swinging the door open and trying to act casual. 'Fancy seeing you again.'

'Fancy.' Henrik stood smiling in jeans and a soft, red jumper, which looked very much like cashmere. For a man of the woods, he didn't scrimp on his clothes. His hair was swept up in a ponytail and he'd combed his beard like a good Boy Scout. I nearly fell into him trying to smell his neck as he walked past.

So good. All woody and fresh. I'd assumed his scent was au naturel, or from some Scandinavian soap, but now I thought about it, that aftershave was nose-on for Tom Ford. He clearly hadn't given up *all* his finance-bro habits.

'I've come to do another check on that wood burner,' he said with a cheeky smile. 'And I brought us some drinks – in case it takes longer than expected.'

My eyes lit up as he pulled a bottle of red from his coat. I couldn't wait to drink like grown-ups, then snog like teenagers.

'That's very sweet of you,' I said, taking it from him.

'Not a problem. Hmm, just as I thought.' He nodded at the picture-perfect fire I had going, where three chunky logs were burning nice and slow. 'It's malfunctioning.'

It looked totally fine to me. 'Is it? How can you tell?'

'At the back there, on the end. Looks like an overactive airflow.' I bent myself double to see around the logs and he laughed. He'd got me.

'Let's open the wine and keep watch,' I said, playing along. 'To make sure it doesn't explode.'

'It isn't wine, but close enough. Sorry to disappoint you twice in one day.'

Bloody hell. 'Not at all! Who needs alcohol, right?'

There weren't any wine glasses, so we made do with plastic tumblers, and the 'wine' looked like Ribena as I poured it out. I missed my daily glass, and occasional bottle, of Chablis, but I didn't miss the hangovers. I had so much more energy since I'd got here which could only be down to cutting out the booze. My candles glowed green and red along the window ledge, and with the fairy lights twinkling and the snow outside, it felt like Christmas as I carried our drinks over.

'How was your tree-hugging session?' Henrik asked, taking his tumbler. My skin tingled where our fingers brushed.

'Good! I think I'm getting the hang of it. The hardest part is letting go, but Willow was warm and welcoming as always.'

He nodded. 'It takes time and practice to master, but you'll get there.'

'You obviously know what you're doing when it comes to your mind and body,' I said, trying to shift the tone. 'Throwing me over your shoulder like that earlier.' My voice went gravelly as I relived it. I'd never envisaged myself as a hapless woman, but actually...

Henrik smiled. 'That's taken time and practice, too. My body didn't look like this when I was in New York. I was living off takeaways and carrying an extra twenty kilos.' He slapped his abs. 'I had that grey, overworked look about me, you know?'

'Only too well!' I said, pointing at my face. 'Being a barrister is non-stop brainwork and I'm always too tired to cook. My exercise regime went out the window a while back.'

'You look good to me,' he said with a wink. 'It's hard to do it all. The closest I got to the gym back then was walking past it twice a day, to and from work.'

I couldn't imagine him pale and overweight. Lucky me, to have this version instead: rustic and outdoorsy, and solid in every way. I tried to see him as anything other than an absolute hunk, but he caught me staring at his arms and cleared his throat. 'So, are you enjoying it here after all? Glad you stayed on?'

'You know… it's not the kind of trip I would *ever* have deliberately booked. No offence. But it's growing on me. I'm glad I randomly found you.'

'High praise indeed! Can we quote you on the website? *Would never deliberately book.*' He sat back and laughed. '*Pappa* will be delighted.'

I threw a cushion at him. 'I'm trying, alright? What can I say? I like an all-inclusive holiday. I wasn't expecting to have to bungee into breakfast and abseil down to dinner.'

'Yet here you are, relaxing at home in a ski jacket. Ready for anything.'

'Ready for something.'

Henrik threw the cushion back at me and caught my glass, knocking it into my lap. We both watched in horror as it toppled over, fake red wine spilling everywhere.

'Arghhhh!' I screamed, lifting my jacket to contain the liquid and dashing over to the sink. Bright red splodges were already soaking into my jeans but it had miraculously missed both the sofa and the sheepskin rug.

Henrik leapt up, mortified. 'Sorry! I'm such a clutz. Take it off! I'll get the salt!'

I unzipped it without thinking, relieved to get some air on my body. The fleecy lining was not designed for indoors. Henrik pretended not to notice me stood there in my bra as he frantically ground sea salt over the stain. It was all very gastropub. I half-expected him to add a sprig of rosemary and pop it in the oven.

'Will salt still work if it isn't real wine?'

He stopped and turned. 'I've no idea. I can't concentrate.'

'Why's that?' I asked, knowing full well. My breathing slowed as his eyes searched mine, waiting and teasing before finally leaning in to kiss me.

'Must be the heat,' he said, eventually, stripping off his jumper and throwing it at the sofa. His chest was strong and sculpted and his skin felt warm against mine.

I smiled into his lips. 'Seems my fire is working, after all.'

Henrik pulled me into him, the two of us lost in each other as we kissed. He took his time building me up, then lifted me onto the kitchen counter. It was a relief to finally give in to temptation; the charge between us had been hard to resist. I shivered in pleasure as his beard tickled my neck. He traced a finger down my spine as he kissed me. My hands went to his abs and his stomach before going lower to undo his belt.

'Much better,' I whispered. Barefoot and bare-chested, in just his battered jeans, he picked me up and strode into the bedroom. 'I could get used to being carried around like this.'

'Just say the word,' he said, laying me down, my legs wrapped around him as we kissed again. He nipped back into the lounge and reappeared with a pair of wine-bottle candles, the soft light casting a shadow over his hairy chest.

'It's been a long time since I had a moment like this,' Henrik said, looking at me tenderly. 'I want to take it in. You are beautiful, Sara.'

'Really?' I hadn't expected him to say something so heartfelt, and it made me quite emotional. I didn't feel beautiful, and I hadn't for a long time if I was being honest. I'd stopped caring about myself and been piling all my self-care energy into work. I strategically draped the bedsheet over my legs and stomach and fluffed my hair forward as he climbed onto the bed. Was I about to have sober sex? Who even was I these days? Henrik seemed determined to take his time, kissing my feet, then my calves and thighs, exploring my body as he made his way back up.

This felt exciting and new. I'd missed the sign that said 'rebound' and was already in way over my head. Henrik was gorgeous and kind and chill, the total opposite of Mark's cold ambition and drive. And his relaxed vibe was clear to see as he devoured me, while I lay back and enjoyed every single second of it.

Nineteen

Thursday 24th September

I was getting good at this.

I hugged Willow tight, and I swear I could feel her leaning into me. She wasn't like the other trees. She was warm and malleable and full of good vibes. Just how I liked my hugging partners.

It was official. I was going mad. I'd be on Sky News next, telling the world how we'd fallen in love and defending our decision to marry. My one tree-love.

There were whoops and squeals coming from the forest, and I followed my ears to find the others. I'd planned in a cheeky five minutes with Willow on the way through, knowing everyone else would be down at the bonfire. That way I could get the benefit of tree-hugging, without the embarrassment of anyone knowing I was doing it.

The group had gathered in a clearing next to the water and everyone was dressed up for a party. There was a queue at the buffet table, with its towers of marshmallows and a rainbow of fruits to skewer up for the fire: strawberries, banana chunks, mango and grapes. And then there was the sauces and sprinkles section. White and dark chocolate sauce, honey, sesame seeds and chopped nuts. I didn't even need a marshmallow – just give me a spoon. Will and Ethel were sat on a log together chatting, and Kimi and Yuto were building marshmallow kebabs.

'Sara!' Greta skipped over, her orange dress dragging on the ground. 'I made this for you.' She held out a flowery headdress, in reds and pinks, that matched hers.

'So pretty! Thank you!' I said, putting it on. 'What's the occasion?'

'It's for the fire dancing. Our ancestors would have danced naked – so we like to make hair and body decorations,' she said, pointing to the daisy chain around her ankle.

'I won't be dancing naked – if at all,' I said, zipping my coat up tight. 'I'll catch my death.'

Greta laughed. 'You must! You don't want to risk angering the Nordic gods!' she said dreamily, wafting around in a circle. 'You're way too young to be so... uptight.'

'It's not uptight to stay dressed,' I said, loud enough for people to hear. And considering how cold this country was, they were over-indexing on activities where you could (but never should) take all your clothes off. Just... keep them *on*, please. There was nobody here I wanted to see dancing naked about the place. Except, maybe... Well. It wouldn't be awful if Henrik got his kit off again, but I wasn't keen to see Tore's todger or Ethel's lady garden, thanks very much. Or to show anyone mine for that matter.

'S'mores, m'lady.' Jonas handed me a bag of marshmallows and a jousting stick.

'Thank you, chef. These are a bit risky, aren't they?' I punctured a couple of white puffs onto the skewer and cast it into the fire. Toasted marshmallows were the best.

'And an oat-milk hot chocolate?' he said, offering me a mug.

'Oooh – yes, please – delicious.' I was being converted to veganism by stealth and would be telling *everyone* when I got home. There was a cool Enya vibe playing and I spotted Celeste in the corner, strumming away on a harp. Greta picked up her flute and Jonas got on the drums to make a transcendental trio, and the music had us all swaying as we stared into the fire on a collective sugar high.

'Evening,' Will nodded over as he dipped his melted marshmallows in dark chocolate sauce.

I smiled; mindful Henrik was also trying to catch my eye on the other side of the bonfire. He was wearing one of Greta's headdresses too, in blues and blacks, and his hair was loose. I gave him a wave, feeling hot at the memory of us together.

'Sara! Watch out!' Will shouted, pointing at my marshmallows, which were now engulfed in flames.

I screamed, dropped my skewer and backed away from the decimated goo. The smell of burnt sugar reminded me of the fire alarm going off when I'd attempted a banoffee pie for Mark's birthday. I was not a natural chef. And anyway, I didn't need to barbecue my marshmallows; I'd just pop one on top of my hot chocolate. Or better still, straight in my mouth.

'I'm the resident fire officer here, ma'am. What seems to be the problem?' Henrik said in a Deep South drawl as he stamped on the gluey white fireball, getting sticky mess all over his boots.

I giggled at his heroics. 'Why thank you, kind sir,' I said, clutching my hands to my chest. Will looked at us both then turned away, leaving us to it.

'Sorry I had to leave so early yesterday,' Henrik whispered. 'I was on morning meditation duty.'

'That's OK. I wasn't expecting you to stay and make me breakfast.'

'I'd have been happy to,' he said, smiling. 'That's the least I could do to thank you for such a great night. I haven't stopped thinking about it since.'

I blushed, suddenly self-conscious.

No matter the butterflies swirling in my stomach, surely last night could only have been no-strings sex – how likely was I to ever come back to Norway? And Henrik hated big-city life. I had to look at the pros of the situation: knowing you can be as wild as you like if you're never going to see each other again. That was how we'd been – reckless and free – so it was slightly awkward standing next to him like this. Knowing the positions of all his tattoos, and the positions I'd been in when I'd seen them. Knowing how he'd pulled me down on top of him with those arms as he'd kissed me. Knowing exactly what his abs looked like under that linen shirt.

'Oooooo, look.' Celeste stopped playing abruptly and pointed up at the sky, but there was nothing to see apart from a couple of glittery stars and a wispy cloud.

'Behold the aurora borealis,' Tore announced, proudly. 'Or as some of you call them – the Northern Lights.' He waved his hands dramatically, like a magician revealing a rhino in a previously empty box.

I squinted up at the night sky. 'Where?'

'There.' Henrik stood behind me, his aftershave giving me butterflies as his cheek hovered next to mine. He pointed at the murky-looking mist swirling overhead.

'The cloud?'

He nodded. I kept trying to see, in case it was like some kind of magic-eye poster. Staring *into* the cloud rather than *at* the cloud, then crossing my eyes to get a different perspective. But no. Nothing. *Nada*. The others were all gasping in delight and taking photos.

What was I missing?

'Are you having me on? It's pitch-black up there. No greens, or purples or blues?'

'The lights aren't always in colour, but there's an app you can download to turn them green if you like?'

'I have to *turn* them green?' I said, confused. 'Isn't that how they come? The Arctic tribes didn't have mobile phones, so how did they see them?'

'Trust me, Sara. I've witnessed the aurora many times, and you're looking at it.'

I tried again to see what was in the framed photos in my cabin. But it was no good – it was just a load of grey clouds.

'Well, if this is what they really look like, I want my money back!' I said, faux-outraged.

Henrik smiled. 'Other colours are available, you'll see.'

'With different apps?' I said, facetiously.

'The lights aren't an on-demand service I'm afraid. They turn up how they like, when they like. Sometimes like this, sometimes green or purple, and sometimes all the colours of the rainbow at once. So, I can understand how you might feel this is somewhat... underwhelming.'

'To say the least.'

A shaft of green light shimmered in the corner of the cloud, and Kimi squealed.

I silently rolled my eyes. *Oh, pur-lease.*

'So young and yet so cynical,' Henrik said. 'You can see the colour trying to break through, yet you still don't believe it? Every version is different – that's the magic of the aurora.'

Henrik's gaze had cast some kind of spell on me, and I couldn't stop staring at him, our eyes locked together. Maybe it was lack of sleep, or a subconscious response to his aftershave, but something carnal inside me wanted to clonk him over the head and drag him back to my cave for round two. I'd been convinced my love life was doomed post-Mark, yet here I was, being drawn to a new man and feeling all those feelings again.

The green flash started to glow brighter, illuminating the cloud from within for a second, before giving up and fizzling out.

'Ladies and gentlemen, I suspect that is the end of tonight's show. An *amuse-bouche* if you will of all the auroras yet to come. I hope you'll get to see a more explosive, exciting version before you go home.'

Hmm. Suspect was right. Celeste started her harp back up, plucking the strings rhythmically next to Jonas on the bongos, and Tore threw a handful of powder into the bonfire, turning the flames a deep blue. They sparkled and flashed for a few seconds before turning back to yellow, then he did it again and the fire turned white, then green. Everyone whooped and cheered as Greta started off the dancing. Barefoot, she untied her hair, shaking it out and swaying to the beat of Jonas's drums, and Tore took to the mic, singing a low, melodic tune.

'*Heiemo og Nykkjen,*' Henrik whispered in my ear. 'An old Norwegian folk song.' I watched as Ethel stood up and the others stepped closer to the fire one by one, moving to the music in different ways. The flames joined in, dancing in the wind, and I shivered with pleasure, feeling an all-consuming calm. I wasn't sure if it was the heat, the music, or being so close to Henrik.

'Are you dancing?' Henrik asked, holding out his hand.

'Yes,' I said simply, all my reservations disappearing, and I followed him over and kicked off my shoes.

The floor was surprisingly warm and spongy, and I could see rubber mats had been laid in a ring around the fire. They'd thought of everything. I closed my eyes and tried to concentrate on the music, breathing deeply, feeling my feet on the floor and the air in my nostrils. Grounding myself in the moment, like Henrik told us to do in our meditation sessions. I felt self-conscious, awkwardly moving to Tore's lament, even though we were all in it together. Yuto and Kimi danced cheek to cheek and Will was either channelling a spirit or having a seizure. Jonas must have slipped a cheeky psychedelic into his hot chocolate. I was curious to see Henrik's moves, but it was difficult to look without being obvious. It would have been much easier to stare at him from the sidelines – even if the idea was to dance like nobody was watching.

Tore stopped singing and Greta went back to her flute as Celeste rejoined the group to dance. The drums pulsated through the trees as everyone started to move in time, and we followed each other around the fire. There was a table of musical instruments we could grab as we went past. Bells, cymbals, maracas, castanets – a random percussion selection to help with our self-expression. I took a tambourine to shimmy along with, then did a few side-slides to see what Henrik was up to behind me. His instrument of choice was a tiny gong, which was tricky to navigate while dancing. Jonas let out a battle cry, which started a chain reaction of whoops and squeals.

'Woohoo!' I called, but my voice was lost in the noise, so I tried again, shouting as loud as I could. 'WOOHOOOOOO!' Nobody turned or looked at me; everyone was concentrating on their own wailing, but the hit of adrenaline released something inside me, helping me dance more freely. I could feel myself letting go of my worry and embarrassment – my fear – and starting to move like I did in my kitchen disco after a few wines. Mark and I had loved a dance at home, but it was a much boozier affair in the flat on my own, usually involving at least one bottle of prosecco.

The music led the pace, starting off slowly as we all got into it, then turning jaunty and getting faster as we sped up the footwork, eventually reaching a crescendo. Jonas paused the drums while Greta played an intricate piece on her flute, then started up again, belting away like his life depended on it. The dancing turned to running as we tried to keep up with each other, and my heart felt fit to burst when he hit his final beat and silence descended. We stopped and clapped, ready to collapse as we bent over and gasped for breath, dizzy with dopamine.

'Glad you did it?' Henrik asked, lying on the floor next to me, panting.

I nodded. 'I think so. I don't really know how I feel; my brain has been disconnected from my body.'

He laughed. 'Excellent. That's the idea – shake the physical up, so your mind can't override it. Active discombobulation.'

'Is that what it's called?'

'That's what I call it. All our activities are designed to discombobulate. It's the Firefly way.'

Twenty

Wednesday 30th September

'It's not for the faint-hearted, but I promise you'll feel amazing afterwards.'

'Are you sure?'

Henrik nodded. 'One hundred per cent. Inside and out.'

I eyed the lake cautiously. This situation was entirely my own doing. I'd been banging on about how much I loved wild water swimming ever since I'd arrived, but I'd only ever done it in Greece, in the height of summer. And now it was just me, Henrik and a freezing cold lake, and it was too late to backtrack. I had to get on with it. Surely a little dip wouldn't kill me.

'How often do you come out here?' I asked, trying to stall him.

'Rarely, these days. I'm not really one for swimming to be honest. Hot tubs and Jacuzzis are fine, but otherwise I prefer to be on the water, rather than in it.'

'Right.' He didn't want to do it either. 'You're going in today though, yeah?'

'No, I'm just the taxi,' he said with a straight face. 'You're the wild water swimming champ.'

'Right,' I said, again. 'Right.'

Henrik laughed. 'Just kidding – of course I'm going in. I can't let you go in there unaccompanied. You might get pulled under.'

'Might I? By what?' This was sounding worse by the second.

'Not really. It's a lake – there are just a few small fish. Maybe the odd trout. I thought you'd done this before?'

'I have, but not in Norway,' I said, starting to panic. 'I'm really not sure about this, you know. My inner child is screaming blue murder, and I like to respect her opinion on these things.'

'Lucky for you wild swimming isn't designed for children,' Henrik said with a wry smile. 'Your outer adult can make the decision here.'

'Right.'

'Oh. Before I forget – I wanted to show you something,' Henrik said, pulling a Polaroid out of his wallet. It was a stunning, multicoloured sky over Firefly farmhouse. 'This is the special aurora I was telling you about. The magical version. Taken on a Polaroid, so no apps involved. Proof the Northern Lights exist in all the different colours.'

I took it from him and looked at the rainbow of light: pinks and purples into greens and blues. It was beautiful. 'No Photoshop?' I asked, still suspicious.

He gave me a look. 'Be serious. We barely have Wi-Fi out here. Can you imagine any one of us Photoshopping rainbows onto Polaroids to placate the guests?'

Fair point.

'That does look pretty cool,' I admitted, begrudgingly.

'Cooler than cool. Hopefully you'll get to see them properly before you head home,' he said, tucking the photo away carefully and zipping up his bag. 'OK. Are you ready for a swim? I'll race you.' Henrik threw off his fleecy tracksuit and ran full pelt towards the lake, which ironically my inner child would have loved to do. It was impossible not to stare at his body. Hot and cold all at once, and super cute in his Norwegian flag swimming trunks. I laughed as he screamed 'Geronimo!' and bombed into the water like an enthusiastic otter.

'I'll just be a sec,' I shouted, my outer adult about to burst into tears. I wanted to enjoy my jumper for a few more seconds.

Bollocksssss. There wasn't even a sauna to warm up in afterwards.

Speed was of the essence here. Get my kit off quick, get in and out quick and get back in the minibus. Quick. Henrik was clearly part frog; he was swimming around, loving it in there.

I shed my clothes in one fluid movement, like a snake crawling out of her own skin. The air was strangely serene and wrapped itself around me as I walked towards the lake. It was bastard freezing of course, but nothing like it was going to be once I was in that water.

'Come on!' Henrik called, impatiently. No doubt shrivelling up like a used balloon. 'Get in!'

There weren't any steps, what with it being *au naturel*, so there was no option but to suck it up and jump. I couldn't loiter in the cold any longer. I stood on the edge of the concrete, my feet like blocks of ice.

'Is it deep enough to jump?' I asked, gingerly. Last chance to tell him to do one. I was supposed to be on holiday after all. *I was in charge here.*

'Like I just did, you mean? Yes! It's very much deep enough. Completely safe.' *And I was completely in charge.* 'Are you ready? One, two, three, GO!'

I held my nose and scrunched my eyes shut, leaping out towards him. Anticipating ten seconds of ice-cold hell before I'd be allowed to wrestle myself back onto dry land. But I hit the water and it was... warm. It was bloody gorgeous, in fact. I'd been faffing about, freezing my tits off while Henrik had been luxuriating in a hot bath. I bobbed to the surface and took a deep breath.

'It's hot!' I gasped, treading water like a happy Labrador, my skin tingling all over.

Henrik frowned. 'Yes – obviously. I wouldn't still be in here if it wasn't.'

'You tricked me!' I splashed him and he laughed, a sound I was finding I couldn't get enough of. The water felt warmer than it had been in Greece. Or maybe the temperature contrast made it seem that way. And it was so clean and fresh. That'd teach me to judge by appearances. 'How did you even find this place?'

'*Mor* and *Pappa* used to bring us here when we were little, if we were good.'

'And were you good?'

He laughed. 'We were very, very good.'

'Yeah right. I bet you and Jonas were an absolute nightmare as kids,' I said, closing my eyes and trying to float. 'Your poor mum.' There was silence as the water lapped around us, doing its thing.

'Yeah,' Henrik said, sighing.

My eyes flew open. 'Sorry, I didn't mean…'

'It's fine,' he said. 'You're not wrong. We were a nightmare.'

'What would I know? I'm sure she was hugely proud of you both.' He stared straight ahead then shrugged. 'Has she been gone a long time?'

Henrik shook his head. 'Three years in December. The 22nd, so Christmas is always difficult.'

'Was it… sudden?' I didn't want to pry. Well, just enough so I didn't keep putting my foot in it. And I wanted Henrik to know that he could talk to me, if he wanted.

'No. Which I'm grateful for, selfishly. We all had plenty of time to say goodbye.'

I didn't know what to say to that. The thought of saying goodbye to my mum and knowing it would be the last time I'd ever see her was heartbreaking. I paddled over and hugged him tight, in case that might help, then left him to his thoughts, swimming to the other side of the lake.

Patches of labradorite twinkled in the rock, and the birds were singing their hearts out as the sun began to appear. I practised my backstroke up and down the lake then made my way back to Henrik. The sky was vast and clear, and the stars were somehow still visible as I propelled myself through the water. A permanent reminder of how tiny we all were. Insignificant grains of sand on a vast beach of universe. The water was silky-soft, and I felt at one with nature as I cut through it, gliding back to Henrik, who was lying nestled in the rocks.

'I've found a water jet,' he said, taking my hand and reeling me in. Thermal streams were firing from all angles, and the more I tried to resist the flow, the more it pushed me into Henrik's lap. I gave up and let it drag me in backwards, spinning me round at the last second so we were face to face.

'Heyyy, smooth move. No need to jump on me though, I think we've established I'm interested.' He watched in bemusement as I tried to back up, thrashing about and going nowhere.

'It was... not... a move...' I said, fighting against it for a few seconds before giving in. There were worse positions to be in than jacuzzi-ing with a Norwegian hunk.

'Well, this is,' Henrik said, leaning in to kiss me. Our bodies glued themselves together, and his kiss was slow and deliberate, making me tremble with anticipation. His expression turned dark with desire as his lips teased me, biting and kissing my neck.

'Do you like that?' he whispered as I quivered beneath his hands.

I moaned into his hair and wrapped my legs around him tight as we kissed deeper and harder, lost in each other as the jets gently gushed around us. We stopped, breathless, and swayed in each other's arms. His hands had woken up my body and I was hungry for more, but the muffled bleating of a mobile phone disturbed the peace. Henrik had an ancient Nokia, and the tune was straight out of the noughties. He didn't move a muscle.

'No interest?' I asked as it started ringing a second time.

'Not when I'm here with you. Tore is the only one who ever calls,' he said dismissively. 'Jonas sends a text.'

'What if it's an emergency?'

'It isn't. He'll be confirming the boat for this evening. The one your man is on.'

'My man?' I said, confused. 'Oh! You mean Mark? He's not my man anymore.'

'More yours than mine,' he said, giving me a nudge.

'Well, you're welcome to him. I don't know what he thinks he's doing gatecrashing my holiday. He's been ignoring my messages. How did he manage to book in anyway? I thought you were full.'

Henrik stopped. 'Are you serious? He told *Pappa* you'd offered to share.'

'He did *what*? The cheeky git!' I was furious. 'What time does he get in?'

'Six-ish. I'll call Tore back when we're on our way.'

'And there aren't any other cabins available?'

Henrik shook his head. 'He mentioned your name and said he was your husband, so with the same surname and everything Tore thought it was legit.'

'We're getting divorced! What was he thinking?' I paused. 'You didn't think that was strange?'

Henrik shrugged, looking past me and out over the lake. 'I didn't think it was my any of business.'

Hmm. I checked my watch and it was already half three. We had to dry off and drive back and I wanted to meet Mark straight off the boat and find out what he was playing at. I did a little stretch then broke into a swim, gliding off into the middle of the lake. I felt so conflicted at the thought of Mark arriving. What could he possibly want that couldn't wait until I got back? There must be some paperwork I'd forgotten to sign. Why else would he bother? He'd been actively avoiding me ever since I'd moved out.

I floated on my back in Henrik's direction. 'Ahh, well this has been lovely, but we should probably think about heading off soon,' I said, stifling a yawn.

Henrik opened his eyes. 'We can stay another hour or so – I'm in no rush.' He frowned. 'Unless you are?'

'No, not especially, but we've got to go back sometime, and I wouldn't mind being there to find out what's going on with Mark.'

'Oh. Yes, sure.' Henrik climbed out of the lake and pulled on his T-shirt which clung attractively to his wet back.

'I didn't mean immediately,' I said lightly, attempting to salvage the moment. I wouldn't mind a few more minutes with my legs wrapped around that back.

'No, no, let's go. You're the guest; I don't want to keep you here against your will.'

Bloody hell. Men and their fragile egos. 'You're not keeping me here. This is bucket-list worthy and has been amazing. Thank you.' I tried to catch his eye, but he threw a towel over his head and started vigorously drying his hair. 'I just need a shower before dinner,' I said, getting out of the lake and shuddering into my Firefly robe.

I didn't want Mark seeing me like this, a bedraggled rat smelling of pond water. My hair was curling up without my weekly blow-dry and the frizzy bits on my hairline were almost impossible to tame. My ginger roots were poking through, and I needed to iron out the kiss curls on the nape of my neck. Assuming there would be a hairdresser here was possibly my biggest regret. I hadn't even packed shampoo. I'd have to use the block of vegan soap on the shelf in the shower. Or worst-case scenario – the vegan washing-up liquid.

Ana and Lars stood on the edge of the boat as it chugged towards the jetty. What a weird existence; boating in and out all day, going around in circles. Although wasn't that what we were all doing? I was on the never-ending King's Cross to Central London loop, which was far less pretty and far more polluted. I wondered what Lars would make of the Victoria Line.

Even if I hadn't known Mark was coming, I'd have known it was him. Even more so because he was arriving by boat. His red curls glowed in the sunshine as he stood tall and sure of himself, with his hands on his hips. Boats were his forever happy place, so why he'd decided to work in 'real estate' was entirely beyond me. I pulled my hat down and fluffed my hair forward as Tore side-eyed me with amusement. I'd done the best I could, but it was irrepressibly wild and woolly without a professional to wrestle it into shape.

'Glad to see him?' Tore asked.

'Glad, no. Confused, yes. Although it's always nice to see a familiar face when you're somewhere strange.'

'Does it still feel strange here? I think you fit right in.'

We waved as the boat got closer, and Ana and Lars returned the greeting. Mark stayed still, surveying the shores like a pirate directing his ship in to land. Waving like a children's TV presenter would have ruined his vibe.

'Mr Pearson, welcome,' Tore said, shaking Mark's hand, while Lars tossed his Armani holdall into the snow.

'Thank you, it's great to be here.' Mark turned to me, then did a double take. 'Look at you!' he said, holding up a piece of my hair. 'Trying out a new style while you're here? I like it.'

'Hey, you,' I said, trying to hide my immediate irritation. We'd get to that later. 'Good trip?'

'Yeah, yeah,' he said, looking around in awe and taking it all in. 'Bet you didn't expect to see me here, did you? How did you ever find this place? It's not even marked on the map.'

'Isn't it?' I frowned over at Tore, who had Mark's bag and had already started walking.

'The forest is listed, of course, nothing we could do about that, but not the buildings. Deliberately so. It's private land and I opt out of giving information to the tech companies when I can. We try and keep the retreat somewhat off-grid.'

'Really?' I asked. 'I didn't know you could do that. How weird that I stumbled across you then.'

'Our business is mostly word of mouth, so there would be no reason to look for our website unless you'd been told about it. I thought your friend had stayed with us. Emma Stone, wasn't it?'

'The actress?' Mark asked.

'It was a misunderstanding,' I said, walking double speed to keep up. 'Em actually stayed at the Firefly retreat in Sweden.'

'*Em?*' Mark repeated, baffled. 'Since when do you know Emma Stone?'

I gave him a coy smile, letting the implication that Em and I were besties hang in the air.

'Synchronicity then,' Tore said. 'Something beyond reason and logic brought us all together. I wonder why. Interesting to observe how the world works once you start to notice these things. People come here for all sorts of reasons – a chain reaction if you like. What brings *you* here?'

Mark looked surprised by the question. 'Me? Oh, right. Same as everyone else I suppose. A quick break in nature. Relaxation, good food – and I knew if Sara was here, it'd be top class.'

'Am I your quality assurance officer?' I said, affronted.

'Yup. The original hotel inspector.' He gave me a friendly nudge. 'She's got high expectations, this one.' His tone made it sound like a bad thing. What was wrong with wanting the best for your holidays? I worked hard every other day of the year; I wanted to make sure it was worth it.

'It is a gift to have a wife who aims for the best in life,' Tore replied, and I could have kissed him.

Mark looked uncomfortable as he nodded. 'For sure,' he said.

Ha! Put that in your pipe and smoke it. Although it felt sad to have a virtual stranger sticking up for me against my own husband – albeit soon-to-be ex. The man who chose me above all others. Before un-choosing me, of course.

'Here is your cabin,' Tore said, pointing to my front door.

'Yes, I heard you'd said it would be OK to stay with me,' I said, eyes flashing. 'There isn't space, Mark. What were you thinking?'

'I'll stay on the sofa; I'm only passing through.'

'You still should have asked,' I said in a huff. Cheeky bastard.

Tore gave an awkward cough. 'As it's still daylight hours, I can give you a tour of the retreat site if you'd like?' Tore said. 'Unless you'd prefer to see it with Sara?'

'No, no – I'd love the personal tour. I'm fascinated by this part of Norway. I've got loads of questions about it.'

'Please,' Tore said, with open arms. 'Ask me whatever you like.'

Mark dumped his bags on my sofa and I hovered by the door. 'Do you want the guest version too?' I asked.

'Definitely. Can we do it tomorrow? I don't want to drag you round the place when you've already seen it – I'm sure you've got better things to do.'

'Cool. I'll see you at dinner.'

I didn't have anything better to do. Especially now Henrik was annoyed with me. It wasn't like I could pop back and finish off my wild water swimming. It was weird having Mark suddenly here in the flesh at Firefly Forest and I wanted to interrogate him in private. I needed to understand why he was here.

Twenty-one

Thursday 1st October

We'd been walking for over an hour, and I was desperate for some water and a flapjack. Firefly Forest had a rich array of wildlife and the further we were from the retreat, the more impressive it got. Puffins flew silently overhead, skidding into the water, next to birds of every shape and colour. Guillemots and gulls flittered with pink-footed geese and oystercatchers, and Mark was in his element, ticking them all off in his bird-watching book. Herds of elk and reindeer ran together in the distance, moving as one for protection, and the occasional eagle swooped past.

It was a joy to be out in the fresh air, but I was still smarting from Mark's bizarre arrival, despite him apologising over dinner.

'*You said I should check it out? When you messaged me?*' he said, seeming surprised that I was annoyed.

'*Are you serious? You thought I meant you should physically come over to check it out and sleep on my sofa? Rather than "checking out" their website, for example?*'

'*Fine, I'm sorry – it was a misunderstanding,*' he said with a bashful smile. '*I'm only here for a few days. I didn't think you'd mind so much.*'

'*Of course I mind!*' I huffed. '*Not that there's much I can do about it now.*'

'In my defence, the cabins looked much bigger on the website,' Mark argued. '*You've been booking our holidays for years, I wasn't really sure how to…*'

'Mark – look!' I whispered, putting a finger to my lips and treading carefully. Three reindeer calves were grazing with their mum next to a pine tree. Little brown, fluffy things, nibbling away at the grass. I silently pulled out my phone and zoomed in. This was going to be my Christmas card. I took a tiny step closer and somehow slipped on a branch, thudding to the ground and sending them scampering back into the woods. Four white bums bouncing off through the air.

'Very slick,' Mark said, watching them through his binoculars. 'This area is huge, you know. I reckon it's still another mile or so to the shore.'

'Yeah, Tore said it was ten by ten or something like that.'

'Did he? Interesting. They're barely using any of it then,' he mused.

'Hmm, I don't know. I've seen loads since I've been here. The activities stretch across it.' I shaded my eyes to see. 'We went alpine touring up that mountain a couple of weeks ago. Then husky sledding over on the west side, near the water. They employ people from the mainland to come over on different days, depending on what we're doing.'

'Nice. A local business model. Keeps everything tight.'

I sat on a chunk of wood that could almost pass for a bench and dug out my water bottle. 'Can we stop for a few minutes?'

'Sure,' Mark said, slipping off his rucksack. He slapped himself hard on the neck then checked his hand. 'Gotcha, you little bastard.'

'Get some of this on you,' I said, handing him my insect repellent.

'Amazing, thanks, I didn't bring any,' he said gratefully, spraying himself all over.

'At least I'm good for something.'

'You are,' he said. 'And what am I good for?'

'Are we in a pantomime?'

He pulled a hip flask out of his bag with a grin. 'Drink?'

'Mark! You're not allowed booze in here!' I said, looking around furtively to check no one was watching.

'Er... yes I am. I'm a grown man on holiday – I'm not here to practise abstinence. Of any kind.'

The sharp whisky fumes punched me in the nose as he unscrewed the cap, and I could taste it in the air as he glugged it down. Not a very gentle option for eleven in the morning.

'No thanks, I'm on a detox,' I said, as he offered it to me.

'A detox, eh? Anything else I can tempt you with instead?' Mark unzipped his jacket like a trench-coat salesman and the pockets were packed with chocolate bars and alcohol miniatures. 'I read it was vegan and booze-free on the website and wasn't sure how long I'd last.'

He was a human vending machine, and my eyes were on stalks as I scanned the options, but I had to stay strong. The Nilsens took the rules so seriously and I didn't want to let them down. I bit into my flapjack and closed my eyes to distract myself.

'Dealing Double Deckers at your age – tut, tut,' I said, shaking my head. 'No booze for me thanks, but I'll take a tonic on the rocks.'

'No tonic or ice, unfortunately. But you can sit on the rocks and drink your water?'

I laughed. 'Fine.'

'I've got a block of cheddar and a pack of pork pies back at the cabin as well.'

'You haven't!' My mouth watered instantly. The vegan food was good, but my insides were missing meat and dairy. I'd had enough pumpkin shots and beetroot brownies to last me a lifetime. I pictured a slice of bear ham with grated cheese for hair, holding out his hammy hand with a wink. It wouldn't take much to tempt me back from my have-a-go veganism. Never again would I travel abroad without an emergency stash of KitKats.

Mark was taking photos like a comic-book photographer, capturing the view from every angle: the forest, the fjords, the sky.

'Are you OK?' I asked, concerned. It wasn't like him to care about remembering a place.

He stopped. 'Yeah, fine. I got this camera for my birthday, and I'm loving it.'

'Oh, yes. Happy birthday for last week.' It was a date that had been etched in my mind for years. Mark's love language was receiving gifts, and I'd treated him to some outrageously generous birthday presents in the handful of years we'd known each other. Tickets to The Ashes in Melbourne, Adele in Las Vegas, a surprise weekend to

Coachella. It felt strange to have barely acknowledged his birthday this year when there had always been such a build-up to it before. But I wasn't too bothered. It was as clear a sign as any that I was moving on. All that past thought and effort – and what was the point? I didn't ask who'd bought him the camera, and I didn't care. Maybe his mum. Maybe he'd bought it for himself. 'Did you celebrate with Millie?'

He rolled his eyes. 'No. It might surprise you to hear she went cold after your little outburst at Harry's.'

I clutched my chest in faux surprise. 'What? Why?'

'Lots of reasons, but mainly her allergy to dogs.'

'Oh really? Nothing to do with you then?' I said archly.

'No. More women are allergic to dogs than you might think.' He laughed. 'At least that's what they keep telling me.'

'Speaking of which, we should call your mum and check in on them.'

'Have you missed them? Being out here?' Mark asked.

'Of course,' I said, thinking of their little snouts. 'My two mini besties. Always full of good vibes.'

'Not when they're with me. They bark non-stop when you're not around. It was a relief to drop them off at Mum's. I don't even think they like me.'

'Of course they do!' I said, knowing full well I was their favourite. 'They only ever want a walk, a cuddle or food – or ideally all three. Dogs are remarkably simple creatures.'

'I've read they choose one human, and all others pale into insignificance,' Mark said, glumly. 'And it's clear I'm not their choice. I'm a means to an end at most.'

'How can you say that?! They love you!'

'Nah. They love treats and pigs' ears. But I get the feeling I'm just their pork supplier. They tolerate me until they can get back to you.'

I was proud of my girls for being loyal in my absence and showing Mark what they thought of him breaking up our little family.

'It's hard for them. It's been hard for all of us,' I said sadly.

Mark didn't respond, picking up his camera and hiding behind the lens to take more photos of the same view. 'Shall we carry on down to the water? Or head back for lunch?'

I was still hungry after my flapjack and hadn't had much breakfast. 'We could go for silent lunch now, then walk along the shoreline tomorrow morning? If we leave before nine it'll give us time to have a swim in the thermal pool.'

'Good plan,' Mark said. 'You always were one step ahead.'

I took a final swig of water and stood up in a burst of energy.

'I'll race you,' I called behind me, getting a head start before his competitive streak had chance to kick in. I was still trying to get his attention, even now, and it made me sad. I didn't really want him to chase me. But I wanted him to *want* to chase me.

'There you are,' Tore said as we ran towards the Orangery, snorting with laughter. 'I was getting worried. Are you OK? Did you get lost?'

'No, we were just exploring,' Mark said.

The restaurant windows were open, and people were already silently tucking into lunch. I tried to catch Henrik's eye, but he seemed very caught up in his courgetti and didn't look my way once – not even when I waved.

Tore blocked the doorway, calm and zen-like, his alpha aura radiating strong.

'Mark, as I mentioned on our tour, we observe quiet during lunch, out of respect for anyone processing difficult feelings.'

'Understood,' Mark said, his face suddenly serious.

Tore nodded slowly, frowning. 'Sorry to ask this, but can I smell... spirits?'

My immediate instinct was to lawyer up and defend our collective criminality. But I managed to keep my mouth zipped. Mark was closest and it was his drinks cabinet – he could handle it. He pulled out his hip flask and waved it shiftily. 'I always take it when I go orienteering, in case of emergency. Better to be safe than sorry.'

The absolute front of him, standing there breathing noxious fumes all over Tore while trying to pull the wool over his eyes. He was like a five-year-old.

Tore eyed the contraband and smiled. 'It's quite safe here, but I understand the logic. I wonder, if under the circumstances, I might speak to Jonas about you having lunch a little later. You probably want a shower and a rest after all your... exploration?'

'Great idea. Thanks, Tore,' I said, linking arms with Mark and dragging him off. 'This way.' He put the hip flask back in his pocket and a Bounty wrapper fluttered to the floor.

I snatched it up as fast as I could. 'Sorry,' I mouthed at Tore, feeling guilty. 'We'll be back in an hour, in a more presentable state.'

He gave me a thumbs up, but I knew I'd let him down. Mark sniggered, so I kept him facing forward and frogmarched him down the path.

'Ha, ha… I got you in trouble with the teacher,' he sang. 'What kind of resort doesn't let you have a few drinks to relax? Is this AA or something? I didn't realise you were holidaying with winos and smackheads.'

'Shh. Let's get some coffee inside you.'

'How about we get something inside *you* instead?' he said, chuckling to himself. 'For old times' sake.'

'Jeez, how many did you have?' I steered him back to the cabin, put the fire on and made a pot of Henrik's special coffee as Mark lay on the sofa. His phone started pinging away as soon as we walked in. 'Have you got signal in here?'

'Yeah, I brought a booster box with me. I got it in Finland last month. I'd have been cut off from civilisation, otherwise.'

'I think that's the idea,' I said, carrying over his coffee.

'Need to stay in touch with work though, don't I?' he mumbled, closing his eyes. Always so worried about work, his brain was forever buzzing with activity, just like mine. Maybe that was part of the reason we got along so well.

'No, Mark, you don't. You're Tore's worst nightmare. Secret aerial on the roof, booze, chocolate… pork pies! You'll be pulling a string of sausages out your pocket next, like a Punch and Judy show.'

'Not a sausage, I'm just pleased to see you,' he said with his eyes still closed, laughing to himself.

'Still rolling out the same old puerile jokes, eh?'

'Sausage,' he replied, then started softly snoring.

Twenty-two

Saturday 3rd October

The coals glowed orange through the ash, giving off a tar-like smell as Henrik raked them back and forth. They'd been laid out on top of the shingle next to the water and Jonas sat cross-legged at the top of the pathway, drumming out a rhythm on his bongos as we walked up. The sun had flooded the sky with burnt yellows and reds, and I could happily have spent the evening with my book, a blanket and a flask of hot chocolate, but instead we were gearing up to walk across hot coals. As you do. The others seemed giddy with excitement but there was no way I'd be putting my little piggies through it. This little piggy would be going wee, wee, wee, wee, all the way home, well before it got to me. I'd play along for a little while, though. I didn't want to give off completely negative vibes.

I tightened my ponytail and tucked it down the back of my dress. It was covered in hairspray, and I didn't want to take any risks while I was flammable.

'Have you done this before?' Ethel asked, taking off her socks.

'Er, no. Have you?'

'Yes, lots of times. Shaking up your belief system is the secret to an interesting life,' she said.

'Is it? You've lost me. How does this link to my belief system?'

'Well, you believe – we all believe – the coals to be hot. We *know* they're hot, in fact. Our eyes tell us so. It goes against logic and our sense of safety to step on them.'

'True.'

'Which makes this less about hot and cold and more of a mind over matter conundrum,' she said, her blue eyes twinkling. 'You'll watch as your friends somehow walk to safety, and your brain will then have two versions of the truth to contend with. Either way you'll be challenging a belief, and once you've done it yourself, you'll feel elated – trust me. That sense of achievement when you get to the other side is addictive.'

'Totally,' Mark piped up. 'I've done it a couple of times myself.'

'Have you?'

'Yeah. In Goa last year. It's easy. Focus straight ahead; don't look down.'

'We did it in Thailand,' Celeste chipped in.

'Cool,' I said, feeling very uncool.

Everyone seemed super casual about running across an open fire and it turned out I was the only one who hadn't done it before. I mean, who didn't have smoking hot coals on their front lawn these days? In which case, maybe I should give it a go. I didn't want to pass up my chance to try it in a safe environment. And then *I* could be all casual about having done it next time I found myself in this situation.

Walking across hot coals? Completed it, mate. But I'd wait until the end, once everyone had checked their soles for burns and confirmed there were none. I needed two fully functioning feet. Walking was a key part of my life.

'Gather round, everyone, please!' Tore clapped his hands together, and we all shushed each other. The coals hissed behind him as Henrik doused them with water. Surely there was a fake section of battery-operated charcoal that we'd run over? My travel insurance wouldn't cover self-harm. *Oh God.* 'There is no pressure at all to do this. It is an exercise in listening to yourself and pushing your limits. Even if that push means you consider the coals, then choose not to take part. That process still takes strength and courage.'

Phew. He'd given me an out. I could tell everyone I'd pushed myself on the inside and they'd never know if I really had. Not that anyone else cared. I just didn't want Ethel to think I was a wimp.

'We will line up here and take it in turns. Henrik will talk you through the technique, then walk alongside as you traverse the coals. He'll even hold your hand, if you ask him nicely.'

'Yes, please!' Mark called out, chuckling to himself.

Henrik gave him a cool stare. 'I'm sure you can manage.'

Jonas had upped the tempo on the drums, and we were about to begin. Ethel went first, hitching up her skirt and taking big, bouncy steps, while Henrik held on to her like a pony. Then Kimi and Yuto went together, hand in hand, skipping in time to the music as they laughed their way across.

'Watch this,' Mark said with a confident smirk, rolling up his trouser legs. He started clapping above his head, like an Olympic athlete preparing to do the triple jump, encouraging everyone to join in – which we felt obliged to do. Absolute cringe. Then he jogged around in a circle, gave Tore a high five and ran at the coals, hopping across them in four easy strides. If only I had his long legs, instead of my chunky skittles.

I was getting increasingly nervous. I'd mentally pushed myself enough. I'd just say no when it came to me. It didn't matter. *No one cared.* Henrik had barely looked at me all evening. He obviously had a love 'em and leave 'em approach to one-and-a-half-night stands, which was fine by me. It had felt good to get all that pent-up energy out of my system. It was a shame not to be able to tee up an encore, but it would be tricky with Mark here anyway.

Everyone was quite taken with the clapping and started doing it for all the firewalkers, chanting their names as they stepped up, to give the walk a sense of drama. Then suddenly they all turned to me.

'Sa-ra! Sa-ra! Sa-ra!' I'd been so absorbed watching everyone else, I hadn't realised I was the only one left and it seemed churlish to say no now. I was going to have to bloody well do it. FUCK.

Henrik came over in his professional capacity as coalmaster. 'Are you OK?'

'Not really.' I laughed.

'You don't have to do it,' he said earnestly. 'There's no pressure.'

'Sa-ra! Sa-ra!' The cheering got louder as everyone tried to encourage me.

'Sounds like it,' I said, my heart thumping wildly. 'It's fine, I'll be fine.'

'Are you sure?' I nodded, feeling sick. 'The trick is not to overthink it,' he said. 'Hold my hand and we'll go together. You'll be done before you know it.'

I nodded again, feeling much better with my hand in his.

The whole experience was bizarre and surreal. The music, the clapping, the chanting, my naked toes exposed to the cold. It felt like I was about to be sacrificed to the gods. I looked for Mark, but he was at the back of the group, swiping on his phone. He must have had a coat hanger down his trousers to boost the signal.

'Ready?' Henrik asked, looking straight into my eyes.

'Yes,' I said, taking a deep breath. These coals were real, and the fire was hot, but I trusted him. I'd watched the others and they'd all taken different routes as they'd made their way across. Some held Henrik's hand, but there was no trickery going on, no safe route he was steering people down.

I ran like a cartoon character, all arms and legs, as fear took hold of my insides. Henrik legged it alongside me to keep up, and I was ten metres beyond the coals when I realised I'd finished.

'Did I do it?' I shrieked. 'Have I done it?' I looked down at the grass under my feet.

'You have,' Henrik said, grinning.

'Woohooooo!' Relief and adrenaline coursed through my veins, and I jumped into Henrik's arms. 'I did itttt! I survived. Oh, thank fuck for that.'

'We wouldn't do anything that might hurt you,' he said, spinning me round, then pulling back, our noses nearly touching.

'You never know what's going to hurt someone. What if I'd tripped?'

'I'd have thrown you over my shoulder and got you out of there,' he said, his eyes dark.

I felt my breath catch. He'd caught me unawares again. This guy was something else.

'Really?'

He nodded silently, still holding me tight. The last time we'd been this close, we'd been kissing in jacuzzi jets, and the flashback gave me palpitations.

'Well done, Sara!' Mark shouted. 'Now you can say you've walked over hot coals too!'

Henrik's eyes changed, the desire gone, and he let go. I felt instantly colder as he stepped away, as well as being all hot and bothered.

Mark bounced over. 'Nice one!'

'Yeah, thanks.' I murmured, watching Ethel's face light up as Henrik congratulated her.

'Fancy a cheeky nightcap?' Mark whispered. 'No point hanging out with this lot drinking camomile and cocoa.'

I absolutely needed a drink. I didn't know what to do with myself, and Henrik was avoiding my attempts to catch his eye. Aside from a few moments ago, he'd been giving me the cold shoulder ever since our tryst in the lake. I felt awful about the situation, but I needed to speak to him one on one to explain – it was still confusing to me, so it must have looked completely bizarre to him, and I didn't want him getting the wrong idea. Mark gatecrashing my retreat had not been on my holiday bingo card.

'Sure,' I said, turning away from the group and following him. I glanced back briefly as we reached the edge of the forest, and Henrik's eyes were fixed on mine from all that way away.

Mark poured me an amaretto and Coke, and it was the sweetest thing I'd tasted in a *lonnng* while. Apart from the cheese and crackers we'd had earlier. I'd got the fire going almost instantly and had successfully turned on the hot tub. I was on the verge of becoming a professional woman-of-the-woods and now knew that dry, battered old logs made the best fires – the uglier the better. Mark and I had jumped in the jacuzzi and were relaxing in the bubbles under the stars. The booze had gone straight to my head and the woozy Henrik-factor wasn't helping. That guy was *so sexy*. I closed my eyes and imagined he was here instead of Mark. He was such a passionate, sexy kisser, and his body was so strong. The memory of him on top of me, nibbling on my ear, sent tingles down my spine. And knowing he was only ten minutes-walk away was torture. I wanted to order room service, but it was impossible with my ex-husband sat next to me, cramping my style.

I opened my eyes and Mark was staring at me.

'I know that smile. What are you thinking about?' he asked, narrowing his eyes.

I sat up and tried to pull myself together. 'What? Nothing!'

'Yeah, right.' He gave me a cheeky nudge.

Funny to think he could still read my mind after all this time – almost. That he knew me and didn't know me at the same time. How had it all gone so wrong? To have been on such a level together and now back to being strangers.

'I was thinking about us running over the coals,' I said, lying through my teeth.

'Really?' he said, a sly smile on his lips. 'Did I look good? Did you get a photo?'

I laughed. 'No. We're not meant to have our phones, remember? Taking photos would defeat the object of it being a personal, physical, *visceral* experience. An inner journey.'

'Yeah, but it's nice to put it on the socials though, eh? Show everyone how it's done. Hashtag serenity. No – I've got it – hashtag life coals.'

I snorted with laughter. 'Too blessed to be stressed.' Our neighbour's favourite hashtag – who was always *very* stressed.

'You'll just have to keep the mental image in your mind.'

Mark slung his arm around me like he'd done a million times before, and I turned and kissed him like *I'd* done a million times before. My muscle memory taking over. It was the same old familiar kiss, but it only lasted a second before Mark jumped back and pushed me away.

'What are you doing?' he said, his face full of panic. 'Sorry, Sara, I shouldn't have sat so close. This isn't what I want.'

'Oh! No, nor me,' I said, sitting up and shaking my head. I'd been snuggled and cosy and wasn't really thinking. Mark's arm had felt so familiar and I was like a coiled spring after being so close to Henrik. 'Let's pretend it didn't happen.'

He was suddenly very sober. 'I thought we were good?'

Mark said *good* in the same tone Mum saved for *dairy* as a lactose-intolerant.

'We are. Calm down, it was an accidental kiss. And you made the first move, with the old arm-around-the-shoulders trick!'

He pulled himself out of the hot tub. 'It's late. I'm going to bed.'

'Bloody hell, Mark! Overreaction, much? It's not like we haven't kissed before.' What was I doing? And more to the point – what was Mark doing in my hot tub in the middle of my holiday? Auto-kissing the ex-husband was never a good look, but it was all Henrik's fault for giving me the horn. And on top of the alcohol and the high of firewalking, I'd been completely discombobulated – in the worst possible way.

Twenty-three

Sunday 4th October

What. An. Idiot. *Why* was I such an idiot? I made my way back to the cabin with a plate of peanut butter cookies, a peace offering. Mark had been snoring on the sofa when I got up, so I'd walked down to the Orangery to ask Jonas for some extras. We had Twiggy and Dots to consider, and I didn't want him thinking I was still in love with him. I wasn't. The sun was out so I'd cracked the windows and doors to get rid of the hangover fug, and I could hear Mark on the phone as I tiptoed into the kitchen. I was in two minds about popping the oven on to warm the cookies through when Mark started laughing and my brain tuned in to his conversation.

'Piece of piss, mate. The old man doesn't even own the land. It's fair game.'

I froze, listening at the door. Mark was speaking in his wide-boy business voice, which he only used when he had information on a property deal and was up to no good.

'You're gonna love it. Absolutely spot on for what you need – loads of space. And once you get rid of all the trees,

I reckon you'll fit fifty houses on here, minimum. And that's without touching the holiday huts, so you can keep the woo-woo retreat going for cashflow if it floats your boat.'

I gave an involuntary gasp. The sneaky little *rat*!

'Yeah, yeah, sweet. We can make it happen as fast as you like – that's the beauty of it. Two signatures and it's ours. I've tracked down the owners and the fella is interested in the three million in principle.' Mark laughed. 'I know. Peanuts for what we'll make long term. He said he'll get the woman on board, no problem.'

Oh. My. God.

'I've got a few loose ends to wrap up before I head back tomorrow. The ex-wife won't be happy when she finds out, but nothing I can't deal with.'

I slammed the door open at that and marched in. Mark jumped and nearly dropped his phone, his smarmy smirk replaced with a look of pure panic.

'Speak-to-you-later-mate-bye,' he said, hanging up. 'Sara? What the hell do you think you're doing? How dare you eavesdrop on my private phone calls!'

'Are you for real? You're in my bedroom, Mark. On *my holiday*. What exactly is going on here?'

'You can't just burst in and ambush me. Look, I'm sorry I gave you the brush-off last night, OK? I know it's made things weird between us.'

'Don't change the subject,' I said, trying to keep my voice steady. 'This has nothing to do with last night and you damn well know it.' Mark side-eyed his phone as it lit up again. 'Tell me what's going on. Right now.'

'OK, OK. You'll find out eventually, so it may as well be now. But no need for the histrionics, alright? It's totally legit.' I pursed my lips and waited for him to continue, scared of what I might say if I opened my mouth. 'It's no secret I've been scouting for land in Scandinavia on behalf of a client who is looking to invest.'

My blood was already boiling at his switch in tone.

'Mm-hmm,' I said, eyeballing him.

'And when I arrived, it got me thinking about whether there might be a mutually beneficial deal to be done.'

I nodded, furious. 'Go on…?'

'So, I called him – literally just now – to float it as an area to look at.' He shrugged. 'That's all there is to tell.'

'Do you think I'm stupid? What a load of old bollocks. You've been sniffing around this place like a dog after a rabbit ever since you stepped off the boat. Holiday, my arse – I should have known better. You've been casing the joint this whole time. Trying to work out how to get your greedy little hands on it.'

'Why are you acting all surprised? It was you who suggested I check it out.'

'As a retreat, you moron, not as a get-rich-quick scheme!'

Mark laughed. 'Don't get all holier than thou with me,' he said, brushing past me into the kitchen. 'You've done far worse. Getting criminals off on technicalities, knowing full well they're guilty. But who cares, as long as you get your bonus – eh, Sara?'

'Don't you dare turn this on me!' I said, getting angrier by the second.

'Don't like it when I hold the mirror up? We're not so different, Sara, remember that.' He picked up a cookie and gave me a wink.

'Why can't you ever just tell me the truth?'

'Fair enough. You got me.' He held his hands up. 'I hadn't heard of this place, and I wanted to check it out.'

'It's been a work trip all along?'

Mark shrugged and half-nodded. 'Kind of. With some bird-watching in-between.'

'And what's the verdict?'

'My client is interested in buying it.'

What *the actual fuck*?

'How can he buy it when it's not for sale?'

'Don't be naïve, Sara. Everything's for sale – we both know that. It's just about agreeing the number.'

'And Tore has agreed to three million?'

Mark paused. 'Not Tore, no.'

Surely Henrik and Jonas wouldn't have gone over Tore's head. They couldn't have. 'Who then?'

'Look. I'll level with you. Again, only because you'll find out anyway. The Nilsen family don't actually own Firefly Forest. Another local family does. The Bakkens.'

I frowned, trying to get my head around what he was saying. 'Meaning?'

He rolled his eyes. 'Meaning any deal that gets done will be with the Bakkens and not Tore. Bjorn Bakken is very interested in the three million.'

It was a double blow. 'I can't believe this. How bloody stupid am I to think you were here for a break? You'd think I'd know you well enough by now. You just used me to book in here and do your dirty deal.'

'Who cares if I did?' he snapped, irritated. 'Why are you so invested? You've only been out here a couple of weeks.'

'Because I feel responsible! It's my fault you've managed to bulldoze your way in here, pretending to be a guest.

Tore took the booking *because I was here*. And now you're planning to swing a wrecking ball through his life and snatch the land his family have lived on for generations.'

'What are you talking about? My investor doesn't want to wreck anything; he wants to make this place bigger and better. Capitalise on its success. Refurbish the cabins, build a proper spa, get some top chefs in. He'll throw loads of money at it and add that layer of luxury you thought you were getting when you booked.'

It was hard to argue when I'd said those exact words to Mark, but now I understood what it was, I felt ashamed for having wanted all that. 'I was an idiot before, and I've changed my mind. Firefly Forest is perfect just as it is, because it's the opposite of all that. The Nilsens have created something unique and magical here. And their vibe and approach – their secret sauce – isn't scalable. The kind of luxury you're talking about would ruin it. This place wouldn't be the same without them.'

'Agreed,' Mark said, nodding.

I felt my shoulders drop. 'You agree?'

'Absolutely! It wouldn't be the same without the Nilsens and my client has no intention of getting rid of them. It's their brand of tranquillity that guests are buying into,' he said with a smile. 'They'll be kept on with full employment contracts and excellent terms and benefits; nothing to worry about there.'

'Employment contracts? To work in their own business?'

'Don't take it so personally, sweetheart. It's quite simple. Tore doesn't own the land and the family who do are keen to sell. It's only fair that they're allowed to do so, don't you think?'

'No, Mark, I don't think that. I think you're meddling and mansplaining where you're not wanted. And don't call me sweetheart.'

He held up his hands. 'Apologies, old habits. Let's just agree to disagree then, shall we? I'm afraid I *am wanted* here by Mr Bakken and I'm dealing with him directly to work out the finer details of the sale.'

'You're not floating it as *an area to look at* then, are you? There's already a deal on the table.'

'Potentially.'

'Is this really what you've become? A wannabe property tycoon, preying on innocent families doing good in the world?' I rubbed my temples in frustration as I tried to think of a way out of this. Where was the win-win? There had to be a way to negotiate a deal.

Mark lowered his voice. 'Look. I get it. This is your retreat. You found it and now I'm making a nice little wedge out of brokering a deal, which doesn't seem entirely fair.'

I put my head in my hands. 'It's not *my retreat*, Mark. For God's sake – listen to yourself!'

'How about I try and swing you a finder's fee?' he said, ignoring me and typing aggressively into his calculator. 'Hmm? Would ten grand make you feel better?'

I gave him a murderous look. I was going to scream.

'OK, OK. Twenty.'

'This isn't about money. You don't get it, do you? Please don't do this – Firefly Forest is special.' I was trying to appeal to his good nature, but I wasn't feeling very hopeful. Was this really the man I'd married? A man who put profit before family? A man who put profit before everything and didn't even want a family?

'Firefly won't be any less special for changing hands. And once the deal is done, Tore can retire and enjoy the spoils of all his hard work. Henrik and Jonas will both get a chunk of cash and won't be tied to a dilapidated old building for the rest of their lives. Think about it. Don't let your ego block a deal that might feel like a lottery win to them.'

I was seething. 'Have you asked them?'

'The Nilsens?'

'Yes. Have you sat the three of them down and told them what your client is thinking? Or were you planning to do a deal with Mr Bakken in secret and buy it from under their noses?'

'I mean, that'll be down to the lawyers to discuss,' Mark said. 'I'm just the estate agent.'

He was an estate agent when it suited him. Mum was right – he *was* a chicken-shit.

I marched up to the Wi-Fi lounge and changed my flight again. Another £200 up the swanny. I didn't want to go back on the same boat as Mark, or on the same plane, or live in the same country. The conniving bastard. Cheating good, hard-working people out of their livelihoods behind their backs. I'd have to tell Tore myself. There was no way Mark would speak to him, and I couldn't let them find out from a solicitor's letter – it would be too late to do anything by then. They needed to know as soon as possible to have any chance of fighting back.

My stomach churned as I made my way up to the farmhouse.

'Sara! Back again even though you know our home is off-limits?' Jonas said, languidly hanging off the door. 'Hennyyyyy! Your girlfriend's here!' he called up the stairs.

'I'm here to see Tore, actually.'

'To ask for Henrik's hand in marriage? I'm happy to speak on behalf of the family when I say – please, help yourself. You can take him with you right now.'

Henrik ran down the stairs, two at a time, his eyes wide and hopeful. '*Hei*,' he said, stuffing his hands in his pockets. His hair was sticking up and his beard was soft and fluffy, neatly nestled into his Scandi jumper. He probably just called it a jumper.

'*Hei!* I was hoping to have a word with Tore. Although, seeing as you're both here, maybe you can join the conversation too? I've got something to tell you all.'

'Sure, come in.'

Jonas and Henrik led the way through their dining room which obviously hadn't seen any guests for a while. An eight-seater glass-topped table with faded leather chairs, a hostess trolley from the nineties and a dusty sideboard with an enormous mirror. Candles waiting to be lit sat in candelabras, next to a box of yellowing silver cutlery.

'Ignore the mess. This is the quickest way,' Henrik said, marching through and creaking the office door open.

Tore looked up from his paperwork. '*Hei*, boys. Sara! Is everything OK?'

'Not really, no. I'm so sorry guys, I don't know where to start.'

Jonas stayed in the doorway, ready to leave as soon as he could, and Henrik perched against the desk. 'Take your time,' he said, relaxed and calm as always.

'I'm just going to say it. Mark didn't come here for a holiday. He's been sussing the place out for one of his clients. A venture capitalist group he works with is looking for land in Scandinavia and Mark is recommending they buy Firefly Forest and invest in the retreat.'

Jonas frowned. 'And how would they do that, exactly?'

'It's not for sale,' Henrik said firmly.

'I know, but...'

'Please thank him for the interest, but we aren't looking for investors,' Tore said with a smile.

I felt awful. The three of them were so unassuming and pure of heart, looking at me with their handsome, beardy faces and matching brown eyes. How was I going to make it clear that Mark was out to shaft them, whether they were open to it or not? I decided on the softly, softly approach.

'He said something about the land belonging to someone else?' I ventured.

'And how the hell would he know that?' Jonas snapped.

'Owning land is a strange concept to us. What right does anyone ever have to claim space as theirs and theirs alone, on this planet we all share?' Tore said. 'We have a lifelong agreement with the Bakkens, which we are all happy with.'

'Is it in writing? Sorry, just putting my legal hat on quickly, in case I can help.'

'Do you mean a contract?' I nodded. 'No, we don't need a contract. I've known Bjorn my whole life. We were at school together and our great-great-grandfathers were the originators of the Firefly concept. We are distant relations in fact, and the agreement has been in place for years. Before either of us were born.'

'The retreat is part of a long line of Norwegian legacy, passed down through Bakken and Nilsen generations,' Henrik said. 'There's no way Mark or any British investor would be welcome I'm afraid.'

'Ain't that the truth. Thanks for the heads-up though, *ja*?' Jonas grabbed his coat and headed for the door. 'I'm meeting Greta in the forest to map out the seating plan. Laters.'

'Are you getting married here?'

'Yes, they're having a winter wonderland wedding.' Henrik ruffled his hair. 'Jonas is dressing up as a penguin, aren't you, bro?'

'Sure. With you as my best man, the Arctic fox.'

'Fitting.' Henrik laughed, as Jonas slammed the door.

I couldn't bear the thought of his and Greta's big day being ruined by Mark's greedy plans.

'Tore, have you spoken to Bjorn recently? Could you maybe give him a call and check in with him? I'd feel better knowing for certain he hasn't heard from Mark.'

Tore beckoned me back into the office. 'If it'll help ease your mind, I'll call him now.'

I held my breath as he dialled the number. Mark didn't lie about money. Conversations were happening and the Nilsens were clearly the last to know.

'*Hei*, Bjorn?' Tore boomed into the phone. '*Ja!* I'm good, and you?'

He nodded along as they chit-chatted, sitting down at his desk.

'I have an odd question for you, but have you heard of a guy named Mark Pearson?'

Tore listened intently for a couple of seconds, then mindful of me and Henrik stood staring, he put his phone on the desk and switched it to loudspeaker.

'He said the lawyers would be in touch to smooth everything over with you before we spoke.'

'About what?'

There was silence as Bjorn realised he'd dropped himself in it.

'About the title deeds for the land. Why would you be phoning me if you did not know?'

Tore stopped in counter-shock. 'We'd heard a rumour…'

Henrik butted in. '*Hei*, Bjorn. We didn't believe it was true. You can't sell the land from under us without any conversation about it. It needs two signatures, remember.'

'Mark explained about the expansion plans and the ambition to monetise Firefly and make the most of what you Nilsens have going there. It sounds fantastic.'

'Monetise Firefly?' Tore whispered.

'Optimise, bring it out of the dark ages. And I completely agree with him, with you all. The place needs a lot of investment and cleaning up. Firefly could make a fortune if it was in the right hands. I'd love to see it happen for all of us, Tore.'

'You don't think my hands are the right hands?' Tore croaked.

'Your hands have done fine work over the years, but we have to face reality. We are old men now. This isn't my conversation to have, it's for them to explain. The investor – Mark – was very charming. He said nothing will change for the worse. You'll all keep your jobs if you want them, and can stay in the farmhouse, if you want to, but with a lot more money to spend. You and me both.'

'That's very generous of you, Bjorn. To let us stay in the farmhouse my great-great-grandfather built. Our family home for six generations. How can you even consider a sale?'

'Is it already agreed?' Henrik asked, sharply. 'What does Nina say about it?'

Bjorn sighed. 'Less convinced but taking some time to think it through. It's a lot of money, Henny.'

'How much? Fifty pieces of silver?' Tore shot back and Bjorn went quiet. 'I didn't think our family legacy was for sale.'

'Don't be an old dinosaur about it, my friend. None of us are getting any younger and it might be nice to retire before we're dead, don't you think?'

I sat quietly watching Tore's face as it dawned on him what was happening. I couldn't let Mark do this. It would break all three Nilsen hearts at once and ruin their family wedding.

'Is there anything we can do at this stage to change your mind?' I asked, gently. 'Even if it's just a chance for us all to discuss the situation in person, before any firm decisions are made.'

'It isn't all down to me of course. Nina needs time to consider the proposal as well.'

'Can we at least all get together and talk face to face?' I said, desperately trying to buy some time.

'You know where we are, Tore. You are always welcome. Let me know when. *Farvel.*' The phone went dead.

Tore put his head in his hands. 'I always feared something like this might happen.'

'There will be a way, *Pappa*. Don't be upset.' Henrik hugged him tight. 'Nina will never agree to it. We'll make Bjorn see sense together.'

Tore shook his head. 'Not if he's made up his mind. He can be a stubborn old goat. Money does strange things to people, Henrik. It changes them.' I thought of the glint in Mark's eye when he'd offered me a finder's fee. As if that would make it OK.

'This is all my fault,' I said, miserably. 'If I hadn't come here, Mark would never have known it existed.'

'There is no blame, Sara,' Tore said. 'Money-grabbers always find a way.'

'Let me see what I can do – please. I have a lawyer friend in Bergen who might be able to help.'

Tore shrugged. 'I imagine it's too late, but you can try.'

'Thanks Sara, but we'll take it from here,' Henrik said. 'We just need some time on our own to figure out what's going on. You understand.'

I nodded. I understood only too well.

Twenty-four

Monday 5th October

'Oliver Lund? It's Sara Pearson from the London office of CSH. You advised me on a case last year?' I said, clutching my phone tightly and hiding behind a tree. I'd had a sleepless night and couldn't sit back and do nothing while Tore's world fell apart. Especially when it was all my fault.

'*Hei*, Sara. Yes, of course I remember you. How are things over there? I hear it's hard going?'

'I'm not in work at the moment, but everything was fine a few weeks ago.'

'Ah, well that makes sense. It's going down with you out of office.' He chuckled. 'I heard you were very impressive in court on the Danny Jackson case.'

I flushed with pride. I had been particularly excellent that week. 'Thank you. He's back in Mauritius now and probably on the rum already, if I know him.'

'It's hard in these fraud cases for people to understand that we are there to focus on the law and not on the crime – that's what they pay us for.'

'To game the system in their favour. Well, we certainly did a good job for Danny.'

'Absolutely. Now what can I do for you? Is everything OK?'

'Not really, no. I'm on holiday near Bergen, at a retreat called Firefly Forest and a legal situation has come up. I was hoping to pick your brains on local property law.'

'Of course. Tell me the problem.'

'It's an ownership question that needs digging into, but the scenario is this: a covenant agreement was struck years ago between the ancestors of the Nilsens who run the retreat, and the ancestors of the Bakkens who own the land it's built on. The agreement states that they each bring their half to the party – the land plus the work efforts – and as long as the retreat makes enough money to wash its face and supports the people who find their way there, the two families share any profits and the legacy of good. In perpetuity.'

'Makes sense,' Oliver said. 'I've heard of similar situations and it's fairly straightforward if there is a covenant in place.'

'The complication is that there's an interested buyer who is speaking directly with the Bakkens about a possible sale, which will of course affect the Nilsens' livelihoods and business.'

'Hmm. These old agreements can get messy. It often depends on who is trying to break it and why. Do you know what this buyer wants to do with the land?'

'Yes,' I said, miserably. 'He wants to chop the trees down and build houses.'

'Residential?' Oliver asked.

'I don't think so. More likely to be holiday homes.'

'Which could be argued as good or bad. I'd need to understand the details and read the proposal. Have you got anything you can send me?'

'Yes!' I lied, desperate to secure his help. 'I'll email everything across. The signal is terrible here, so it'll be later today once I get into the office. Is that OK?'

'Sure. No rush my side. Send it on when you can and I'll take a look.'

'Thank you, Oliver, I really appreciate it.'

The good news was I had him on side, the bad news was I had nothing to send him other than the few snatches of conversation I'd overheard from Mark. The farmhouse door flew open and an angry Jonas marched down the path, followed by Henrik, who was trying to calm him down.

'That asshole is not leaving until he tells us everything,' Jonas said. 'Filip sent a text to say he'll be at the jetty in ten minutes. As if *Mr Pearson* thought he could book a private speedboat and disappear without us knowing. We need to straighten out a few things before we see him off the premises.'

'*Pappa* doesn't want any bad publicity, remember, so try and keep it civil.'

Jonas laughed. 'No chance, bro. He lost the right to civil when he tried to steal our home. Screwing us behind our backs while we walked him over hot coals.'

'I get it, but let's stay focused on what we need from him. And that's the proposal and plans.'

'Which I will help myself to, while you hold him down.'

They walked out of earshot. *Shitttt*, this was an actual nightmare. Maybe I could influence the situation somehow. Get Mark to see sense and talk his client out of it. I tiptoed out of my phone signal nook and followed them down to the water, hiding tree to tree as they walked through the forest and down to the jetty. Filip was heading straight towards us in his speedboat while Mark paced anxiously, his bags packed next to him. I hurried the rest of the way to bear witness to Jonas and Henrik seeing Mark 'off the premises' and presumably throwing him in the sea. For the courts.

Mark's face dropped as he saw the boys heading his way. 'Hey, big fellas,' he said, a look of terror in his eyes as he checked Filip's position and willed him to go faster. The last time I'd seen that expression, we'd found ourselves alone in a field with a bull on a romantic country walk. Mark had pushed me forward to 'make eye contact' because I was a girl.

'*Hei*, Mark. What's going on, buddy? Leaving without saying goodbye?' Jonas asked.

Relief flooded Mark's face at Jonas's friendly tone. 'Yes! Sorry, didn't I say? I'm heading back to London, mate. My bill is all settled though – I sorted it with Tore last night and added a nice big tip for the staff. Thanks for looking after me.' His wink was so cartoonish, I could see it from my spyhole.

'This isn't about your bill,' Henrik said evenly. 'We need to understand what conversations have been had with Bjorn and Nina Bakken before you leave.'

Filip arrived in a puff of diesel as he steered the boat alongside the jetty with a noisy put-put-put. He threw the rope towards the boys and Jonas caught it, hooked it and knotted it with no more than a cursory glance.

'Ah, lads, I'd love to stay and chat, but this is my ride,' Mark said, holding his bag out to Filip, who gave him a curt nod and ignored it.

'It'll only be your ride once you tell us everything we need to know,' Henrik said as Filip stepped ashore. 'It's a small community out here, you see, and the reason it works so well is because we all look after each other.'

Mark's smug smile faded as he looked from Henrik to Jonas and then Filip, and realised he was very much still on his own. The situation hadn't gone from two-on-one to two-on-two. It was now three-on-one, and he was outnumbered on all sides.

His tone changed immediately. 'Absolutely, guys! We're all friends here aren't we? Anything you need to know, just ask!'

'We're not all friends here, no,' Jonas said. 'And we need to know it all. Start from the beginning and tell us exactly what is going on.'

'Honestly, I would if I could, but the lawyers will put my bollocks in a blender – you know how they can be. Especially the girls,' he said, rolling his eyes. 'Total control freaks!'

Henrik ignored him and continued. 'We need copies of the financial proposal, the development plans and any formal paperwork or draft contracts you've shared with Bjorn and Nina.'

'Right,' Mark said, nodding. 'OK, well I will absolutely check if I'm allowed to share those with you...' Jonas stepped forward. 'I don't have paper copies on me,' he said, hurriedly. 'But I can email you once I'm back in the office.'

'No.' Jonas was getting annoyed. 'Whatever Bjorn has seen, we need to see. Today.'

Mark gulped. He was in way over his head. 'There was only one certified copy for the landowner as they were authenticated in ink, but I have PDF copies on email – you can print them out?'

Jonas and Henrik were getting increasingly agitated, and it felt like a good time to pop my face in, so I jumped up from my hidey-hole and walked along the jetty.

'Going without saying goodbye?' I called, and Mark looked over in relief. A rabbit cornered by three foxes. Or should I say a rat.

'Heyyy, of course not. I've been trying to call you,' he said, holding his phone in the air. 'It's impossible to do anything around here. I don't know how you can stand it.'

'Tick tock,' Jonas said. 'Your flight won't wait, and you're not leaving until you hand over the information.'

'How can I give you what I don't have?' Mark was trying to look innocent, but I could see he was almost enjoying this. He didn't consider these guys to be anywhere near his level of intelligence. He'd spit out his soy Frappuccino if he knew about Henrik's rainmaking career.

'You can't expect us to believe you don't have a second copy?' Jonas said. 'You came all this way with no backup? That feels like extremely poor planning on your part.'

'Is it on your laptop?' I asked.

'Yes, but they don't trust me to email it over once I get signal.'

'I'm sure you can understand why,' Henrik said, with a wry smile.

'How about I scan the files on my phone,' I said, swiping through my apps. 'Then you can email when you get signal in Bergen and Filip can check we've got everything through before you get off the boat.'

'Great idea,' Henrik said, nodding. 'Thanks, Sara.'

Mark forced a smile. 'Yes, *thanks*, Sara.' He was clearly livid to have been cornered when he thought he was home free, but there wasn't much he could do about it. He flipped his laptop open and bashed the keys furiously to bring up the proposal. I smiled at him as I scanned, saving the files onto my phone.

'Anddd... done,' I said, snapping the last one. 'We can make a start with these.'

Mark rolled his eyes. 'Oh, come on, Erin Brockovich, you're not getting involved as well, are you? Is this to piss me off?'

'Not everything is about you, Mark.'

He laughed. 'Isn't it?' he said. There was a malicious glint in his eye. 'You weren't saying that in the hot tub the other night.'

That was a low blow.

'You wish,' I said. It was a weak response, but if I got too defensive I'd look guilty of something I hadn't done. Well, only half done. Henrik was staring at the ground, his hands in his back pockets.

'Anyway – thanks for the recommendation, Sara. It's been fun!' Mark said, full of pep. 'I'd love to stay longer, but you know how it is... people to see and work to do. I'll catch you guys soon, yeah? All the best.'

He was talking into the wind like a deluded politician. Filip glared at him and Jonas and Henrik had already turned their backs and were walking along the jetty. Mark didn't warrant a Firefly farewell, but he couldn't care less. He had no interest in any of them. And he clearly didn't have a shred of respect for me anymore, either.

He slapped Filip on the back as if they were old friends and grabbed his own bags. 'Let's be off my good man, and don't spare the horses!' he said with a laugh as he jumped on board, and Filip revved the engine and sped off. I waved when no one was looking, physically unable not to, but he didn't wave back. Funny how he'd somehow painted me as part-villain in this situation, while taking zero responsibility himself. I wanted to help the Nilsens but felt like *persona non grata* as I trotted back to the farmhouse after the boys, going over and over in my mind what to say.

'Henrik?' I called, as Jonas disappeared inside.

He turned with a look of irritation, which was quickly replaced by a professional smile. 'Sara! How can I help?'

'Don't be like that,' I said softly. 'I'm on your side. At the very least I need to send you these scans.'

'Fine.' He held the door open, avoiding my eyes as I passed him.

'It was nothing with Mark, by the way. Just a misunderstanding. I don't know why he said that.'

Henrik shrugged. 'None of my business.'

'It kind of is. I don't want you thinking I'm bingo bonking my way around the retreat.'

He nearly smiled at that.

'It's been tough having my ex sleeping on the couch uninvited, and I've spent the whole time wishing you were there instead. Well, not on the couch. Mark kind of got in the way while I was thinking of you.'

'I'm not sure how to take that,' Henrik said. 'Jonas heard you guys shouting in the hot tub. Saying it was just a kiss.'

'There was an accidental half-kiss, but it was a silly mistake. I promise it was nothing. Mark is well and truly in the past now. We share dogs and that's it.'

We walked through to the office where Tore sat rubbing his eyes, his glasses on the table. Jonas was speaking in Norwegian and stopped when he saw me.

'Back again, Sara! Are you following us?'

I waved my phone. 'Thought you might want these photos. Shall I airdrop them to you?'

'Oh, yeah. I suppose,' he said, despondently. 'Not sure they'll help. I doubt we'll understand what any of it means if it's in English legalese.'

'Email is best,' Henrik said quietly. He wrote the Firefly address down and handed it to me.

'This is hopeless!' Tore slammed his hand down on the table. 'I can't believe Bjorn would do this to us. He's never seemed money-motivated before. What is going on with him?'

The mood was sticky, but I had to speak up before I left them to it.

'Look, guys, I put a call in to my lawyer friend in Bergen and he is happy to help. His name is Oliver Lund and he specialises in property law, so he would at least be able to clarify our – your – position to make sure everything is being done in the right way.'

'You got us into this mess, we don't need you fiddling about in it any further,' Jonas snapped.

'Hold on,' Tore said, putting his hand on his youngest son's shoulder. 'Sara, it's truly kind of you to offer. Thank you for making the call. We'd love to accept help from your friend.'

'*Pappa!* We need to decide these things together!' Jonas raked an angry hand through his hair. 'We don't know anything about this Oliver guy. It could be another one of her *friends* looking to take advantage.'

Henrik spun round on his chair. 'Have you got any better suggestions?'

Jonas huffed. 'It's just bollocks. How can it be so easy for someone to take everything off us?'

'Let's read through and understand everything before we get upset,' Tore said. 'Sara said the proposal still had us in jobs and living in the farmhouse, so let's not assume it's all doom and gloom until we know what we are dealing with.'

'Greta is going to freak when she finds out. The wedding is two months away and based on what that prick was saying, the sale could go through before then.' Jonas was clearly freaking out as well.

'If you send everything over to Oliver, he can advise you. These sorts of questions should be easy to answer. Do you have a copy of the original covenant? Mark might be acting on the assumption there isn't one.'

Tore tapped the table with his pen. 'Let me check *Besta's* chest,' he said, slowly standing. 'It's in the cellar somewhere. It hasn't been opened in years, but all the family papers should be in there.'

'*Pappa's* grandpa,' Henrik said, translating for me. 'Our great-grandfather.'

'OK, well that feels like a good place to start in terms of an action plan,' I said, putting my legal hat on. 'Henrik, if you email the documents to Oliver then he can advise on the property law position. I'll read everything through at the same time and check for any loopholes. Tore will look for the original agreement between the Nilsens and the Bakkens. And between you all, try and gather as much ammunition as possible to help Oliver put an argument together. Should you maybe visit Bjorn and Nina as well, to talk it all through?'

Jonas snorted. 'No chance.'

'Maybe not you then,' I said. 'Who has the best relationship with them?'

'Henrik,' Tore said, without missing a beat. 'They are his godparents.'

'What? Oh wow! The plot thickens.'

'Doesn't it. Unbelievable, eh?' Tore replied. 'I can't face them right now – I'm too angry.'

'Nina hasn't given her blessing yet, remember. Maybe she can be persuaded,' I said, looking for the win. Nina might be it for Firefly. 'I can come with you if you like, as a neutral pair of ears?'

Henrik nodded, a flicker of light back in his eyes. It wasn't completely hopeless. We had avenues to explore. And we would find a way through. There hadn't been a case that had beaten me yet.

Twenty-five

Tuesday 6th October

'Do you go everywhere in this thing?' I asked, looking out at the vast snowscape as Henrik hurtled along in the twelve-seater minibus. 'It's a bit big for the two of us.'

'I very rarely have just one person in here with me. It's usually a busload for the retreat programme. But to answer your question – yes, I do. Unfortunately, there isn't a Maserati in the underground garage that I drive at the weekends.'

'I didn't know you had an underground garage?'

'We don't.'

'Oh. Ooo, can we get some peanut M&Ms?' I asked, spying a petrol station.

'I'd rather not stop unless it's urgent,' Henrik said, staring straight ahead. 'This isn't a minibreak.'

'Fair enough,' I said, staring longingly at the shop as we whizzed by.

'Sorry, I just want to get there.'

I couldn't blame the guy for being tense. 'How about some music?'

He sighed, then clicked the radio on, filling the car with The Weeknd, which seemed to shift his mood.

'I love this guy!' I said, singing along. 'I went to one of his gigs in Hyde Park last summer. Have you ever seen him?'

He half raised an eyebrow. 'I have as a matter of fact. A couple of times. Madison Square Gardens – a few years back now.'

'With the New York girlfriend?'

'God no, she hated him. On my own.'

'That's a shame. I'd have gone with you.'

I was trying to make nice, but he was still a bit twitchy. I didn't want to bring Mark up again, but he clearly didn't believe that nothing had happened.

'So... have Bjorn and Nina always been your godparents?' Henrik looked at me like I'd totally lost it and I laughed. 'Sorry. All this silence is making me nervous! I'm just trying to make conversation.'

'Yes. They have *always* been my godparents. Is that not how it works in the UK? Do you switch them up every now and then?'

I giggled. 'No, it's the same. It just seems crazy to me that your actual godparents would whip the carpet out from underneath you all like this when they're supposed to protect and guide you.'

'That's why we need to find out what they've been told.'

'Presumably they're invited to the wedding?' Henrik nodded. 'And they will know about your special trees. They were probably there when your dad planted them.' My heart broke for him. What an awful situation. 'Are they your mum's friends, or dad's?'

'Both. They all went to school together. But as *Pappa* said, he and Bjorn are also very distant cousins – four times removed, or something like that.'

'Wow, OK.' I was dreading meeting these people. What kind of godparents-best-friends-cousins would even consider doing this? I tried to focus on the view and tune out my thoughts. What would be would be and I wouldn't see landscapes like this again once I was back in London. But it would have been nice to have some M&Ms at the same time. Then Henrik pinched me.

'Ow! What was that for?'

'Yellow car,' he said, as if that made sense. He rolled his eyes. 'Whoever sees the yellow car first can pinch whoever they're with.'

'Is this how you vegans amuse yourselves?'

'Yes. Pinching. It's the only thing that brings us any pleasure as a collective – you should try it.'

'Hmm… I think I'll stick with cheese, thanks.'

I pinched his cheek and tried to lift his mouth into a smile. His skin was warm and soft, his fluffy beard neatly groomed.

'Nope. I'm not sold. But if pinching's your kink, I'll bear it in mind.'

Henrik slowed down and finally turned off the road we'd been on for an hour. It felt like we were driving into nowhere as we followed the track up a snowy hill towards a smattering of cabins, his Tonka truck tyres and chains working hard.

'Here we are,' Henrik said, revving the bus up the final part of the drive and parking next to a battered old Volvo. It was a relief when he switched off the engine; I'd been half worried we might have to get out and push. 'Remember, you're the ears. I'll do the talking.'

'Charming.'

'Sorry, I didn't mean it like that. I'm just anxious it goes well.'

'It will! They're your family.'

We were barely out of the van when a willowy, silver-haired lady came rushing over.

'Henny!' She hugged him, a torrent of Norwegian pouring out.

'*Hei*, Nina. This is Sara. She's English.'

'Ahhh, well then we speak in English. Hello, Sara. My godson has an eye for a beautiful woman.'

'Oh, thank you.' I blushed as she hugged me, unsure of whether to correct her.

'Just a friend,' Henrik said and Nina nodded, clearly unconvinced.

'Come in, come in,' she said, putting an arm around each of us. 'I want to hear *all* your news. I've made us a *troikakake*.'

'My favourite,' Henrik said.

'Chocolate cake,' she mouthed, shooting me a wink.

This woman couldn't possibly be planning to ruin Tore's life – she baked cakes! I was desperate to get inside and warm up, but the cabin didn't feel much different to being outside so I kept my coat on.

'Now, let me look at you.'

'Where's Bjorn?'

'He's here,' a gruff voice shouted down the corridor. 'How's my favourite godson?' Bjorn was wearing an oversized knitted cardigan in a similar style to Nina's, plodding slowly towards us with a stick. He stopped when he saw me. 'Oh! A new girlfriend at last!'

'Not quite. This is Sara, she's one of the guests at Firefly.'

Bjorn frowned. 'Are we part of the retreat programme now?'

'She's also a lawyer,' Henrik said quietly.

Nina jumped up and scurried off into the miniature kitchen as Bjorn harumphed his way into the chair by the fire. 'I see. And do we need a lawyer present as well?'

'I hope not. Sara's not *our* lawyer; she's not representing us.'

'I'm just here as ears,' I said. Henrik gave me a look. 'I mean, to listen.'

'Ideally we'll figure this out by talking it through,' Henrik said. 'And by *we*, I mean me, *Pappa*, Jonas and you. Both of you.'

I glanced around at them all. This conversation needed professional mediation.

'Anyone for cake?!' Nina hurried over with a tray of coffees and a raspberry-covered chocolate cake, then busied herself handing out cups and fussing over the milk and sugar. She danced around getting everyone sorted, until eventually there was nothing left to do but sit down. 'So!' she said, awkwardly. 'How have you all been?'

'Not great, to be honest. *Pappa's* worried sick.'

'Then why isn't he here?' Bjorn asked.

'He's too upset. He's worried he'll say the wrong thing, so I offered to come in the first instance and find out what's going on.'

'We haven't seen you in nearly two years, Henrik,' Bjorn said. 'Or your father.'

'Yeah, I know,' Henrik said, jiggling his leg. 'I should have been to visit sooner. The weeks and months just keep disappearing. Time flies by somehow, we're all busy with the retreat – it takes up every hour of the day.'

'And yet there doesn't seem to be any money coming in.'

'There must be some?' Henrik said, stroking his beard. 'I leave the finances to *Pappa*, but I know the upkeep is expensive. Jonas uses good quality ingredients for the food. And there's the maintenance and bills; water, fuel, washing, it all adds up.'

'It does. And the profits each month do not add up to very much at all.'

Henrik nodded. 'I've told *Pappa* we need to be more money-minded. Is that why you're considering selling?'

'Of course! All our wealth is tied up in that land and we are sitting here growing old in the cold.'

'Why haven't you spoken to us about it before now?'

'We never hear from you. Tore shut down when your mother died and we've only seen him twice, maybe three times, since the funeral. We've lost touch. I'm sorry for the situation, Henny, but Nina isn't well, and we must look after ourselves before we look after you.'

'Absolutely, you must. I totally understand, honestly I do. But I'm still not completely clear on what's been agreed. Mark told me and Jonas one version of events, but I want to hear it from you. I don't trust him.'

Nina gave me a silent smile before stuffing a wedge of cake in her mouth and Bjorn stirred a sugar into his coffee. 'It's as I said to your father. There is an offer to buy the land that Firefly Forest is built on. Not just the retreat patch but the whole forest area. And it is serious and sizeable, and we have to consider it. Don't we, Nina?'

She nodded into her coffee.

Henrik pushed, gently. 'It's not yet decided then?'

'Ninety per cent decided, yes.'

'And the other ten per cent?' Nina took a large slurp of her coffee instead of answering. '*Tante* Nina? Can't we talk things through at least? We can take a loan out on the land if it's cash you need, rather than getting third parties involved. Especially property developers.'

Nina cleared her throat to speak. 'Henrik, my darling, Bjorn and I are old.'

'What? No, you're not.'

She smiled. 'Yes. Yes, we are. We are the same age as your father, who I'm sorry to tell you is also now officially old, although he'd never admit it. But unlike Tore, we don't have any children. We only have each other. Our cabin is falling to pieces, and the car is on its last legs. We are surviving week to week on our pensions, but we don't have any money.'

'And can't work our way out of it,' Bjorn said, pointing to his stick.

Henrik looked crestfallen. 'I had no idea you were struggling like this.'

Nina put a hand on his arm. 'It isn't for you to worry about. We've had our life and enjoyed it, and it's on to the next generation now.'

'Except we don't have a next generation,' Bjorn said. 'Nobody cares about us. So, if there's a chance we can access our family money before we go, then I think we should.'

'What do you mean nobody cares? They do! I care about you.'

Nina's smile stayed fixed as she nodded. 'And we care about you.'

It felt like a good moment to chip in and change the tone. 'Can I ask a question from an information-gathering perspective?'

'You can ask...' Bjorn picked up his pipe and tapped it on the table to loosen the tobacco.

'Do you have a copy of the original covenant between your families to show what was agreed?'

He chuckled. 'Now that's the kind of information-gathering both parties need to do.'

'*Pappa* has our copy,' Henrik said earnestly. 'He's going through *Besta's* old papers to find it.'

'And are you all clear on the specific terms of the agreement or is it more of a word-of-mouth situation, passed down through generations?' Even if they knew but wouldn't say, it might help us understand their position.

'It was what the English would call a gentlemen's agreement between my great-great-grandfather and Tore's great-great-grandfather, and they shook on it so long ago that I don't imagine there's any record of it left. And even if there was it wouldn't be legally binding.'

'When do you think you'll make a decision?' Henrik asked, clearly scared of the answer.

'Two days,' Bjorn said, glaring at Nina, who started clearing the plates.

'More coffee? Cake?' she asked manically, then turned to me. 'Would you prefer a tea?'

I shook my head.

'We're fine, *tante*. We should head back before it gets dark. I'm working the evening shift and Sara is supposed to be on holiday.'

'Of course.' Nina looked like she might cry.

'If we could get you the money from somewhere else, would you be open to a different kind of deal?' I asked, to try and keep the conversation open.

Bjorn laughed. 'Absolutely. Money is money.'

Henrik nodded. '*Only when the last tree has been cut down, the last fish caught and the last river poisoned, will we realise we can't eat money.*'

He paused for effect.

'Beautiful,' Nina said, tearing up. 'Your mother would be very proud of you.'

Bjorn puffed on his pipe then snorted out the smoke. 'We're not planning to eat the money, Henny, we'll buy food with it and eat that.'

Twenty-six

Wednesday 7th October

Tore put Oliver on loudspeaker so we could all hear what he had to say.

'I won't sugar-coat it,' he said, clear as a bell. 'The land registry has Bjorn and Nina Bakken listed as sole owners of Firefly Forest and legally it is theirs to sell.' Jonas screeched his chair back and stomped over to the window. 'We are therefore looking at three possible scenarios as far as the law is concerned. Option one, you find the covenant to prove the arrangement currently in place is legally binding in perpetuity. In that scenario any sale or changes to the agreement would need to be signed by both parties. If there is no proof of covenant then option two could be that you reach a financial arrangement with the Bakkens direct and draw up something legally binding between you. Option three – they sign with Mark Pearson's investors, whoever they are, and you become sitting tenants and subject to whatever terms Bjorn and Nina agree as part of that deal.'

'FUCK!' Jonas shouted.

'Calm down,' Henrik said. 'We just need to find that damn agreement.'

'I've looked everywhere!' Tore said, exasperated.

'Have any of you ever seen it?' I asked. 'Do you know what you're looking for?'

The three of them shook their heads.

'*Pappa* always said it was a promise etched in stone, and I'd never need to worry about it,' Tore said. 'What an idiot not to have *something* that proves this place is ours. We have just as much right to claim the land as the Bakkens do.'

Oliver cleared his throat, and we all looked down at the phone. We'd forgotten he was there.

'I'll leave it with you,' he said, cheerfully. 'If you find anything send it through.'

'Bye, Oliver, thank you so much!' I trilled, trying to keep the vibe up while the others stared despondently into space.

'*Ha det!*' And he was gone.

'We need to look again,' Henrik said. 'We have to believe it's here somewhere.'

'*Pappa* would know if it was here,' Jonas snapped. 'Face it, Henrik, we're fucked.'

'I can help too, if you need another pair of eyes.'

'Thank you, Sara, you are very kind to offer,' Tore said gratefully. 'Why don't you and Henrik check the attic? We are searching for a needle in a haystack, but if there are two of you up there, it will be easier. Jonas – you and I will go through *Besta's* chest again. My tired old eyes may have missed it. And I'll check the office and the safe and some of the other places your mother used to put our important things.'

'Great idea,' I said. 'Could it be with your passports or your banking information?'

Jonas cocked his ear up at that. 'Do not tell her where we keep our banking stuff. What exactly are you trying to pull here, Sara?'

'Nothing! I just feel so responsible and I'm trying to help you think through where it might be.'

'Jonas!' Henrik glared at his little brother. 'That's enough.'

'What? For all we know, she's in on it too. Mark is her husband after all. They could be a pair of con artists working together.'

The idea that the Nilsens might suspect me as a thief broke my heart. I could see where Jonas was coming from, though, and his anger was totally justified. If it was happening to my parents, I'd be just as furious and suspicious. All I could do was stand there and hope I could somehow magic up a solution. Would Mark listen to me if I appealed to his good nature? Could I blackmail him with a sex tape? (There was no sex tape.) And if there was he'd have no issue with me releasing it to my seventy-eight followers on Instagram. Strutting around like a peacock with nothing to hide.

'Jonas, relax,' Tore said. 'Sara isn't the enemy here.'

'Come on,' Henrik said, leading the way upstairs. In another reality, I'd be following him into the bedroom, and I got a burst of butterflies just thinking about it as I skipped up the stairs. The attic was weirdly clean and virtually empty, a carpeted space with six big boxes stacked neatly on top of each other. Maybe it was me who should be worried – whose attic looked like this?

'This is very… tidy,' I said, opening the first box and eyeing the piles of paper. 'Where are all the spider's webs? And piles of crap?'

'*Pappa* likes to keep things organised. Even more so since *Mamma* died.'

'Do you think it's in here somewhere?'

Henrik shrugged. 'There's as good a chance as any. We've got to at least try, right?'

'I suppose. I don't know how much help I'll be, but I'll give it a go.'

We each took a box and got to it, sifting through all the random pieces of the Nilsen family history that had been preserved over the years. Anything I was unsure of went into my miscellaneous pile as we worked through the boxes one by one.

'Peace offering?' Jonas called, waving a flapjack through the hatch.

'How many have you got?' Henrik asked. The hand disappeared and came back with a plate of four. 'Yes. You may enter.'

He popped up and pushed two coffees in our direction. 'Keeping it very methodical up here,' he said, looking at the two of us working diligently through the papers.

'I like to be organised – it's my lawyer brain.'

'And Henrik's a control freak.' He chuckled. 'You're well matched.'

'Jonas only has two settings in life: slob or sloth,' Henrik mused, scanning through one of the papers. 'He doesn't understand what it means to be ordered and meticulous.'

'You've missed out chef, drummer, skipper. Lots of precision needed for all those. Don't be pissed at me, bro, I'm stressing about the wedding.'

Henrik gave him a long, cool look.

'Listen, Sara, I'm sorry about earlier,' Jonas said, offering me a flapjack. 'I shouldn't have spoken to you like that. I know you're only trying to help.'

'I accept your apology and your delicious-looking peace offering.'

'I'm worried about *Pappa*, and where we're all going to live. But mostly I'm worried about the wedding.'

'We *know*, Jonas. You've mentioned it a few hundred times. Have you told Greta, yet?'

He shook his head. 'I can't even think about it. I'm hoping it will somehow get sorted before I need to. There's no point worrying her unnecessarily.'

Greta was lucky to have a man whose first thought was to shield her like that. Mark had always shared any and every problem with me – no matter how stressed out it made me. I sometimes wondered if he enjoyed seeing how far he could push me before I cracked. A real-life game of Buckaroo. Just one more tiny weight on my shoulder, then watch me crumble.

Jonas slowly ate his flapjack while the two of us worked. 'A smidge too much honey,' he said, looking at it carefully. He took another bite and sucked in his cheeks to taste. 'Any sign of anything?'

'Not yet, but we've still got two boxes to go,' Henrik said. 'Are you sure it's not in *Besta's* chest?'

'One hundred percent sure,' Jonas said. 'I'll leave you to finish up here. Holler if you find Wonka's last golden ticket.'

'Will do,' Henrik said, barely lifting his eyes.

We kept going, trawling through page after page. I put a playlist on and Henrik nodded along to it every now and then, mouthing the words to himself.

The family photos were beautiful, but nosing through them was clearly outside the remit of the task. Henrik had his mum's cheeky smile and dimples, and there were hundreds of pictures of the four of them: skiing, swimming, climbing trees, playing tennis. A happy, healthy, outdoorsy family who clearly adored each other. The two boys were a melting pot of their parents, with Audhilda's sparkling brown eyes and Tore's dark blond hair. Henrik caught me looking at one of the photos for a little too long.

'Sorry,' I said, putting it down and moving on to the next pile.

'Show me,' he said.

I turned the photo round and almost heard his heart break as he looked at it. The four of them stood in front of a Christmas tree, Henrik and Jonas each holding up a ski while Audhilda and Tore beamed into the camera. No wonder all the memories had been packed away so tightly. They were still too devastated to share them. Of course they were.

Henrik smiled sadly. 'I was twenty-one in that photo. My first pair of touring skis.'

'Such a cute picture. Do you want to keep it out and get it framed?'

'I want to get them all framed. They shouldn't be up here gathering dust and getting ruined.' He yawned and rubbed his eyes. 'I've got pins and needles.'

'Well, I'm done. My boxes were mostly books and photos, a few paintings you and Jonas did when you were little. Some other bits and bobs. This is the pile of randomness I couldn't work out.'

'Cool, let's have a look,' Henrik said, taking it from me.

'I wasn't sure with all the Norwegian, but then why would it be in there? You wouldn't put something as important as that covenant in a box of old school reports.'

'No idea, but if it's not in any of the places it should be, it must be someplace where it shouldn't.'

'If it exists,' I said, starting to doubt the whole thing. It was late, and I'd been sat on the floor for too long. I'd have to launch myself headfirst down the stairs at this rate.

Henrik was immersed in the final pile, speedily scanning each page. 'No, no, no,' he muttered, placing each document back in the box once he'd checked and rejected it. I thought about sending Mark a message while I had Wi-Fi, but the damage was done. If he pulled out now, Bjorn would find another buyer. Mark had meddled with the status quo and a seismic shift would now have to happen one way or another. Henrik was still and studious as he carefully checked every last detail of every page, a tiny frown on his face. Another *no* went in the box as he picked up the next, which had a manila envelope paperclipped to the back. He opened it and unfolded the paper inside, his eyes flicking back and forth, working overtime.

There was no point me sitting watching him. 'I think I'm going to head back…'

'Hang on,' he said, his frown deepening as he read. 'I've found something.'

I opened my eyes wide. I sat completely still on my numb bum, in case I jinxed it.

'Have you? Have you found it?'

'I don't know…' he said, still scanning. 'It's a handwritten letter that mentions it.' He flicked to the second page and then the third. 'Oh. Hang on. There's something more official looking attached to it. And it's signed.'

'Oh. My Godddddd!!!! Is it IT?' I crawled over to have a look.

'Yes! Two signatures – a Bakken and a Nilsen. This is it, Sara! This is IT!'

We screamed with excitement and stood up, hitting our heads on the ceiling. Laughing and hugging, relief palpable as it flooded through us both. Henrik pulled back and kissed me on both cheeks. Then I kissed his cheeks, and our celebration kiss turned into a full-on snog, just as Jonas popped his head up.

'Sorry!' he shouted, bobbing back down. 'Don't worry, I didn't see anything.' We stopped, flustered and breathless, staring at each other. I wasn't sure how that had happened, but I'd been enjoying it and didn't want it to stop.

'What are you screaming about?' Tore yelled. 'Come down here.'

'I've found it!' Henrik shouted, his eyes hot and hungry. 'Actually, Sara found it and I translated.'

Jonas popped back up again. 'You're shitting me.'

'Come down immediately!' Tore shouted again. Jonas reversed down the ladder and Henrik followed, waving the letter in the air like a winning lottery ticket. Which was exactly what it was.

The four of us sat around the kitchen table, red-faced and excited for different reasons.

'Read it out then,' Jonas said.

20th February 1842

My dear friend Ivan,

Today is a blessing for both our families. The day my daughter marries your son, and the Bakken and Nilsen clan become one. In honour of this occasion, I want to put in writing our agreement on the future of Firefly Forest. It is a magical place that gives solace and healing to all who visit. My family have owned the land, and your family have worked the land, for generations, and the forest is part of the dowry that will forever belong to our descendants. The covenant attached makes this so.

Yours,

Aksel Bakken

Twenty-seven

Thursday 8th October

'In short, it *is* legally binding, and there's nothing they can do about it,' Oliver said, delighted with the outcome. 'Any decisions to do with Firefly Forest have to be jointly agreed between Tore and the Bakkens. Fifty percent to each half, not fifty-fifty between Bjorn and Nina.'

'Yesss!' Henrik punched the air, then high-fived me.

Jonas was stood with his arms around Greta and squeezed her tight. Once we'd found the covenant, he'd updated her on the situation.

Tore let out a huge sigh of relief. 'Thank God. *Thank God*. And thank you, of course, Oliver. And Sara for bringing you to us.'

'It was nothing,' I said, beaming. My record was still unbeaten.

'And very much my pleasure,' Oliver added. 'Firefly Forest is a special, protected place, and it didn't take long to formalise an objection, once we had proof of covenant. Certified copies have been sent to Mr Pearson and Mr Bakken, along with a cease-and-desist order. I've also made it clear that should they decide to reopen negotiations, Mr Nilsen, senior – Tore – you would need to be part of those conversations.'

'How can we ever repay you?' Tore said, his voice cracking. 'I thought we'd lost it all. I haven't slept for days with all the worry.'

'No payment necessary. Sara is a friend and I've been happy to help. Perhaps I'll come and visit sometime and experience the magic for myself?'

'Please! You must! Consider it an open invitation for anytime you'd like to come. Bring your family and friends. Anyone you like! Just let us know.'

'Greta and I would also like to invite you to our wedding,' Jonas added. 'As our honoured guest.'

'Oh no, no. That's too much…'

'We insist!' Greta said. 'You don't need to decide right now – we'll send you an invite. We want to thank you properly. In person.'

'OK, well that's very kind of you both. I'll leave you to celebrate the good news. Sara – call me when you're back in London. I'm thinking of opening a satellite office there and would love to pick your brains.'

I laughed. 'Will do! Thanks, Oliver.'

Tore hung up and we all jumped around screaming. That winning feeling of pure elation – there was nothing like it. But it felt different this time. I wasn't getting a master criminal off on a technicality. We'd done a good thing for good people and stopped the baddies for once. There was no big fat bonus waiting for me post-win, just a warm glow inside.

'Time to celebrate,' Tore shouted. 'On the boat!'

'Yesss! To the boat!' Greta said, grabbing some champagne flutes and following Tore and Jonas through the patio doors. I prayed he wouldn't fill them up with sparkling apple, like he did at dinner.

'Will we all fit on the dinghy?' I whispered to Henrik.

'Not the dinghy,' he chuckled. '*Pappa's* boat.'

'You've got two boats?'

'*Pappa* bought it when we were small,' Henrik whispered. 'He's been doing it up for years. We had a party for our Norwegian national day in May, and he finally let us see it, but he's yet to officially take it out.'

'Somewhere to hide from the guests,' I said with a smile.

'Or to take them,' he quipped, putting his arm around me. I could just about make out his smile in the dark and it made my insides melt. I was so relieved to be back in his good books.

'It's a shame I've only got two days left,' I said, lacing my fingers through his.

'We'll make it count,' he said, kissing me on the head as we walked down to the water.

Tore and Jonas were already popping corks when we got there, next to a beautiful speedboat shored up on their private jetty. Greta had disappeared downstairs and I hopped onboard behind Henrik. The stars were out in force and the air felt clear and calm. It was still freezing cold, but I was dressed for the weather in my Firefly jacket, all bundled up and cosy.

Greta had switched on the lamps and was lighting candles to hygge up the lounge, while the champagne glasses waited to be filled. I felt like an A-lister arriving at a private party as I sat on the cream leather sofa, surrounded by stripy, knitted cushions.

'Your handiwork I presume?'

Greta smiled. 'I've obviously got a "style". I can't help myself. I'd crochet the whole boat if Tore would let me.'

'You're keeping everyone warm – it's important!'

'Speaking of which – that jacket looks great on you. Henrik is such a sweetie, isn't he?'

I looked down at it. 'Oh yeah, it does the job. He ordered a load for the staff and managed to bag me one.'

Greta smiled. 'Is that what he said? He's too shy to admit his massive love bomb. Those jackets are handmade in Trondheim and they cost a fortune. A friend of mine weaves them on a loom.'

'Does she? I thought it was a nice finish for a uniform.'

'They are designer coats by *Ildflue* and the firefly is her logo. Henrik bought one for you as you were so cold those first few days and didn't have any proper clothes to wear.'

'What?' I was stunned. 'He didn't say. I'd have been happy to pay for it.'

Greta rolled her eyes. 'It was obviously an under-the-radar gift. And it worked – you've worn it every day since.'

Henrik reappeared with Jonas and Tore and a bottle of champagne in each hand. 'Who wants a drink?' He filled up the glasses and Jonas handed them out. No doubt it was sham-pagne, but I'd have to get on with it.

Tore cleared his throat to speak. 'First of all, I want to say thank you and cheers to all of you – we had a few scary days there, but we all pulled together and got through it and I'm so proud of you all.'

'Cheers!' we chorused, clinking our glasses together. The champagne tasted… real. It was dry and delicious and expensive. Had it always been this good or was it because

I hadn't had any in a while? I nudged Henrik and held it up with a silent frown and he nodded. I was immediately giddy with excitement. Maybe champagne was better kept for special occasions after all.

'Henrik, Jonas, my boys, I have something to show you, but I've been waiting for the right moment. And I can't think of a better day or moment than right now.'

That piqued their interest.

'What is it, *Pappa*?' Jonas asked.

'I finally got round to naming the boat,' Tore said. 'Come and see...' He walked back upstairs, and we followed him out into the cold air with our champagne.

'Aurora is trying her best tonight,' Henrik said, pointing to a blur of green on the horizon.

'Allow me to present...' Tore ripped a sticker off the side of the boat, revealing intricate gold lettering underneath. '*Audhilda*. Our beautiful family boat. Your mother would have loved zipping along the water in this baby, and I couldn't call her anything else.'

Jonas nodded quietly and Henrik slapped Tore on the back.

'Love it, *Pappa*.'

'Greta – I thought you could act as ceremonial godmother while we bless the boat,' Tore said. 'We don't want to risk the wrath of Poseidon.'

'I'd be honoured,' she said. 'To the sailors of old! To Audhilda!'

'Audhilda!' Tore repeated and drank, and we all followed.

'To the sea! To the sailors of old! To the sea!' Greta continued.

'The sea!' Henrik said and drank, and we all followed.

'To the sea! To the sailors before us! To Audhilda!'

'Audhilda!' Jonas shouted and drank, and we all followed.

Tore took a third bottle of champagne, shook it violently and smashed it against the bow of the boat; it exploded with fizz and foam as we all cheered into the night sky.

Twenty-eight

Friday 9th October

My last night in the Norwegian wilds.

I wandered from the bedroom to the kitchen, then back into the lounge, staring out of the windows to breathe in each view and lock them in my memory. A herd of reindeer were on the edge of the forest, chewing away on the willow tree leaves like they had all the time in the world. Which of course, they did. It was just me who didn't.

How could I hold on to this place and the feeling of peace it had given me? I didn't want to leave and let it go. I photographed every inch of the cabin so at least I'd have some pictures to look back on. Had I really been here a whole month? A month that had desperately dragged for the first few days, then flown. I looked around my cosy little nook and reluctantly pulled down my Louis Vuittons, embarrassed at the brashness of my matching designer luggage. Their shiny gold zips were out of place next to the lovingly handmade wooden furniture. I'd had my last silent lunch, my last icy dip and sauna combo, and it was time to put the last few logs on the fire. I was a fussy fire starter these days, always on the lookout for a dry lump of wood that would catch easily, then burn slowly. The only way to make a fire last. I opened both suitcases and laid them on the bed. My wetsuit and karate outfit were still fresh and clean, folded up next to my Jimmy Choos. What was I thinking? I wrapped my labradorite rocks in my knickers and tucked them inside my trainers, remembering that first accidental hug with Henrik when the geothermal pool had delivered me straight into his arms.

'Sara, are you home?' Greta called through the bedroom window. I'd left it open despite the Baltic conditions. The heat from the cabin was keeping the cold at bay, and I wanted to feel everything as deeply as possible before I left.

'For now,' I said, opening the door and giving her a hug.

She was holding a huge parcel wrapped in brown paper and tied with gold ribbon.

'I've got you a little something,' she said, handing it to me.

'Have you? What for?'

'Because it's your last day and I'm going to miss you!'

'Stop it! You're too cute!' I said, feeling bad that I hadn't been as thoughtful.

Greta laughed. 'You haven't seen it yet.'

I waved her in, and we sat by the fire. I couldn't take her gift without giving something back. What could I give her? My kimono? A pair of Jimmy Choos?

'Honestly, you didn't need to do this,' I said, a lump in my throat as I untied the beautiful bow. How exciting to get an enormous, surprise present. It was soft and squidgy, with a flash of purple, then green and red. 'Oh, Greta!' It was one of her crocheted blankets in all the colours of the aurora. Allegedly.

'As I said, I can't help myself,' she said with a smile. 'And I don't want your sleep patterns interrupted when you get back to London. A magic blanket will help – and remind you of us all.'

I unfolded it and held it up to the window, feeling its weight in my hands. Rows and rows of rainbow colours had been woven together and dotted with luminous fireflies. 'It's gorgeous,' I said, totally gobsmacked. 'It must have taken you hours and hours to make.'

'You're worth it,' she said, giving me another hug.

Each firefly had a flash of gold thread running through it, giving the pattern an overall sparkle. It was more than a blanket – it was a work of art. 'Thank you so much, I love, love, *love* it.'

'You're welcome. Enjoy it and don't forget us,' she said. 'Henny is going to miss you so much.'

'Do you think?' I hadn't allowed myself to believe that Henrik might have genuine feelings, even though I knew mine were painfully real. I wanted to keep all our wonderful memories safe and protected. I didn't want to sour them with a sad conversation.

Greta searched my face, confused. 'What do you mean? Absolutely, he will.'

'He'll be on to the next one in no time.'

'Not Hen. He hasn't had a girlfriend for years, not since he moved back from New York. The way he's been with you has been completely... different. He's clearly smitten.'

'Really? But he's so smooth. I assumed it was part of his schtick.'

'Not. At. All. He has no schtick. He is schtick-less and totally genuine. Can't you see? His heart is pure and golden, and ordinarily he's very protective of it. We all are.'

'He is lovely,' I murmured, thinking about some of the moments we'd shared. 'I hadn't really let myself think it could ever be anything...'

The wood burner popped loudly, and the gently lolling logs burst into flame, spitting fiery flecks at the glass. I'd had a golden heart, once, too. Open and trusting, with no room for cynicism. Where had it gone?

'You could totally sell these on Etsy, you know,' I said, changing the subject. I covered my knees in the blanket and posed. '*For the stylish thirty-something couch potato*. Get a production line going.'

Greta smiled. 'I *could*. But I only make them for my special potatoes. The magic can't be crocheted in en masse.'

'Well, it's perfect. I'm proud to be one of your specials and to have a little piece of Firefly Forest to take home.'

'Welcome to the final dinner. The end of your transformation programme. I hope you have enjoyed your time with us here at Firefly Forest,' Tore said as Jonas and Greta handed out champagne flutes full of sparkling lemon and lime. 'We have one final surprise for you all, if you'd like to bring your drinks outside and follow me.'

The sun had already set, and the air was cold and fresh as we marched single file behind Tore, past the thermal pools and into the forest. I hadn't really dressed for an Arctic trek and my Chelsea boots had had just about as much as they could take out here, getting even more wrecked as we scrambled over wet leaves and muddy branches. A line of lemmings playing follow the leader, leader, leader, without question.

Eventually we arrived in a glade, where a circle of trees had been decorated with fairy lights and three glass igloos were glowing gold, cream and white in the dark. It could easily have been a proposal set-up or the backdrop for a romantic photo shoot – except it wasn't. It was just us having dinner together. We were the occasion. Each igloo had a table inside set for dinner, with white tablecloths, gold cutlery and sheepskin covered chairs. The candles were already lit and welcoming and yellow forest flowers gave a pop of colour in silver vases. Pine cones and holly decorated the ceilings, and a mini wood burner crackled quietly in each corner.

'Wow!' Celeste said, skipping down to the first igloo. 'Where have you been hiding all this?'

Ethel gave me a knowing smile – she'd seen it all before. 'Fabulous, isn't it?' she whispered, not wanting to interrupt the awe-struck reverie of the group.

I walked down to the clearing, slowing my steps to take it all in. An enormous chiminea was blasting out heat in front of the igloos and a makeshift kitchen had been set up outside. The spicy smell of vegetable chilli being cooked over an open fire carried through the air. Huge paella pans of rice were being tended to by Jonas, in between flipping homemade pittas on the griddle. And then I spotted them. At first I thought it was the wind rustling the fairy lights in the trees. But it was too bright for that. Thousands of tiny lights flashing randomly, illuminating the forest. They weren't fairy lights. They were fireflies.

'Pretty cool, huh?' Henrik appeared next to me, looking up into the trees.

'Are they... real?' I asked, getting as close as I could.

Henrik laughed. 'Very good, eagle eyes. We use little lights in winter to give the effect while they hibernate. All solar of course.'

'Still cool to see the light show.'

'The trees are full of fireflies and glow worms in the summer – fascinating little creatures.'

'I did wonder where the name had come from. I'd love to see them.'

'Then you'll have to come back,' Henrik said with a wink. 'We get a few different varieties here in Norway and each one lights up differently. They all have their very own flirtation dance.'

'Is that why they do it?'

'Not the only reason, but I suppose the light patterns are like languages. The same species can chat together: one flash for yes, two flashes for no.'

'Seventeen flashes for *there's a spider over there*.'

Henrik laughed. 'Exactly. And to attract the right mate. The men light up and the women reply if they're interested.'

'What if the woman is interested first?'

'I don't think the men are fussy. They put their lights on for everyone then see who replies.'

'Sounds like Tinder.' I laughed. 'My mate Kat says men are like taxis. They put their lights on when they're ready for a relationship. She has a nose for a single man.'

'How do I put mine on?' Henrik asked, suddenly serious.

I felt myself blush under his scrutiny and shrugged. 'You'll have to ask Kat.'

Tore banged a huge gong to get everyone's attention. 'Ladies and gentlemen, dinner is served. There is a table plan for this evening, so please find your place and take your seat.'

I poked my nose into the first igloo where Yuto and Kimi were in fits of laughter and there were two spare chairs. 'Evening! Am I in here with you?'

'These seats are for Jonas and Greta,' Kimi said.

The middle igloo was being hosted by Tore and already had everybody seated, so I carried on walking up to igloo number three, where Celeste and Will were sat with Ethel and Henrik.

'This must be me,' I said, peering in.

'Best seat in the house,' Henrik said, patting the empty chair next to him.

'A Nilsen in every room,' Ethel said, raising her apple juice in a toast. 'Thank you for a wonderful few weeks, Henrik. The retreat was as magical as ever and I'm already booked in for next year.'

'A pleasure having you here, *tante Eth*, as always.' He smiled around the table. 'I hope you've all enjoyed it too?'

Celeste's eyes filled with tears. 'Yes,' she managed.

'We're very emotional about leaving,' Will said, putting his arm around her. 'It's been incredible.'

A loud humming drowned out the conversation as the igloo roofs slid back in unison, the glass panels folding in on themselves to reveal the October moon and a sky full of stars. More stars than I'd ever seen before.

'The hunter's moon,' Ethel said, closing her eyes to bask in the lunar glow.

'Almost full,' Celeste added. 'Make a wish at midnight, everyone.'

The cold air battled against the heat from the fire, the woody smoke homely and comforting. I took a sip of my fizzy lemon and lime. Ice-cold and delicious. It tasted just like the Sprite I'd had the day I'd seen Mark on his date with Millie. I was consumed with anxiety and sat around in my pyjamas all day, eating doughnuts for dinner; well, look how far I'd come.

'I'll be your waiter for the evening,' Henrik said, standing up and tossing his napkin over his shoulder. We clapped and cheered, and he took a bow. 'First things first. Starters.'

'Starting with the starters makes sense,' Will said.

'Can we help?' I asked, feeling bad he couldn't relax.

'No, no. Leave it to me. Henrik Nilsen at your service, one last time.' He took my hand and gently kissed it, a look of pure longing on his face. The moment passed and off he went, my heart still racing. It was all becoming real. I was going home, and this was the final night. Our final night. My last chance to do something – but what?

'That boy is an absolute marvel,' Ethel said, dabbing her eyes. 'He works so hard, always going above and beyond for his family. His mother would be so proud.'

'Did you know her?' Celeste asked.

'You could say that. Audhilda was my little sister.'

'What?! I didn't know you were family?'

'You're Henrik's aunt?' Will said, looking into Ethel's brown eyes. 'Hmm, yeah, I can see it, actually.'

'Guilty as charged. This is my annual pilgrimage to keep an eye on my nephews.'

'Here we are...' Henrik reappeared with four small plates, balanced on his arm. 'Homemade hummus with carrots, cucumber, spinach and not to forget… the humble radish. Remember these?'

'The seeds we planted on our first day,' Celeste said, bursting into fresh tears.

'Almost. These are from the group before you, and yours will be served to the next group in a few weeks' time. Continuing the cycle.'

'Will they be fully grown by then?' I asked, surprised.

'Oh yes,' Henrik said. 'Some will be ready before.'

'Growth happens quickly in the right conditions,' Ethel added.

The pink and white radish fanned out in front of me looked so dainty on the plate. Hard to believe it had been a tiny brown seed just a few weeks ago. I'd pushed handfuls of them deep down into the soil, thinking they'd take forever to grow. Yet here we were.

'It feels mean to eat them,' Celeste said as Will speared a forkful into his mouth.

'Not at all,' Henrik said. 'That radish exists to be eaten, I promise you. And if you don't eat it, someone else will.'

'It's a radish-eat-radish world,' I said with a smile.

'I have a leaving present for you all,' Henrik announced while we munched our salads.

'I've already had a lovely gift from Greta,' I said, starting to feel overwhelmed.

'It's only a very small thing,' he said, pulling four envelopes from under the table and handing them out. There was a Polaroid inside each of them and mine was a photo of me on the husky sled, holding on for dear life, eyes bright, my hair frizzy and flowing as I laughed. A perfect picture of adventure and freedom, with Henrik and Kaspar blurry in the background. Tore must have taken it as we'd skidded in towards him at breakneck speed and I barely recognised myself. I looked so rested and happy.

'You're welcome to share them with each other, if you like,' Henrik said. 'We've tried to capture your spirit in a photo. A moment of joy for you to take home. And there is something written on the back of each one.'

'Holding on,' I read, eyes shining.

'Snow angel.' Celeste went next, with an aerial shot from the fire and ice experience.

Will was tucking into a mushroom stroganoff, looking devastated. 'Is it all vegan?' he read aloud, and we all laughed.

And lastly Ethel. Her Polaroid showed her running over hot coals, full of joy and light, and she smiled as she said her word. 'Believer.'

There were squeals of delight and thank-yous directed at Henrik for his thoughtfulness. I wondered if I'd ever see a husky again. It wasn't the kind of pet you could get away with in London. Life was going to feel so different when I got back. I couldn't think of the nearest tree to my flat in King's Cross, let alone an actual forest.

'Ready for your main courses?' Henrik whipped away our plates and returned with two small cauldrons: vegetable chilli and steaming hot rice. My mouth watered as he ladled out our portions, and Jonas popped in with a platter of toasted pittas, guacamole, salsa and homemade tortilla chips. What a feast.

Ethel gave a little cough. 'I also have a small gift to share with the group,' she said, loading her chip up with guacamole. 'There are enough for everyone actually, Henrik, not just these three, so you can give them out.' She delved into her velvet tote and handed us each a sage bundle tied with string. Mum would be delighted.

Celeste smiled. 'A smudging stick.'

'This is so kind, Ethel, thank you,' I said, giving her a hug. 'Have I missed something? Were we all supposed to bring a sharing gift?'

'We didn't bring anything either,' Will said, looking clueless.

'Nothing has been missed,' Henrik said. 'The gifts are from our family to yours as a memento of your stay. Think of us sometimes and come back one day. Maybe you'll tell your friends, and they will tell their friends.'

'My parents have already booked to come in the spring,' Celeste said. 'And we'd love to come back, wouldn't we?'

Will nodded. 'What's a smudging stick?' he asked, holding up his sage.

The chilli was delicious. Spicy and chunky, with beans and onions all fresh from the vegetable garden. Everything tasted good. Wholesome and nutritious, but still moreish. The five of us scoffed our faces, happily eating as much of our last supper as we could. I was not looking forward to going back to the meal merry-go-round of Itsu, Deliveroo and the supermarket three-for-two.

There was a murmur from the other igloos, and we looked over to see everyone moving towards the chiminea, like zombies, staring up at the sky.

'Finally,' Henrik murmured. 'She's here. Aurora on the edges of the clouds through there, can you see?'

We followed Henrik's gaze, gawping up at the sky together. I wasn't expecting much, having been disappointed twice. If the only way to enjoy the Northern Lights was through a magic looking glass, wearing 3D glasses, by the light of the strawberry moon – or any other such nonsense – then I wasn't interested. Although... Oh. My. God.

'I can see them!' I shouted into the air at no one in particular. The silver edge that Henrik had pointed out was now pale pink and spreading fast across the sky. We watched as it deepened to red and was joined by purple and pale blue, the horizon shifting slowly in front of us, full of different colours.

Tore put his arms around Jonas and Henrik. 'It's a good one tonight, boys.'

'Rare to see the multicolour,' Jonas said. 'Greta's put an order in with *Mor* for the wedding.'

'*Mamma's* favourite,' Henrik replied. 'She'll sort it for you if she can.'

Twenty-nine

We stood still, staring up at the sky until our necks got sore, then one by one, people made their way back to the igloos, cold and keen for dessert. Henrik brought in a slab of chocolate brownie and a bowl of forest berries to share, with a much-needed pot of hot coffee.

'I'll leave you all to enjoy. I've got to get ready for the show,' he said, mysteriously.

'There's a show, as well?' Will asked, biting into his brownie.

'The Firefly Forest finale,' I said sadly. 'Is it a crying workshop?'

Henrik laughed. 'Maybe. Depends how it goes.' We didn't have to wait long to find out. We'd barely finished our coffees when the folk music started, and Tore launched into a song.

'Ladies and gentlemen, for one night only, may I present to you the *Nilsen family band*.'

Everyone whooped and cheered.

'All the way from Firefly farmhouse we have the man, the legend – can you believe he's really here? – it's

Henriiik Nilsen on the hardanger fiddle!' We screamed. 'By coincidence, he also hails from Firefly farmhouse, with lungs like a blue whale, playing on the bukkehorn tonight we have none other than Jonaaas Nilsen!' We all cheered. 'And finally, we are delighted to announce our lead singer tonight, singing all your favourites, you'll know him as the king of the swingers – the Firefly folk legend himself – it's meee, Toreee Nilsen!' We went wild with applause as Tore swung his microphone around, then caught it with a thrust of his hips.

Henrik got the beat going with his fiddle and everyone clapped along. I loved watching him get into it – he really was the poster boy for clean living. Fit, muscly, musical, real. As well as kind and thoughtful. But first and foremost, he was fit, and the fiddle showed his arms off to perfection. Henrik was the closest I was going to get to a rock star this evening and I suddenly felt full of fizz. Light and energetic – high on life. The rhythm was powerful and tribal and had us all up dancing straight away. By the time Tore started singing, we were really going for it, spinning each other round and letting ourselves go. Aurora was shining down on us in all her colourful glory and the fire was burning bright. It was nothing short of magical.

'And now for an a cappella number to finish,' Tore said, humming the first few bars of A-ha's 'Take on Me'. I barely recognised his slow, haunting version of the normally upbeat song as Henrik walked towards me and held out his hand.

'*Hei*,' he whispered into my hair.

'Nice work on the hardanger,' I said, sinking into his chest. There was no point resisting when we only had a few hours left together.

'It's quite easy for me. I have quick fingers and strong arms.'

I laughed. 'They must come in useful. And a great sense of rhythm.'

'That too.' He held on to me tight, one arm pulling me in and the other brushing the curls out of my eyes. 'You're going home?'

I nodded, but my heart felt sad.

'For real this time? You said it before then stayed.'

'For real. I've got to go back to work.'

Henrik nodded, slowly turning us around. Tore's song choice couldn't have been more spot on. *You're shyin' away. I'll be comin' for you anyway.* Henrik sang the words into my ear as he held me, and I emptied my mind of all other thoughts. I wanted nothing more than this. To be dancing here together, his arms around me as the cold air mixed with the warmth from the fire and the Northern Lights shone down. There would never be a more perfect moment.

Tore finished singing and everyone clapped, but Henrik and I carried our slow dance on, staying close and connected as we danced to our own song. I didn't want it to ever stop.

'Shall I walk you back?' he asked eventually, and I nodded into his chest. We couldn't stay here all night, and the others had already started disappearing back to their cabins. It was empty and quiet. 'I can carry you if you like?'

'Is this how you keep your arms in such good shape? Carrying women around?'

'The service isn't open to everyone,' he said softly. 'Just you, in fact.'

I smiled up at him. 'Go on then. One last time.' My heart felt full as he leant forward, pausing to stare into my eyes, and kissed me. Slow and sensual, hitting all my hotspots at once and making me tremble. An owl hooted in the distance, and Henrik picked me up and wrapped my legs around his back.

'I'm "holding on",' I said, smiling into his hair.

'Good,' he said. 'Don't let go.'

'How fast can you get us back?' I whispered. He gave me a look then started to run, his head down, tunnelling through the trees like a newborn rhino. I held on tight until we got to the other side of the forest, laughing as the wind whipped at my face.

'It'll be faster if we both run,' he said breathlessly, putting me down. 'I'll race you.' He disappeared down the pathway, all legs and arms, leaving me swaying on the spot, lusty and woozy. His taxi light was on, and it was up to me to flag him down and get in. Thank God the cabins were so remote. We could make as much noise as we liked. I couldn't wait to get him back in my tiny double bed. Suddenly its size was a good thing: we'd have to stay close together to fit in. And once we were in, we were staying in. I was not checking out until I absolutely had to. Not until my Louis Vuittons were being lobbed onto the boat by Lars.

The front door, *my* front door, was closed when I got there. I took a giddy breath and knocked, suddenly uncertain.

Henrik opened it just a crack. 'Not today, thanks,' he said, slamming it shut.

I laughed and knocked again. 'Let me in!'

It seemed to reopen by itself, and the cabin was warm and glowing. Henrik had already fired up the wood burner and was pouring out two glasses of champagne.

My eyes lit up. 'Where did you get that?' I whispered.

'The boat stash,' he said. 'It's for special occasions.'

'Are we about to have a special occasion?'

'We're already having one,' he said, sending me all wobbly again. 'This is it.' He handed me a glass and kept eye contact as we clinked. Slow dancing, fast running, and now this painfully slow conversation. The delayed gratification was killing me. How was he doing this? With Mark everything was immediate. Fast and done, then on to the next thing. My body tingled as I waited for him to make his move. This was new territory for me. I was used to planning ahead, always knowing exactly what was going to happen next. What I was going to do and say and when. But I didn't need to control this, and I didn't want to. I wanted to wait and see. Henrik had this mesmerising effect on me. A way of reducing me to a mumbling, quivering wreck with his eyes.

He stroked my face, his lips on mine as he wound my hair around his hand and tipped my head back. I unbuttoned his shirt, my hands on his chest as I turned and kissed his neck. I wanted to feel his skin on my skin and his body on mine. Now. The clock bleeped to tell me it was midnight, and I made my full moon wish.

Dear Moon, I wish to have the best sex of my life. Right now. Do not let me down.

Thirty

Saturday 10th October

I woke up in a tangle of arms and hairy legs. Just when I'd thought this bed couldn't get any better, it had. Henrik's heart was beating next to mine and our naked bodies were wrapped around each other. The hunter's moon had gone above and beyond in granting my wish and I was exhausted. We were so entwined, my brain couldn't work out what was where, and I didn't want to ruin it by moving to find out. Although I'd have to at some point. The boat was due at 11 a.m.

There was a knock on the door. My very last breakfast basket.

'*Frokost* for two!' Jonas called through the letterbox. 'You in there, Henny? Not working today?'

'*Gå bort*,' he shouted. *Go away.*

'Just kidding,' Jonas replied. 'I've brought you over some pants and something else I thought you might need. Wink, wink. You're welcome.' His footsteps disappeared off down the path and Henrik rolled his eyes.

'Morning,' he said, cuddling me in.

I wriggled in delight as he stroked my back, then kissed my shoulder. 'Is it morning already?'

'I'm afraid so. The end is nigh.' He leapt out of bed and grabbed a towel. 'Stay right there. I don't want to break the spell.'

I hid under the blankets and closed my eyes. I didn't want it to be morning. I wanted to light all the candles again and pretend it was still last night. Pretend we still had time.

Henrik reappeared with a smoking-hot mug and put it on the table next to me. 'Coffee, splash of milk, half a sugar?'

'Perfect.' He'd remembered how I liked it from my very first day.

'I'm doing us breakfast in bed. I want to spoil you while I can.'

I don't think a man had ever made me breakfast, in or out of bed. Apart from my dad. I'd shopped, cooked and cleaned for me and Mark, in between working, so it felt strange to lie around waiting for a man to wait on me.

'Here we go…' Henrik said, bringing in a tray with more coffee, blueberry muffins and croissants. He'd chopped up strawberries, apples and grapes, with a dollop of coconut yoghurt.

'This is incredible service. Five stars. I'll mention you in my Tripadvisor review. What's your name again?'

'Henrik. With a k.'

'Got it.'

'Jonas wasn't being quite the bellend I'd thought earlier. I got you something and he must have spotted it in my room.'

'*Another* something? I've already had my Polaroid.'

'Everyone had one of those. This is something special for you.' He went back into the kitchen. 'Close your eyes and hold out your hands,' he called.

And I did. He rustled back in, and I could smell Christmas as he put a small pot in my hand.

'You can open them, now.'

It took a second for my eyes to adjust. It was a little plant. A seedling.

'Oh wow! I love it!' I said, trying to work out what it was. 'Is it a… radish?'

He smiled. 'No, but you can have one of those as well if you like. This is a cutting from Willow. I thought you might like to grow your own hugging tree at home.'

'Really?' I was touched. 'Are all these kindnesses a traditional Norwegian thing?'

Henrik shook his head. 'They're a me-and-you thing.'

'Well, they're incredibly thoughtful. Thank you.' I kissed him on the cheek. 'Although it might take a while to get this little dude up to Willow's size.'

'Let's call him Lil' Will for now.'

I laughed. 'I'll do my best to keep him alive.'

'Water, light and love. That's all any of us need.' Henrik's phone vibrated on the table, and he snatched it up. '*Pappa? Hei. Ja. Ja. Ja. OK.*' He nodded and hung up. 'Tore needs me back at the house.'

'Noooo, can't you say there's a guest emergency?' I kissed his chest, then his abs, and then his stomach. He lay back down, no longer in a rush.

'I guess I could… What kind of emergency?'

'An important customer relations issue. You're going to have to go above and beyond to sort this one out. It's going to take some time.'

'Have you been dissatisfied with your stay?'

I nodded. 'Extremely. When I first arrived, the cabin was far too cold. And now I'm *realllly* hot,' I threw the sheets off and straddled him.

'There's just no pleasing some people,' he said as he slid his hands around my back and pulled me down on top of him.

Thirty-one

I was much better prepared for the flight home and arrived at Bergen airport with plenty of time to indulge myself in the business lounge. Starting with a massage and a mini-mani, then half a bottle of champagne and a smoked salmon platter. As much as I'd grown to love the stripped-back experience at Firefly, it was nice to indulge a little before I returned home. Never had smoked salmon tasted so good – with prawns and fresh crab and crusty bread and butter. It turned out I wasn't vegan after all. It was time to start prioritising pleasure again, and cheese was top of my list. Top of my *food* pleasure list at least. I was going to thoroughly enjoy *all* the little things on this business class flight. It would be the last one for a while without a legal case weighing on my mind. I'd soon be back to panic-working between panic-eating and panic-sleeping.

'Welcome back, Ms Pearson.'

'Thank you so much,' I said, smiling.

Which reminded me. I needed to change my passport back to my maiden name. I didn't want to be a Pearson anymore.

Lil' Will was sat next to me on the table, and Henrik had even organised an official phytosanitary certificate to make sure it sailed smoothly through security. I wouldn't have thought twice about popping it in my handbag, but apparently it's not that easy to smuggle plants in from other countries. His thoughtfulness levels were something else. I'd have likely been arrested for attempting to poison the ecosystem without the paperwork.

I opened the door to my flat and it felt cold and unwelcoming. The smell of paint was strong and noxious, and I felt my sense of Firefly freedom deflating almost immediately. At least the painting had been done, and the flat was clean and decorated. I whacked the thermostat up and opened all the windows so the air could circulate; I needed a breath of fresh air.

Me: Hey Abs, thanks for overseeing everything with Jimbo. Was he OK?

Abi: Yes, all fine. Do you like it?

I walked from room to room, turning on the lights. Did I like it? He'd done exactly what I'd asked him to do. He'd used the greys and the blues; the exact same shades Mark and I had in the house on the King's Road. Colours I'd loved. We'd loved. Back then. I ran in and out of all the rooms and tried to imagine new beds and a sofa, but I could only think of our old furniture. Our love seat from John Lewis, our Heals dining table. The thought of it made my stomach turn. It was all wrong. The colours and shades were all wrong.

I didn't want my flat to be a smaller, shitter version of my old home. A daily reminder that I didn't have the big Chelsea house anymore, or the big swinging-dick husband. That the future we'd planned together had all been a fantasy. I wanted my place to represent the me I was now. To be a vibe. Abi had said it was all transitory anyway. That it was only paint and we could change it anytime. So that's what we'd do.

Me: Not 100% sure. Can you come over tomorrow?

Abi: Of course. Desperate to hear all about it. Shall I bring my paints?

Me: Please!

Abi: Shall I bring Jimbo?

Me: Lol. You know me too well.

Sunday 11th October

HIIT me up Group Chat

Kat: Are you back?

Abi: She sure is – I'm heading there now with Jimbo.

Me: Got back last night! Come too and bring your roller.

Kat: Erm, OK... sounds fun.

At least I'd have the girls to distract me from my pining. Bad joke. The last few days had completely thrown me. My mind was so full of Henrik, I didn't know what to do with myself. Everything about him had felt so different and real. The gifts, the looks, the breakfast. The rescue missions. His never-ending patience. How could anyone else I dated compare to He-Man Henrik?

I unpacked my suitcases into three piles. Dry cleaning, washing, bin. This time there were also things that could go straight back in the wardrobe. I lay all my Norwegian trinkets out on the bed and breathed in the scent of the crocheted blanket, slowly unfolding it to appreciate its full size and all the effort Greta had put in. The double-dyed colours, the alpaca wool, the luminous thread she'd used for the fireflies. It didn't feel right using it as a blanket; it needed framing and hanging in a gallery. I washed my labradorite rocks and placed them on the windowsill in descending order to air-dry. Lil' Will had survived the journey home in a carrier bag, but the central heating was a bridge too far. I popped him in the sink to freshen up, gave him a long drink then put him next to my bed, so he'd be the first thing I saw every morning. It would take years for a tiny seedling like that to get to huggable status, so I'd have to settle for stroking his leaves for now.

The London traffic droned loudly outside my window as the pollution tried to cough its way in. The stars were hidden behind a fug of fumes and the rain smattered against the skylight, quickly turning into a downpour and hammering the windowsill with water. London in October was the worst.

The intercom buzzed. The cavalry had arrived.

'Hello?'

'Hellooooo!!!' Kat, Abi and Jimbo collectively cooed. Hurrah!

I buzzed them all up and threw on some clothes to give the illusion my day had begun. It wasn't like me to still be in my pyjamas, positioning plants at 11 a.m.

'I missed you girls!!' I screamed, opening the door and hugging Kat and Abi at the same time. 'Thanks for coming straight over. You too, Jimbo.'

'Not a problem, pet,' he said, smoothing his hand down the wall and admiring his own handywork. 'Lovely job, this. The paint went on like a dream.'

'Tea? Coffee?' I shouted, pointing at them all like an out-of-control air stewardess. 'Tea?'

'Yes, milk, three sugars. And then you need to *spill* the tea,' Kat said, eyes gleaming. 'Don't miss anything out. I want all the gossip. My cup needeth to be filleth-ed.'

'Coffee for me and Jimbo – both white, no sugar.'

I put the kettle on and got straight into the tricky part of the chat to get it over and done with.

'Jimbo, you have done an amazing job. Exactly what I wanted, no complaints – it's perfect.'

'Champion!' he said, beaming widely. 'I was worried there for a minute when Abi called.'

'Well, that's the thing. This is exactly what I *did* want, but it's no longer what I *do* want.'

'It's not?' Jimbo said, exchanging a look with Abi. 'You've lost me.'

'I'll pay for it twice, obviously, because I want to change all the colours.'

I locked eyes with Abi, and she immediately understood.

'Don't worry at all,' she said, fixing me with her 'we can do anything' smile.

Jimbo was still puzzled.

'It's a re-brief,' Abi whispered. 'Double bubble on the cash.'

His face lit up at that. 'Well, why didn't you say?' he said, rubbing his hands together. 'Nay problem, pet, we'll get straight onto it and have it done in no time.'

'I don't want a mini version of my old house on the King's Road; I want a King's Cross original.'

'Amen, sister,' Kat said, holding her roller aloft, ready to do battle.

'I'm thinking lots of greens in different shades – grassy, emerald, racing car – with stark white walls.' I showed them the Pinterest board I'd put together.

'Ooo, yes, that'll look fab,' Abi said, swiping through and zooming in to check against her colour swatches.

'Then, Kat – I was thinking maybe we could go shopping with your PR discount and get some furniture. Floating shelves in pine, a rustic dining table with hand-hewn chairs, see what else there is – maybe a wicker basket for my blankets?'

Kat gave a low whistle. 'Someone's got their mojo back,' she teased, putting her roller down. 'That is a *huge* relief. I'm much better at shopping than painting.'

'I LOVE these colour combos. Very *rumble in the jungle*,' Abi said. 'I know you weren't keen before but can I please, *please* do you one of my murals? I've got a brilliant idea.'

She was desperate to get her hands on my naked walls. And really, what was the worst that could happen? It was only paint after all.

'Yeah, go on then,' I said, giving her a hug.

'Squeeee! Really? Shall I tell you what I'm thinking?'

'No. Surprise me.'

'Even better,' Abi said, clapping her hands in delight. 'My favourite.'

It was time to shake things up. Kat was right, my mojo was back. I'd found it in Firefly Forest.

Kat dragged me in and out of every house-y shop on Oxford Street. Furniture, beanbags, fresh new sheets, blankets, cutlery, tea towels. It was like getting married again. Except this time, I didn't have to compromise. It didn't matter what anyone else thought, I was having my flat exactly as I wanted it. And I wanted it like my cabin in Firefly Forest. Warm, cosy, homely. Soft and snuggly. Hot baths full of oils, beeswax candles on the go, and a wilderness of big, leafy plants. No more fakes. I wanted the real deal in every aspect of my life and to have the time to enjoy it.

'Can we *please* stop for a drink? I'm desperate.' Kat was laden down with bags and had slowed to a stumble. She was flagging. We both were.

'Yeah, let's grab some lunch. Mildreds?'

'Is that Italian?'

'Vegan.'

'Bloody hell, Sara! No. Lunch without cheese is like toast without butter. And vegans can't have that either. How about we compromise and go for sushi. That's healthy?'

'I'm only joking, I don't want vegan either. Let's tuk-tuk into Soho and see what takes our fancy,' I said, flagging down a man in a pink feather boa who was blasting out

Whitney Houston. The pair of us sat on the furry seat and clutched our bags to our knees.

'Dean Street please!' I shouted as the man stood up and tried to get going. 'Kat, tell me honestly – do you think me getting a bread maker is taking it too far?'

'Taking what too far?'

'My new "woman of the land" vibe. Making my own food. Living off-grid.'

Kat rolled her eyes. 'I don't want to burst your bubble, babe, but King's Cross is about as on-grid as it gets. And why on earth would you want to make your own bread when they sell it in the supermarket?'

'To bake it fresh.'

'Waitrose bake it fresh.'

'I want to get rid of all the nasties – the additives and preservatives.'

'I'm pretty sure that's the stuff that makes it taste nice.'

'I could always make the dough by hand, I suppose.'

Kat turned to me in shock. 'Am I hearing things? The queen of takeaways is now baking her own baguettes. What have you done with my friend Sara?'

'It's time for a change, Kat. I've been eating myself into type-two diabetes for too long.'

'If it's a health thing then bread should probably be off the menu anyway. Why don't you start small? Get a window box and grow your own tomatoes?'

'I can do that as well, but I really want to make fresh bread every day.'

'Realistically? You won't have time for all that once you're back at CSH. You'll be working twenty-four-seven on your next case. And if you do end up with a spare half hour, do you really want to spend it kneading dough?'

'Yes! I do. Work should facilitate my life, not the other way around. I shouldn't be giving up my spare time to work my bollocks off, helping criminals who don't deserve it. Arguing reasonable doubt when I know damn well they're guilty.'

'Easy to say but that's why they pay you the big bucks.'

'What's the point in money though, if I don't have time to enjoy it? I'm fitting a tiny bit of life in around my work, rather than doing a job that works around the kind of life I want to live. That's a major red flag.'

Kat shrugged. 'Is it? You love being a lawyer and you're brilliant at it. You've got an amazing flat in central London – and unbelievably cool friends.'

'The best, and thank you. But I can tell that story a different way. I'm thirty-two and divorced – nearly – and I keep bad guys out of prison. I'm so burnt out I've been signed off work and when I go back I won't have enough time between working, sleeping and commuting to make a loaf of bread. That's more than a red flag, Kat, it's the red bloody sea.' My breathing had gone off kilter, and I could feel a panic attack coming on. Physical red flag. I was allergic to London.

'It's OK, look at me.' Kat held my hands, breathing with me to try and calm me down. 'It's alright, you're fine, I'm here. Of course you can order a bread maker. Let's go and buy one now. Whatever you want to do,' she soothed. 'How much is it?'

'Two hundred,' I said, as Whitney hit a high note.

'Pounds? Two *hundred* pounds? Before you've bought any ingredients? Then add on the butter, eggs, sugar...'

'Isn't that a cake mix?'

'Probably. I've no interest in trying to do something Mr Warburton has spent decades perfecting. You'll be fashioning your own shoes together next and putting Jimmy Choo out of business.'

'You're always so am-dram.'

'Just looking at the bigger picture, babes. By the time you've bought all the stuff you need to make the bread, you'll have spent four hundred quid and could've had eight loaves a week delivered to the flat by Tesco. For a year.'

Thirty-two

Tuesday 20th October

Abi stayed up all night working on the mural in the bathroom and wouldn't even stop at midnight when I finally succumbed to sleep. She wanted to keep going while the flow was flowing. I'd brushed my teeth over the kitchen sink as she wanted it to be a surprise, but I wasn't about to wee in it as well. I tiptoed down the corridor for a quick stealth wee before she arrived, but she was already up and in the bathroom, rustling about.

'Morning,' I croaked through the door.

'Morning!' Abi and Jimbo said at the same time.

'You're here early,' I said. 'Or didn't you go home?'

'I slept for a few hours,' Abi said, sliding her way into the corridor with her Starbucks. 'Then Jimbo brought me my rocket fuel an hour ago and I got going again.'

'I'm an early riser, me,' Jimbo added. 'Paint while the sun's out, then knock off at four.'

Abi was blocking the bathroom door.

'I'm going to need to get in there,' I said.

'You can't look at anything – you'll freak. It's in a very unfinished state.' She disappeared back in and came out holding my froggy-eyed headband. 'In fact, would you mind wearing this?'

'As a blindfold?'

She nodded.

'Yes, I would mind! Don't be so ridiculous – I'll just close my eyes.'

'Fine but make it quick. I'm on a schedule to get it finished before I go back to LA next weekend, so every second counts. You don't want a half-painted wall!'

'Nooo! You're not going back already? That's gone so quick. Although you'll get to see your two boys I suppose – well, one man, one dog.'

'I know. I've missed them both. Three months filming in Brazil has felt like forever – for Tony and for me! But it's all finished now and he's on his way back. He said he'll bring Nero with him to pick me up from the airport.'

'Ahh, how sweet.' I was so glad Abi had found her one in Tony. They doted on their Italian dog, Nero, and were such an adorable little threesome. Wholesome and happy. Despite living in LA LA Land.

I didn't even peek at the bathroom floor, shading my eyes as I went in and out – a prisoner in my own home. Already back on the boring breakfast treadmill of Crunchy Nut Cornflakes and tea, I debated going to Mum and Dad's for a shower while Abi and Jimbo did their thing, then had another cup of tea and watered the plants. It was 8.30 a.m. in Norway, so Henrik was awake over there – why hadn't he been in touch? I checked every inch of my phone for the thousandth time since I'd left, but there was nothing.

Text, email, WhatsApp, Facebook, LinkedIn. Fifty ways to communicate with your lover. I'd already sent three messages – none of which he'd opened – and I didn't want to look unhinged. As I stared at my phone it lit up, and for a millisecond my heart stopped, thinking it might be him. But it wasn't. It was work.

Cheryl: Hey stranger. How are things? Are you feeling up to a call?

My insides went all funny. What day was it? What date was it? My time off couldn't be up already, surely? Cheryl had poked her head through my protective force field and was trying to reconnect me with the real world. I thought back to that last day in the office: the call with Danny Jackson and his desperation to have us represent Micky Maloney. I half-wondered where the case was up to, but the fire I'd had around keeping it all for myself, and away from Bobby, had gone. I'd been trying to prove myself to the partners for far too long when my win record spoke for itself. Every one of my cases was just another meaningless gold star – in a forever line of meaningless gold stars – towards a promotion that was never going to happen. I loved being a barrister, but not at all costs. Not anymore.

Me: Really good! I'm back from my retreat and feeling refreshed. Sure, let's have a call. Tomorrow afternoon?

I nearly dropped my phone as it started ringing, I stared at it for a few seconds, knowing I had no choice but to answer.

'I'll take that as a now then, shall I?'

'Time waits for no man – or woman – Sara, *tempus fugit* and all that.' Cheryl's low drawl was as familiar to me as my own mother's. 'How are things? How are you feeling?'

'Good! Fine! Happy, relaxed.'

'Any more panic attacks since you've been off?'

'Nope.'

'OK, that's good news. Look, Sara, I'm going to shoot straight with this as we're both busy people and I respect you too much to pussyfoot around. Antony wants me to offer you a redundancy package. It's your choice entirely and we can massage the narrative to be whatever you want it to be – but we're dropping headcount this quarter and he thinks it's only right you have first refusal when you haven't been well.'

'What?! Why? I've only been out for a few weeks.' I couldn't grasp what she was saying. Was I being fired?

'The firm has some serious money issues – hard to believe with the hourly rate we charge, I *know*, but we're going through a process and need to cut costs by twenty per cent asap.'

I was shocked and… scared. I'd be having money issues too if I lost my job. 'I had no idea. Antony's never mentioned any problems before.'

Cheryl sighed. 'Consider yourself lucky. One of the many benefits of *not* being a partner. Believe me, it's not all it's cracked up to be.'

'Can I come in and see you both? Have a meeting to discuss it?' My heart was racing as I tried to take it all in.

'You absolutely can. Although you're still signed off for a few more weeks, so legally we couldn't see you until then. We need to make sure you take the full two months before you come into work. But honestly? It's a clusterfuck here right now. You're best off out of it. We're letting a lot of people go, and Antony and I are in non-stop meetings trying to sort it all out.'

I pushed my feet into the floor to try and ground myself, as the blood rushed to my head, but I couldn't feel my feet or the ground. My whole body felt centred in my lungs and my breathing had gone shallow. I couldn't control it.

'As I said, your package is an option – unlike the others.'

'And if I opt to say no?'

'Then we'll save the money elsewhere.'

'Right.' I was totally stunned.

'Why don't I email the details over and you can have a read through and think about it?'

Like I had a choice. 'Sounds like a plan. Although I'm blocked on work email. Can you send it to my personal email – chocolate cake at Gmail dot com?'

'Sure. Very professional. I'll be in touch in a couple of weeks if I don't hear from you before. It's a generous offer, Sara. See it as an opportunity.'

Easy for you to say, I thought, as I silently hung up.

Thirty-three

Tuesday 27th October

'Oliver? It's Sara.'

'Sara! To what do I owe the pleasure? Not another Norwegian crisis I hope?'

'More of a personal crisis, this time.'

'I'm listening.'

'It was something you said when we had the wrap-up call with the Nilsens and I thought it was worth a conversation. Were you serious about opening a satellite office in London?'

'Completely. Why? Would you be interested?'

'CSH are making redundancies and I've been offered the option to take a package, which I'm considering. To be honest it's made me stop to think about what I want the rest of my life to look like, so I might be open to having a conversation.'

'My firm is tiny compared to CSH, so I couldn't offer anywhere near the kind of money they'd be paying you.'

'As I said, they're offering me a package, so money isn't my main motivator here. I'm looking for an interesting next move.'

'OK, well why don't I send you some more information on what I've got planned, and we can have another chat from there?'

The door buzzed and the postman called up. 'One to sign for.'

Weird. I hadn't had a registered delivery since Mark had sent the decree nisi to kick off the divorce. Normally everything went to work – because I was never in to sign for anything. I ran downstairs and scribbled for the brown envelope with the gold handwriting, knowing what it was straight away. I'd seen Greta and Jonas working away on them at the farmhouse, cutting and gluing and stuffing and sticking each one. It was a wedding invitation, and I held it to my heart all the way back upstairs, giddy with excitement. I didn't want to rip it open straight away. I wanted to savour the moment.

'Abs!' I hissed, through the bathroom door.

'Two more minutes – I'm almost done,' she shouted, her voice echoing off the tiles.

'I've finally heard from him. From Henrik.'

She cracked the door and one of her eyes looked at me and then at the envelope.

'What is it?'

'An invitation.'

'Looks like a special one!' she sang, eyeing the gold lettering. 'Is it from the palace?'

'Better. A wedding,' I said, eyes shining. '*The* wedding.'

'At Firefly Forest?'

I nodded.

'Why the hell are you waggling it around then? Open it!' she screamed, slinking out of the bathroom and closing the door behind her.

We ran into the kitchen, and I slit the top open with a knife, like Dad did with all his letters, the pair of us saving the world together, one envelope at a time. Although this was a special one. I was going to keep this brown envelope forever. Even if nothing ever happened between me and Henrik – nothing *else* – it still felt like the most romantic thing that had ever happened to me. The invite was four big leaves pressed together and sprayed with glue, and I felt like a princess in a fairy tale as I read the words out loud.

'Ahem. *To the fabulous: Ms Sara Pearson* – that's me.'

'Obvs.'

'*We would love you to join us at our winter wonderland wedding on Saturday 5th December. Dress code: Nymphs and Centaurs. Midday till midnight.*'

'Amazing. Who doesn't love a fancy-dress wedding? Is it from Henrik? Or Greta?'

'Not sure,' I said, pulling out the rest of the bumf. Directions, gift list, RSVP postcard, dried petals… and a flash of bright white that didn't belong in there. An alien piece of paper folded up at the back. My heart was in my mouth as I opened it.

Hei, Sara,

It's only been three days and I'm already missing you like crazy. (It's Henrik, by the way.) Another snowstorm has hit, and our connection and Wi-Fi is now completely dead – no surprises there – so I thought snail mail might reach you as fast while we wait for the technician.

I want to invite you as my guest to Greta and Jonas's wedding. They would love you to be there and more important – as important – I would love you to be there too. I want you on my arm and in every other way. I keep expecting to see you around and am disappointed daily when I remember you've gone.

I'm coming to London to collect your RSVP in person. I'll be staying at The Soho Hotel on Saturday 31st October – would you join me there for dinner? Say, 8 p.m.? I'll book us a table and hope to see you.

It's a lot to ask you to come back again to Firefly Forest so soon for the wedding, I know. I wish I could send a helicopter, like we did for Emma Stone.

Looking forward to your answer.

Henrik x

'Oh. My. Gadddd!' Abi screamed, then hugged me. 'This is so cool and romantic. I LOVE HIM ALREADY. A hot date and then a wedding on top!'

I was in shock. 'He's coming to London?'

'To collect your RSVP,' Abi said with a wink. 'And the rest!'

'Seems a bit much, doesn't it?'

'Bloody hell – make up your mind. You've been moaning that you hadn't heard from him for two weeks!'

'I don't think I'm ready for a one-on-one date.'

'What are you talking about? You've just spent a whole month with him!'

'That was different. A date is serious.'

I hadn't been on a date with anyone other than Mark for four years.

'A date will be fun. This is his GRG Sara! His grand romantic gesture! I love that he's coming over here to see you so soon – he's obviously keen. Don't put pressure on it – it's just dinner with a hot guy.'

'With a *really* hot guy! Argghhhhh!'

We both screamed.

'It's a good recap opportunity – then if the date is a disaster, or you don't like each other in the cold hard light of London – you can decline the wedding invite and leave it at that.'

'True.'

'But if you do accept the invite, I'll have to do your nymphy make-up.'

'Yesssss!'

'Via Zoom though, I'll be back in LA.'

'Zoom isn't really an option with the dodgy Firefly signal.'

'I'll do you a *get ready with me* video then, as backup.' She laughed. 'Get nymphy with me. Honestly, I wish we had a dodgy signal. Tony doesn't get a second to himself. We're seriously considering splitting our time between LA and Italy to get some peace. But onto more important stuff – *what are you going to wear?*'

'No idea. What does a nymph look like these days?' I squealed in her ear. 'Underwear as outerwear and a jacket?'

'Erm... no. That doesn't sound wedding appropriate. But actually... you could be in luck, my lucky duck.'

'How so?'

'My friend Benji did the wardrobe for *A Midsummer Night's Dream* at The Globe over the summer. He might be able to pull me a favour.'

'Really?' I could feel tears in my eyes. I'd been unhappy for such a long time. It was overwhelming to suddenly have something so fabulous to look forward to. 'That would be incredible, Abs. Thank you so much.'

'Leave it with me,' she said, nodding to herself. 'And in the meantime, I'm ready to show you what I've been doing in your bathroom, so to speak.'

I did a happy little wiggle and ran after her, excited to see it. Jimbo had done an amazing job on the rest of the flat, and the blues and purples had gone. It was like Jurassic Park, minus the dinosaurs, with the walls in different shades of green. He'd put up my floating shelves, which were now covered with floating plants, and added some colour and excitement to the white walls. I'd spent a fortune on greenery and needed to keep it all alive for as long as possible. Lil' Will was doing well at least, enjoying his sunny spot by the window and starting to shoot up already.

'Right, stand there. Let me do one last check,' Abi said, disappearing behind the bathroom door. She had paintbrushes sticking out of her ponytail and flecks of blue all over her dungarees. She'd been working non-stop for three days, so whatever it was and whatever it looked like, I had to love it. I mentally prepared myself. 'OK, come in, come in!'

I walked in smiling, but my jaw dropped when I saw what she'd done.

Abi had painted all three walls as a forest glade. The shower was running to add to the effect, and she'd worked the water into the design, so it looked like a waterfall. The bath was on the edge of a thermal pool, and there were conifer trees on either side, dotted with tiny birds in different colours. It was way beyond anything I'd been expecting.

'Abi! This is so cool and beautiful! I don't even know what to say. I thought it'd be a couple of crocodiles painted on the wall.'

She laughed. 'Thanks for the vote of confidence.'

'I had no idea this is what you meant. I've seen your mural, and the one you did for your friend Holly, but that was a nursery; it wasn't the adult collection.'

'Sounds a bit dodge.'

I took a closer look. The birds were all different, each one full of intricate detail. A kingfisher, a hummingbird, a woodpecker. I spotted some brown animals snuffling in the trees. 'Is it a family of deer?'

'Kind of,' she said, pointing at their wide snouts. 'Reindeer. And then, wait for it…' She pulled on the light cord, which had a dragonfly hanging off it, and the bathroom went dark. Apart from the ceiling. Tiny flashes of green glowed on and off randomly, giving the illusion of something very familiar. 'And… my creative vision is complete.'

'Fireflies?' I said, gazing up at them in wonder.

'Yup. I did what I could, using the photos you shared in the group chat.'

'It's amazing.'

'You can light your new candles and imagine yourself there.'

She turned the light back on, and the fireflies disappeared.

'This is so incredibly thoughtful, Abs, thank you.' I swallowed hard, trying to hold back the tears that were forming.

She smiled. 'I'm glad you like your place again – it's my housewarming present.'

'It might be time to get the boxes over from Mum and Dad's,' I said, looking around.

'Yep,' she said, giving me a hug. 'Time to unpack. Me and Kat will help, you're not on your own, you know. We're so proud of you.'

'Are you?'

'Yes! Mark really messed you around and you did nothing to deserve it. Between you meeting, marrying and now going through a divorce, he's been non-stop. Never quite sure, always busy, off with his mates. You've put up with so much. You deserve a fresh start and a home that fills you with joy. Somewhere you can relax and feel safe.'

I was touched. 'That's how I felt at Firefly.'

'But not here?'

'Not yet.'

'It'll come. You've only just got back. Give it time.'

'I hope so,' I said, looking around. 'This definitely helps.'

Abi gave me a hug. 'Good. Now. Let me get on to Benji, while you RSVP with a carrier pigeon, or smoke signals, or however you and Henrik plan to communicate without the luxury of technology. Then we can plan your outfit and get styling!'

'I'm so glad you're here, Abs.' The flat was feeling more like home, but I couldn't quite put my finger on why. Was it because Abi was here? It was hard to feel alone with one of my besties in the room next door. Home was having my people around me, and the truth was that Mark's place had always been Mark's place. Even with a lick of paint and my clothes hanging in his wardrobe. We hadn't chosen it together and it was never really mine. But this flat had been my first big purchase once I could afford to get on the property ladder, and I'd worked day and night to get the deposit together and pay the mortgage on my own. But you don't get the big bucks without the big amount of work to go with it, which meant I barely saw it once I'd moved in. A quick shower and out to work in the morning, then back at night for another quick shower and off to bed. It had been like living in a hotel room.

Being a barrister hadn't given me any respite. Ten years of hard slog with no time to rest. I didn't regret it, but maybe it was time for me to be something else. These burnout attacks weren't going to stop by themselves. They were a warning sign from my body.

The front door buzzed again.

'It's like Picadilly Circus in here,' Jimbo shouted from the bedroom.

I laughed. 'I know! I'm not expecting anyone – it's probably the wrong flat.' I pressed the intercom. 'Hello?'

'Hey, Sara, it's me.' I switched to video and could see Mark stood on the doorstep holding a bunch of flowers.

'Oh. Hi,' I said, flatly. He was the last person I wanted to speak to.

'Any chance I can come up?'

'Erm… not really, no. I've got someone here. Wait there, I'll come down.' I didn't want him in my freshly painted space. This flat was a Mark-free zone. He wasn't welcome in my life anymore.

I ran downstairs without a coat and stepped outside in my slippers. He couldn't keep me talking for too long in the freezing cold.

'We're still technically married, and you won't even invite me in?'

'That's right,' I said with a smile. 'I've invited you in plenty of times. It's time to stop now. Not that you deserve any explanation after what you pulled at Firefly. Those people are my friends.'

Mark held the flowers out. White roses, my favourite.

'I'm sorry. I know I fucked up. I wish I'd never gone out there. The whole thing has been a disaster, and I accept all responsibility.'

'As if you could blame it on anyone else.'

'I hadn't planned to confuse you or toy with your emotions out there either. Firefly Forest looked like a great investment opportunity all round, but it seems I read it wrong.'

'You did.'

'Can we at least be friends?'

I looked at him stood there, stumbling over his terrible apology, knowing he'd done this to hundreds of people like Tore over the years to make money. Money I'd once enjoyed as well. It felt good for him to get a taste of his own medicine, but there was no point being at war when we had the dogs between us.

'Only for the sake of our hairy children,' I said, taking the roses. 'It was a snake move and a really shitty thing to do – there's no getting away from that.'

'I know. I'm sorry. And funny you should mention the dogs...' My internal alarm bells started ringing. 'I wanted to float something by you.'

'Did you indeed.'

'Yes. I was wondering if you might consider full custody?'

'Really? How come?'

'I don't have time for them, Sara. When it was both of us living in the house it was different. We made it work between us. But this co-parenting thing is too messy. It's a pain for us and unsettling for them. I think it would be best all round if they had one home.'

This was amazing news! Mum and Dad loved the dogs and had missed them desperately. They could help me look after them and then Mark and I would be out of each other's hair for good.

'Let me think about it,' I said, and Mark smiled, knowing that ninety-nine per cent of the time, that meant yes.

'Cool,' he replied. 'Shall we hug it out?'

My gut said no but it was a moment in time, and I needed the closure as much as he did. I held my arms out and we had one last hug. He was the same Mark I'd married, but he felt like a stranger somehow, a man I didn't really know anymore. Just like he didn't really know me. And our hug had no heart in it.

'Thank you for the flowers.' I breathed in his *sorry and goodbye* present and smiled.

'Anytime,' he said. 'Let me know about the dogs.'

He walked off into the drizzle, pinging open an umbrella to protect his curls, and I felt a weight lift. I hadn't wanted us to part on bad terms, and we hadn't. We were finally done, and I knew that would be it now. I could close my chapter as Mrs Pearson and go back to being Ms Lee.

Thirty-four

I'd written back to Henrik to accept his date but had no idea if he'd received my letter. How had people ever got together in the eighties – or ever, in fact – before technology existed? I suppose you just had to marry your neighbour in those days and that was that.

I was completely out of my comfort zone as I walked into the restaurant at The Soho Hotel and anxiously scanned the crowd. Even though I knew Henrik, it still somehow felt like I was on a blind date. The bar was packed with beautiful people supping cold beers and cocktails and singing along to 'Pink Pony Club', but I couldn't see Henrik anywhere. *Was I in the wrong place? Was there another Soho Hotel? Had he changed his mind? Was I too late? Too early?*

'Are you joining us for dinner?' A lady in a smart cream suit interrupted my spiralling thoughts as I hovered by the door.

'Hi!' I said, wide-eyed. 'Er... yes. At least, I think I am. Nilsen at eight o'clock?'

She scanned her iPad to check, as I felt his arms around my waist.

'Hi,' Henrik breathed into my ear, spinning me round.

I was completely stunned. 'Are you really here?'

He kissed me gently on the lips. 'Looks like it, doesn't it?' he said with a cheeky smile. His hair was loose and lion-like as he towered above me, sexy and stylish in faded cords and a well-cut suit jacket. He looked like a rock star.

'If you'd like to follow me.' The maître d' took us to a candlelit table in the corner, away from the noise at the bar. It was decorated with tiny pumpkins and beautifully laid with black and white plates and fresh flowers. 'We have a special Halloween menu tonight, or you can stick to the ala carte,' she said, handing us menus. 'Can I get you some drinks?'

'Shall we start with a glass of champagne?' Henrik asked.

I smiled and nodded. 'Another special occasion so soon?'

'Yes,' he said, giving me one of his slow smiles.

The lady left us to it as his feet scooped mine up under the table.

'Well, this is a nice surprise,' I said. 'Having you all to myself in London town.'

'You forget I was once an international jet setter. I have no issue with hopping on a plane and I'm a big fan of London, in small doses. I used to stay here a lot in my past life.' He poured us both some water and an Omega watch peeped out from under his sleeve, reminders of his past life suddenly everywhere.

'I'm worried you're a mirage.' He grabbed my hand under the table, tangible proof that he was real.

'How has it been being back?' he asked, staring at me in wonder.

'Noisy,' I said, as the singing at the bar reached a crescendo. 'I found the silence stifling when I first arrived at Firefly and now I crave it.'

'I'll record the meditations for you if you like. Then you can close your eyes and pretend you're back in the Sun Hut.'

'Sure,' I snorted. 'And then I'll lie underwater in the bath with a fish and pretend I'm in the Maldives.'

He laughed. 'It might work! It's good for the nervous system to immerse yourself in calm, however you choose to do it.'

'True. Your meditations were working like a charm at Firefly, so it's worth a shot. You could record them straight into my phone.' I liked the idea of his throaty voice lulling me to sleep each night. Deep and sexy.

'Sure. I'll do it for you tonight. Meditation and spending time in nature are both good habits to cultivate. Even if you got nothing else out of the retreat.'

'Oh, I got plenty out of it. I can light a fire with my eyes closed, for a start.'

Henrik laughed. 'I'm pretty sure our insurance doesn't cover that.'

The champagne arrived and the waitress took our order.

'I've missed you,' Henrik said, holding his glass up and clinking mine.

I couldn't stop smiling. 'It's going to take me a minute to get over the shock of you being here.'

'Take your time – we've got all night,' he replied.

'And tomorrow morning,' I said, taking a sip of my champagne.

'It's nice to just concentrate on us. Even being able to look at you without a roomful of people sat watching us is a new experience. Cheers, Sara! Here's to lighting many, many fires.'

I clinked my glass with his and couldn't stop a goofy smile spreading across my face. 'I'm supposed to be back at work next week, but I've had some weird news,' I said, thinking back to the call I'd had with Cheryl. 'They are making redundancies and I've been offered a package to consider.'

'Is that good news or bad?' Henrik asked, concerned.

'Interesting question. It was a shock at first, but the offer is generous, and I've been there a long time. More than long enough. Maybe it's a sign to move on.'

'Would you do something different? Or work as a lawyer for someone else?'

'I've worked too hard to become a lawyer to change career completely. Oliver is planning to open a satellite office in London, so I rang him last week to ask what the situation was with that.'

'What did he say?'

'He's sent me through his business plan and we're having a chat on Tuesday, so there might be something interesting there. How about you? How are things at Firefly Forest?'

'Same old, same old. Except for the first time in years, I'm feeling lonely out there. The tech not working has been a nightmare. Not being able to contact you has been driving me mad. It's made me realise I've been hiding out there for too long. Hiding away from getting on with my life.'

Our food arrived and Henrik tucked into chunky halloumi fries with salsa, while I had a spicy tomato soup with a balsamic spider's web. We chattered away non-stop, laughing and gossiping and swapping life stories, and before we knew it, eyeball truffles were being served with coffee, and I was willing the clock to turn back. It got to eleven and I'd been eking out my coffee for half an hour, while Henrik stroked the inside of my wrist. It was probably time to say goodnight and go home, but I didn't want the night to end.

'Do you want to go to a club?' I asked.

Henrik looked horrified. 'Not after all that ghoul-ash and bump-lings. I'd rather have a nightcap and record your meditation.'

'Oh. OK, well that sounds good too,' I said, grinning from ear to ear.

'We need somewhere quiet to do it,' he said. 'My room has a small lounge area?'

I nodded. 'Makes sense to be somewhere private,' I said. 'For the sound quality.'

'Exactly. What's your poison?'

'Brandy please.'

Henrik ordered two brandies and signed for the bill, then we walked through the hotel, which was like an art gallery. As soon as the lift doors closed I jumped on him. We kissed frantically for the few seconds of alone time we had and I couldn't have been happier to be back in his arms.

We chased each other down the corridor, holding our drinks out to balance them like an egg and spoon race. His room was beautiful, with high ceilings and sash windows, heavy velvet blackout curtains and a plush pink carpet. The headboard took up half the wall and looked like its own art installation, with soft flowery blankets over cotton sheets. Shiny copies of *Vogue* and *Wallpaper* magazine sat on the table in the lounge area, next to a rolled-up *Big Issue*, and there was a Nespresso machine next to the bed.

'Wow, this is alright, isn't it?' I said, slipping off my heels and taking a seat in one of the leather armchairs.

'They upgraded me – they must have liked my face.' He took a sip of his brandy and switched on the radio.

'I like your face too,' I said, picking up the *Big Issue* and flicking through it. 'Was this in your room? How cool to see hotels buying copies and getting them into the hands of the hoi polloi.'

'Sadly not – I bought it from a guy outside the tube.'

I rolled my eyes, disappointed. 'I thought it was too good to be true. So how do we do this, then? Do you need to do some mouth exercises? Or gargle with vinegar to prepare?'

'Vinegar? For what?'

He looked so confused; I couldn't help but giggle.

'Recording the meditations.'

'Oh, that. I thought you were about to put me through some kind of cleansing ritual. How about we do the meditations in the morning,' he said, kissing me again and taking the magazine. 'I'm not sure you'll want to kiss me with vinegar breath.'

Frank Sinatra started crooning on the radio and Henrik offered me his hand to dance.

'Tomorrow morning, before you go back to Bergen?'

'Yep. Back to Firefly tomorrow. Which reminds me – I haven't had your official RSVP to the wedding.'

'Well, Jonas and Greta have, and my nymph outfit is already cleaned, steamed and hanging in the wardrobe,' I replied, snuggling into him.

Thirty-five

Thursday 3rd December

Abi had leant me a truckload of make-up to go with the nymph outfit and everything was packed in professional-looking cubes as I travelled back for the wedding. A stage-quality costume with film-star make-up – it was like going to the Oscars. The plane started its descent, and I felt a rush of excitement and nerves knowing Henrik was waiting for me at arrivals. He'd suggested we stop in Bergen for a night before heading to Firefly Forest and I couldn't wait to see what he had planned. We needed an off-site liaison to have some no-pressure alone time now that the entire wedding party knew we were a thing.

I waltzed through with nothing to declare and there he was, a head taller than everyone else and holding up a *Welcome Sara* sign. It looked like it had been splashed together with paint and glitter, and I couldn't decide if it was cute or cringe. But then his face lit up when he saw me and he gave me an enthusiastic wave – he could only ever be in the cute category.

'Welcome back to Firefly!' he said, his dimples showing.

'Why, thank you very much,' I said, grinning like an idiot.

'What brings you back?' he asked, stroking a curl from my face and staring at me as if he'd never seen me before.

'The bread,' I said, wrapping my arms around his neck. 'Among other things.' He pulled me in and kissed me until I melted. Yep. One hundred per cent *cute*.

'Greta's goddaughters made you something,' he said, handing me the splodgy sign. 'They spent all day on it yesterday.'

'That is so sweet!' I said, loving his kind, semi-uncle vibes. 'How many are there?'

'Two. Ella and Kaja. They are verrry excited about the wedding.'

'Me too. I've got quite the nymph outfit to wear.'

'I can't wait to see it,' he said, kissing me again and picking up my bags. 'Let's go. I've got a surprise for you.'

'Well, that is a coincidence, because I've got a surprise for you too,' I said, thinking of my skimpy Norwegian-flag underwear. 'Although I feel bad keeping you away for the night if people are already arriving for the wedding?'

'Not at all – it's perfect timing. Gives me a breather from the chaos and means I get you all to myself for a while.'

We jumped in the Firefly minibus and sped out of the airport and onto the highway.

'Do I get any clues?' I asked. It was only five, but we'd already missed daylight. There was very little sunlight in Bergen in the winter, but it wasn't pitch-black outside – more a melting pot of different shades of blue where the sea became sky.

'Nope. But you won't have to wait long to find out. It's quite close.'

Henrik slowed the minibus and turned off down a country lane. It was hard to see down these narrow roads, without any streetlights, but Henrik obviously knew the route. We clearly weren't staying in the centre of Bergen or going out for dinner and there was nothing to do but sit back and wait.

'I'm glad you know where we're going,' I said, checking my phone, already knowing there'd be zero signal. This area was a nightmare for connection. Henrik turned another corner, and there, lit up below us along the water's edge, was a row of little glass houses.

'Oh, wow!' I said, wide-eyed. 'Is this where we're staying?'

He nodded with a shy smile. 'Got it in one. Our very own star-gazing pod. Well, until tomorrow lunchtime,' he replied. 'And later tonight we'll be served a delicious four-course tasting menu paired with wine, and then we sleep beneath the stars.'

I had a lump in my throat. This was the most thoughtful thing anyone had ever done for me. Ever. It looked like aliens had landed in ice-cube spaceships and parked up to take in the view.

'Henrik! This is too much! I've never seen anything so beautiful.'

He leant over and kissed me. 'You are way more beautiful, and you deserve it. I hoped you'd like it. I wanted us to have something special to remember. The wedding will be magical of course, but it isn't our occasion. Tonight is just for us.'

The view out into the ocean was stunning, like a multi-textured oil painting. Lights blinked on and off the boats travelling across the horizon and the waves crashed gently on the shore, lulling the world to sleep. The moon was enormous, mirrored in the water, and the stars were already out and ready for gazing. Quiet and calm. 'I won't get a wink of sleep.'

'That's the idea. Another good reason not to go straight to Firefly.' Henrik parked next to the final glass hut and turned off the engine. 'This one is ours.'

'How do we check in?'

'Already done,' he said, holding up a luminous blue fob.

Henrik bleeped us in, and the glass door slowly slid open. It was like walking onto the set of a Hallmark movie. There was a huge bed made up in crisp cotton sheets and chocolate brown furs, a fluffy red sofa with puffed-up cushions, and a soft, velvety rug in front of a roaring fire. And to top it all off, sat quietly in the corner was a fully stocked minibar and a glass jar of peanut M&Ms.

'What have we got here!' I said, delighted my backstage diva-demands had finally been fulfilled.

'Your favourite,' he said, with a smile. 'We aren't at the retreat anymore. We're allowed a drink and chocolate. And look at this.' Henrik pressed a button, and a pane of smoky glass dissipated to reveal a heated patio area with a smoking-hot Jacuzzi.

'We can spa under the stars.'

'We can do whatever we like,' Henrik said, checking his watch. 'We've got a couple of hours before they serve dinner. Shall I bring the bags in, and we can have some drinks by the fire?'

'Gin and tonic?'

Henrik nodded, leaning down to kiss my cheek. He had such a warm, gentle way about him. 'I've also got us a nice bottle of French red.'

I was in heaven. Locked away in a toasty, cosy Rubik's cube, as close to nature as it was possible to be, with a mesmerising view and my favourite Norwegian for company. Ironically, this was exactly how I'd imagined Firefly to be when I'd booked. It was a roundabout way of getting things done, but I'd got here in the end. I swizzled us up a couple of G&Ts and turned the fire up a notch, glad to get my boots off and sink my feet into the rug. Our first tiny home together. The sofa was feathery and soft, cuddling me in, and it felt good to curl my legs up and relax.

Henrik carried the suitcases in like they were cartons of milk – no sign of the struggle I'd had wrestling mine on and off the plane.

'Cheers,' I said, handing him his drink.

'Skål,' Henrik nodded, looking into my eyes as he took a sip. 'I've missed you, you know? Firefly isn't the same without you.'

'Oh realllly? How so? No one shouting across the room at silent lunchtime? No one moaning about the cold and then the hot? And then the cold again.'

Henrik laughed. 'The customer is always right. No, I've missed seeing your face.' He reached out and stroked my cheek, his touch making me tingle.

'I've missed you too.' I couldn't resist getting closer, until our noses were almost touching. Teasing each other with what was about to happen. He brushed my hair back then held my face in his hands, kissing me as if he never wanted to stop. My hands were in his hair as I climbed into his lap, feeling him go hard against me as our bodies pressed together.

'Thank you for arranging this. You're so thoughtful – I didn't think I'd get you all to myself for a night, so this is a real treat.'

'We both get to have each other,' he breathed, his hands sliding under my jumper and making me shiver for all the right reasons. 'I can't stop thinking about you.'

'I'm the same,' I said, unbuttoning his shirt and kissing his chest. I couldn't keep my hands off his body. His back, his shoulders, his arms – I wanted to touch all of him all at once. I threw my jumper off in the direction of the bed, revealing my Norwegian flag bra. Tight and pushed up, my tits spilling over the edge and looking fantastic.

'Oh, Sara,' he moaned, burying his face in them.

'I've got the matching G-string, too,' I teased. 'Wanna see it?'

He nodded, eyes shining and I stood up and led him over to the bed, pushing him back to enjoy the show as I peeled off the rest of my clothes.

'Do you like it?'

'Yes,' he said urgently, switching our positions to lie me down while he stripped. 'I like it very much.'

I lay back on the pillows gazing up at the stars, and a whoosh appeared in the dark. 'Oh wow! A shooting star,' I said, pointing up at it. 'Oh… hang on, it can't be… the line is still there.'

Henrik looked up as the smoke broke open and emptied a green haze into the sky. 'It's the lights,' he said. 'Aurora is with us again. You are lucky to see them so many times.'

The luminous green shimmered and curled, getting brighter as it spread across the sky.

'I thought I needed an app to see the green?'

'Not every time. Just that time.'

Henrik slid under the covers and pulled me into him, the two of us tangled up together, kissing.

'Why don't you enjoy the light show, and I'll take a closer look at this G-string,' he said, breathless, kissing my neck, then the insides of my arms and nibbling along the edge of my bra. The sky was exploding with light above us, and I tried desperately to keep my eyes open as Henrik went lower, untying the G-string laces on each hip, and using his fingers and then his tongue to make me shake with pleasure, over and over and over again.

Thirty-six

Saturday 5th December

'Not that one, the pale pink!' Abi said, panicked, as I brushed a stripe of brown on each cheek.

'Oh no! The screen froze. I thought you were giving me a thumbs up!' I peered into the mirror and tried to rub it off. 'I knew this would be a disaster over Zoom.'

I'd bought the dongle and booster kit Mark had recommended but the signal still wasn't brilliant, and we were only very precariously connected.

'It's fine – there's time to fix it,' she said. 'But you need to concentrate. You're a natural ginger, remember, and your skin is extremely pale. The only powders going anywhere near your skin should be the peaches and pinks.'

'Sorry,' I mumbled, putting the bronzer away and grabbing a baby wipe.

'Now get your foundation brush and buff back over the bit you've just wiped.'

I buffed as best as I could, trying to mirror what Abi was doing on screen.

'Good, that's good.' Her nose was up close to the camera as she watched me. 'Leave that now and warm up the nib of your white eyeliner.'

I copied her as she scribbled into her palm, then coloured in part of my eyelid and shaded the corners, adding gold dots either side. I could see my inner nymph starting to emerge, but I didn't want to go too Hollywood with the make-up. Abi was so talented – she could make me up all the way from LA with her eyes closed, but I wanted to stay recognisable.

'I need to start getting dressed,' I said without moving my lips as I applied the correct pink blush to the apples of my cheeks.

'Up, up, up!' she squawked. 'Upward strokes, small and light. Yes, put your dress on now, then finish your eyeliner once you're laced in.'

I couldn't wait to put my nymphette costume on again. 'You're going to love it! Benji sorted me out the full kit and caboodle. Although I've had to tone it down slightly – there's only so much side boob one should have on show at a wedding.'

'And that amount is zero,' Abi said, looking alarmed. 'Show it to me.'

I propped my phone up on the dressing table and carefully unzipped the dress, slipping it on and standing back to give her the full effect. It was long and layered in dark blue silk, with a strapless bodice that was tricky to tighten up on my own.

'Sara! That is… wow. Just wow. It's a beauty. You look absolutely gorgeous.'

'I don't know how nymphy it is, but it makes me feel like a princess.' I gave Abi a twirl and the layers fluffed up all fairy-like, before gently dropping.

'There is a bit of boob overshare though. Well, more neck exposure really. It's an optical illusion because it's strapless. Have you got a scarf or some necklaces you can wrap around the top?'

'I've got some gold wings with a big ribbon I can tie in a bow?'

'Shut up!'

I laughed. 'I have – I told you, Benji gave me the lot! But I think that would be pushing it. I'm wearing this...' I pulled out the sequined jacket I'd bought from Liberty, which was long and loose and covered in purple flowers.

'Sara – that looks stunning. My work here is done!'

'It's not too much?'

'Nope. Perfect. Glamorous enough for a wedding without being over the top. And completely on theme. I can't wait to see what everyone else is wearing. And by everyone else, I mean Henrik.'

'He's been up since six on best man duties, making breakfast for everyone and polishing up his speech. The bridal party are all up at the house getting ready, but I can't imagine the boys are going over-horsey for the centaur theme.'

Abi snorted. 'Please let Jonas and Henrik arrive as a pantomime horse.'

I laughed. 'Thank you so much for sorting out my outfit and painting me a nymphy face.'

'Any time. You've got the big eyes for it. Right, I better run. Tony's already down at breakfast and keeps messaging me.'

314

'Go, go, go. Sorry for interrupting your New York shag fest. Have a fab time and let's swap photos when we're both home.'

'*Ciao, ciao,*' she said, and blew me a kiss.

It was weird being back in my old cabin again. Henrik had made sure it was allocated to me, and I'd had an overwhelming sense of comfort walking through the doors. Of coming home. This time the heating was on, and he'd even popped a bottle of champagne in the fridge. The wedding was a special occasion, after all.

I finished off my eyeliner and stood back to have one final check. I felt nervous going into the wedding on my own. I knew everyone would be friendly and full of joy and happiness for the day ahead, but the last wedding I'd been to was my own. I took a deep breath and put one hand on my solar plexus and the other on my heart, to acknowledge and channel the nervous energy. To reframe it as excitement and anticipation. *All was well and all would be well.* Just as Henrik said in our meditations.

The dress was long enough to cover my little wellies, which were not very nymph-like, so I could make it safely over the snow. There were flame-lit torches wedged into the ground, illuminating a path from the farmhouse to the forest, and glamorously dressed guests walked in twos and fours towards the pine trees. A wooden arrow with *Happily Ever After* chipped into it pointed us in the right direction, and the ceremony had been set up in a little dell in the middle of a clearing. Rows of wooden chairs with a red crocheted blanket over each had been lined up either side of the aisle, and fairy lights were strung through the trees. There was a wooden altar at the front with a simple lectern for the registrar and a rose-covered backdrop with more fairy lights looped around in the shape of a heart.

I'd managed to avoid weddings up to now, and I couldn't help but feel sad at how much hope I'd had for my own. Every wedding was special, but this felt extra magical. The guests were full of colour: buttercup yellows and golds, shades of blue and pink. The ethereal dresses made it look like a living, breathing flower garden amid all the fir trees, and there were varying levels of effort on the theme. A full-blown Tinker Bell and one or two absinthe fairies on the bride side, with plenty of dark brown suits for the men.

'Sara!' I turned and Ethel was stood behind me in a long mint dress and a cream fur cape. 'I thought it was you,' she said, giving me a kiss. 'Shall we sit together?'

'Yes, please! It's so lovely to see you – I was worried I'd be sat on my own.'

'Not at all! You'll know lots of people. Nina and Bjorn are here, of course, and Oliver Lund is coming too, plus me and the whole of the top table. You are a star guest, Sara. I can't remember the last time Henrik brought a guest to a family event.'

'It's kind of him to invite me,' I said, feeling my cheeks turn pink. 'I love your outfit by the way. Aunty Nymph.'

'You like it?' She shrugged off the fur. 'Vintage market in Helsinki. I like to keep an eye out. Not much to complain about here, I think?'

'It's like a dream. I can't wait to see Greta's dress. Have you had a sneak preview?'

'As a matter of fact, I have. Greta is such a darling, thoughtful girl. She invited me to her bridal appointments with her mother Ingrid, to represent Audhilda. I saw the dress she fell in love with, but she's so imaginative and creative; naturally she wanted to customise it a little.'

'Are we expecting a crocheted robe of some sort?'

Ethel's eyes twinkled. 'You'll have to wait and see.'

The violinists struck up a tune as Jonas and Henrik walked down the aisle, both reflecting the beauty of the trees around us in matching chocolate suits. Jonas was beaming and mouthing hellos, but stopped when he saw Ethel, and came straight over.

'*Tante Eth*,' he said, wrapping her in a hug and squishing his red rose buttonhole. Henrik was busy welcoming guests across the aisle so I couldn't catch his eye.

'You look so handsome,' Ethel said, wiping away a tear.

'Everything looks beautiful,' I added.

'The fat lady hasn't started singing yet,' Jonas said with a laugh, nodding at Tore who was adjusting the microphone stand.

'Is your dad doing the opening number?'

'He's doing all the numbers, so fair warning if you want to put tissues in your ears. Thank you for coming all this way, Sara.'

'Wouldn't have missed it.'

Jonas moved on to the next row and Henrik put a reassuring arm around him when they reached the altar. They hugged and Henrik whispered something that made Jonas laugh. The two brothers stood tall and broad, with their matching man buns, looking happy and relaxed. He'd truly picked the best man for the job.

There was a second hush as the registrar stood up. '*Mine damer og herrer vær så snill reis dere for bruden.*'

'Ladies and gentlemen, please stand for the bride,' Ethel whispered to me.

Henrik turned to look at me as the violins took it up a notch and started playing a jolly jig. Finally, he'd remembered I was here.

'Hi,' I mouthed, and he put his hand on his heart. His dimpled smile made me melt and I couldn't help but reflect it back. I was proud to be here with him, and he looked so handsome all dressed up.

Tore took to the microphone with a folky version of 'Thinking Out Loud' and Ethel gasped. 'This was Audhilda's favourite. She played it on repeat towards the end.'

The musicians led the procession, swaying and spinning as the music got louder, followed by a lady who could only be the mother of the bride in a beautiful gold dress, the two little flower girls in rose red silk, and finally Greta, clutching her dad's arm and beaming bright. Her blonde hair was piled high, and she looked radiant in silver, with a diamanté bustier and a long, layered skirt. Her bridal crown was covered in tiny bangles that clinked along to the music, and she touched it and mouthed 'thank you' to Ethel as she walked past.

'My *brudekrone*,' Ethel said, filled with emotion. 'Audhilda's too, of course. A Balke family heirloom passed down through generations. Greta is wearing it for Jonas's mother.'

Tore's voice wobbled as he caught sight of his daughter-in-law-to-be wearing the crown, and he closed his eyes to try and keep it together. Greta was glowing, the picture of elegance and grace as she glided down the aisle, holding a bunch of long-stemmed red roses, tied with a white ribbon.

Jonas turned to look at her. He'd waited long enough. His mouth dropped as their eyes locked, and Greta giggled.

318

'Wow,' he said, mesmerised. 'You look incredible.'

'So do you,' she said, kissing her dad and taking Jonas's hand. Her dress was equally fabulous from the back: a delicate gold train that looked like it had been spun from gossamer, covered in hundreds of tiny crystals, see-through and luminous as it floated along the aisle.

They looked happy, relieved and full of love for each other. Their moment had finally arrived to become Mr and Mrs, and it was beautiful to witness.

'Wow is right,' I breathed, and Ethel nodded, wiping away more tears.

'I might burst with joy,' she whispered.

The registrar started speaking in Norwegian, and I followed everyone else as they stood up and sat down. Listening in another language made it bearable, as it felt so different to mine. The beats of the ceremony were the same, so I could kind of follow where we were and what was happening, but I couldn't understand it completely. I'd kind of forgotten Henrik spoke Norwegian; his English was so pitch perfect. I'd have to get myself on Duolingo.

Greta and Jonas looked so happy, and I could tell from the way they were standing that it was time to say their vows. Henrik had stepped up with the rings. Tall and handsome in a three-piece suit, his beard trimmed and on point. He looked like a Viking warrior. *My* Viking warrior.

Thirty-seven

'I'll translate,' Ethel said as the registrar stood and opened her book.

Greta looked at Jonas with big eyes and repeated everything the registrar said.

'I pledge my love and loyalty to you,' Ethel whispered. 'As enduring as the mountains and as deep as the fjords.'

How beautiful.

'With this oath ring, I vow to stand by your side, through storm and calm, now and forever.'

They kissed and then Greta put his wedding ring on the wrong hand. *Eek!* Third finger *left* hand I telepathically communicated, hoping the registrar would correct the situation before there were any awkward laughs. But she didn't. She went straight on to Jonas, who had tears in his eyes and had stopped to take a breath. Henrik put a comforting hand on his shoulder, and Jonas struggled through his vows, smiling with relief once he got to the ring. Which he also placed on the wrong hand.

'Left hand,' I whispered to Ethel, thinking she was in the best position to intercept. The marriage might not count if the ritual was wrong.

'What? No, it's right.'

'The ring should be on the left hand,' I insisted, trying to help.

'Not for us,' she whispered, holding up her wrinkled right hand, a gold band firmly wedged on the third finger.

I stopped, surprised. Well, that was as good a reason as any to marry a Norwegian. My English wedding finger was far too sensitive to have another ring on it anytime soon. Possibly ever.

The registrar said something in a loud jolly voice and Jonas dipped Greta down for a glamorous Hollywood kiss. I couldn't help but have a little tear at that myself, as everyone cheered and Tore launched into 'Romeo and Juliet' by Dire Straits.

The new Mr and Mrs Nilsen danced their way down the aisle, smiling and waving and kissing. Henrik ushered the little bridesmaids out in front of him, blowing Ethel a kiss as he walked past, and Greta's mum and dad linked arms to complete the bridal party.

'I loved that,' I said, relieved that I'd survived the ceremony without having a breakdown. 'What a gorgeous couple.'

'They are very much in love. And now it seems Henrik is smitten, too.'

'Does it?'

'I don't think I've ever seen him blow a kiss to anyone in his whole life.'

'That was to you, Ethel, surely.' She looked at me, archly. 'Wasn't it? To both of us then.'

'I know my nephew, and public displays of affection are *not his thing*,' she said.

We followed the crowd to a second clearing in the woods, where three giant tipis had been erected. Two were packed with long trestle tables and decorated with fairy lights and flowers, and the third was a bar, with a dance floor and soft seating. The floor was covered in cowskin rugs and a table of champagne greeted us. I took two glasses and followed Ethel as she strutted with her stick towards the biggest of the chairs and flopped herself down.

'Champagne for the lady,' I said, offering her a glass.

'Not for me, thank you, I don't drink anymore.'

'Oh, sorry, shall I get you something else?'

'Not for now – you're OK.'

There weren't any tables close by, so I stood there like a lemon, double parked, and tried to drink one of the champagnes as quickly as possible, so I didn't look like an alcoholic.

'My two favourite ladies.' Henrik appeared with a big smile and kissed Ethel on both cheeks. 'One who is obviously very thirsty.'

'It's a special occasion,' I said with a shrug as he kissed me too. I didn't mind being champagne-shamed, but two small kisses weren't enough. I felt drawn towards him and had to control myself as his aftershave swept over me. The scent reminded me of our game of naked Twister the night before. Our bodies touching as we pretended to concentrate. Henrik's attempt at *left hand, red*, had been our undoing and we'd collapsed in a heap of giggles, with me on top, just how he likes it.

'It is a special occasion,' he said, repeating it back to me and staring into my eyes.

'OK, OK, I think we've established that,' Ethel said, rolling her eyes.

'Sorry, *tante*,' Henrik said, kissing her hand. 'Oh, Sara, did you know Oliver is here? He caved when Jonas and Greta sent the third invitation. Over there, by the bar.'

'Yes, Ethel told me earlier.' I followed his gaze to where Oliver was holding court, short and round and laughing loudly. 'Excuse me for a minute while I go and say hi.'

I made my way over and tapped him on the shoulder.

'Guess who?'

'Hmm... English, female, expensive perfume – Sara! I'd recognise that voice anywhere. How are you?'

I gave him a big hug. 'All the better for your help. Thank you so much for coming to my rescue with this place.'

'Anytime. Have you had chance to consider my proposal?'

'I have, and I'm interested if the offer's still open?'

'Well, that's wonderful news! Why don't we set up some time to chat while you're over here – maybe tomorrow?'

'Perfect.'

'Oliver is such a sweetheart. I haven't seen the table plan yet – am I sitting next to him?'

'No. You're sitting next to me. With Aunt Ethel on my other side.'

I blushed, taken aback. 'I can't sit on the top table with all the family – people will wonder who I am! I'm fine hanging out with Oliver – I don't want to be in the way.'

'You're not in the way; you're my guest. And nobody will wonder who you are, because I've already told everyone the beautiful girl from London is with me.'

I blushed even harder at that. He pulled me in and kissed me on the lips. 'Isn't she beautiful, *tante*?'

'Very,' Ethel agreed. 'And a force to be reckoned with. It's a miracle you managed to sort out that situation with Bjorn. He had dollar signs in his eyes.'

'It came down to the covenant in the end,' I said. 'The paperwork was legally binding so there was nothing they could do about it. Although, I do agree with Bjorn that this place could be making you all a lot more money.'

'I feel for Nina and Bjorn,' Henrik said, nodding over at them in the crowd. 'We should find an investor and buy them out. They don't have anyone to pass the covenant down to and they deserve to enjoy their retirement.'

'I've been giving the situation some thought as it happens,' Ethel said conspiratorially. 'You know how much I love this place; I've been coming here for years. And I've noticed it getting increasingly tired, while you try and keep it affordable. I don't have any children either, so all my money will go to you and Jonas in the future, Henny, but it could make sense to buy out Bjorn and Nina with it instead, then gift you their half of Firefly Forest. That way we keep the retreat forever, and I leave a legacy behind from the Balke side of the family too – your mother would have liked that.'

Henrik was welling up. 'That is an incredibly kind thought, *tante*, but we can't ask you to do that.'

'You haven't asked. I'm offering. And I like the idea of my money spreading future good in the world.' Ethel gave Henrik a kiss on the cheek. 'I will want one thing though,' she said.

'Anything,' Henrik said.

'A tree planted for me.'

Henrik smiled. 'Done.'

'We can discuss it another day with Tore, Jonas and Greta,' Ethel said. 'Let's enjoy today for now, and worry about tomorrow, tomorrow.'

'An excellent mantra,' I said as Tore made an announcement in Norwegian, and everyone bustled through to the dining tents. 'Can I come with you two, seeing as we're seat buddies?'

'And the rest,' Henrik murmured in my ear as he led the way. It was a room full of happiness and joy, and I felt privileged to be part of it – even more so to be sitting at the top table. I waved at Greta's parents as Tore took to the mic to welcome the bride and groom, and the tipis vibrated with clapping and whooping as Jonas and Greta made their entrance.

'Is it a vegan wedding?' I asked Henrik as we all sat down.

'I hope not. Jonas is a hardcore carnivore.'

'Is he?' I said, surprised. 'Greta too? The whole vegan thing is an act?'

Henrik smiled at me. 'It's not an act – it's part of the offering for the retreat.'

'You watched me suffering through asparagus stew, while you were stuffing down sausage rolls up at the farmhouse? No wonder it was out of bounds for guests,' I said, swigging my champagne.

'Yes, sausage rolls day and night – a top Norwegian snack.'

'*Hei*, Sara,' Greta called, waving down the table.

'You look so beautiful!' I shouted. 'Congratulations!'

An army of groovy-looking waiters, with imaginative moustaches surrounded the tables with small plates. They were wearing three-piece tweed in claret and looked like a foodie flash mob, putting on a show.

'*God ettermiddag!*'

'Good afternoon,' Ethel said, giving me a wink.

Our waiter had a blond handlebar moustache and mischief in his eyes. 'To start we are having a Nordic shrimp toast, with rye kernel and tarragon salad,' he said, while two other waiters did the rest of the top table.

'*Takk*,' Henrik said, then leant in and whispered, 'Jonas went to chef school with these guys. They own a restaurant in Copenhagen and their food is unbelievable.' He tucked in and did an A-OK sign, his leg wrapped around mine under the table, our chairs as close as they could be. There was no mistaking our body language.

The starters were melt-in-the-mouth delicious and so were the main courses. I'd been unsure about roasted reindeer with pickled herring dumplings, but it was a taste sensation.

Henrik tinkled his champagne flute with his fork, and everyone joined in until Greta and Jonas stood on their chairs and kissed. But the speeches were the real surprise. It was a total free-for-all, and anyone could make a toast. Greta's parents kicked things off, followed by Tore, Jonas and Greta. I couldn't understand a word, but I could see Henrik shuffling his speech and scribbling in new lines as people told funny stories and offered words of wisdom.

I tried to laugh in the right places, but I was always two beats behind everyone else. Eventually Henrik rang the glass for himself and stood up.

'Ladies and gentlemen, it is my turn to make a toast.' He turned to me and smiled. 'I hope you don't mind it being in English. My girlfriend Sara is here and it's important to me that she can understand it too.' The guests tinkled their glasses in approval and my heart leapt. Jonas and Greta stood on their chairs again to kiss, and Henrik kissed me at the same time. His *girlfriend?!*

'I want to raise a glass to my little brother Jonas – my Jo-bro – and his beautiful bride Greta. They share the kind of love we all aspire to. They laugh and play together, champion each other, and encourage the best versions of each other to grow. Jonas – thank you for being a wonderful brother to me. *Mamma* would be so proud of you today... of the man you have become. And I know she is watching over and celebrating with us. Some of you will know that *Pappa* always called my mother his little firefly...'

The champagne flutes started tinkling and Tore stood up and raised his glass to the sky.

'...because she was busy and buzzy and lit up every room she ever walked into. And just as fireflies light the way in the darkness, *Mamma* lit the way for us too.'

Henrik looked down at me with a smile.

'Greta – I have seen you do the same for Jonas. You are a Nilsen firefly. You carry light and warmth within you, and your kind heart and wonderful spirit radiate energy wherever you go. Even your magic blankets keep us all warm. You've looked after not only Jonas, but me and *Pappa* ever since *Mor* left us, and I want to thank you for that. For coming into our lives and shining so bright. We love you so much, and even though you've been part of the family ever since you first put that goofy smile on Jonas's face, I want to join *Pappa* in officially welcoming you as a Nilsen. Congratulations to Jonas and his firefly bride, Greta! Wishing you both a happy forever and may all your dreams come true.'

Everyone stood up and cheered as Henrik shouted, '*Takk for maten-tale!*', clinking their glasses and repeating it after him.

'It means *thank you for the food*. We say it at weddings – don't ask me why,' Ethel said, as Henrik sat back down. 'Excellent speech, Henny, well done.'

'Too cute!' I said, kissing his cheek. 'I didn't know that about your mum. And I heard you got a girlfriend!'

'Yep,' he said. 'And not just any girlfriend – she's a firefly too. How does it feel?'

'Surprising.' The champagne had me answering with complete honesty.

'Really? In what way?' Henrik crossed his legs, removing any physical touch between us.

'Just that we haven't had the conversation.'

'What was last night?'

I gave him a coy smile. 'It certainly wasn't a conversation. I barely said a word.'

'Then let's have it now. I thought I'd been very clear with how I feel, so I'm sorry if you are in any doubt. Shall I kneel?'

'Absolutely not.' Oh no. Served me right. My heart was bouncing all over the place. And now he was going to tell me how he felt. And then I'd have to tell him how I felt. Argh! *How did I feel?* Why had I done this to myself?

'Sara Pearson... actually, what is your real name? Your maiden name?'

'Lee.'

'As in the gateau?'

'Uh-huh.'

'Sara Lee. You are an enigma to me.'

'Ooh, this is rhyming,' I said, giggling.

'And from the first time I saw... thee, I thought she's the kind of girl, I want to be... with.'

'Ahhh, and it was going so well. I thought you might get ha, ha, ha, hee, hee, hee, in there somewhere.'

Henrik laughed. 'I had to get you smiling somehow when you arrived.'

'Well, it worked.'

'Do I need to ask you to be my girlfriend then? Is this a permission thing? Shall I phone your dad and talk him through where we're up to on the physical front?'

'Er, no, that won't be necessary, but feel free to ask me, officially.'

Henrik took my hand and looked at me very seriously. 'Sara Lee, of the non-gateau Lees, will you make me the happiest man on earth and agree to be my girlfriend?'

I pretended to think about it, then took his other hand. 'I will. And will you, Henrik Nilsen, of the Firefly Forest Nilsens, consider the position of my boyfriend? To have and to hold?'

'I do... accept thee's... proposal.'

'Then it is done,' I said, and kissed him.

'Good. Can we have dessert now?'

There was a table full of cakes in the middle of the tipi and every single one had been made by a member of the family. *Bløtkake* – cream cake – cheesecake, chocolate cake, lemon cake, every flavour and shape and size imaginable was in there somewhere. And then there was the wedding cake. The *kransekake*. An enormous cone of cake rings that got smaller as they reached the top.

'What a beauty, eh?' Henrik plucked out one of the decorative Norwegian flags and stuck it in my dessert.

'In case I forget where I am?'

'The flag just makes me think of you, now. It's burnt into my brain.'

'Funny that,' I said, raising my eyebrows.

Greta and Jonas cut the cake, laughing as it nearly toppled over and the mustachio-men chopped it up and passed it round with more champagne. Everyone drank and talked and laughed until it was finally time for the first dance.

'Remember the drill?' Henrik asked, holding my hand.

I nodded. Greta and Jonas had asked the family to join them once the first dance was a few lines in. They didn't want to be alone on the dance floor for more than twenty seconds.

Tore was doing well in his role as master of ceremonies, among all the other roles he was performing, as he announced the new Mr and Mrs Nilsen for the final time and invited them onto the dance floor.

Jonas twirled his way into the middle of the crowd and held out his hand to Greta. Her silver and gold dress sparkled in the candlelight; the train now bustled up at the back as she curled into Jonas's chest and he put his arms around her. The violinists had been joined by two guitars and an accordion, and the whole room went quiet as they started to play, watching another Nilsen love story unfold in front of them. A moment in time that would never be repeated as the newly-weds stared into each other's eyes, dreamy and lost. I was so touched that I totally missed our cue – not that the happy couple seemed to have any idea who was dancing and who wasn't.

'May I have this dance?' Henrik asked, holding out his hand.

'Yes you may.'

We joined Tore and Ethel, Fredrik and Ingrid and Bjorn and Nina in a slow dance, full of smiles as the music washed over us all.

'Have you enjoyed it?' Henrik asked.

'Yes. More than enjoyed it. I've loved it.'

I glanced behind him at this magical place and felt so lucky to be here. There were ribbons and decorations strewn all over the tipi and candles on every table. A glitter ball slowly turned adding a sparkly light to the dance floor.

'What are you thinking?' Henrik asked, holding me close.

'I'm wondering how easy it would be to bring two dachshunds to Norway and whether they'd need doggie passports. I'm also thinking that I don't know if Henrik even likes dogs.'

His eyes lit up. 'Are you? Well, let me reassure you on that,' he murmured. 'Henrik likes dogs very much. He loves all animals. He's a live and let live kind of guy.'

'I thought he might be.'

'Do you think you might take the package from work?'

'I already have,' I said staring up at him. 'I won't get that kind of opportunity again. It was just a shock when they offered it to me out of the blue. I had no idea the firm was struggling so badly.'

'It's like I always say – when life offers you a cash lump sum – take it.'

'I don't remember that mantra in the meditation sessions?'

'What?! That's the lead message in my money meditation. You were probably asleep. It must have been that time you woke yourself up snoring,' he said, teasing. 'Don't worry – you'll get another job easily.'

'I might already have one.'

'See! I knew it. A smart cookie like you doesn't hang around.'

'Do you remember I told you Oliver was opening an office in London?'

Henrik nodded, listening carefully.

'Well, he's offered me a job.'

'Of course he has!' Henrik said, but his tone was flat. 'Makes perfect sense. Congratulations.'

There was a kerfuffle among the guests as we stared into each other's eyes, and we looked over at the same time. Flashes of pink, purple and blue were flying across the sky like rockets, and then came the greens, luminous and rich. A rainbow of magic spreading out above us, filling the air with colour. The rare rainbow version of the Northern Lights had appeared to bless the wedding, just as Greta and Jonas had hoped. Their wedding wish to feel Audhilda was watching over them and celebrating from up above.

Henrik nodded slowly to himself. '*Hei, Mamma*,' he said, putting his arm around me. We stood completely still, watching the miracle of the Northern Lights as they put on a show.

'It's a sign,' he said, eventually.

'What is?'

'This. Mother Nature showing off all her colours at the exact moment you were talking about changing your life.'

'You think?'

'I know it. Most people will never witness what we are looking at right now. It's a sign you're making the right decision, even if that's to stay in London and run Oliver's satellite office. We'll just have to manage long distance for a while.'

'Well, that's the interesting part of the offer, because Oliver wants to set the London office up himself. He's moving over for six months to recruit the team and get it up and running. The job he's offered me is as acting partner to look after things in Bergen.'

Henrik's expression changed completely. 'Really? In Norway.'

'Yes,' I said, feeling giddy. 'In the *Norwegian* Bergen. The one and only.'

'And what did you say?'

'I said… yes.'

The look on Henrik's face was so cute, I had to kiss him. 'It just feels right being here. I love it.'

It was a different triple F to the 'Financial Freedom Forever' I'd hoped for with my promotion, but 'Firefly Forest for the Foreseeable,' felt just as exciting.

'And we love you being here. *I love you being here.* You can loan yourself to Norway for a while and see how it goes. It doesn't have to be a forever thing.' I leant in and kissed his handsome face, feeling more at home than I'd ever felt before. 'Unless you want it to be, of course.'

Epilogue

Six months later

Twiggy and Dots were barking blue murder as the postman cycled off in panic.

They were the other side of the front gate, so he was safe enough, but the two of them howling like the world was ending was ruining my morning meditation. I tried for another minute or two, then gave up. There were only so many times I could acknowledge the thought 'SHUT UP, THE PAIR OF YOU!' and send it on its way.

I straightened the picture of Henrik's family Christmas on his photo wall, where it sat pride of place, and marched out the front door.

'What is all this noise?' I chided affectionately, but I couldn't help but smile as my two little sausages looked up at me, their tails thudding on the tarmac. It was nice to get any kind of post, but there were three letters with my name on today. I'd used Henrik's address for my redirection. Two cards and an official brown envelope that I ripped open first.

University College Hospital
Euston Road
London

Dear Ms Lee,
I'm pleased to confirm we are discharging you from our care with immediate effect. Your recent tests have shown vast improvements in your anxiety levels, and I am pleased to hear your panic attacks have now stopped. Your blood tests have all come back clear and your blood pressure is back within the normal range.
Whatever you're doing – keep doing it!
Best wishes,
Dr R Fielding

What a relief. I was starting to think I'd never get back to myself.

'Anything for me?' Henrik stuck his head out the bathroom door, steam billowing into the corridor.

'Nope. Happy New Home cards from Kat and Abi, and the official all-clear from Dr Fielding for me.'

'Well, that's good news – we should celebrate.'

'Yes, we should! With a whole *troikakake*?'

He laughed. 'I don't think the doc would approve of chocolate cake.'

Henrik disappeared back into the bathroom, and I put the kettle on. I still had my morning coffee, but I'd cut out the Red Bull and Berocca. Luminous drinks were trouble. It was a beautiful summer's day full of sunshine, and the birds were singing as I opened the patio doors. The dogs flew past, leaping over each other and down the steps into the garden. Their days of tight-lead London walks were now well and truly behind them. Lil' Will smiled at me from his corner of the patio and was now up to my waist. Still too thin to hug, but leafy enough to tickle.

It had been three months since I'd moved to Bergen as caretaker partner for Oliver while he set up his London office, and three months since Henrik had moved away from Firefly Forest and back to the city. Except it wasn't the Big Apple this time, it was the little Bergen version. He'd rented a house near the mountain, and I'd rented a flat in the centre of town which gave us the best of both worlds and plenty of space to get to know each other. I didn't want to jump out of one serious relationship straight into another, even though that's exactly what had happened. It was all still so new, but it meant we could enjoy the buzz and energy of the city when it suited us, go on dinner dates and to late-night bars, and relax in the countryside whenever we wanted to, as well. It was a two-home, two-dog relationship and Tore, Jonas and Greta were just a boat ride away whenever we wanted to visit.

Henrik's phone buzzed on the table, and *Pappa* flashed up on the screen.

'It's your dad,' I called.

'Can you grab it?'

'*Hei*, Tore!' I said, putting him on loudspeaker.

'Ahhh *hei*, Sara. *Hvordan har du det?*' he said cheerfully, asking how I was.

I'd been practising. '*Jeg har det bra! Hvordan har du det?*'

'*Greit, takk.*' OK, thanks. He chuckled. 'Your accent is impressive – the Duolingo lessons are working!'

I laughed. 'I'm not sure how far *I'm fine, how are you?* will get me, but the owl is on my case and she's a harsh taskmaster.'

'Don't give up and you'll get there. Fluent by Christingle! Now then. I've decided to throw a party for my sixtieth birthday in August and wanted to check you can both make it before I go any further.'

'Of course we can. Your birthday weekend is already blocked out on the calendar.'

'Excellent. Now that I've taken a back seat with the retreat, I've got time to organise it, so I want to start planning.'

'Will you be singing?'

'Undoubtedly. But I need my band with me. Jonas and Greta have already said yes, so with Henrik on the hardanger, I wondered if you might play the tambourine?'

'Sure! I'll be on percussion.'

'Just the tambourine is fine, I think.'

Oh. No building up my part allowed. 'Count us in.'

'Maybe the Northern Lights will come out for me, hey? The *ildflue* are awake again and decorating the trees.'

'*Hei, Pappa,*' Henrik called, barefoot, in his jeans, scanning the kitchen and grabbing his fleece from the radiator. 'I'm on my way in.'

'You're all doing a fantastic job, Henny. Firefly is looking so smart these days, I barely recognise it.'

'Seems to be working so far,' I said. 'The foodie themes, the new-style meditations, the fancy hot tubs.'

'I know! I joined Greta's Tibetan singing bowl meditation last week and it gave me such a wonderful sense of peace and calm. I'm still feeling the effects now.'

'Sounds like it's time to put the prices up,' I said.

'We already have,' Henrik said, lacing up his boots. 'As you both know.'

'There might be room to put them up a little more, Henny, but I leave the decision up to you.'

'It's important we stay affordable for the people who need us, *Pappa*. Burnout can happen to anyone. I want Firefly to be accessible.'

'Always so caring, Henny. I know you'll get the balance right. It's exciting to watch the transformation. Jonas is experimenting with the menu and Greta has done wonderful things with the spa. The retreat feels fresh and modern again – like it was when your mother and I took it over. I'm so proud of you all.'

Ethel's investment had been a lot more than anyone was expecting and had meant a full refurb for the retreat. The cabins had been stripped and redecorated. Each one now had its own hot tub – and an inside bath. Henrik, Jonas and Greta had committed to a three-year plan to get the profits up and it was the ultimate win-win situation. Jonas on the food, Greta in charge of the spa and Henrik running the show. They'd taken on more staff to give them all a better work-life balance, and the business was already turning a corner. They'd always been fully booked – but now they were fully booked and making money. Tore could stay in the farmhouse and the Bakkens had gone off on a three-month cruise around the Caribbean.

'Glad to hear it, *Pappa*.'

'I won't keep you – enjoy your day. *Farvel!*'

'*Farvel*,' Henrik and I said at the same time.

'Jinx,' I said, holding out my little finger. 'Make a wish.'

'What do I need to make a wish for? I've got everything I ever wanted,' he said, putting his arms around my waist and twirling me round.

'Me too, actually,' I said, tugging on his beard and kissing him. 'Me too.'

Acknowledgements

BIG THANKS to my agent Rosie Pierce and all the team at Curtis Brown for their brilliant support, and to my editor Aubrie Artiano for helping me hone and polish the book into what it is today. Thank you to Holly, Sophie and everyone at Head of Zeus who has played a part in launching this book into the world, with a special shout out to Gemma Gorton for the beautiful cover.

I'm very lucky to have a fabulous group of writers who read early copies of my work and give me lots of feedback, and I want to thank you all. Liz Webb, Katherine Tansley, Marija Maher-Diffenthal and Sarah Lawton. As well as Rachel Lyon, who introduced me to Bergen many moons ago and has been a non-stop sounding board as I've written this book. Thank you for enduring my endless three-minute voice notes.

To my Norwegian friends who have always been so lovely and welcoming, and helped with the language, name ideas and the local nuances – Caroline and Jon Inge, Barb and Sven. Thank you for the trips to Oslo, to the cabin in the mountains and for all the inspiration.

Thank you to my sister, Claire, who always makes me laugh, for reading the first and last drafts and giving me loads of brilliant notes (importantly not to overuse the word nipple). To my brother, Justin, for his creative feedback and to my fabulous mom for her endless encouragement. I was very lucky to experience the Northern Lights with Mom a few years back in Iceland, and we still laugh about the naked spa showers and the app we had to download to 'see' them, today.

To my lovely Rob, who supports me every day, and delivers treats to my desk, thank you for walking beside me on this creative path, with my hairy writing partner pups – Ziggy and Bruno. I love you my little family, thank you for looking after me xxx

About the Author

CARRIE WALKER is a Brummie born rom-com lover with a lifelong passion for travel. She has lived in a ski resort, by a beach, in the country and the city, and travelled solo through Asia, South America and Europe. Her own love life was more com than rom until she met her husband a few years ago and settled down with him and their dogs Ziggy and Bruno in a small pub-filled village in Essex.

Stories to fall in love with.

Aria

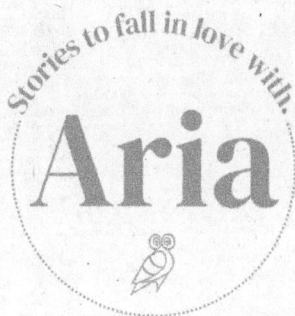

Thanks for reading!

Want to receive exclusive author content, news on the latest Aria books and updates on offers and giveaways?

Follow us on X @AriaFiction and on Facebook and Instagram @HeadofZeus, and join our mailing list.